When Sparks Fly

A PINEGROVE FD NOVEL

LIBBY KAY

When Sparks Fly
A Pinegrove FD Novel
Copyright © 2025 Libby Kay
All rights reserved.

ISBN (ebook) 978-1-964636-38-2
(print) 978-1-964636-39-9

Inkspell Publishing
207 Moonglow Circle #101
Murrells Inlet, SC 29576

Edited By Yezanira Venecia
Cover art By Emily's World By Design

DEDICATION

To my husband, who makes every day sparkle.

LIBBY KAY

PROLOGUE

One month earlier

Whitney Kerr lounged on the couch in her sister's cramped apartment. She'd managed the perfect placement for her afternoon of self-loathing. Four purple fluffy cushions surrounded her, a blanket draped over her legs. Perched on her tummy was a bowl of popcorn, a package of peanut butter cups, and bag of M&Ms, a glass of white wine nestled precariously by her elbow. Clad in her favorite pajamas, her dark curls were tucked into her Savannah Bananas hat. She was the poster girl for living the adulting life.

The reason for binge eating in a pillow fort was simple—Whitney had had her heart broken last month. Yes, it was undeniable that her ex-boyfriend, Baxter, dumped her after nearly three years of dating. Yet, what really got Whitney was the loss of her previous life—a life living in his condo with her own space, and most importantly, a closet to herself and shelves for her romance book collection. Now she crashed on her sister's sofa, her belongings stacked in boxes. As if that was depressing enough, she was back on a budget, hence her Girl Dinner of movie theatre snacks.

At the beginning of the summer, Whitney had been reading on the balcony with a view of the Savannah River, reveling in the security of their shared life. By shared, she basically had been living there rent-free and under his lease. The son of Georgia real estate moguls, her ex didn't have to work hard for his home.

Employed by his parents, Baxter hardly stuck to a schedule that folks would consider normal. He'd sashay into the office after sleeping in, Starbucks in hand, and looked busy enough to avoid his parents' scrutiny. In hindsight, Whitney should have guessed that careless behavior would leak into his personal life. But she'd been blinded by his charms, his place, and her desire to be loved.

Whitney had fallen into the trap she'd sworn she'd avoid like the plague: depending on a man for her livelihood. On their first anniversary, Baxter had popped the question— *Whitney, would you move in with me?* Granted, she'd been hoping for a different question, but at the time, she figured Baxter had a greater plan.

Curled up around her snack bowl, Whitney sighed when her fingers reached the bottom. "Shoot," she muttered, sitting up and swiping a cluster of popcorn kernels from her chest. They clattered to the floor, bouncing under the coffee table and the couch.

"Xena!" Whitney called out, adding a quiet whistle to lure her sister's maniac cat out for a snack. Unlike her namesake Warrior Princess, this Xena was a coward, and a bit of an asshole.

Since moving in, Whitney and the feline had come to an unspoken agreement. Whitney would not touch the beast in exchange for the occasional treat of fallen human food. Last night the pair dined on shrimp Pad Thai from Whitney's favorite shop around the corner.

Whitney was incredibly grateful her sister, Winnie, was out of town on business. If she were to walk in on this sad scene, she'd likely call health services. Between Whitney's mental state and current lack of hygiene, she was certainly breaking some law or at least a local ordinance.

Finally, Xena flounced out from her corner of the apartment and snarfed down the fallen popcorn without a glance. Whitney settled back into the cushions and began flipping the channels. Usually the food competition shows kept her attention, but Whitney wasn't feeling much at the moment.

Her channel changing stopped when she found a Savannah Bananas game. She had been a fan since the team was founded in the mid-2010s, and going to games had been something her sister and she did with their parents before they retired to Florida. Whitney had tried to talk Baxter into joining her, but he always shrugged off the invites. Her ex was a bit of a snob, and slumming it in the cheap seats in the hot Georgia sun was never high on his to-do list.

That was why, when the camera panned to the audience, Whitney almost choked on her wine. There, smack dab in the middle of the stands, was her ex-boyfriend. While their break-up had added five pounds to Whitney's already curvy frame, Baxter looked polished and happy. His strawberry-blond hair was swept back, his gaze fixed on a gorgeous, lithe blonde.

As if her brain had already put the pieces together, Whitney's pulse skyrocketed as the camera zoomed in on Baxter. He slowly lowered to one knee as the blonde fanned her face, eyes already glistening. Currently she was better suited for a beauty pageant than America's pastime.

"No," Whitney breathed, empty glass clattering to the floor. Xena did not appear pleased at the noise and darted out of sight into Winnie's bedroom.

"Uh-oh, y'all!" the TV commentator whooped. "Looks like we've got ourselves a seventh-inning stretch proposal!" Sound effects were piped over the image of Baxter and the mystery woman embracing. Cartoon hearts popped as the audience cheered.

Whitney didn't remember much after that, save for her darting to the bathroom to lose her Girl Dinner. An hour later, her stomach empty and her eyes finally dry, she padded out to the couch and flopped onto her back. She stared up at the ceiling, a million questions roiling through her mind.

Who was this woman?
Why had Baxter rebounded so quickly?
Had she been the other woman all along?

She simultaneously yearned for Winnie's company and thanked the good Lord she wouldn't be back for a week. She understood her older sister meant well, but she wasn't like Whitney. While Whitney was scatter-brained and currently unemployed and homeless, her sister was a high-power attorney out touring sites for her law firm's expansion.

Winnie was only two years older, but she'd managed to live a lifetime more than Whitney. Once the ink was dry on her college diploma, Whitney got placed with a temp agency, eager to find *just the right fit* for her career. Unsure of what her degree would get her, she'd expected exciting placements at law firms, museums, or at least a corporation with a view of a historical Savannah park. Instead, she'd been sent to windowless basements or filing rooms with towers of paperwork to organize and file. Every once in a while, they'd send her to retail shops during sales or grand openings, but nothing seemed to stick.

Now the trouble was, she'd been placed over and over again for six years and had nothing to show for it except a dwindling bank account and no discernable skills. She hadn't found her passion, and after turning down the last three placements since the breakup, she didn't even have a job.

Whitney scrubbed her face and blinked back a fresh round of tears. She truly did not want to be marrying Baxter Hollingsworth, but that didn't mean she wanted him marrying someone else so soon. Unable to stand her own thoughts, she popped the cork on another bottle of wine.

Deciding she did in fact need to speak with her sister,

she dialed and prayed she'd answer. Unfortunately, her sister's career ambitions won out, and Whitney was left leaving a slurring voicemail.

Throwing her phone to the floor, she fell asleep on the couch. The last thing she thought as her eyes drifted shut was *What am I going to do now?*

*

Trevor Mays was the unluckiest man alive.

"I'm sorry, son," Chief Warren said, running a hand over his mustache. "We've decided to promote Hastings to Captain. You understand, right?"

No.

No, Trevor did not understand how this was happening, again. For the second time in as many years, he was being passed over for a job he could do in his sleep. He was the son of the previous chief, and if his father hadn't had a penchant for hot dogs, cigarettes, and beer, he'd still be sitting in Warren's seat.

Trevor had grown up in this fire station, planned his entire career based on his father's, and even considered his teammates his best friends. When other young boys had been in Little League or Cub Scouts, Trevor had been on ride-a-longs with his dad and the man sitting in front of him now. He'd missed his senior homecoming dance because there had been a five-alarm fire that took all hands-on deck. He'd eagerly swapped his rented tuxedo for his father's spare bunker gear to sit guard at the station and help dispatch with calls.

Trevor lived and breathed for this fire station, but apparently the relationship was one-sided. *And sadly that wouldn't be the first bad relationship he'd been in this year.*

Trevor took a deep breath, unwilling to break down in front of his boss. Things were embarrassing enough lately. His life was starting to feel like that meme of Chris Farley falling down the hill. Every time he thought he was done, he'd bounce off another rock and keep on spiraling downhill. The only problem was that Trevor wasn't laughing.

"I'm curious, Chief." His throat closed, but he kept his composure a moment longer. "What could I have done differently over the last year to warrant getting passed over?" He left out the word *again*, since both men were painfully aware of his track record around the station. "Am I missing any benchmarks in my performance reviews? Are my physical fitness requirements slipping?"

For all the stories of nepo babies in Hollywood, Trevor would have loved a little of that right now. He'd served as a fireman in this station for nearly a decade, was promoted to driver five years ago, and within months was made lieutenant. It was time for him to take on more responsibility, but apparently that wasn't going to happen yet.

Chief Warren grimaced and reached for his coffee mug, downing its contents in one go. "Son," he said, clearing his throat.

Trevor bristled. "Lieutenant Mays. No point being casual when we're speaking about my career." Under his breath, he muttered, "Or lack of one."

"Lieutenant Mays," Warren corrected, sliding his mug to the corner of his desk and not making eye contact. Trevor wanted to pick up that damn mug and crush it to smithereens in his hands. He'd bought the chief that mug when he'd been promoted. Trevor was still mourning the loss of his father, mentor, and boss, yet he had the gumption to do something nice for a man who had always had his back. Apparently Southern manners only got Trevor so far.

Chief Warren continued, although Trevor had missed the first part of the lame excuses. "You know how things go around here with city council. They write our checks, and so we must keep them happy."

What wasn't being said was that the new captain was engaged to the city council president's daughter, Virginia.

The city council president wasn't Trevor's favorite person, least of all since his daughter had trampled all over Trevor's heart. Just last year, Virginia had been wearing Trevor's ring all around Pinegrove. He didn't want to unpack that cluster at the moment, so he clenched his jaw and prayed for patience—or maybe a time machine?

Above all, Trevor loathed politics. He didn't want to scratch someone's back *hoping* it would lead to success down the road. He wanted to be nice and help people for the sake of doing it, period. Wasn't that the cornerstone of a good fire captain? Well, apparently not in Pinegrove, Georgia.

Scott Hastings was a tool, plain and simple. He'd barely made it through the academy and lived for pulling pranks on people and slacking off on the job. Trevor had bailed him out of trouble more times than he cared to remember, and that only made this bitter pill impossible to swallow.

Trevor squeezed the armrest, feeling the fabric protest under his grip. He needed to get out of here; he would not break down—or break anything—in front of the chief. Nope, he would do what he could to save his dignity.

"Is there anything else?" he asked, standing up to his full height and squaring his shoulders.

"No, son, urm, Lieutenant. You're dismissed. Take the rest of the day off."

Trevor's shoulders slumped. "I'm working on those arson reports. I thought Javi and I were …" But his words faltered, mentioning his buddy and coworker in a tone more suitable to a whiny teenager. Clearing his throat, he amended, "It was my understanding those reports had a deadline of …"

Chief Warren shook his head, muttering something under his breath that was mostly profanities. "Lieutenant, Captain Hastings has asked that we shift the team around. All that logistics can wait a day. Why don't you go home, have a drink, and blow off some steam?"

Gritting his teeth, Trevor tried to ignore the bile rising up his throat. He didn't want to drink his feelings—

although the option was tempting—he wanted to work. But judging from the chief's sullen expression, that wasn't an option.

Trevor nodded once and left the office, anger coursing through his veins. If his father were alive, he would no doubt be disappointed that his son's career was stagnant. It was humiliating at best, soul-crushing at worst.

Smoothing down the front of his uniform shirt, Trevor stalked out into the bullpen. He made sure to avoid eye contact with his coworkers, as their pitying looks would only push him over the edge.

Things needed to change around here, and fast. Trevor didn't know how much longer he could pretend everything was okay.

CHAPTER ONE

"Hello, is this Ms. Kerr?" a stranger's voice bellowed through the line.

Whitney twitched. Her neck ached from how she'd slept funny on the couch. The ringing phone had woken her up from her restless night, a peanut butter cup wrapper stuck to her cheek. Peeling the paper from her skin, she tossed it in the general direction of the trashcan before sitting up and finding her voice.

"Yes. Who is this?" she asked, clearing a lump of peanut butter from her throat.

The man on the other line cheered at this news. "Oh, excellent. Ms. Kerr, you are listed as the backup contact for Mr. Hollingsworth here at the shop."

Interrupting the happy interloper, she asked, "I'm sorry, the shop?"

"Yes, ma'am. Peach City Motors. Mr. Hollingsworth's Mustang is ready for pickup."

Whitney snorted, recovering quickly. She could tell this stranger exactly what to do with Baxter's prized possession, but she was a lady and wouldn't be that rude before having coffee.

"I'm sorry, but why are you calling me?" she asked, her

finger already hovering over the red *End Call* button.

The sounds of papers shuffling echoed through the phone. "Mr. Hollingsworth listed you as backup contact when he got an account with us last year." He hesitated a moment, and asked, "So can you please pick up the Mustang?"

For all the crap and drama Baxter left at her feet, Whitney would be damned if she played errand girl for her ex. Nope, he and his car could burn in Hell as far as she was concerned. "Well …" She huffed, annoyed with herself for answering an unlisted number.

"Oh, please, Ms. Kerr. It's been here a week, and we need it out of the shop. I wouldn't be calling his backup contact otherwise."

Then a delicious thought occurred to Whitney. She *could* pick up Baxter's beloved car, and maybe take it on a little joy ride. She wouldn't do anything rash, but suddenly this opportunity seemed destined. Not only had the bastard already proposed to someone new, but she never got the closure she craved from the breakup.

"You know what, I think I do have time to pick up the car. What's the address?"

An hour later, Whitney was behind the wheel of Baxter's Mustang, a gift from his sixteenth birthday. The car sparkled like a ruby as she coasted down the highway, the expensive detail job certainly worth the money. The black leather roof shone in the sun, the red paint flashing at every angle. They'd even sprayed some of that fancy air freshener reminiscent of new car and upscale hotel lobby.

Whitney leaned back, resting one hand on the steering wheel and the other fiddling with the radio. Once she found a country station, she cranked up the volume and turned on the back road toward her sister's place. Pulling into a spot, she turned off the ignition and sighed. She'd picked up the car, but now what?

She'd be damned if she dropped it off at his place with a bow on the hood, but she didn't want it with her either.

Deciding it was a problem that could wait another hour, she grabbed her purse and headed inside. Once the door slammed behind her, Xena meowed and nudged her food bowl with her nose.

Scoffing, Whitney filled the dish and sighed. "I know we've both been on a binge lately, Xena, but we need to get ourselves together."

The cat seemed completely disinterested in Whitney's advice, devouring her kibble in record time. Whitney reached down to try to pet the cat, to gain an ounce of connection from another living being, but that had been a step too far. Xena lurched back, hissing like Whitney was the devil himself.

And this was just one of the reasons Whitney needed to figure out her life and move out. One of the biggest reasons she was still beaten up over the breakup was the loss of Baxter's apartment.

Of course, the primary reason was love—*barf*—but the other reason was that his place felt like hers ... at least more than her sister's apartment did. She'd had the space to make herself at home, but now she lived out of suitcases. She'd gone from Cinderella in the castle to sitting on a pumpkin long after the magic died.

While Baxter's childhood was spent at country clubs, golf courses, and river cruises, Whitney was raised on late '90s television, weekend trips to Tybee Island, and frozen pizzas. She felt like she'd won the lottery when she'd met Baxter at a zoo charity event in Atlanta. She'd been visiting a girlfriend who invited her to hobnob on her dime. They threw a couple bucks at the pandas and made their exit.

On the way out, Whitney's heel had caught on a paving stone and she'd fallen right into Baxter while he waited for the valet. She was hypnotized by his crooked grin and piercing green eyes, and Baxter was enamored with her ample cleavage and hip-hugging skirt. In a matter of days, they'd been on their first date and the rest was history.

Whitney shook the pleasant memories of Baxter from

her mind as she opened the fridge in search of something comforting that wasn't booze. Not that she was embarrassed by her alcohol intake over the last few weeks, because she wasn't, but Whitney knew she needed to stay sober. At least until she figured out what to do with Baxter's car ...

Her musings were interrupted by her cell phone. At first, she hesitated, fearing it was Baxter calling to ream her out for taking his car, but curiosity won out and she checked the screen. It was her sister. Answering right away, Whitney said, "Win, what's up?"

Winnie laughed. "Um, I don't know. Nothing interesting has happened in the last twenty-four hours. I thought I would reach out and see what's new." After a second, she added, "Cut the bullshit. How are you holding up? I got back late from a dinner thing and heard your message." Her sister paused. "Baxter is more of a dick than I realized."

Whitney snickered. "You're only now discovering this fun fact?" She pinched the bridge of her nose and sighed. "You can take me off suicide watch, if that's what you're worried about," Whitney said, rummaging in the pantry for a snack. Coming up with only a bag of popcorn, she gave up and went to the couch. *She'd seen enough popcorn lately* ...

"I'm more worried about homicide at this point."

"Actually, that's fair. I never really wanted to die. I want to get even."

"And has that urge dissipated, or should you keep me on retainer?" Winnie asked, her tone still light.

"You're a corporate litigator. Would you even be able to defend me in a murder trial?"

"Pfft. For my only sister, I'd figure it out." Confidence dripped from every syllable. For as listless as Whitney was, that was how steady and professional Winnie was. Whitney envied her big sister, craving that level of certainty in her professional life.

As if reading her mind, Winnie asked, "Did you call the agency and get another placement lined up?"

"Nope," Whitney said, letting the *P* pop. "I have no desire to answer phones and do filing in a gray cubicle farm. I have enough saved up that I can wallow another few weeks."

"Whit," Winnie said, her tone turning harsh. "You've worked there for over six years. I'm sure if you call and beg, they'll get you scheduled someplace new by Monday."

"Win," Whitney mimicked. "If you're about to scold me on my work habits, I can hang up and call our parents. Or better yet, I could just hang up."

"Mom and Dad are only worried about you, like I am. You can crash with me as long as you need, but I think you need to get a job."

"Um, need I remind you that Baxter just proposed to someone on national television?"

"Honey, it was local TV, and Baxter was always a tool."

"Fine, whatever. Why else did you call?"

Muffled voices drowned out Winnie's voice as she changed rooms. "That was all, only checking in. I'm due in another meeting in a moment, so I have to go. Promise me you'll get out of the apartment, get some fresh air, and clear your head. Maybe take a little road trip or something. Okay?"

"Yeah, yeah. Good luck with your meetings." Whitney disconnected and tossed her phone across the room, where it landed on a stack of dirty laundry, and slid to the floor. The notion of going on a quaint road trip made Whitney laugh to herself.

BB—Before Baxter—Whitney loved to plan random road trips around the south. She'd drive with girlfriends or boyfriends, and once Baxter even joined the fun, but those memories were starting to fade. That adventurous side to Whitney hadn't visited in a while, and she wondered if Winnie was right. Perhaps it was time to do something different?

An hour later and Whitney was still restless. She didn't want to sit and mope anymore, but she didn't know what to do. Winnie's advice rattled around her head. Fresh air usually required exercise, and Whitney wasn't about to make herself even more uncomfortable. Her curvy frame had picked up a few extra switchbacks from her post-relationship binge. She'd get back on track with her diet eventually, but that wasn't her biggest concern.

Stalking back into the kitchen, Baxter's keys twinkled from the countertop. She *could* get some fresh air with the top down, and that level of pettiness would likely be a balm to her ravaged soul. She'd noticed the tank was full and, suddenly, Whitney didn't know why she was standing in the apartment. It was time to joyride.

Whitney snatched the keys and headed outside. The mid-June sun hung heavy above her, but she craved the wind in her hair, so she yanked the top down. After tossing her purse on the passenger's seat, Whitney slid behind the wheel and got moving.

Now that she was on the road, she had no idea what she wanted to do. The longer she sat in the driver's seat, the more she thought about Baxter. And, honestly, she was done thinking about him. Imagining him with his new fiancée made her queasy.

Whitney bristled, her skin crawling with discomfort. He had moved on, and she needed to as well. The trouble was, she still didn't feel like she'd gotten the closure she craved.

Her stomach rumbled. In her haste to leave, she'd forgotten to eat lunch. Passing an exit that promised a pizzeria, Whitney turned off and into the parking lot of a mom-and-pop shop. Twenty minutes later, she had an extra-large supreme pizza and a Coke.

The box was heavy in her hands, the beginnings of a grease pool forming through the cardboard. This right here was why Baxter banned any food in the Mustang. He never wanted to jeopardize anything happening to his girl, he used to cry.

"It's too bad you never cared that much for me, asshole," Whitney muttered as she dropped the box on the front passenger's seat. It landed with a thud, the grease already puddling, and Whitney beamed.

Pulling back onto the winding road, she flipped the lid and helped herself to slice number one. "Hey, Baxter!" she shouted out to no one. "I'm eating in your car, and I forgot napkins!" She took a greedy bite, grease trailing down her chin as she chewed. It wasn't even the best pizza, but it was the best meal for her current mood.

Looping back toward Baxter's house, she planned to drop the car in the driveway with a few spots of pizza grease on the buttery leather interior. But as she drew nearer, memories flooded her crowded brain, and Whitney second-guessed her decision. She didn't want to do anything too wild, mostly because Baxter would likely take her to court, but she needed to leave her mark.

Whitney craved a little destruction. She wanted him to return to an inconvenience. Licking a blob of marinara from her thumb, she looked down at the pizza box. An evil grin cracked her face as she picked up another slice. Taking a bite, she chewed thoughtfully and hummed the tune of "I Will Survive."

After finishing the second slice, she decided it was time for action and eased the car into the driveway. Turning it off, she rested her head on the headrest and sighed. Her little joyride had provided a nice distraction, but vengeance was far from hers. Lifting the corner of the pizza box, she saw a satisfying orange tint to the beige leather. Baxter would be livid, but it wasn't enough.

Stepping out of the car, Whitney walked around to the passenger's side door. Flinging it open, she reached for the box and tested its weight in her hands. There were six slices of greasy cheese and red tomato sauce begging for some attention. Opening the lid, Whitney turned the box over and smashed it into the leather upholstery. The squelching sound of cheese making contact with the interior filled her with a sense of unbridled joy.

"This is for the engagement," she hissed through her

teeth as she leaned into the task. Her arms shook with rage, but she also felt lighter the more she pushed the box. When she was satisfied, she stepped back and grinned.

Not wanting her handiwork to be washed away by rain, she pulled the top back into place on the car. Just then, another thought occurred to her, and she jogged to the garage door panel and tested the code. The door rose, presenting Whitney with a final revenge. She carefully backed the car into the garage before retrieving her purse.

Pulling out her favorite red lipstick—a color Baxter used to love—she popped off the cap and circled to the windshield. In careful scrawl, she wrote *Congrats on your engagement* across the pristine glass. It would be the first thing that asshole would see when he arrived home, and it filled Whitney with the glee she usually only experienced after sex or a tub of butter pecan ice cream.

Stalking around the car, she tossed the keys onto the driver's seat and slammed the door. Retrieving her cell phone, she ordered an Uber to take her home. It was time to grab her own car and get out of town for a few days. Whitney would take her sister's advice. She only hoped it would bring her back to herself.

*

"Pack up, man. Our shift is over, and I refuse to watch you mope another minute without a beer in front of you," Lieutenant Ortiz, aka Javi, said.

Trevor groaned, logging out of his computer and tossing his empty coffee cup in the trash. His buddy was right, but he wouldn't admit that fact sober. "Give me a second to …" His words were cut off when his least favorite person sauntered into the bullpen.

"Mays, you're on hose duty tomorrow," Hastings said from his perch at his new desk. The son of a bitch had the nerve to look smug while delivering Trevor's death sentence. Hose duty was the most boring busy work imaginable, a task saved for rookies or staff on probation.

"Sure thing," Trevor said, grabbing his messenger bag from his desk drawer.

Hastings made a show of cupping his ear, leaning closer to Trevor. "I'm sorry, Lieutenant, what did you say?"

Stifling an eye roll, Trevor squared his shoulders and met Hasting's beady gaze. "I said, sure thing, Captain." An evil grin crawled up Hastings' face, and Trevor bit the inside of his cheek to stop himself from saying something that could get him fired … or arrested.

"Sorry, man," Javi said, joining Trevor at his desk. "Dude's a dick, but an order is an order." His voice was low, so no one else overheard. "We all wish you were captain, trust me."

Trevor ran a hand through his hair, leaving the russet waves at an odd angle. It wasn't a secret that very few people were thrilled with Scott's promotion, but it was cold comfort now. All Trevor knew was that it was another obstacle to his professional ambitions of taking over his father's command.

"Thanks, Javi."

Javi held up his fingers, which were crossed. "I'm hoping he'll screw up and get canned sooner rather than later. I mean, familial connections can only get you so far, right?" Javi winced as soon as he asked the question.

Trevor shook his head. "Real nice, man."

"Tell you what." Javi sighed and clapped Trevor on the shoulder. "I'll apologize over a pitcher of beers at The Pecan Pit. Let's get drunk."

The pair hopped into Javi's pickup and turned onto the highway. The town of Pinegrove, Georgia, wasn't huge, but it was home. Trevor had lived here since he was knee-high to a grasshopper, and he never thought about leaving. His mother was here, his best friends were here, and he'd be damned if he gave up on his dream of taking over the chief rank in his father's station. Station 33 would be his someday, it had to be.

Javi drummed his thumbs on the steering wheel as he took the exit for their favorite pub. It wasn't much, but The Pecan Pit was their watering hole of choice. The nachos were amazing, the beer was cheap, and the crowd was all friends and family. Right now, it was exactly what Trevor needed.

Following Javi inside, Trevor blinked at the dim lighting and exhaled. The Fourth of July was only a couple weeks away, but already the tiny hamlet was crammed with visitors. Since The Pecan Pit was one of the few bars in town, it usually filled up fastest. Trevor was relieved to have a break from crowds, even for the moment.

Javi clapped him on the shoulder, and said, "You grab a pair of stools, I've gotta hit the head."

Trevor nodded and snagged the last two stools at the end of the bar.

Before he took a seat, a pair of mugs were slid in front of him. "Here ya go, man." The gruff voice belonged to Buster, the owner of The Pecan Pit. He was about forty years old and was built like a retired NFL linebacker. You didn't mess with Buster.

"Thanks," Trevor said, pulling out his wallet and sliding his credit card across the sticky bar top. "Let's start a tab and an order of nachos, please."

Buster took the card in his meaty fingers and nodded, disappearing into the kitchen.

Trevor sipped from his beer, waiting for his frustrations to wash away. He tried to shake the feeling of inadequacy weighing him down. His father had risen up the ranks to chief at the speed of light, never once stumbling on his way to the top. In stark contrast, his only son couldn't get beyond the rank of lieutenant despite years of training and experience.

"You better start drinking faster, man," Javi teased as he slid onto his stool. "You look like crap, and I want to get lucky tonight."

Trevor sniffed, perking up when Buster appeared with

their nachos. "On the house, Trev. Sorry to hear about captain." He rapped his knuckles on the counter before Trevor muttered his thanks.

Javi was delighted with their bounty, snatching a stack of chips and shoving them in his mouth. "Oh, extra guac. You should get screwed over more often."

Trevor nudged him aside and took a handful of chips for himself. "Thanks. I'm glad the demise of my career is worth it."

Through a mouthful, Javi replied, "Do you know how expensive avocados are?"

Stifling a grin, Trevor went to work devouring the nachos. They ate in silence for a few minutes, gazes locked on the dwindling pile of fat and carbs. Around them people laughed and threw darts; their lives continuing as normal. Trevor hadn't felt normal in quite some time, and he was sick of it.

"You guys want another round?" A female voice asked over the din.

Trevor looked up to see Julia, one of the waitresses and a woman who had been asking him out for about a decade now. To be fair, she usually asked out everyone from Station 33, but she'd always been the most persistent with him. They were acquaintances at best, going through high school together before putting down roots in their hometown. Julia was sweet, and not bad to look at, but Trevor never caught a spark. That didn't mean she didn't shoot her shot every time she saw him.

Javi, aware of Trevor's feelings toward the waitress, nodded. "That'd be great. Thanks, Julia."

She returned with fresh beers and a sour expression. Glancing over her shoulder, she said, "I'm so sorry about the promotion, Trevor. Scott's an asshole and only got the job because he's sleeping with that tramp." Immediately realizing her mistake, she clapped a hand over her mouth and grimaced. "I'm so sorry, I shouldn't have said—"

Trevor took mercy on Julia and shook his head, cutting

off her rambling apology. "It's fine, thanks."

Julia was incredulous, squaring her shoulders and popping her hip to the side. "It sure ain't fine. What Virginia did to you was horrible. Cheatin' on you while wearing your ring—it makes me mad as anything. And to do it with such a loser, ugh! Whenever you're ready to get out there again, you know where to find me." She angled her shoulders in a way that showed off her cleavage. She might as well have dangled road kill in front of him, for as little as Trevor was tempted.

He picked up his beer and chugged down a third of its contents before Julia took the hint and left.

Javi slid his own beer closer before eating the last chip from the tray. "You gotta hand it to her, she's tenacious."

"I wish she would get the hint and drop it."

"I get that she's not your type, but you've got to get out there again." Javi sipped from his mug for a moment before soldiering on. "I mean, I get that you're a wreck about the breakup, but if Virginia …"

Trevor slammed his hand down on the bar top, gaining the attention of a few onlookers. "I'm not still a wreck about Virginia," he insisted, draining his beer and motioning to Buster for a third. He hadn't driven there, and he was ready to drown all his sorrows in malt and barley.

Javi lowered his voice. "You're allowed to be, man. She left you for freaking Hastings."

Trevor slapped his cheeks in mock surprise. "Oh really? I nearly forgot my fiancée left me for my work rival, and just in time for promotions. Thanks for reminding me."

"We're going to need a couple pimento cheese burgers to go with this pity party, Buster." Javi ordered before turning back to Trevor. "It's been six months, and I think you're due for a little action. If you don't want to date Julia, that's fine, but you need to find someone."

"Where? This is Pinegrove. All the women my age are taken, or I'm not interested."

"Pfft, you're missing a very important fact," Javi urged,

slurping from his beer.

"And what's that?" Trevor asked, turning his beer in his hands.

"It's almost the Fourth of July, man. This town is swarming with hundreds of out of towners. It's the perfect distraction from, well, life."

Trevor merely grunted and downed the last of his second beer. Pinegrove was known throughout the South as the perfect summer destination. Their forests brimmed with hiking trails and watering holes, not to mention their fireworks and parade on the Fourth rivaled any of the big cities. It was small-town charm meets patriotic festivities.

"I don't know. I'm no good with strangers. I get awkward, and I hate one-night stands." The admission sat bitter on his tongue, but Trevor knew it was true. He was uncomfortable with people he didn't know, and he always said the wrong things. Add on getting dumped by his fiancée and losing another promotion, and Trevor's confidence was in the toilet.

Javi wasn't deterred. "You'll figure it out. I heard from my buddy that all the motels have been booked for months. Everything is chaos since the Peachy Keen Resort closed and the mayor added more festivities. They started some of the smaller events this week already. Apparently Pinegrove will be patriotic from Flag Day to Halloween. It'll be the busiest event yet." He waggled his eyebrows. "You only need to wear your uniform and flex your biceps, man. The chicks flock around you like bees to honey."

Trevor tried to listen to his friend drone on about the upcoming festivities, but his heart wasn't in it. He was lonely, and more than a little depressed. The idea of trailing around after faceless women didn't appeal.

Just when he was about to suggest a topic change, the door to the pub opened. A woman about his age strolled in, wearing a matching expression of concern. She had a mess of black curls and curves that went on for days. Her gray gaze swept around the pub until she found an empty seat.

"Are you even listening, man?" Javi asked, waving his hand in front of Trevor's face.

"Huh?" Trevor muttered, not blinking for fear this gorgeous woman was a figment of his imagination. *The way his life was going lately, he wouldn't be surprised ...*

Javi spun on his stool and saw the woman, letting out a low whistle. "Okay, if you're not going to buy her a drink, I call dibs." He made a show of pushing off his stool and running a hand through his dark hair. Damn near half the women in the pub turned their way when Javi stepped away from the bar, and it soured Trevor's stomach.

Trevor shook his head slowly, willing his mouth to work. He wanted Javi to back off, yet he wasn't sure why. Picking up strangers wasn't his scene, but he knew Javi would have that woman's number before he could settle the check. Damn trouble was, Trevor was the nice guy, the passive guy. He didn't approach women and ask for their numbers or shower them with praise and cocktails.

Javi nudged Trevor on his way toward the gorgeous brunette. "I'll be right back, or maybe not." He winked and Trevor's pulse points in his temple throbbed. Without another word, Javi closed the distance between him and the mystery woman. Trevor swallowed past the lump in his throat, telling himself he'd made a tremendous mistake.

CHAPTER TWO

Whitney had been inside pubs like The Pecan Pit before, so she wasn't caught off guard by the noisy, or nosey, clientele when she stepped inside the dimly lit bar. She'd left her duffle and travel suitcase in the car, but she clutched her purse to her chest as her eyes adjusted to her new scenery—'90s country music droned from a classically cliché jukebox in the corner, and waitresses in denim shorts flitted between tables delivering baskets of hush puppies and greasy cheeseburgers.

Her stomach rumbled a reminder that it was beyond dinner time, so she strode up to the bar in need of sustenance and liquid courage. She hadn't stopped in Pinegrove on accident, oh no. Somewhere between Atlanta and Columbus, she'd had the brilliant idea to head toward her hometown of Peach Springs. She hadn't been back in over a decade, but the pull to the cozy surroundings of her youth was irresistible.

The only problem with her lack of a plan? Her beater of a car kept overheating on the backroads of Georgia, threatening to leave her stranded. A part of her lamented her maturity in returning Baxter's Mustang—albeit in worse shape than she'd received it—but there was no use crying over spilled milk now. Instead, she flagged down a burly man and asked for a menu.

"Here you go, darlin'," the man said, his cheeks popping with a smile. "I'm Buster, and I'll be right back for your order." He knocked his fist on the bar top once before sauntering off to another table.

"Thank you," Whitney said to Buster's back before looking for comfort food.

It was no secret that Whitney Kerr was a comfort eater. She was also a stress eater, regular eater, and occasional binge eater. Her weight was always a sore spot, but she decided to lean into who she was and try to stop fighting it. Granted, that didn't help her own criticisms of her body, but she was too worn out to obsess over the calorie count of a double cheeseburger and fries.

"What'll ya have, darlin'?" Buster asked a moment later, sliding a cold glass of sweet tea toward her. Whitney thanked him before sipping from the tea and savoring its sweet punch.

"What do you recommend?" she asked, tapping the menu. "I'm torn between the double cheeseburger and the fish fry."

Buster cocked his head, studying her a moment. Whitney struggled not to squirm in her seat; she wasn't used to strangers giving her a once-over. She liked to blend into her surroundings, but that clearly wasn't an option now.

"I'd get the burger," a male voice boomed beside her. "Buster should have taken the fish off the menu five years ago."

Splaying a hand over his chest, Buster sighed theatrically. "Javi, you wound me." Turning back to Whitney, he said, "But he's got a point. No one in their right mind orders the fish here. I'd say the double burger, or the hot chicken sandwich are best."

Whitney snapped the menu shut and handed it to Buster. "Double burger, medium rare, with extra pickles."

Buster saluted Whitney with the menu. "Comin' right

up." He disappeared into the kitchen, leaving her alone with the stranger.

Whitney spun on her stool, finally taking in the man beside her. He was on the tall side, but not one of those giants she read about in her romance books. He was strong, with cords of muscles popping on his arms as he leaned against the bar. A tangle of black curls, much like her own, sat on top of his head. His smile was warm, yet promised trouble if she wanted it.

She didn't.

"Hello," she said, her voice sounding tired to her own ears. She wasn't in the market for trouble, or at least not more than she was already in. At the proverbial crossroads of unemployed and single, Whitney knew she had a lot to figure out for herself before she hopped into bed with anyone, even handsome men like this.

The man extended his hand, smiling when she slid hers into his grip. He shook it gently before introducing himself. "I'm Javier Ortiz, but my friends call me Javi. And you are?"

Whitney bristled against the Southern manners she was raised with and finally gave in. "I'm Whitney. It's nice to meet you, Javier."

Carefully placing her hand back on the bar, he slid onto the stool beside her. "Please, Whitney, call me Javi."

Whitney was incredulous. "I'd hardly say we're friends."

"But we're no longer strangers," he countered, the glint in his eye promising more than friendship.

Whitney had to stop her eyes from rolling. This guy was as smooth as an unopened jar of peanut butter, but she wasn't in the mood to play games.

"I'm sure you're a nice man, but I'm not looking for anything other than a cheeseburger and a hotel for the night." Realizing what she'd said, she quickly amended, "To sleep, *alone*. I mean when I say I'm not looking for funny business." She waggled her fingers in his direction, striving to keep her tone light.

Javier wasn't deterred. "I hate to break it to you,

Whitney, but that hotel room is going to be hard to find."

Whitney frowned. "What do you mean?"

Javier gestured around them, to the crowded pub. "Fourth of July festivities started." He held up his hand, counting on his fingers as he spoke. "Tomorrow is the duck race by the creek, followed by the Uncle Sam costume contest, and the pie eating contest starts this weekend. Pinegrove is the busiest place east of the Mississippi."

She scrambled her brain trying to remember what would cause half of Georgia to flock to this small town when she remembered. "Oh damn, it's the fireworks extravaganza." Whitney covered her face with her hands and sighed. She'd forgotten all about festivities in her haste to get on the road.

Back when she and Winnie were girls, their parents took them a few towns over for a long weekend of fireworks, parades, games, and more food than anyone could eat in a lifetime. Part of her was pleased to see the event was still a mainstay for Pinegrove—and growing—but the other part of her was angry she'd have to keep driving.

All she really wanted right now was a warm bed, a hot shower, and a steamy romance novel. Instead, she had a well-meaning flirt and a long night on the road ahead of her. Oh well, at least a greasy burger was on its way.

"Wait, what about the Peachy Keen Resort? We stayed there once when we were kids." She held her arms out high over her head. "That place was huge." Granted, her memories were based on the world surrounding a young girl, but Whitney recalled the place was at least five stories high with a wrap-around porch and rocking chairs. It had felt like half the state of Georgia could reside and there'd still have been room to play.

Javier sucked through his teeth. "Peachy Keen closed years ago. The family couldn't keep up with the maintenance and the place was shut down. There's talk of a big corporate hotel coming to town, but nothing's happened yet. It's basically a couple motels on the outskirts of town and a handful of rentals. This year the mayor added some more activities, so it's basically going to be chaos here for weeks."

"Oh, well, damn." Whitney couldn't believe the old mainstay was gone. There went her plans for recreating childhood memories on a rocking chair, the warm summer breeze blowing through her curls.

"You're familiar with the festivities?" Javier asked, inching closer despite Whitney leaning away. His dark eyes sparkled with mischief, and Whitney wished she was interested. He was probably just the man she needed in her life, albeit temporarily. He'd be a good time—a pleasant distraction from her solo state—and she'd be on her way, but her heart wasn't in it.

Licking her lips, Whitney offered her nicest smile. "Look, Javier—"

"Javi, please," he interrupted.

"Javi. I'm sure you're a nice guy, but I'm not interested in what you're offering."

Voice dipping dangerously low, Javi raised an eyebrow, and asked, "What exactly do you think I'm offering?"

Whitney gestured between them, and said, "A roll in the hay and a few sweet words. I'm not in the market for a hasty sexual encounter that may or may not add to my emotional burden. I'm coming out of a relationship, and I ..." Whitney's words faltered when she realized she was pouring her soul out to a stranger. "You know what? I don't have to explain anything to you, or to anyone. Bye!" She pushed her stool back and hopped to her feet. Reaching out for her iced tea, she marched to the opposite end of the bar and plopped down.

Cheeks flushed with annoyance, she made a show of fumbling in her purse for her phone ... aka the international sign of *Leave me the hell alone*.

Javi spluttered in her wake, and she was proud she could still stand up for herself, despite the happenings of the last several weeks. A moment later, Javi took a step closer and began apologizing when another man joined him. "Whitney, I didn't mean to—"

His excuses were cut off by another stranger. "Leave her be, Javi." The other man's tone left no room to argue. He glanced over to Whitney and grimaced. "We're sorry for intruding on your evening." He nodded once before dragging his buddy back to their end of the bar.

Whitney appreciated the man's efforts of giving her space, but she'd be lying if she wasn't intrigued by his wavy hair, a reddish-brown reminiscent of burnt terracotta, or the lopsided grin that made her belly flop. Throw in a chin cleft that Cary Grant would envy, and she was almost smitten.

This man was her type, but she wasn't about to stir up trouble now that he'd free her from it. Besides, nice men like that usually were already married off with half a dozen children, gay, or absolute tools like Baxter Hollingsworth. Better to stay single for as long as humanly possible, handsome faces aside.

Buster chose that moment to appear with her dinner, and glowered at her empty seat. "Javi, did you scare away my customer?"

The other man gestured toward her and mumbled something to Buster. Just then a crash erupted from the kitchen, taking all of Buster's concentration. "Son of a biscuit. Trevor, can you help me out here?" He shoved the plate into the other man's hands before storming back into the kitchen.

Whitney watched in fascination as he closed the distance and slid the plate in front of her. "Sorry about that," he said, reaching over the bar to snag her a stack of napkins and a bottle of ketchup. "Buster is training a new line cook, and let's say it's not going well." He chuckled, and Whitney leaned into the sound of his warm laughter as it melted over her like caramel on her favorite sundae.

"Thank you," she said. Unable to meet his gaze, her eyes fixed somewhere over his broad shoulder.

"You're welcome. Enjoy your dinner, and I'm sorry again about Javi." He offered her another nod before going back.

Whitney took a bite of her burger and groaned with delight. It was perfectly cooked, still juicy, and covered in enough pickles to embarrass a normal person. While she devoured her burger, she idly scanned through Airbnb listings hoping to find an option close to where she was. The last thing she wanted to do was head back to Savannah with her tail between her legs. She was craving adventure, or at least a break from reality.

Planning for the near future was interrupted by a group of women in their forties and fifties barging into the pub. They were giggling like teenagers, a woman in the front striding ahead to a table set for ten. "Ladies, over here." She flopped down and patted the chair to her right.

The women filed in around her, and soon, a waitress brought over a few bottles of white wine. Each of the women held a paperback novel in their hands, and Whitney recognized it. It was a new historical romance she was dying to read, promising a brooding Duke and swoon-worthy happily ever after.

Before Whitney's curiosity got the better of her, the group's ring leader called out to the man at the bar. "Trevor!" His cheeks flamed red as he jumped off his stool and strode toward the rowdy women. At first Whitney feared it was his wife, and she chastised herself for feeling even the hint of butterflies.

She dragged her attention away from the crowd and went back to the matter at hand—finding a room for the night. Everything else—her curiosity included—could wait.

*

"Momma, you're causing more of a stir than usual." Trevor greeted his mother, leaning down to kiss her cheek and earn *oos* and *awws* from her friends. "Y'all ready for book club?" He nudged one of the books with his finger, inwardly wincing at the image on the cover. A man with wildly long hair had a woman draped over his arm with what could only be described as a heaving bosom.

"Daisy, that boy has too many manners for his own good," Joan announced to the table. "Why Virginia left for Scott, I'll never understand."

Trevor flinched at the comment, despite appreciating the comradery. "Thank you, Ms. Joan."

Daisy sat up straight and shot a glare at her friend. "Bless your heart, Joan. Why bring up something like that now?" The other woman looked chastened, but Daisy wasn't finished. "Would you like to bring up my late husband or Kim's dead dog while we're discussing upbeat topics?"

Joan shuddered, clearing her throat. "No, of course not." She looked up to Trevor and offered an apology. "I'm sorry, Trevor. I get one glass of chardonnay in me, and I get all stupid."

Kim, who just lost her beloved show dog, Watson, snickered. "Then what is your excuse when you're sober, honey?" The table dissolved into laughter, all hurts forgiven.

"I'll leave you ladies to it," Trevor offered, attempting to pull free of his mother's grasp.

"When will I see you this week, sugar?" his mother asked, her eyes shining.

Trevor cleared his throat, not wanting to break his mother's heart, let alone in public. "I'll get by soon. Work has been busy." He nearly choked on the lie. Not only was work not busy, but it was starting to be a slog. Never had Trevor hated going into the station, but that was his current reality.

His mother couldn't possibly understand the difficulty of seeing his nemesis sitting one seat below the chief; one seat away from his father's spot. He couldn't tolerate stilted conversation in the family home while his mother smothered him in love and deep-fried platitudes.

Yanking his hand so he was forced to lean down, Daisy whispered in his ear, "I know it's been awful since you lost the promotion, but please don't shut me out."

"I'm not, Momma. I've been ..." He hesitated. He'd

been what? Hiding out with Javi and drinking his feelings? "Busy?"

"Busy being sour. Now, come by tomorrow morning before work, and I'll fix you a nice breakfast." She squeezed his hand before releasing it. "Tell Javi I said hello."

Trevor took his cue and left the table, striding back to Javi. "I'm telling you, man. If I was twenty years older, or had a thing for cougars, I'm pretty sure I'd have a shot at that group."

Trevor rolled his neck, the bones popping back into place. For as much as he enjoyed his nights with Javi, the other man could be exhausting. "Need I remind you, my mother is at that table?"

Javi took a pull from his beer. "I love Ms. Daisy like my own mother, so, clearly, I was leaving her out of this discussion. Besides," he added, signing off on the check before Trevor protested, "I'm pretty sure Chief Warren has his sights set on your momma."

His friend's statement brought Trevor up short, causing him to clutch the counter edge so he didn't fall in a heap to the floor. "I'm sorry, what?"

"C'mon, man. Like you don't see it? Chief is always swinging by Daisy's place and taking care of things. Remember last month when you didn't get around to fixing those loose floorboards on the porch? Chief was out at dawn on his day off with a hammer and nails. And don't forget about—" Javi was silenced by Trevor's hand slicing through the air between them.

"Think long and hard before finishing that sentence," he warned, his pulse racing.

Unlike other children who lost parents who served, Trevor's dad passed without warning from a heart attack. He wasn't injured in the line of duty, which in some ways was a blessing. One minute his dad was laughing with the crew, leaning against the doorway into his office, and the next he was clutching his chest and falling to the floor in a sickening thud that Trevor still heard in his nightmares.

While never a prankster, his dad's sense of humor took all forms. For an instant, everyone froze and waited for their fearless leader to pop up and start laughing. When it became evident he wasn't about to do much of anything, Trevor called 911 while Javi performed CPR.

That was over two years ago, but the loss still felt as fresh as a brand-new paper cut. It stung when he least expected it. Swallowing down emotions that were not suited for a bar, Trevor prayed Javi let the issue drop. It was no secret that Chief and his mother were close, but any mentions of romance made Trevor's skin prickle.

And speaking of skin prickles, the woman from the bar was packing up her bag and leaving a stack of bills next to her empty plate. Trevor watched as she checked her reflection in her compact, fluffing her gorgeous dark curls off her face. Her skin was flawless, the color of his grandmother's fine porcelain.

She waved Buster down to pay him, holding up her phone and pointing at the screen. Buster shook his head and gestured around them before frowning. She offered a tight nod before hiking her purse up her shoulder and striding toward the restrooms.

"Buster!" Trevor shouted when she was out of earshot. "Is she all right?"

Javi perked up at his question, leaning in to hear the answer himself.

Buster shrugged. "Poor girl was looking for a place to crash tonight, but everything in a fifty-mile radius is booked for the Fourth of July." He lifted a shoulder. "Who knew the duck race would bring in these crowds?"

"Whitney could stay at my place," Javi quipped, waggling his eyebrows.

Trevor elbowed him in the ribs, hard enough to prove a point.

Trevor swallowed past the growing lump in his throat, struggling to understand why the thought of this woman leaving town gutted him. Before he had too much time to figure it out, Whitney came out of the restroom and stopped to chat with his mother and her ruckus friends. They could call it a book club all they wanted, but he knew a group of drunken women when he saw one.

Javi beat Trevor to the punch and practically skipped over to the book club, his smirk already in place. "Oh boy, here comes trouble," Daisy announced to the group. "Javi, dear, what are you up to?"

Trevor sprinted faster than a summer Olympian track star to catch up and was greeted to a shy smile from Whitney. "What's going on?" he asked, winded by his sprint.

"Did you know that Miss Whitney here has read all of Darla Champaign's books?" Daisy asked, as impressed as if she'd witnessed Whitney walk on water.

"Urm, no?" Trevor said, rubbing the back of his neck.

Javi, sensing an opening, stepped closer to Whitney and beamed. "You don't say? You read all of Ms. Champaign's catalog? Why, that must be close to a dozen books."

Joan had either sobered up from her chardonnay haze or was already tired of Javi's bullshit. She reached out and pinched his bicep between her gnarled fingers until the he whimpered. "Javier Ortiz, I won't have you interrupting book club with your flirting and nonsense. We all know Darla Champaign has written over forty-five novels. Now mind your business and find another pre-menopausal woman to flirt with."

The mere mention of menopause was enough to send Javi scampering back to his perch at the bar, but Trevor was rooted in place. Daisy and Whitney were talking in hurried hushed tones, and it brought the hairs on the back of his neck to rising.

"Everything okay?" he asked, his attention locked on his mother. If anyone at that table had answers, it was Daisy Mays.

"Yes, of course. I was figuring out the logistics of Whitney staying with me."

Now that knocked the wind from Trevor's sails.

"Staying with you?"

Whitney interjected, a lovely flush crawling up her cheeks. "Your mother was very kind to offer her guestroom, but I really don't mind looking for a hotel."

"Which you won't find anywhere near Pinegrove this time of year, especially since Peachy Keen closed and the mayor and city council added the new events. Pinegrove is as busy as Atlanta when it hosted the SEC championship. Rooms booked up months ahead of the Fourth of July festivities," Kim said, quickly becoming Trevor's favorite person for reasons he wasn't ready to explore.

"Oh." Whitney sighed, her shoulders slumping so low, her purse slid off and onto the floor. Before she stooped down to grab it, Trevor was on the move. He'd crawled through burning buildings and climbed into infernos with less grace than he displayed in that instant. He was determined to help this woman in some way, even though he didn't understand why it was important.

"Here you go," he muttered, placing her purse into her waiting hands.

"Thanks."

His mother's gaze drilled a hole through his back, but he pretended to be oblivious. "You can trust my mother," he insisted, feeling as awkward as his teen years.

Joan threw in her two cents. "Of course you can. Daisy is the late fire chief's wife, and she's been a staple of Pinegrove since she was born."

"I'm also good at reading people," she said, holding up her book, "and reading books. If you're a fan of Darla Champaign, then that's all I need to know."

Whitney was incredulous. "Ma'am, I really do appreciate the offer, but we're strangers. How do you know I'm not an ax murderer?"

Kim leaped out of her seat in excitement. "Are you? That would certainly liven things up around here." She turned to Daisy. "Although I don't want to see you get murdered, honey."

"Thanks for that," mother and son said in unison, earning a smile from Whitney.

"My son is a firefighter, and he won't let anything bad happen to me," Daisy assured Whitney, who was still looking more worried than relaxed. "And besides, it's too late to drive around looking for a hotel. Follow me back to my house, and if you're not happy with what you find, you can try somewhere else."

Whitney nibbled on her bottom lip a moment before nodding. "Well, I guess it won't hurt to take a look."

Daisy clapped. "Wonderful. I'm glad that's settled. Ladies, the meeting is adjourned. Next time we're reading that book with the hockey players."

Kim scooted out of her seat and gathered her book. "Is it spicy?"

Trevor was afraid to ask but couldn't hold his curiosity at bay. "Spicy?"

Daisy chuckled. "She means smutty. Yes, Kim. This book is five out of five chili peppers."

Kim fanned herself with her paperback and grinned. "Good Lord, I better prepare myself."

"In more ways than one," Joan muttered, following the other woman outside.

That left Daisy, Whitney, and Trevor, the other readers had abandoned ship a half hour ago. "Whitney, would you like to follow me to the house? I'm out back in a blue pickup."

Whitney fiddled with her purse strap a moment before agreeing. "Sure, but, Ms. Daisy? Please don't let me put you out. I'm a stranger, and you don't—"

"You're hardly a stranger. You're from Peach Springs, so we're practically neighbors."

Trevor's ears perked up. "You're from Peach Springs?"

Whitney finally met his gaze, and it was like a punch to the gut. Her eyes were troubled, yet he didn't believe she was a bad person ... more likely a good person in a bad stretch. *Lord, he related to that.*

"Yes, I grew up there with my parents and older sister. I haven't been back in ages, and it felt like the right time to…" She didn't finish her thought, her gaze now off in the distance meeting an old memory. "Anyway, I really don't mean to cause any trouble."

For reasons he couldn't explain, Trevor needed to hear his name on her lips. He extended his hand, fingers itching to touch her, even for a heartbeat. "I'm sorry, we weren't properly introduced. I'm Trevor Mays."

His mother gathered the last of her things and chuckled. "I'm sorry, Whitney. I raised my son to have more manners than that." She flicked his arm and tutted.

Covering the spot with his hand, he chuckled. "It's hard to introduce yourself when Javi's got his flirt on."

"Trevor, it's nice to meet you," Whitney said, finally placing her hand in his. A bolt of heat surged up his arm and through his core. This woman was a walking matchstick. "Your friend is certainly charming, but I appreciate you intervening."

"Javi means well, but he certainly is a ladies' man." Lowering her voice, Daisy said, "Not my Trevor though. He's like his daddy—loyal, sweet, and totally devoted."

A flush crept up Trevor's neck, and he wanted to crawl under the table and die from embarrassment. Instead, he let go of Whitney's hand and tried to hide how much she affected him. "Thank you for the glowing testimonial, Momma. I sound like a golden retriever."

Daisy was undeterred. "Well now, since we're all friends, can we head out?" She craned her neck and sighed. "I think your ride is leaving, sugar. Care to snag a ride with me?"

Trevor turned to see what had his mother's attention. Javi was propped up against the bar, giving his A game to a pair of tourists in high-waisted shorts and sparkles in their eyes. He'd be in no mood to drive Trevor home now. "Yes, ma'am. I'll take that ride, please."

"And you're sure this isn't too much?" Whitney asked, flapping her hands between herself and Daisy. "I really don't mind finding something outside of town."

"Sugar, you're coming back to Casa de Daisy." His mother looped her arm through Whitney's and led the way outside. "You head to the truck, Trevor. I'm going to walk Whitney to her car."

And with that, Trevor watched his mother walk Whitney to an old beater that had seen better days. Whitney glanced back at him once and smiled before turning her attention back to her vehicle. He wasn't sure what the hell was going on, but suddenly life in Pinegrove was a lot more interesting.

CHAPTER THREE

Whitney thought she might have officially lost her mind. She had no reason to be following a sweet lady and her handsome son home. Wait, he wasn't handsome. Okay, that was a lie. He was a walking firefighter fantasy, with broad shoulders, biceps that could crush cinder blocks, and that little divot in his chin that …

"Knock it off, Whit!" she scolded herself, hands squeezing the steering wheel. "You don't have time for that nonsense." The mini pep talk did nothing to calm her nerves.

Whitney appreciated this situation for what it was—a kind woman helping her out. Daisy's son, no matter how attractive, was not hers to moon over. This wasn't her life, and it certainly wasn't permanent.

Knowing Winnie would have an unholy fit if she didn't keep her in the loop, she hastily dialed her sister and waited for a reply. It was after nine o'clock, so she might already be in bed at the hotel. Despite being a workaholic, Winnie appreciated the need for her beauty sleep.

To her surprise, a sleepy voice greeted her. "Whit, what's up?"

"Sorry to call late, but I wanted to keep you in the loop."

The sound of rustling sheets and a light clicking on came through the line as Winnie woke up. "You're fine. It's the life of an attorney, I guess. I'm up with the rooster and passed out after dinner. What's up?"

Whitney chewed on her bottom lip for a moment before summoning her courage. "I, um, took your advice."

"You're back to work? That's great! What is your new placement?"

Oops, perhaps her sister wasn't the target audience for her news. But then again, Whitney really didn't have anyone else to call. It wasn't that she didn't have friends back in Savannah, but they were people she'd met through Baxter's circle. The thought of calling these women now felt uncomfortable, like when she ate the entire package of Oreos. And not for nothing, but those women didn't come calling when he dumped her. There was radio silence on both sides.

"No, Win. I took your other advice—I'm on the road."

"Oh! Where to? Did you take Xena with you?"

A lump the size of a peach pit lodged in Whitney's throat, and she had to cough three times to find her voice. "No, erm. Xena is with your neighbor, Mrs. Rodgers in 4A."

More silence. Even through the lack of sound, Whitney could *feel* her sister reacting. "Where are you?"

Forcing a laugh she didn't feel, Whitney strived to sound casual. "Believe it or not"—she added a maniacal giggle— "I'm in Pinegrove, you know, that little town near Peach Springs."

"Pinegrove?" There was no mistaking the shock in Winnie's voice. "But why?"

If Whitney had the answer, she would have shared it. "Not sure, really. I got in the car and decided to head west, I guess. The point of this call is to let you know I'm fine, Xena is fine, and I'll keep you posted on when I'm coming back."

"Where are you staying? Did you get an Airbnb?"

Part of Whitney considered lying to her big sister, spin

the truth to meet her needs and hope for the best. Then there was the rational side of Whitney, who watched *Dateline* and *Law & Order,* and she needed someone to know her location. "Well, actually ..." She laughed again, and this time Winnie called her out.

"Yeah, I'm going to need details. You're about to hyperventilate on me, and that can only mean one thing."

"And what's that?" Whitney countered, death grip still firm on the steering wheel.

"You're lying about something. Spill it, Whit. Now."

Whitney groaned, hating herself now for calling her sister. "Okay, but you're going to freak out."

"Too late," Winnie warned.

Whitney lifted her chin, needing to feel in control even if Winnie couldn't see her. "I'm staying with a sweet woman I met at a bar."

Winnie snorted so loudly, Whitney was surprised she couldn't hear it across the state line. "Honey, please tell me you're not switching teams because of Baxter. I know that man was an absolute letch, but I don't think you'd like my side of the dugout."

Winnie was bisexual and had dated her fair share of Georgians since coming out in law school. "First of all, that's a terrible baseball analogy. But I agree, and it's nothing like that. Her name is Daisy, and she runs a romance book club in Pinegrove. She's Mom's age, give or take."

"This is getting weirder and weirder. Why are you staying with Daisy?"

"Remember the Fourth of July festivals Pinegrove used to do when we were kids?"

Winnie sighed wistfully. "Of course. Those are some of my favorite childhood memories. Are you saying you're going to the fireworks show?"

"Among other things," Whitney admitted, cautious to keep her attention on the road as she took a turn a little too quickly to follow Daisy's pickup. "Look, I got in the car and started driving. I didn't have a plan; I didn't think of where

I was going." Even through the phone, she sensed her sister's answering eye roll.

"Whit, you're going to stay with a stranger and watch the fireworks? I know it's been a rough month, but you need to think this through. What do you even know about this woman?"

I know that her son is gorgeous and protective of his mother. I know that I'd love to run my fingers through those dark red locks. I know it'd be nice to just avoid my life for a little while.

"I know enough. Her son is a fireman, and everyone at the pub vouched for her."

"Oh, well, if a few drunks at a bar vouch for the woman, I'll relax."

"Win, that's not fair."

Winnie cursed under her breath and sighed. "You're really going through with this, aren't you?"

"Yep, it's why I'm calling. When I get to the house, I'll text the address so you know where I am."

"You mean so I know where your corpse will be buried?" Winnie deadpanned.

"That's real nice."

"Says the woman that called to wake me up and tell me she was on an odyssey to our childhood?" Under her breath she muttered, "And you didn't take Xena with you."

"It's better than sulking back in Savannah." Since she was feeling feisty and already pissed off at her sister, she spat, "And Xena hates my guts. She'll be happier with Mrs. Rodgers until you come back."

"Mhm, sure. And this has nothing to do with the fireman son you just mentioned?"

"No!" Whitney's response was too quick, and much too loud. Winnie snickered as Whitney rallied. "I mean that she's a nice lady giving me a place to crash."

"Please be careful, Whit. I'm serious."

"I will be, and I love you."

"Love you too." And with that, Winnie hung up and Whitney tossed her phone onto the passenger's seat. Her hands flexed around the steering wheel as she followed Daisy and Trevor into a small neighborhood. The houses were mid-century with manicured lawns and mature trees flanking the road, and it was like she'd driven onto the set of *Leave it to Beaver.*

She simultaneously felt at home and on edge as she pulled up in front of a small cottage with white shutters and pink and yellow flower beds. This house was a home, and right now that's exactly what she needed. The lunacy of the moment be damned.

*

"Momma, I don't mean to tell you your business," Trevor said, leaning forward with his head in his hands. The four beers he'd crushed had caught up to him, and his head pounded in time with the turn signal.

"But I have a feeling you're about to, son." Daisy's voice was light as she made the final turn into their neighborhood.

"Are you sure this is wise, Momma? You don't even know this woman, and she could be a whole mess of trouble." *For his mother and him …*

Daisy waved away his concern with a flit of her wrist. "Now, come on, when was the last time I've done something foolish?" She shot him a sideways glance. "And choose your words carefully, Mister I'm-drunk-on-a-weeknight."

She had his number and there was no denying it. "Fair point, but I'm worried about you."

"You needn't be, considering you'll be crashing in your old room. If Whitney does turn out to be an ax murderer, I trust my big, strapping son to protect me."

Trevor sat upright and cursed under his breath. He needed a pair of aspirin and a dark room pronto. "Momma, I thought you'd take me home."

Daisy huffed. "After nine o'clock? You know I hate driving at night." That was a lie, and Trevor wasn't sure what his mother was up to. His apartment was less than five minutes down the road, seeing as how Pinegrove could fit on a postage stamp.

"What about work tomorrow? How will I get to the station?"

"You can borrow my car. I have nowhere to be until Bingo on Thursday."

Trevor was incredulous. "Bingo? Aren't you a little young for that game?"

The first thing that scared Trevor after his father's death was what would happen to his mother. She and his daddy had been high school sweethearts, never leaving the other's side in over thirty years. He'd watched what happened to his grandmother when his granddaddy passed, and he didn't want Daisy to become an old widow before it was time.

"It's a laugh, I'll tell you. Paul has been taking me. Didn't he tell you?"

Javi's observation from the bar raced back with gusto as Trevor tried not to barf in his mother's pickup. "No, he didn't," he said through clenched teeth. "I didn't realize you were seeing that much of Chief Warren."

"Ain't much of a surprise, son. We have been friends since high school." That wasn't news to Trevor, as there were no secrets in Pinegrove.

Except for this secret, which Trevor was quick to solve. "So, what does that mean?"

"What does what mean?" Daisy asked, putting the truck in park in the driveway.

Realizing he had about thirty seconds to get to the bottom of his mother's love life, Trevor went straight for the truth. "Are you dating Chief Warren, Momma?"

Daisy turned to face her son. Even in the light from the porch, her gaze was warm and her smile forgiving. "A lady never kisses and tells." That was all she gave him before throwing the door open and bounding out of the truck. "Whitney sugar, you can park right there."

The sound of Whitney's name brought Trevor back to

the present, leaving his mother's dating concerns for another time. Scrambling from the passenger's seat, Trevor nearly fell to his knees when he stepped down from the truck.

Whitney stood in front of her car, arms wrapped around her waist as she waited for them to join her. Her eyes darted around her, taking in the house and the neighborhood. "Are you sure it's all right if I stay here tonight?" she asked, worrying her bottom lip. It took all of Trevor's strength not to reach out and run his thumb over the plump skin to soothe her nerves.

Woah, man!

Clearing his throat, Trevor motioned to her car. "It's no trouble at all. May I carry in your bags?"

"They're in the trunk. I packed light."

She wasn't kidding. All Trevor found was a small duffle bag the color of pink cotton candy and a wheely suitcase. When he'd traveled with Virginia, this would have been the size of her makeup bag, not all her belongings for a trip. He admired Whitney a little more as he hoisted the bag on his shoulder and led the way up the driveway, only stumbling twice.

Daisy had run ahead, turning on the lights of the house so Whitney wasn't greeted by darkness. "C'mon in, sugar!" Before Whitney joined them, their basset hound, Gus, bounded out the door to relieve himself. "That rude fella right there was Gus. He's sweet as pie but has a bladder the size of a pecan shell."

Glancing down at the dog, Whitney smiled before turning her attention back to the human owners of the house. "Thank you," Whitney muttered as she crossed the threshold. She took in the surroundings, and for some odd reason, Trevor hoped she liked what she saw.

The house was modest, but it had been home his entire life. The floors had divots where he and his sister had played with their toys, the walls were covered in tiny slashes to mark their growth spurts, and the curtains in the kitchen were the same as when his mother had decorated after moving in.

Trevor stepped ahead and strode into the guest room, carefully placing Whitney's bags on the corner of the bed.

The guest room had been his sister Jessie's when she was a girl. It wasn't that Jessie didn't want to visit often, but since joining the Peace Corps out of high school, her visits home were few and far between. He missed his sister, but Trevor wasn't going to focus on that fact now.

"This is lovely," Whitney cooed, stepping inside and studying the display of his mother's prized figurines. She'd collected one every time they went on vacation. The shelf of souvenirs was basically a snapshot in time of their family trips. Whitney peered down at one of a peach on a little waterfall. She gasped, gently picking up the piece to study it. "I have this exact one," she said, cradling it to her chest.

Trevor's own chest expanded at the look of wonder on her lovely face. He wasn't sure, but he guessed Whitney was about his age, on the sunny side of thirty, give or take. Her eyes sparkled and her lips were turned into an adorable smile.

Daisy joined them, sitting on the side of the bed with a grin. "That's from Peach Springs's bicentennial celebration. My late husband and I took a weekend trip away to stuff our faces with peach jam and cookies. Have you ever had their spiced peach preserves? I'll tell you, best jam I've ever eaten. And what about those peach waffles?"

Whitney placed the figurine back and eased down on the bed opposite Daisy. She clasped her hands together as if in prayer and sighed. "I was only a little girl then, but I remember my grannie bringing Winnie and me over for the bake-off. I've never seen so many peach pies, and I've lived in Georgia all my life."

It was clear his mother was just as enchanted by Whitney as he was. Her eyes were focused, her smile eager, and the questions kept flowing. Leaning against the doorjamb, Trevor tried to school his features so he didn't give himself away. "Who is Winnie?" he asked, genuinely curious about Whitney and her life.

She turned toward him, and her smile lit up the room. Two rows of pearly whites gleamed at him, and another chunk of Trevor's resolved chipped away. "She's my sister. She's a lawyer out in Savannah. I've been, uh, staying with her these last few weeks."

Trevor didn't miss how her cheeks flushed at that admission, which only brought more questions. *Why was she staying with her sister? Was she in trouble? Was* she *trouble?*

Either oblivious to Trevor's questions or uncaring, Daisy shifted the conversation back to safer topics. "It's nice you're close to your sister. My youngest, Jessie, is off saving the world. I do wish she'd visit more, but here you are." His mother's casual shoulder lift hid years of sadness over missing her only daughter.

Whitney tucked a dark lock of hair behind her ear. "I'm lucky. Winnie's always been there for me."

"That's what family does," Daisy said as she pushed herself off the bed. She walked to the far side of the room, then picked up a framed picture of their family about fifteen years ago. Jessie and Trevor were only two years apart, but they could have been twins. Daisy had forced them to wear matching shirts and denim shorts, their pairs of gangly limbs on full display. Both siblings had mouths full of metal, their braces glinting in the photo.

Trevor could have done without that glimpse into his awkward past, but there was no stopping Daisy Mays when she set her mind to something. You had to hold on for the ride and hope for the best. "This is our family. My late husband, Nick, and my youngest, Jessie."

Whitney winced at the mention of his father, and she offered her condolences. "I'm so sorry for your loss, Daisy." Handing the picture back to Trevor, she added, "And to you as well. I know it's not the same, but my parents moved to Florida a few years ago. I miss them every day."

Daisy saved them all from the tension of the moment by

shifting gears. "Do you have a lot of kin in Peach Springs?"

Whitney shook her head. "Not many anymore. My father is William Kerr, and my mother is Janet Kerr, née Rollins."

Daisy gasped, clasping her hands over her mouth. "Is your aunt Anita Rollins?"

Whitney laughed. "She is, but it's Waysmith now. She married my uncle over twenty-five years ago. They just retired to Arizona."

"To Colin Waysmith?" At Whitney's answering nod, Daisy's mouth dropped open as she gawked. "My, my, what a small world. I used to go to band competitions with your momma and auntie. I'll need to give them a call." Turning back to her son, she pointed at him and raised an eyebrow. "See, son? I told you Whitney wasn't a stranger."

Trevor held his hands up in surrender. "You're right, as always. I'll never question your judgment again." *Unless it has to do with dating my boss,* he mused.

He wasn't certain, but Trevor thought he saw Whitney relax at this realization, proving she was as nervous with the temporary housing situation as he was. When Daisy walked toward the door, he noticed Whitney yawn behind her hand.

"Momma, maybe we should let Whitney get some rest? I'm sure she's had a long day."

"Of course, how silly of me." She held up a finger and jogged out of the room, leaving Trevor and Whitney alone with dozens of ceramic eyes watching them. If he were honest with his mother, he hated most of those souvenirs. He wanted the memories connected with them, but not their creepy gazes and mismatched shapes and colors.

A moment later, Daisy strode back in with an armful of towels. "The sheets were washed last week, and no one sleeps here anyway." She plopped the towels on the bed. "And here's some towels."

"Thank you so much. This really is quite generous of you, Daisy."

"My house is your home, sugar. Now we'll get out of

your hair so you can rest. If it's all right with you, breakfast is at eight. I want to get Trevor fed before he heads off to work."

Whitney snagged his gaze and offered a slight smile. "You're spending the night, too?"

Trevor opened his mouth to reply, but his mother beat him to it. "Oh yes, ma'am. Can't have my only son drinking and driving."

Trevor ran a hand down his face and stifled a groan. "Momma, I'm hardly fall-down drunk right now." *Not to mention being in close proximity with Whitney sobered him right up.*

"Nonsense. Go over to your room and get some shuteye." Turning to Whitney, she said, "Your children hit thirty and suddenly they know it all." She winked and left the room, leaving Whitney with a goofy grin and enough towels for a three-month stay.

"Thank you, Trevor. I know this whole situation is a little odd."

The thing of it was, he would have agreed with her an hour ago. Yet now, standing in his childhood home surrounded by the unfamiliar scent of Whitney's lilac perfume, he couldn't imagine the space without her.

"Not odd at all, Whitney. My room is at the end of the hall. Give a holler if you need anything." He nodded once before closing the door behind him.

As Trevor collapsed on his childhood bed, he stared unblinkingly at the ceiling. Not only was tomorrow a long day of tedious work, but he was emotionally wrung out. There was something going on in his ribcage, and it had everything to do with the curvy brunette down the hall. Squeezing his eyes shut, Trevor prayed for sleep. As he drifted off, his dreams were filled with lilac fields and a laugh that sounded like music for his soul.

CHAPTER FOUR

Morning came earlier than Whitney expected. Slices of sunlight peeked through the blinds as she rolled over on an unfamiliar mattress. She nuzzled into the pillow, smelling a detergent that wasn't hers, and her eyes flashed open. "What in the ...?" She sighed as she pulled herself to sitting. A decorative throw pillow fell onto the floor, landing with a small thud.

It took a moment, but memories of the last twenty-four hours collided back into place. Baxter's car, the impromptu road trip, sweet Daisy and her painfully handsome son. Oh boy.

Finger-combing her curls, Whitney slid out of bed and rummaged through her bag for her toothbrush and makeup case. There was no way she was facing either of the Mays without looking her best ... or as close to her best as possible. Cracking the door open, she peered into the hall and didn't see anyone. Holding her breath, she tiptoed into the bathroom and closed the door with a click.

Exhaling, she went to work looking more presentable. After brushing her teeth, washing her face, and putting on enough makeup to look fresh, she was ready for her day. *No matter what it brought ...*

Down the hall came the heavenly aromas of bacon and cinnamon. Whitney surreptitiously wiped the drool from her chin and headed toward sustenance. As she reached the doorway, she heard Trevor and Daisy talking.

"Momma, I think that's enough food," Trevor said. He had a mug in his hand with a fire station logo, his dark red hair slicked into place like he was on his way to work. Gus dozed at his feet, ears splayed out to the side and a trail of slobber puddled under his snout.

Daisy tutted, adding another egg to the pan. "Hush up now. It's nice to cook for a crowd."

Trevor snorted but recovered quickly. "I know you miss having a full house, but I don't think Whitney and I can eat that much. I'll have to invite over half the station to help."

Daisy whirled around, her lavender apron flapping into place. "Funny you should say that," she started, before noticing Whitney. "Good morning, sugar. I trust you slept well?" She wasted no time pouring a mug of coffee and sliding it across the table to an empty place.

Whitney joined the duo, quickly adding a splash of cream and a generous spoonful of sugar to her caffeine fix. "Good morning, Daisy. This all smells heavenly." She slurped from her mug before bracing herself to meet Trevor's gaze. The man had this effect on her belly, like she was about to go down the first hill of a rollercoaster, and she wasn't sure she liked it. "Morning, Trevor."

He dipped his head in greeting, lips quirking into a smile. "Morning, Whitney. Was everything to your liking in the room?"

It was sweet of him to ask, especially since Whitney wouldn't complain if it wasn't satisfactory. "Oh yes, it was great. I had no idea how much I needed to get away until last night." She flinched at her words, hoping the Mays clan wouldn't expect her to pour out her heart over a short stack of pancakes. *Although if anything could get her talking …*

Her musings were interrupted by a knock at the front door and a familiar voice. "Good morning, Ms. Daisy!" Javi strode into the kitchen and joined Daisy at the stove. He kissed her cheek and washed his hands at the sink before pulling out a seat at the table. He turned his megawatt grin to Whitney. "Hello again, Whitney. How are you on this fine morning?"

Trevor didn't give her a chance to answer. "What in the hell are you doing here at this hour, Javi?" His question was answered with a playful swat to the back of his head from his mother, and Whitney nearly choked on her coffee.

"Hush up, I invited him. I changed my mind about you borrowing my car. Plus I knew I'd cook for a crowd, and I haven't fed Javi in weeks."

Trevor rubbed the back of his head and flipped off Javi as soon as Daisy's back was turned. Javi rolled his eyes and poured his own coffee. "I'm surprised you're even vertical. You were still at The Pecan Pit when the three of us left."

Javi flashed a look to Trevor that Whitney could hardly decipher. She wagered he'd either had a good night or a *really* good night. "Don't you worry about me, man. All I need is a little caffeine and a dose of Ms. Daisy's fine cooking."

That earned him the first helping of eggs as Daisy filled a bowl with a worrisome amount of yellow fluff. "Here you go, Javi." Daisy took a break from serving breakfast to top off Whitney's coffee mug.

Suddenly realizing her manners, Whitney pushed to her feet and tried to step over to the stove. "Let me help you with this. Where on earth are my manners?"

Before she took a step, Trevor reached out and carefully cupped her elbow. It was barely a caress, but Whitney felt his touch from her hairline to her toes. On wobbly knees, she fell back into her seat. "Momma's got it. She lives for fussing over people, so it's best to do as she says." He pulled his hand back and smirked.

"My son is right. Please make yourself comfortable. I so rarely get to spoil people with food."

Javi doused his eggs with hot sauce before shoveling in a massive bite. Through a mouthful, he moaned and leaned back in his chair. "Ms. Daisy, is this a standing invitation to breakfast, because I'm in love."

Trevor pointed at his friend with a piece of bacon and sighed. "You're in love about a dozen times a day, Javi. And my mother's not your personal chef."

"Although, if you ever need help, you know where to find me," Daisy teased as she flipped the last pancake onto a platter.

Placing the dish on the table, Whitney felt like she was in the middle of a Martha Stewart magazine photo shoot. Trevor handed Whitney a plate of bacon, and she pinched one slice for herself. Frowning at her meager helping, Trevor slid three more pieces onto her plate. "You'll never get out of here alive if you're not bursting with cholesterol," he warned.

This was new for Whitney. Never had a man in her life *encouraged* her eating. Baxter was famous for taking her to fancy restaurants known more for their elite clientele and micro meals than their lavish portions of comfort cuisine. On too many instances to count, he'd left the pantry and fridge bare of anything that wasn't from a tree or plant, forcing Whitney to hide her own cans of Pringles or Cheetos in the linen closet.

Yet here was Trevor, a man who had known her for a matter of hours, ensuring that not only did she get to eat, but she ate to her heart's content. "Thank you," she said, fingers trembling as she plucked a piece and took a bite.

"You're welcome. You need some syrup for those hotcakes?" Trevor didn't wait for her to answer, passing her the bottle.

Everyone tucked into their breakfasts, *ooh*ing and *ahh*ing over the spread. Daisy flushed with pride and kept piling plates until Javi leaned back and rubbed his protruding belly. "I don't think I'll ever eat again," he lamented, muttering something in Spanish before waving his napkin in the air like a white flag.

"I'm with Javi, Momma. You outdid yourself."

"I can't think of the last time I ate this well, especially on a weekday," Whitney agreed, stacking empty dishes to carry over to the sink.

Trevor helped her clear dishes while Javi put away the syrup and hot sauce bottles. "I hate to eat and run, but my boy and I need to get to work."

Groaning, Trevor covered his face with his hands. "Please, don't remind me."

With his shoulders slumped in defeat, he hardly painted the picture of the happy community fireman.

Whitney cocked her head and studied him a moment before asking, "You don't like being a fireman?"

Her question sucked the oxygen from the warm kitchen, and she immediately knew she'd stepped on an emotional landmine. Javi whistled under his breath, and Daisy shoved plates into the dishwasher without glancing up.

Whitney shook her head and backpedaled. "Forget I asked, that's a personal question from a stranger. I should probably pack and hit the road anyway."

That statement shot three pairs of eyes in her direction. "Hit the road? But you only just got her, sugar. I was hoping you'd come with me to town this morning. I wanted to show you Kim's shop and the bookstore. It's called the Cracked Spine. They recently had renovations, and their romance section is to die for."

"We're only getting to know each other. Don't let me down now," Javi pleaded, his signature grin in place. Whitney was pretty sure this man could talk almost anyone into almost anything.

Whitney looked to Trevor, who was studying her with an unreadable expression. He either wanted to shove her out the door or pull her into an embrace. Honestly, she was hoping for the latter.

"Yeah, you should stay a while," he said, his voice low.

Daisy wasn't having it and rushed to Whitney's side. "We never asked you, where are you headed?"

Whitney opened her mouth to respond, but nothing

came out. Where was she going to go anyhow? She wasn't ready to head back to Savannah, and the thought of missing the fireworks and parade made her chest tighten. Over the years she'd remembered Pinegrove with fondness, but up until now she hadn't realized how much she missed it.

"Well, I ..." but she was never good at thinking on her feet. She looked like a goldfish out of water as she opened and closed her mouth an alarming number of times.

Finally, Daisy took pity on her. "Whitney, if you're worried you're overstaying your welcome, don't be. It's so nice having someone in the house again, and you're more than welcome to stay through the Fourth."

Trevor's eyes had never left her, and Whitney couldn't explain the pull to this man. They'd hardly shared more than a handful of sentences, but there was a charge between them. As ludicrous as it sounded, she wasn't ready to let him go. "If you're sure I won't be in the way."

"Sugar, I wouldn't ask if I didn't mean it," Daisy insisted.

Trevor leaned forward and rested his hand on her shoulder, giving it a reassuring squeeze. "What Momma said, you're more than welcome to stay."

Javi and Daisy exchanged a look that made Whitney's toes curl in her socks. They were onto something she wasn't aware of, but she ignored it for now.

"Well, okay. But I insist on paying a nightly rate, like any other hotel or Airbnb."

Daisy ushered Whitney down the hall. "We'll discuss logistics later. Why don't you get ready for a day in town? I'd love to talk about books with a new reader. Maybe grab some lunch?"

Giving in, Whitney went into "her room" and changed into a sundress, all the while telling herself she was making the right decision. It was good to get outside her comfort zone, especially with people like this. There was the sad notion that she was lonelier than she'd realized, and vowed to rectify that situation. Baxter had broken her heart and shaken her self-esteem, but Whitney was ready to start piecing herself back together. Starting now …

*

"You might as well say something," Trevor grumbled from the passenger's seat. His traitorous best friend was behind the wheel, slurping from his mother's favorite to-go mug. It was covered in daisies and puppies, and for some reason, it made Trevor's blood boil. "And why did you take Momma's mug?"

Javi shot him a glance before placing the mug back in the cup holder. He raised an eyebrow and chuckled. "Okay, man, so you want to talk about the merits of coffee vessels? I'm game." He tapped his temple as he pondered all the options. "Well, I've never been a big fan of Styrofoam. It's hard not to chew on it, first of all, but I feel like it's probably giving me cancer. I don't mind a good paper cup, but only if it has the sleeve on it, otherwise I burn my hands. Of course there's always …"

Trevor covered his face with his hands and moaned. "You know what's ridiculous?"

"This line of conversation?" Javi asked, lips quaking with mirth.

"The fact that I know you'd drone on about coffee cups until we get to the station, and even then, you'd only take a break if we got a call."

Javi shrugged, picked up the floral cup, and took a long pull. "I mean, you're not wrong. I'm only trying to figure out why you're so pissed."

"Really? You don't understand why I'm pissed?" Trevor's voice rose, despite not understanding his own mood swing. Ever since he'd laid eyes on Whitney, he'd been a walking, talking contradiction. He simultaneously wanted her on the road and in his bed. No woman had even turned his head since Virginia stomped on his heart.

"Wouldn't have asked if I did." Javi turned down the radio and hummed to himself for a minute until Trevor broke.

"Okay, I'm pissed about a lot of things. This whole thing"—he paused and flapped a hand in front of the windshield—"is just a bridge too far. I can't handle this on top of my work bullshit. It's too much, Javi. She seems nice and …" Tripping over his own tongue, he couldn't find all the words to list every single one of Whitney's *nice* attributes.

Javi mimicked his gesture and sighed. "First of all, that's probably the best thing that's happened since Virginia pulled a runner."

Trevor scoffed. "A stranger coming to town to bunk up with my mother is a good thing? How do we know she's not crazy and some type of grifter?"

"Pfft, if Whitney is a grifter, then she can grift me for all I'm worth." That statement earned Javi a punch in the shoulder from Trevor that caused the car to jerk. "Easy, man," Javi said, rubbing the sore spot. "For someone who's not into her, you're sure protective."

And he knew it. Trevor couldn't explain why he was so worried about Whitney for her sake, not his mother's. Daisy Mays could not only handle herself, but she didn't trust just anybody. If Whitney passed the Daisy test, she was likely a good person.

"I can't explain it," he muttered, staring out the window as Pinegrove flew by.

At least it was summer, his favorite season. The town was alive in every possible way. The trees were green and lush, the air was warm and welcoming, and Main Street was bustling. He had so many fond memories of summers in his hometown, they threatened to choke him in his current state.

Last night when he struggled to fall asleep, he thought about Whitney and showing her how much had grown and changed since her girlhood trips to Pinegrove. He wanted to take her out for cotton candy and watch the fireworks, take her down to the creek for the duck races, to steal her away into the woods for stolen kisses.

Trevor's musings were interrupted when the fire station came into view. Javi pulled into his normal spot and clapped Trevor on the back. "Look, man, I'll drop the Whitney thing for now."

"Thank you."

Holding up a finger, he urged, "But you need to see this as the gift it is. You've been in a funk since Virginia left, and clearly the Hastings promotion is bullshit. Whitney is hot, nice, and could provide the perfect distraction." He waggled his eyebrows, earning another shoulder punch before they got out of the car.

Chief Warren was in the bullpen getting the team ready for their morning huddle. Every shift he'd meet with the group to share their tasks and objectives for the day. Unfortunately for Trevor, he knew that involved nothing but hose duty and inventory. He dropped his things at his desk and joined Javi and teammates Dylan Flax and Malcolm "Smithy" Smith by the coffee maker.

"Listen up, team," Chief said, clapping his hands to get everyone's attention. "Hastings will pull a small team together to investigate that fire in the warehouse district. I know that several of you have shown an interest in this project, and Hastings will follow up if you've been selected." His gaze landed on Trevor for a split second before he continued. It was all the recognition he got, and it curdled his stomach. Suddenly his momma's hotcakes were cement blocks in his gut. *Damn Hastings.*

The man himself stood and went beside the chief, hands on his hips and smug expression on his face. He took a moment to look at everyone before listing the teams. "When Chief is done, I'd like Ortiz, Flax, and Smithy to join me in my office." His voice was reminiscent of a football coach on Friday night, and Trevor bristled. He'd give up his entire career for one swift punch to that idiot's jaw.

"Thank you, Captain," Chief Warren said, clearing his throat. "I'd like Mays to assist our probie Maxwell with inventory today. We'll regroup with new projects later this week."

The group was dismissed, and Trevor sighed. It was impossible not to be disappointed to be on probie duty. Granted, Tiffany Maxwell was a damn good firefighter. She'd transferred to Pinegrove from Columbus, eager to put down roots with her husband and their growing family. Despite having given birth the year before, she still bench-pressed more than half the men in this room.

"Hey, Mays, want to meet in the garage for inventory?" Her blue eyes sparkled with excitement over the mundane task, and Trevor's shoulders sagged. It was not her fault his career was stalled, and he wouldn't take it out on her.

"Great idea, Maxwell. Give me one minute to get more coffee." She shot him a thumbs-up and headed toward the garage. Trevor took a moment to gather a clipboard and inventory form before filling his coffee and heading out.

Despite the mundane task at hand, he was eager for a distraction from Whitney, his libido, and his jacked-up heart. The last thing he wanted was more drama, and it was in that exact moment that Chief Warren waved him down. "Lieutenant, can I have a moment?"

Trevor wanted to tell his mentor that now wasn't a good time. His emotions were raw, his skin too tight, and, honestly, he was angry with the world. "Sure thing, sir." He pivoted toward the chief's office and collapsed into the seat opposite the desk. His finger tapped a rhythm on the clipboard until Chief Warren sat down.

"Son, I know this isn't easy." He waited for Trevor to acknowledge his statement, but he remained silent. "But we'll find some bigger projects for you to work on. This is a temporary glitch."

Trevor ground his teeth together, struggling not to vent his frustrations on his superior. "I'm sure they will, Chief." He didn't mean it, because he knew that Hastings's promotion set him back years. There were not a lot of retirements planned in this precinct for quite some time, so unless someone quit, he was stagnant. He bristled and made to stand, eager to end this impromptu heart-to-heart.

And that fact made him even angrier. His time with Chief Warren had been among his favorites. The man had been in Trevor's life for as long as he could remember, and when the chief took Trevor's father's position, it felt like the only thing that made sense. Now, though, Trevor was listless and alone. It was a horrible sensation he couldn't shake.

Chief studied Trevor another moment before he sighed and scratched his chin. "Look, I know this isn't what you'd want, but I can put some feelers out to other stations outside this precinct. There will be other promotions sooner than this station, if you don't mind relocating."

Correction, now Trevor really felt like crap.

"You want me to leave Pinegrove?" He edged forward in his seat, heat coloring his cheeks as he wrapped his head around the idea of leaving his hometown, family, and friends.

Holding up his hands, Chief shook his head. "No, that's not what I want. Not only are you an excellent lieutenant, but I know it would kill your momma to have you far away. She's already sad Jessie doesn't come home often."

This statement brought Trevor to his feet, nearly knocking the chair to the floor. He knew Javi was right about Momma and the chief, but hearing the chief discuss *his* family was setting Trevor on edge. All he'd ever heard Daisy say out in company was how proud she was of Jessie for traveling and helping others with the Peace Corps, yet the chief had firsthand examples of his mother's true feelings. It was just too much.

"Is there anything else, Chief? Maxwell is waiting on me in the garage." Trevor's back was ramrod straight; his hands clenched into fists at his sides. He didn't think he could take much more of the world laughing at him.

Chief studied him a moment before shaking his head. "No, son. I'm sorry it's been a rough few months, but we can figure this out. Things have a way of working out, we need a little faith."

"Faith." Trevor snorted. "No offense, sir, but I don't have a lot of that right now." He turned to leave, but Chief's last question stopped him in his tracks.

"Keep an eye on your new visitor, will you? Daisy is excited to have the company, but I'm always wary of out-of-towners."

The hair on the back of Trevor's neck stood up. Very few people knew Whitney was staying with his mother, so she must have called him herself. Trevor's head dipped down until his chin rested on his chest. The whole world was spinning and living without him.

"I don't think we'll have any problems." He let the door close behind him with a snick and strode to the garage. He only hoped that counting hoses, ropes, tools, and helmets distracted him from the cluster that was quickly becoming his life.

Four hours later, Trevor's back ached from hunching over stacks of supplies in the garage. Sweat dripped from his temples, and he wondered why the air conditioning wasn't churning at full power. It was just one of many little things he'd noticed since Hastings took over, small details other captains would notice.

"Did you get that last pressure valve?" Maxwell asked as she leaned against the pump panel. She flipped to another page on the clipboard, sweat beading on her upper lip. "Did we count five cones or six for truck number four?"

Trevor strode over to the collection of cones and recounted. "Yep, it's six."

Maxwell nodded and clicked her pen closed. "Then inventory is officially done. Not bad for a day's work." She pushed off the side of the truck and smiled.

Lord, how Trevor envied her positive attitude. They'd spent an entire shift counting and sorting through myriads of firefighting equipment. He was grateful that Chief had teamed him with the bright-eyed probie, because otherwise Trevor probably would have grumbled through the entire project. "Thanks for your help, Maxwell. It's good having you on the team."

Maxwell covered her chest with her hand and pretended to swoon. "Oh! Knock it off, Mays. Otherwise, I'll think you have a heart."

She'd started at the station the week Virginia left him, and Trevor hardly pretended to be polite when Maxwell had peppered him with questions. Once Javi shared the horrible news, she backed off and relied on other teammates for training and support. That didn't sit right with Trevor, because he normally relished the chance to train new recruits.

"Pfft, the jury is still out on that, Maxwell. Seriously, thank you for your help with this. We got it done faster than I thought."

"Let's celebrate with some candy, my treat." Maxwell pulled out her wallet and tossed a few bills at Trevor. "You mind grabbing me a Twix?"

Trevor took the cash and saluted. "You got it."

Trevor went inside to the vending machines and got Maxwell a Twix and himself a Snickers bar. Maybe a little afternoon pick-me-up would put him in a better mood. He hated the notion of coming home to Momma and Whitney with a bad attitude.

Before he had a chance to dissect that thought, he heard a voice that used to make his heart sing. "Oh, baby, not now." A familiar giggle punctuated that sentence, and Trevor nearly ran back into the garage, ready to strangle himself with a utility rope.

Slowly turning around, he spied his ex-fiancée and Hastings in a lip lock better suited for an R-rated movie. "How can I keep my hands to myself when you show up looking like this?"

"You're messing up my makeup, baby," Virginia warned, pulling back to adjust her hair.

The whole damn team was at their desks, pretending to work. Smithy typed on a laptop that wasn't even turned on, his eyes locked on the drama. Javi caught Trevor's eye and mouthed *Sorry* as Trevor walked past. Maxwell joined him and took her candy, patting his shoulder in sympathy as she went to her own desk, one Twix already shoved in her mouth.

Trevor kept his head down and hoped that Virginia and Hastings finished their PDA session without giving him notice, but of course that wasn't to be.

"Oh, shoot, hey, Trevor!" Virginia waggled a manicured hand in his direction. "How are you doing, honey?" Her voice dripped with insincerity, her frown as fake as her nails.

"Good afternoon, Virginia. I'm doing well, thanks."

She waited a beat in case he was going to inquire about her, before stepping closer and lowering her voice. "I'm so sorry it didn't work out with the promotion, but you know how things go with city council." Her lips pursed in an approximation of sadness before she went back to her default setting of casual indifference.

"I sure do," Trevor said, forcing the biggest grin as he chomped into his candy bar. A peanut broke free and clattered to the floor.

Hastings, displeased that his girl was talking to her ex, shouted, "Mays, knock it off."

Trevor stifled a sigh and finished his snack, molars mashing into the chocolate with more force than was necessary. "Not sure what you mean, Cap." He tossed the wrapper in the trash and swiveled his chair to face his computer. He just dismissed the whole situation, and silently begged for Hastings to leave it all alone.

No such luck.

"Don't you disrespect my girl like that." In three quick strides, Hastings was at Trevor's desk, his chest heaving.

Trevor remained seated, looking up at his captain with a saccharin-sweet expression. "I'm sorry, but I don't think I did anything wrong. I had a brief conversation with Miss Virginia, but now it's time to get back to work. Didn't you tell us not to bring our personal lives into work, sir?" He raised an eyebrow in challenge, savoring the sight of the throbbing vein in Hastings's neck.

Right after Hastings and Virginia got together and he got the promotion, he spent ten minutes of a staff meeting droning on about how no one in the station should discuss their personal lives on the clock. It was a clear attempt to avoid probing questions about the musical chairs between Virginia and Trevor, but nonetheless he pushed the issue.

Trevor knew he was in the right, and so did Hastings. "I don't like your tone, Lieutenant."

Now Trevor was on his feet. Behind him, Javi left his desk to join his buddy. "Captain, I think this is all a misunderstanding," Javi urged.

Apparently bored with the outburst, Virginia linked her hand through Hastings's elbow, and said, "Baby, can we go back to your office? I need to tell you about our dinner plans at Daddy's club."

Hastings wasn't having it. "You're getting written up for insubordination, Mays. Right now." He stabbed his finger into the air, spittle falling from his mouth. He looked more rabid dog than man in that moment, and Trevor was almost afraid. *Almost.*

"I don't see how I'm being insubordinate, Captain."

The air in the bullpen was thick with tension, and only the sound of the ticking wall clock was heard. "Get in my office, now."

"Do we have a problem here?" Chief Warren asked, emerging from his office to investigate the hubbub. "Captain, what seems to be the issue?"

"Mays is being disrespectful to me and my fiancée."

Fiancée?

That was the last straw.

Only together a matter of months, and Virginia was already engaged? Trevor quickly glanced down to her left hand, and sure enough it held a diamond that sparkled like the sun. It was twice the size of the one he'd given her a year ago, and his stomach roiled. Granted, he didn't want

Virginia back, that was a fact he'd accepted months ago, yet his pride took a beating that she was able to move on that quickly from him.

"Congratulations," Trevor muttered to Virginia, who finally had the manners to look embarrassed.

"Thank you, Trev." She tucked a lock of blonde hair behind her ear, averting her gaze from everyone.

"My office," Hastings insisted.

Chief raised his voice. "No, how about my office." He looked at Trevor, and said, "Dismissed for today. We'll discuss tomorrow, first thing." Turning back to Hastings, he said, "Please see your fiancée off, then come to my office." Looking back out to the bullpen, he added, "And everyone else get back to work."

Everyone scurried to their corners, and Trevor grabbed his messenger bag and stomped out to his car.

He vibrated with nervous and angry energy. He needed to clear his head, and he knew just what to do.

CHAPTER FIVE

Whitney was currently in a dream sequence from a Hallmark movie. She strolled arm-in-arm down Main Street in Pinegrove with Daisy, gabbing like a couple of teenagers. Birdsong echoed around them, the air scented with pine. She hadn't been this carefree and smiley in, well ... far too long.

After the best breakfast she'd had since getting her first training bra, Whitney and Daisy piled into the pickup to explore the town. While Daisy drove, Whitney texted Winnie proof of life so she didn't worry.

All is well in Pinegrove, Win. Spending the day with my gracious hostess. I'll call tonight.

Winnie responded with a thumbs-up emoji, as well as a screenshot of a background check on Daisy Mays of Pinegrove, Georgia. *Don't be pissed, but I wanted to make sure you wouldn't be tied to a porch post and forced to play the banjo.*

Whitney snorted and replied with *I think you're referencing too many movies ... but thanks for caring*. With a few hearts, and an eye-roll emoji, added at the end.

"Everything okay, sugar?" Daisy asked as she turned onto Main Street and parked in front of a charming little café. The storefront had a scattering of small tables and chairs, where a group of young mothers congregated. A half dozen baby strollers flanked the women, with a variety of babies and toddlers cooing and being adorable. One of the women recognized Daisy and waved before handing a juice box to a kid with a finger up his nose.

"Everyone is so friendly here," Whitney marveled, loving the feel of small-town life again. Savannah was hardly Manhattan, but it was still a city to her.

Daisy tugged a straw hat on and closed the car door. "Oh, that's Pinegrove for you. There's a reason Nick and I stayed here after high school. It's relatively safe, the cost of living isn't bad, and we wanted the kids to feel like they grew up in a postcard."

"I'd say you succeeded," Whitney agreed as she hiked her purse up her shoulder and followed Daisy into the first store.

It was a women's boutique with two gorgeous picture window displays. Whitney wouldn't admit it to Daisy, but the fashions skewed toward the over-fifty set. "We won't stay here long, but the owner is holding a new blouse for me. You met her last night, it's Kim." Daisy held the door for Whitney, and they were greeted by a stout woman with gray hair and a warm grin.

"Daisy, how good to see you again." The older woman pulled Daisy into a hug before turning toward Whitney. "And it sure is nice seeing you again. Winnie, right?"

Whitney held out her hand and smiled. "Good guess, as that's my sister's name. I'm Whitney, ma'am. Ms. Daisy is nice enough to be showing me Pinegrove today."

Daisy draped her arm around Whitney's shoulder when the other women were done shaking hands. "And she's staying with me through the festival. It's nice to have guests again."

Whitney hoped she didn't come across as a free-loader, but she forced a wider smile.

"Well, isn't that perfect? I'm Kim, the owner of Kim's Creations, and I'm sure glad to meet you officially,

Whitney."

"Same, Kim."

Kim motioned around to the store. Save for a few shoppers, their little trio was alone. "Please, make yourself at home. Poke around, have a drink, whatever you'd like!"

Daisy steered them toward a drink station at the counter. "You help yourself to some lemonade while I check on my blouse. I won't be a minute."

"Take your time," Whitney urged, helping herself to some lemonade in a charming paper cup covered in wisteria flowers.

While Daisy and Kim gossiped and tried on her new outfit, Whitney strolled around the shop inspecting the jewelry section. There were necklaces her mother would adore, long chains with charms and rhinestones. A choker caught her eye, and she pictured Winnie pairing it with one of her power suits. Glancing at the price tag, Whitney quickly realized she'd need to watch her pennies during her little road trip from reality. Without a job, she'd need to make every dollar count.

"What do you think, Whitney?" Daisy asked as she stepped onto the main floor. The blouse was fitted at her waist but had short flowy sleeves, the fabric a mix of red and blue stars.

"It's lovely and perfect for the Fourth of July."

Daisy twisted to see herself in the three-way mirror before nodding and turning back to Kim. "She's right, I'll take it."

Kim beamed and pointed to the register. "You get changed, and I'll meet you up there. I need to help these ladies over in shoes."

Daisy and Whitney waited at the counter while Kim flitted around the shop. There was a pair of women roughly Daisy's age with shopping bags looped around each arm, and an elderly couple browsing the jewelry counter. Whitney watched with a frown as Kim tried to serve everyone at once, even as the bell over the door chimed another arrival.

"Is she usually shorthanded?" Whitney asked, her voice barely above a whisper.

Shaking her head, Daisy grimaced. "Never like this."

"Excuse me, do you work here?" One of the customers asked Whitney. She held a stack of clothes and motioned toward the dressing rooms with her free hand. "I'd like to try these on."

Whitney was about to shake her head when she had an idea. "Follow me," she said, taking the clothes and striding to the fitting area. She'd noticed a key chain hanging from the counter and snagged the keys then let the woman into a room. "You leave what you don't want right there, and we'll take care of it. There are some gorgeous bracelets out there if you like that orange dress. It'll match your skin tone beautifully."

Before Kim reacted, Whitney strode over to the older couple looking at necklaces. The husband's hands shook as he attempted to latch the tiny clasp. "Let me help with that, folks." She smirked as she deftly secured the chain and stepped back to admire her handiwork. "That is a great length, isn't it? It draws the eyes to your gorgeous smile."

The woman rested a hand on her chest and giggled; her husband nodded. "She's right, isn't she, Frank? What do you think?" She turned her head this way and that before Frank pulled out his wallet.

"I can't argue with that smile." He turned to Whitney and handed her his credit card. "We'll take it, miss."

By the time Whitney was back at the register, the woman from the dressing room was ready with all the clothes, Kim hot on her heels. "These all worked out great, thank you. Could you show me that bracelet you mentioned?"

Kim checked out the older couple while Whitney paired a ring and bracelet set with the customer's new dress. "And think, these will work well into fall when you're ready for those pumpkiny outfits," she suggested and found the woman the proper ring size.

Ten minutes later, and the shop was empty. Whitney

leaned on the counter to catch her breath. "I'm so sorry, Miss Kim. I hope I didn't overstep."

Kim was incredulous, her eyes bugging out from behind her bifocals. "Are you kidding, honey? You sold over five hundred dollars' worth of merchandise in the time it took me to help one person. Are you looking for a job?"

Whitney's jaw hung open so far, she feared she'd catch flies. "A job?" The irony wasn't lost on Whitney, as all she really needed was a job and stable income, but they were hours from Savannah. "I don't live here, and you don't even know me," she said with a frown.

Kim waved away her concerns as if a six-hour roundtrip commute was standard. "I'm not worried about that. I'll take what I can get at this rate. If this one here vouches for you," she said, hitching a thumb at Daisy, "then that's good enough for me. I need all the help I can get this month, especially with the festival growing at the speed of sound. Pinegrove is hopping."

"Oh, well." Whitney chewed her lip, struggling to decide the best way to let this sweet woman down.

Daisy had other plans. "You've shocked the poor gal, Kim. Why don't we swing by on our way out of town? I promised Whitney lunch and a tour of Main Street."

Kim nodded, satisfied. "I'm here all day." She turned back to Whitney and pulled her into a brief hug. "Thank you for your help. You saved my bacon this morning." Another customer entered the shop, and Kim got back to work.

Daisy held the door for Whitney, and they headed toward the bookshop. "That was very nice of you to help Kim like that. Most people step back and watch the chaos."

"Oh, it was nothing. I don't mind helping," Whitney said, pleased she was able to do something.

"I don't know about nothing. Do you want to think about Kim's offer? I know she won't make you a millionaire, but she would be fair." She peeked at Whitney from under the brim of her hat. "I never did ask you, are you working now?"

Whitney shook her head and strived not to look too depressed. Discussing her career goals was about as much fun as unplanned oral surgery. "Well, actually, I'm in between things at the moment."

Gesturing back to Kim's Creations, Daisy said, "You clearly have retail experience."

With a shrug, Whitney agreed. "Yes, some. I've been a temp for years, hopping along to various jobs in Savannah. I like the variety, but I know it's time to make a plan and put down roots."

As soon as the words were out of her mouth, she flinched. The truth had come out, and Whitney wasn't ready to dissect what it all meant, especially with Daisy.

The other woman hummed to herself while they walked past the bookstore. "Why don't we postpone our book browsing and grab lunch now? There is a great sandwich shop up on the corner, and we can beat the rush."

Despite eating breakfast fit for an army, Whitney's stomach grumbled at the suggestion. "Why not?"

At the counter, Daisy ordered a Reuben and a side salad while Whitney settled on the chicken salad with a side of coleslaw. When the cashier gave the total, Daisy quickly handed her credit card to the clerk and shooed away Whitney's attempts to pay. "Whitney, you're my guest."

"Exactly, you're giving me a place to stay. I should be paying you."

Daisy carefully pushed away Whitney's hand as she clutched a fistful of bills. "I know it might not look like it to you, but you're doing me a favor."

"I am?" Whitney didn't believe her.

"You are." Daisy took off her hat and fluffed her hair with her free hand. "Let's grab that table by the window, and I'll tell you my tale of woe." She chuckled as she walked, proving the conversation would be lighter than it sounded.

"Thank you," Whitney told the waitress as she slid their plates across the table. Daisy chose a table for two with the perfect view of Main Street. A pair of joggers sprinted past, avoiding a herd of teenagers on their cell phones. She took a greedy bite of her sandwich and savored the tang of the mustard dressing. "This is heavenly," she said through a mouthful.

Daisy nodded, already tucking into her salad. "I won't argue with you. This place is perfection." She chomped on a tomato before speaking. "As you know, I lost my husband a few years ago."

Whitney finished chewing, eager to show manners. "Yes, ma'am. Again, I'm sorry for your loss."

"Thank you, I appreciate that. Nick was a wonderful husband and father. I know a lot of widows say that, but it was true. He was the fire chief, and his heart attack sure came as a surprise." She lifted her Reuben, which dripped with dressing and cheese. "Granted, after a lifetime of eating these, I shouldn't be so surprised." She mused as she took a bite. "Hence, the salad to balance things out." She laughed at herself and wiped her fingers on a paper napkin.

"Was he the chief at Trevor's station?"

Daisy dabbed a blob of sauce from her lips and nodded. "He was, but we don't need to go into all that now. There is time to fall down that rabbit hole." She smirked and sipped from her iced tea.

Suddenly Whitney wanted to know everything about Trevor, about the man who shaped him. It was already clear from their brief interactions that he cared deeply for his family, and that must be a hard loss to recover from.

Her musings were interrupted by Daisy's question, which was only fair, since she'd poked into her past. "So, sugar, why are you on the road right now?"

Whitney's sandwich froze halfway to her mouth, and she swallowed. "Well, how much time do you have?" she teased, buying time by taking a massive bite of chicken salad.

Daisy threw her head back and laughed, the sound as melodic as wind chimes. "Whitney, I like you. Have I mentioned that?" She slid her plate away and leaned back in her seat. "You don't have to tell me anything you don't want to, but since we're two gals gabbing over lunch, I thought I would ask."

Whitney didn't want to lie to Daisy, but she also wasn't ready to open a vein and hope for the best. Eating the last bite of sandwich, she chewed thoughtfully before sharing the abridged version of her life.

"Well, when I said I was in between things at the moment, I meant it. I recently got out of a three-year relationship, and I've been temping all over Savannah for a while. I lived with my ex, so right now I'm crashing on my sister's couch. Winnie insists it's time for me to grow up and find a career, but I'm not sure what feels right. In case you couldn't tell, not much is feeling right lately."

Daisy nodded along as she spoke, giving her time to find her words.

"I suppose a part of me thought I'd have it all figured out by now. But ..." Unsure how to finish that thought, she waffled her hand back and forth.

"But you need a little more time?" Daisy wagered, her smile kind. "I don't see anything wrong with that. I won't tell Trevor's story, it's his to share, but you two have a lot in common."

Whitney choked on her Diet Coke. "We do?" From where she sat, he was a sweet man with a career and devastating good looks, while she was a little plump, homeless, with a dwindling savings account, and no job prospects.

Well, that wasn't true—she had Kim's offer. It was madness, but Whitney really wanted to accept the job. She had nowhere to live, and her life was back in Savannah, but sitting here in Pinegrove with Daisy ... it felt like where she needed to be.

As she was about to share this new revelation with Daisy, a tall, skinny blonde approached their table. Her hair was swept off her face in perfect ringlets, humidity be damned, and she had a designer purse looped through her arm. The smile she gave Daisy was kind, but the returning smile from the other woman was anything but.

"Daisy, I thought that was you." The blonde leaned down and air-kissed Daisy's cheek. The older woman recoiled.

"Good afternoon, Virginia."

"I was running errands and thought I'd stop by for a salad. Everything here is lovely." She sighed and rested her left hand over her heart.

Daisy's eyes bulged for a fraction of a second before she schooled her face. The ring on the woman's fourth finger was big enough to be classified as a heliport, the diamond catching the light at all angles.

Virginia caught Daisy gawking at the ring and smirked. "Oh! Did you see my ring? Isn't it divine? Scott only gets me the best." She fluttered the hand over her chest, which Whitney staked was artificially enhanced.

Shoving her chair back so quickly it squeaked, Daisy collected her purse and held out her hand for Whitney to join her. "I'm sure Scott's new job helped pay for it. Bless your heart." If Virginia heard the venom in Daisy's voice, she didn't let on.

"Well, thank you, Daisy. I'm so pleased you're happy for us."

Daisy tugged on Whitney's arm, who stumbled to her feet, a fork clattering to the floor. "I didn't say that. Goodbye, Virginia."

Virginia frowned, hand falling to her side. "Goodbye? Daisy, I'd like us to try to be friends again." Her words were strained, the polished veneer of before had melted away.

Whitney stood as still as a statue, squeezing Daisy's hand for support. "My momma raised me with manners, Virginia," Daisy said, taking a long exhale, "but I cannot so easily forget how you hurt my son. I won't wish you ill, but I certainly cannot be your friend." Gesturing to Virginia's hand, she spluttered, "And I won't congratulate your union."

Blonde hair bobbing, Virginia shook her head. "Oh,"

she muttered, gaze locked on the floor. "I, um, understand."

Daisy blinked rapidly, her clear eyes misting over. "Sugar, I don't care if you understand. We all make choices in this world, and this one is mine. Enjoy your salad." And with that, she pulled Whitney out into the balmy late June heat.

"Of all the ridiculous, underhanded …" Daisy muttered under her breath until they were across the street and at the car. "Friends. She wants to be *friends.*" Daisy bitterly spat the last word out. "Do you mind if we cut our shopping short, Whitney? Let's go for a drive, I need to clear my head before I punch something."

Whitney shook her head, concern etched over her face. "Not at all. Is there anything I can do?"

Her question shook the other woman from her stupor, and she looked at Whitney for the first time since leaving the café. "Sugar, I have a feeling you're already doing it."

When they were safely in Daisy's pickup, Whitney gathered the courage to ask a question. "Urm, if you don't mind me asking …"

"Who was that ghastly woman?" Daisy grunted, turning too quickly at a four-way stop sign. The car to their left honked their horn as Daisy cut them off, but she paid them no mind.

"If it's too painful to discuss, I'll mind my own …"

"That awful woman is Trevor's ex-fiancée. She broke his heart and is already engaged to that dim-witted, jack wagon Scott Hastings."

"Oh," was all Whitney mustered. She had no clue who Scott was, and right now she couldn't care less.

All her ears heard was *Trevor's ex-fiancée.*

Turns out she and Trevor had more in common than she realized. Trouble was, she had no idea what to do about it.

CHAPTER SIX

When Trevor was a boy, one of his earliest memories was made in this very kitchen. His father, fresh off a double shift and as ravenous as a racehorse, welcomed him and his younger sister to this sanctuary by the stove. Escorting Daisy away to put up her feet, he sat both kids down and shared their culinary adventure for the day.

"You know, kiddos?" he asked, his smile popping beneath a week's worth of stubble.

"What?" Trevor and Jessie had giggled, their toes a foot off the floor.

"When I was at the station this weekend, all I thought about was …"—he hesitated for effect, holding his hands up as if to keep them in place—"breakfast!"

Jessie, being four at the time, laughed like he'd told the funniest joke ever heard. "But, Daddy, it's suppertime." She pointed out the kitchen window, where the sun had dipped below the tree line. A cozy purple hue filtered through the curtains.

Nick held up his finger, his grin infectious. "Yes, baby girl, but do you know what else?" Jessie shook her head, her reddish curls bouncing on her cheeks. "We're here, at home, and we can make up any rules we want."

Trevor was incredulous, as earlier that day his mother had made him do all his math homework before he watched his cartoons. "No way," he said, crossing his arms over his tiny torso.

"Yes way." Nick ruffled his son's floppy hair. "Daddy is making the rules tonight." He lowered his voice. "Don't tell Momma."

Both kids tittered while their father went to work. He pulled out every bowl, plate, whisk, and canister their kitchen held, lining everything up on the counter. Just as he was about to start cracking eggs, he slapped his forehead.

"What is it, Daddy?" Jessie had asked, fidgeting with excitement from her perch.

"I forgot my lucky apron, and you kids forgot to wash your hands." He helped both kids off their stools and ushered them down to the bathroom so as not to disturb his prep work. By the time Trevor and Jessie returned, their father was clad in his signature *Kiss the Cook* apron their mother had given him the Christmas before.

"Can we help?" Trevor asked after he helped Jessie back onto her seat. He took a moment to ensure she wouldn't wobble off, as she tended to do when excited.

His father patted his shoulder and sighed. "Good boy, Trevor. It's important to look out for the women in your life. Don't forget that, son."

Trevor had covered his heart with his hand and nodded, as if taking an oath. "I promise, Daddy."

Jessie, being Jessie, ruined the moment with a high-pitched squeal. "Can we *please* start cookin'?" Her tiny hands were clasped in front of her in prayer. "I'm about to faint."

Nick tossed his head back and laughed before leaning down to kiss his daughter's cheek. "Well, we can't have that. Who wants to crack eggs? And who wants to measure the flour?"

Jessie was given flour duty, a task that had rendered her reminiscent of Al Pacino in *Scarface*. Nick had dusted a flour smudge from her cheek as he took the bowl.

Trevor had focused all his efforts on perfectly cracking a dozen eggs into two bowls. "How are these, Daddy?" he asked, always eager to please his old man.

Nick nodded and gently patted his son's back. "Damn near perfect. Good work."

"What are we making?" Jessie asked, bouncing her feet against the stool legs. Any other time Trevor would have told his sister to knock it off, but then he didn't care. They cherished those moments, the three of them cooking something delicious.

"Sausage gravy and scrambled eggs."

"Yummy!" the children sang in unison.

"And pancakes with chocolate chips!" Nick did jazz hands, and Jessie almost fell off her stool as she screamed in delight.

Back in that day, Nick was a low man on the roster at the fire station. He served as cook most of the time, making things like soup, chili, and hot dogs. For some reason, the men rarely wanted breakfast for dinner, Nick's absolute favorite. After long or taxing shifts, he'd come home and scoop up his children to make hot cakes, eggs, and bacon.

Those memories were some of Trevor's favorites, and when the world got a little too hard to handle, he fell back into those familiar patterns.

Back in the present, he surveyed the mess he'd already made. There was a small part of him that wished Jessie was in town to help him make breakfast for an army, but he remembered who was going to walk through that door. He wondered what Whitney thought of two breakfasts in one day? It was nonsense, but Trevor saw this as a test. Granted, she was all but a stranger, but he was eager to see her thoughts on heavy Southern breakfasts.

Ever since he left the station, he was beside himself. No, he didn't want Virginia back, of that he was certain. It was more than that; this feeling of inadequacy. He wasn't enough for Virginia, and that stung. It stung even more that freaking Hastings put that gawdy ring on her finger.

Hastings who didn't know the difference between a rack hose and a double jacket fire hose. *Idiot.*

Thinking about that lugworm caused Trevor to crack an egg too forcefully and the shell splintered into the bowl. Muffling a curse, he sifted out the shells and started again. He wanted to channel his father right now; wanted to feel the calm that came with mixing pancake batter in the dwindling daylight. If he closed his eyes, he almost heard the old man humming a nameless tune. *God, he missed his father.*

Grief was positively a bitch. Two years had certainly dulled some of the pain, lessened the sharpness that came with loss. At the beginning, Trevor couldn't even eat, let alone fathom making pancakes and cooking. Yet, as the days passed, his mother reminded them all that Nick would have hated to watch his favorite people wither away. He was a man of action, a man who loved to be out in the world and soaking up every opportunity to have fun.

So, Trevor started small and ate one meal a day. They weren't grand feasts, but he'd force himself to pull out a bag of salad mix or dice up some fruit, anything to fuel his body. Javi and Smithy used to come by his place nearly every day after work for a month with pizzas, wings, or takeout from The Pecan Pit.

Unfortunately, that was also the time Jessie went MIA. He couldn't blame his sister, really. She was always a wanderer, and the loss of their father had been too much to take. They weren't prepared to bury their father before he reached his sixties, before his hair went fully gray and he collected his first Social Security check.

Trevor missed Jessie, nearly as much as his father, but he knew she'd come back when she was ready. The harder he and Daisy pushed, the longer she'd stay gone. Trevor bided his time and always made an extra pair of hotcakes, just in case she decided to come home.

Lost in memories of happier times, Trevor hadn't noticed the sun dipping lower in the sky. Whitney and his mother had been gone most of the day, and he wondered how they were fairing. By the time he got the biscuits out of the oven, the griddle was ready for pancakes.

The deadbolt turned and the rattling of keys echoed into the kitchen. "Hello?" his mother's voice rang out from the hallway, and Trevor's shoulders relaxed a tad. Yes, he was a grown man, but seeing his momma never got old.

"In here," he shouted over his shoulder. He carefully dropped a blob of butter to the griddle and ladled on the first round of hotcakes.

Daisy was clad in her straw hat, her hair sticking out from under the brim. "Well, I'll tell you what. Did we stumble into an IHOP?" Her voice was light and teasing, but Trevor knew she understood the need to cook breakfast in the evening. She'd lived through countless nights of French toast under the moon and never questioned the Mays clan when breakfast was served.

Whitney followed Daisy into the kitchen, her gorgeous eyes wide at the scene in front of her. "Oh my gosh," she exhaled, snagging Trevor's gaze. "Are you expecting company?"

"Yes, and they just arrived." He rummaged in the drawer for a spatula. "You ladies wash up, and I'll holler when it's ready."

Daisy studied the scene, frowning. "Whitney, sugar, you wash up first. I need a minute." A look exchanged between the women that made Trevor nervous.

"Sure thing, but I want to help when I'm back," Whitney said over her shoulder.

Trevor turned the heat down on his pan and faced Daisy, arms crossed over his chest. "Spill it, Momma."

Gesturing around the messy kitchen, she asked, "I take it you're aware of a certain Pinegrove engagement?"

Trevor scoffed. "You could say that."

Her frown slid away, concern replacing her anger. "I should have assumed as much as soon as I smelled the biscuits from the driveway." She reached out and took a biscuit, pinching off a bite. "Did it help?"

Trevor's shoulders slumped and he dropped his arms to his sides. "A little. Nothing a night of binge eating and talking with you girls won't fix."

Daisy cocked her head to the side, chewing the rest of her biscuit in silence.

"What is it?"

"I'm going out to see Joan and Kim. You two stay, eat, and get to know each other."

Whitney rejoined them, her hair pulled back, her face scrubbed free of makeup. Her complexion was smooth as silk, and Trevor had to ball his fists to stop from reaching out and trailing a finger over the dips and swells of her cheeks.

"What can I help with?" she asked, eyes pinging back and forth between mother and son.

"You can help my son with the fruit salad. I'm going to meet a couple of friends for dinner."

Whitney's eyes widened, but she recovered quickly. "Oh, you're not staying?"

Trevor couldn't figure out if she was relieved or petrified at this development. Perhaps the plan of a night alone with a strange man wasn't her idea of a good time. He could hardly blame her.

"I think it's high time you kids got to know each other."

Whitney and Trevor looked at each other, both unsure where Daisy was going.

"You suddenly have an issue with biscuits for dinner?" Trevor asked.

"Not at all, sugar. It's just that Joan and Kim texted, and they invited me to supper."

This was quite possible, as Daisy often shared meals with her girlfriends, but Trevor thought it was all a little too convenient. Judging from Whitney's confusion, he wasn't alone.

"Don't worry, sugar. Kim said she's ready for you tomorrow if you want to take her up on her offer."

"Offer?" Trevor was even more confused, and now

Whitney looked faint.

Resting a hand over her neck, Whitney argued, "But I haven't made a decision."

Daisy shook away her concern. "And you don't have to now. Just know that the spot is yours if you want it." She flapped her hand in the air, backing away toward the door. "I need to get going." Stepping back a few more paces, she said, "If you don't mind, Gus still needs a walk. It's a gorgeous night, maybe you two could take him out after supper? Talk about job offers, life, whatever." She winked at her son, although Whitney still struggled to keep up.

Trevor chuckled, watching his momma bound away faster than a jack rabbit. "Subtle as a freight train, Momma."

Trevor was dying to get to the bottom of this discussion, but Gus interrupted. Now that the kitchen was lively, the hound joined the activity, setting up in the corner ready for something to fall to the floor. He barked twice to get Trevor's attention, who mindlessly tossed a burnt corner of a biscuit.

"You mind a little light chopping, Whitney?" Trevor asked, motioning with his elbow toward a stack of fruit.

Shaking her head, Whitney helped herself to a chef's knife and cutting board and carefully diced an apple, banana, and strawberries into a bowl. Trevor was about to suggest adding a touch of honey when she pulled the bottle over and drizzled it onto the fruit. "Hope you don't mind a little added sweetness," she said, offering him a smile that melted butter faster than his griddle.

Trevor had to clear the lump in his throat before answering. "Not at all. In fact, the sweeter the better."

Whitney's cheeks flushed as she placed the bowl on the table. "What else can I help with?"

Trevor pointed to the fridge with his spatula. "Can you get out the pitcher of tea and that slab of bacon?"

"Absolutely." She retrieved everything and went to work finding glasses. She poured two healthy portions of tea before snagging a frying pan and cooking the bacon.

For a moment, the only sounds heard in the kitchen were sizzling pork fat and the clock over the stove ticking away. Horrendously out of practice with women, Trevor struggled to start the conversation up again.

"You and Momma do anything wild today?" he asked, flipping a pancake and missing the edge of the griddle. The poor little cake went from a perfect circle to a lumpy pile in an instant. The reject received the honor of being another snack for Gus.

Trevor whistled for the old hound, who hadn't gotten far. Gus sauntered over, ears dragging on the floor and jowls hanging damn near as low. He snarfed up the misshapen pancake and turned his attention to Whitney and the growing pile of cooked bacon.

"Can I?" she asked, holding up half a slice. Trevor nodded, his lips quirking up in a smirk. Whitney got down on her knees and fed the bacon to Gus, rubbing his back and cooing words of encouragement like the dog didn't beg for scraps every day.

When Gus was done with his treats, he shamelessly rolled over for belly rubs. Whitney happily obliged, causing his rear legs to twitch in delight. Trevor couldn't lie to himself; he'd kill for merely one minute of that type of bliss with Whitney. Any attention she shared was a gift, and he prayed he found a way to be less awkward; find a way to be like his old self.

Sensing his moment in the sun was over, Gus sneezed and strode back to his doggy bed under the bay window. He snuffled into the pillow and was asleep before they sat for supper.

"Whitney, breakfast is served." He was still so raw from Virginia's news, but having Whitney as his dining companion was exactly what he needed.

"This is so fun, thank you." Whitney beamed as she sipped from her sweet tea. "When I was a girl, my parents did breakfast for dinner sometimes. It's always a treat." She fixed herself a biscuit, sliding the gravy bowl toward him.

For the first few minutes of dinner, the pair discussed safe topics like their favorite breakfast foods. Dangerous topics like feelings and job offers stayed in the periphery, much like a sleeping basset hound. Trevor loved sharing a meal with anyone, since living alone meant his company was usually whatever was playing on ESPN.

Whitney praised everything she ate, giving Trevor the confidence boost he'd been missing. "How do you get your biscuits so fluffy?"

Trevor opened his mouth to share the recipe, to go over the pros and cons of sifting flour and baking powder. But when his eyes locked onto her gray gaze, he couldn't pretend he wasn't a mess. Biscuit measurements were not enough right now; he was finished with polite conversation.

There was no earthy reason for feeling this way, but Trevor knew he could talk to Whitney—share thoughts and frustrations that kept zipping through his addled brain. "I'm assuming you met my ex today," he said, going for broke.

Whitney's fork clattered to her plate. "Um, yes." She hastily picked up the utensil and nearly choked on the bite of pancake. "I'm so sorry."

Her apology was barely heard over the hammering of his heart. He hated even bringing Virginia into any conversation. Anything associated with Virginia felt tainted, rusted over with bitterness. Whitney was like a breath of fresh air, and Trevor wanted to breathe her in and be like his old self.

"No need to apologize," he said, reaching out to cover her hand. Despite the warm kitchen, Whtiney's hand was cool and smooth, like the rocks he used to snatch from the creek as a boy. Their eyes locked for a moment before they focused on the feast between them. "Anyway," he said with a chuckle. "It's in the past, and I really don't have feelings for Virginia anymore. I'm more pissed off she doesn't see how this looks, how it makes me feel." Striving to lighten the mood, he asked, "Can you pass the syrup, please?"

Whitney handed him the bottle, and their fingers grazed.

The blush on her cheeks became nuclear, and Trevor saved that little tidbit for later. She was clearly as affected by him as he was by her, and that did funny things to his belly.

Whitney looked like she was going to say something else on the matter of their love lives, but Trevor interrupted. "What else happened in town? You two were gone long enough that more than clothing was to blame. What was that offer Momma mentioned?"

Whitney nibbled on her lip, drawing his attention to how kissable her mouth was. Trevor wanted to close the distance and taste the syrup from her lips, wanted to ...

"Kim offered me a job at her boutique."

"Oh wow, that's great! Right? I mean, you're considering it?"

Trevor was intrigued. The woman had only been in town one day, and he didn't realize she was thinking of staying. That notion brought the biggest smile to his face. He wasn't sure what he was feeling for Whitney, but he was pleased to think she might be sticking around after the fireworks burned out.

Whitney's finger trailed over the condensation on her glass of tea, her eyes slightly unfocused. "I'm thinking about it, but there's a lot of other things to consider."

"Such as?"

"I don't live here, Trevor. My life is back in Savannah, with my sister."

Trevor had a lot of questions about this sister of hers, including Whitney's need to stay by her side. But his musings were put on hold when Gus barked three times and plopped himself by the door. The old hound had about five minutes before he made a mess Trevor would like to avoid. "Tell you what—how about we discuss job offers while we take Gus out for his walk?"

Quickly, Trevor gathered the dishes and put everything in the sink. Whitney put away the butter and syrup before tugging her sneakers back on her feet. Gus, already hearing the *W* word, thwapped his tail against the wall and whimpered until they joined him.

Trevor grabbed Gus's leash on the way out of the kitchen, whistling for the hound. "C'mon, Gussy. Walkies."

As they stepped into the cooling evening of summer, Whitney by his side and Gus dragging them ahead, Trevor could get used to this. This was the life he'd wanted with Virginia, and he didn't realize how much he'd mourned that loss until he had a chance at it again. Whitney was still a mystery to him, but Trevor was ready and willing to get some answers.

His first question—would she be staying in Pinegrove?

CHAPTER SEVEN

The air smelled like pine and juniper, and Whitney sighed happily as they stepped onto the sidewalk. Gus led the way, his rump keeping time with their paces. Trevor was beside her, one hand holding the leash, the other precariously close to her own. It took Herculean strength not to reach out and snatch it up.

"This is a lovely neighborhood," she observed as they crossed the street headed toward a fire hydrant. Gus's footfalls gained speed as he approached and marked his territory.

Trevor nodded, glancing over at her with a smile that made her belly turn. In the fading light, his hair was almost purple, the dimple in his chin appearing nearly black. "It's a great place to grow up. Jessie and I were very lucky, and I'm glad Momma stayed. We have a lot of good memories here."

"I bet. My parents sold our childhood home when they moved to Florida. It was kind of like this," she said, sweeping her arm out toward a grove of trees. "We had pine and maple trees flanking the road, and the houses were basically the same style, if a little smaller."

"What part of Florida?" Trevor asked, gently tugging on the leash when Gus was done with the hydrant.

"Outside Destin. I like the Gulf, and I've thought about moving down there to be closer to them, but it's not for me." She lifted a shoulder. "I guess I'm a Georgia girl."

"Nothing wrong with that," he quipped. "There's a reason I never followed my sister out of state, I like it here. I'm not a snow person, so avoiding the winters is a plus. The beach is fun, but the sand isn't. Not to mention, my friends and Momma are here. Eventually Jessie will come home, I know it."

"You miss your sister?" Whitney related to that notion, as she thought of Winnie daily and craved one of their nights on the town or cozy evenings watching bad '90s sitcoms. Their dynamic had shifted since Whitney moved in, and she missed how carefree they'd been when they both had their own homes.

Trevor stared ahead, not quite seeing the houses in front of him. "Yeah, I do. Not as much as Momma, of course, but I wish she'd come around more. Even for the holidays would be nice, but I won't push the issue."

"You're a good brother, I can tell." She nudged him with her shoulder, and he leaned into her for a moment before Gus pulled him forward in pursuit of a stick on the sidewalk. The hound nearly tripped over his own ears in excitement.

"Do you like living with your sister?"

Whitney shook her head, making a mental note to call Winnie for a proper update. So much had happened in the last two days, she damn near had whiplash. "I guess. Don't get me wrong, I'm grateful for the place to crash. She's always working and is rarely there, so sometimes it's like living alone."

"Doctor?" he wagered.

"Lawyer, and for as much as I don't seem to have career ambitions, Winnie has them all. She's a couple years older, and I think she came out of the womb with a five-year plan."

A little seed of doubt had been planted in Whitney long ago that she wasn't meant to find her way professionally. She'd watched her sister go through her life with such determination and thoughtful planning, Whitney never thought she could have that too. Now, though, after meeting Kim and seeing the shop, that seed took root. Instead of doubt, she experienced a wave of inspiration.

"That's why I'm considering Kim's offer."

Whitney's admission had Trevor tripping over a bump in the sidewalk. "You don't say?" he asked, lips quivering. "You think you'd stick around a while then." He said it as a statement, and Whitney knew before she started nodding she did want to stay, even if only for a little while.

Taking a moment to study his profile, she took in his square jaw and strong nose. This man was ridiculously handsome, and could cook—and, more importantly, he seemed keen for her to stick around. "I think I will, even just for seasonal work. I need to do something, and I think I can really help with this summer rush."

Trevor's smirk morphed into a full grin at that. Knees wobbling, she hadn't realized how much she wanted to see that smile until she was the cause. "Sounds like a good plan to me."

They reached a fork in the road and Trevor gestured to the right. "If we go this way, we'll be back home in a couple minutes, but if we hang left, we'll see the older part of the neighborhood."

Gus was already pulling on his leash to keep walking left, and Whitney wouldn't argue with him. "Let's follow Gus, if you don't mind. I'm enjoying this." She offered a shy smile before focusing back on the hound. She was falling for this goofy dog, and she needed to be careful not to fall for his owner.

"I'm enjoying this, too."

They strode past a pair of joggers, Trevor reaching out to rest a hand above the small of her back so she didn't stagger. His fingertips practically burned through the cotton of her dress.

She was so focused on his touch, she missed his question. "Hmm?" she asked, clearing the lump in her throat. If she wasn't careful, she'd swallow her own tongue if he kept touching her.

"I asked, what excites you about working at Kim's Creations?"

Now Whitney's pulse galloped for other reasons. Trevor showed an interest in her, as a person. As ridiculous as it was, she was unaccustomed to men in her life showing that much genuine attention. All Baxter cared about was that she had been available for him, not how she'd spend her free time. It took a moment for her to catch her breath and give a thoughtful response.

"Well, at the risk of sounding crass, I could use the money. But it's more than that. I like helping people, I like styling and clothes, and it would be nice to do a job because I'm interested." She wrinkled her nose, and added, "Which I'm sure sounds lame, since you're so career focused."

She couldn't be certain, but Trevor flinched at her last statement. He coughed into his fist before saying, "I try to be, but sometimes situations are out of my hands." He sighed so loudly, she was surprised he didn't blow away. Whitney knew there was more to the story, but she wasn't going to push, not now anyway.

They walked the next block in companionable silence, but Whitney craved a topic change. "Turns out we have more in common than you might think," she said, stepping over a crack in the sidewalk.

Trevor reached out to steady her by the elbow, keeping his hand there longer than necessary, her skin about to combust from his proximity. "Is that so?"

Whitney exhaled, readying herself for the truth. There was no use hiding her pain when the man was clearly in the midst of his own. Plus, she wanted to tell her full story to Trevor. More had brought her here than a need to escape her sister's jerk of a cat and lack of a social life. Just as with her over-filled suitcase, Whitney was ready to unpack.

"I recently got dumped myself."

Trevor's footfalls faltered, and he nearly face-planted in

the middle of a neighbor's lawn. "You did?"

"Yup, last month."

"I'm sorry, Whitney. I wouldn't wish that pain on anyone."

Whitney nodded, but she wasn't done unloading. "It gets worse," she teased.

"Oh boy, worse how?" Trevor's dark eyes shown in the street lamp light, his hair falling down his forehead in burnish waves. His strong arms hung by his side, but he was quick to reach out and steady her anytime her footsteps slowed. He was in tune with her movements, ready in a flash if she fumbled. If, God forbid, she found herself in a burning building, she'd want Trevor bursting through the blaze to save her.

"Do you know the Savannah Bananas?" she asked, giggling at his confused expression. "This is going somewhere, I promise."

Trevor's eyes bulged. "Did your ex leave you for a Banana?"

Whitney choked out a laugh, patting her chest to catch her breath. "Oh Lordie, no. Yet that would have been less upsetting, frankly."

"What happened?" Trevor asked, taking her hand as they crossed the street. It was a gentlemanly gesture; one Whitney had been missing. She squeezed his hand once before letting go, already missing his touch.

"He proposed to another woman during the game, right there on the jumbotron." She held her arms up as if projecting the scene. "It stings, because we'd barely been broken up a month at that point."

Now Trevor stopped entirely, spinning her to face him. "You're kidding."

"Sadly, no. It's likely he was cheating on me. Or heaven forbid, with me." She shuddered, discomfort wrapping around her like a snake, threatening to suffocate her.

"First of all, I'm going to need Baxter's full name and his address so I can drive over to Savannah and kick his ass from here to Mobile." Sensing Trevor's frustration, Gus barked his agreement. He was hardly a dangerous animal, but Whitney respected the support.

Whitney smirked. "I appreciate the offer, but I got closure my own way."

Trevor's lips quirked. "I gotta hear this."

Whitney told him about her joyride, from the pizza to the lipstick love note. With every detail, Trevor's smile grew, and he laughed as if he was watching a comedian's TV special, complete with tears pooling in his eyes. Dabbing away at a stray tear, he reached out and pulled her toward his chest in a bone-crushing hug. "Remind me to stay on your good side, Whitney Kerr."

His breath tickled her ear, and she shivered at their close contact. Every cell in her body was screaming for more, screaming to turn her head only slightly and kiss him. But the voice of reason in her head—*who should really mind her business*—told her it wasn't the right time. Instead, she savored the sensation of being enveloped in Trevor's strong arms and leaned into his comfort. Right now, that was more than enough.

*

Trevor was not happy that Whitney was heartbroken, but he was happy to learn she was single—and planning on sticking around a little while longer. He hated himself for that, but it was true. Sensing she was still raw from her admission, he decided to go for broke himself. They had at least another ten minutes of walking, and there was no time like the present.

"Well, if you'll allow me to repay your honesty, I can tell you about Virginia."

Whitney scoffed but recovered quickly. "You mean there's more?"

"Oh yeah," he said on a long exhale. Trevor couldn't decipher why, but he was suddenly desperate for Whitney to know everything about him. He wanted baggage out of the way, or at least seen, before they moved forward. Granted, he had no idea where they were going, but her landing a job in Pinegrove meant she was staying. He liked that idea … a little too much.

"This doesn't need to be a tit-for-tat situation," she promised, carefully nudging his side with her elbow.

Trevor paused while Gus marked another fire hydrant. "I know that, but it only seems right." He looked at Whiney, her expression filled with concern. "So, I got turned down for a promotion recently at the fire station. I was going for captain."

Whitney covered her heart with her hand and gasped. "I'm so sorry, that's terrible."

"Thank you, I won't disagree." He forced a chuckle he didn't feel before continuing. "To make a long story short, Virginia is now engaged to the man who got the captain's job."

Whitney skidded to a halt, and they walked right into Gus, the hound yipping at the change in pace. "You're kidding?"

"'Fraid not."

"Pardon me for saying this, Trevor, but you're describing the plot of a romance novel," she mused, absorbing everything. "I mean, mean-hearted ex gets with work rival. The book practically writes itself!"

"Well, if you know of any aspiring authors, let me know."

Whitney shook herself, splaying a hand over her chest. "No, I don't mean to make light of your situation. Truly."

"I know you don't. It doesn't look like your style." Granted, he hardly knew this woman, but she didn't seem to have a mean bone in her body. *Well, unless she was humiliated on TV by an asshole.*

"How are you holding up with everything? Today must have been rough." Whitney began walking again, having taken Gus's leash when Trevor wasn't paying attention.

Trevor stretched, his head falling back to stare up at the night sky. Clouds were rolling in, and he hoped by the time the Fourth of July came, the weather cooperated. "Honestly, not too bad, all things considered. I'm over Virginia, I really am, but the fact that she's now engaged to the man who has my dream job, it's just …"

"It's a bitter pill to swallow?" she wagered, reaching out and taking his hand with her free one. She held firm, squeezing so he knew she was there. "Dreams are funny, aren't they? You make plans and have these grand ideas, but sometimes all it takes is one person's carelessness to dash it all to pieces."

His palm grew slick with sweat, but Trevor wouldn't let go. "How are you handling Baxter's engagement? I can't imagine that's an easy thing to bounce back from."

Whitney snorted, the unladylike sound charming him. "Oh, I'll get there. Right now, I'm firmly in the rage portion of things. I'm looking back at some of the things he said, some of the things he did, and I know it wasn't meant to be." She nibbled her bottom lip a moment before continuing. "But the change of scenery helps. Being here helps." Feeling braver than he was, she added, "Being out on this walk with you helps." She stopped and faced him, her eyes searching his for answers. "Thank you for opening up your family home to me, Trevor."

He opened his mouth to say it was nothing, but she clamped her hand over it. Gus plopped down in the grass beside them, already bored with their conversation.

"I know this entire situation is bizarre, but you and your momma offered me kindness when you didn't need to. It's certainly putting me in a better head space, and I found an opportunity I never would have found otherwise with Kim." She dropped her hand and smirked. "You may speak now."

He laughed and gently tugged on Gus's leash. "You're welcome. I'm glad we're able to help. And I know Momma has already said this a million times, but you're welcome to stay as long as you need. Especially if you're working for Kim. I think you made Momma's year with that turn of events. She's been worried about her for a while."

They spoke about Kim and the shops on Main Street until Daisy's house came into view. Gus pulled ahead and barked when they reached the front door. Trevor let them inside, stepping back as Gus leaped through the doorway. Walked, fed, and happy, Gus shuffled off to his dog bed and was asleep in seconds.

Whitney stood awkwardly, watching Trevor pull his keys from the lock. "I should probably head back. Tomorrow is an early shift."

"Thanks for dinner and the walk and the talk." Whitney seemed flustered, and she couldn't keep her mouth shut. "I know it was a rough day, but hopefully it ended on a high note."

Trevor closed the distance in two strides. Reaching up, he tucked a curl behind her ear. His finger grazed her ear lobe as he pulled back, and she shivered. Every cell in his body was on alert at Whitney's proximity.

"Tonight was perfect. I can hardly remember why my day sucked." The admission came easily, and he was incredibly grateful at his mother's matchmaking skills.

"I'm glad." Whitney breathed, goosebumps erupting down her neck.

"Good night, darlin'. I'll see you soon."

"See you," she agreed.

Trevor strode to his car and got behind the wheel with a lightness in his step. When the day had started, he'd been certain it would end in disaster. Yet now, with Whitney in town, things just felt better … more hopeful. He hadn't realized until he parked his car that he'd been singing along to the radio the whole drive home.

Yeah, Trevor was going to be all right.

CHAPTER EIGHT

Whitney rubbed the sleep from her eyes as she shuffled into the kitchen. She went to bed before Daisy but was unsurprised to find the other woman in a cheerful mood. "Good morning," she said as she covered her yawn.

Daisy whirled around, the trim of her apron catching on a drawer handle. "Morning, sugar! Did you sleep well?"

Whitney nodded and fell into her chair. Daisy filled a mug with coffee and slid the much-needed caffeine fix across the table. After adding a spoonful of sugar and enough cream to make it the color of toffee, she slurped and sighed. "Yes, but this will help me wake up."

"Trevor texted—the boys are needed at the station early, so it's us chickens in the hen house this morning. You thinking French toast or eggs?" Daisy tapped her chin and studied the array of ingredients on the counter.

Whitney took another sip of coffee before standing and surveying the scene. "I'm thinking you sit down and let me cook for you." Daisy fidgeted and looked ready to protest, when Whitney begged, "Please? You've done so much for me already."

"Oh, all right. But that means I do the dishes."

Whitney shot a thumbs-up and began cracking eggs. She

wasn't a horrible cook, but she knew she couldn't hold a candle to the delights Daisy and Trevor had already whipped up in this kitchen.

"You know," Whitney cleared her throat, not wanting to overstep with an observation. "When I got up last night to get a cup of tea, you weren't in. Your girls' night go long?" She glanced over her shoulder as Daisy took her seat at the table. She filled her own coffee cup and hummed a moment.

"Everything is lovely, sugar. Dinner with Joan and Kim was great, but I was out with another friend after that."

Whitney wasn't blind, and she certainly wasn't a fool. She recognized that glint and dreamy expression anywhere … even if she hadn't seen it on her face in far too long.

"Wait a minute," Whitney gasped. "Were you out with a man last night, Daisy?"

Daisy's smile only grew with the question. "Yes, as a matter of fact, I was."

Whitney giggled as she dropped a fat pat of butter in a frying pan. After scrambling the eggs, she scattered on some cheddar and chives, then slowly combined the mixture together. "You need to spill, because I'm sorely in need of gossip."

Trailing her finger across the wood grain on the table, Daisy hummed to herself. "Well now," she said, attention focused on the tabletop, "I haven't told Trevor the details, but I'm overdue for some girl talk."

"I won't tell a soul. I'm a vault." Whitney crossed her heart with her finger and beamed. She was quickly growing fond of these times with Daisy. Having her own momma far away and Winnie busy didn't leave a lot of interactions like this in Whitney's life. Regardless if she stayed a while in Pinegrove, she made a promise to herself to keep relationships like these.

Daisy sighed, shoulders relaxing as she began to tell her, their story. "Well, I was out last night with Paul Warren. He's the fire chief and an old friend of the family."

Whitney pushed a couple slices of bread into the toaster

and found an array of jams to put on the table. By the time the toast popped up, she'd plated a sunny pile of eggs. Refilling their coffees, she joined Daisy and settled in for girl talk. "How long have you and Paul known each other?"

"Oh, since high school. We all grew up here in Pinegrove. Paul and his ex-wife, Patti, were high school sweethearts, like me and Nick. Then he and Nick went to the academy together after graduation and the rest is history. Nick was chief for a decade before his heart attack, and Paul was always his captain."

"That must be so hard for both of you, losing Nick so suddenly." Whitney sympathized with grief, even though she had never lost a partner. Enough family members had passed to leave a void; their absences felt acutely by those left behind.

Daisy patted Whitney's arm. "Thank you, you're so sweet to listen to me prattle on." Taking a bite of her eggs, she said, "And this is delicious. Thank you."

"You're welcome. Now, how did we go from friends to whatever happened last night?" Whitney winked.

"Well, Paul and Patti divorced about ten years ago. It was one of those things where we were all sad, but no one was surprised. You know what I mean?"

"Painfully," Whitney agreed through a mouthful of eggs. "I'm betting that's how my parents and sister felt about Baxter."

Daisy leveled Whitney with a glare. "We both know that meathead is more dog than man, but I see your point."

Whitney slathered strawberry jam on her toast and marveled at how the mention of Baxter was causing less and less pain. Sure, she was still embarrassed and hurt over his betrayal, but it was quickly becoming a memory rather than a wound.

"When did things start to shift for you and Paul?"

"About six months ago? It was an ordinary Wednesday evening, and Paul stopped by after a bad day at the station. He was struggling with city council over funding and some position changes, including Trevor's, and he wanted a sympathetic ear." Daisy smiled to herself. "Those are the types of interactions I miss the most with Nick, the everyday ones where you share the burden, or the joy, of the day."

Whitney nodded, not wanting to interrupt Daisy's story.

"So, I asked him if he'd like to stay for dinner. Coincidentally I was making pork chops, which I know are his favorite. One minute we were talking and eating, the next he was helping with the dishes and sharing a bottle of wine on the deck. When it came time to leave for the night, we hugged each other, which was nothing new, mind you, but the way I felt afterwards was. I wasn't looking at Paul and thinking *friend*. I looked at Paul and thought *man*."

Leaning forward in her seat, Whitney couldn't contain her giddiness. "Then what happened?"

Daisy's cheeks turned an adorable shade of peach as she glanced into the distance. "Either my pork chops were better than I realized, or Paul felt it too, because he came back the next day with flowers and the fixings for lasagna, which is my favorite dinner."

Whitney clapped and squealed like a teenager at a Friday night football game. "Oh my gosh, he didn't! That is so romantic, I can't stand it." She fanned herself with her napkin.

"It was, and we started dating. Granted, nothing grand or showy, because we don't want the town or our families in our business just yet. But things are getting serious, and I want to tell Jessie and Trevor. They're my family, and I want them to share in this."

A cozy sensation rippled over Whitney at this news, at knowing a secret about her new friend. "Thank you for telling me. I'm honored you trust me with something so special." Whitney reached across the table and squeezed Daisy's hand.

She covered Whitney's with her other hand, tears brimming in her eyes. "Thank you for listening, and more importantly, for coming into my life at the perfect time. I didn't appreciate how much I needed a new friend until you, Whitney."

Now it was Whitney's turn to fight back tears. "Oh, Daisy." She sniffed, wiping her cheek with her napkin. "I feel the same way, and that's what I wanted to talk to you about." She shook herself back to the moment and squared her shoulders.

"Yes?" Daisy's eyes were pinched, her smile fading fast.

"I've decided I'm going to take the job at Kim's shop. I don't know what that means in the long run, but I'm not ready to leave Pinegrove yet."

Daisy whooped and jumped in the air, her chair skittering across the tiled floor. Gus heard the commotion and sauntered into the kitchen. Finding no danger, or more importantly, no treats, he sniffed the air twice before going back out to the living room.

"But!" Whitney shouted over the sound of Daisy's tap dance routine. "I want to discuss something with you first."

Daisy slumped back into her seat and frowned. "I have a feeling I'm not going to like it." She pouted.

"If I stay here—" Whitney started.

"Which you can, for as long as you'd like," Daisy interrupted.

"I'd like to pay rent and help with the groceries. I don't want to take advantage of anyone, but especially you and Trevor."

Daisy nodded. "Fine, that seems fair. Rent is ten dollars a week."

"Daisy, be serious. We can negotiate something once I speak with Kim about salary, but I want to earn my keep."

"Fine, fine." Daisy rose and started collecting dirty dishes. "If you're truly worried about helping out around here, it looks like Gus is ready to have a moment of nature." She raised an eyebrow as Gus loped back into the kitchen and barked, his tail flapping against the doorframe.

"I'm on it. Come on, Gus!" She leaned down to rub his jowls before clipping on his leash. On the way out the door, she grabbed her cell phone, ready to tell Winnie her news.

Despite the early hour, the Georgia sun turned the outside into an oven. June was winding down, but the oppressive heat was here to stay. By the time Gus and Whitney reached the end of the driveway, her shirt was already stuck to her back. She dialed Winnie and cradled the phone to her neck, her attention split between the call and the hound currently smelling anything in his path.

"Whit? You okay? I only have a second."

Whitney relaxed at the sound of her sister's voice. "Yes, everything is fine. Great, actually."

There were voices in the background and Winnie's breaths as she walked. "Sorry, I'm heading into a client meeting, and I'm late."

"That's not like you." Whitney observed, knowing her sister's penchant for setting not two, but four alarms every morning.

Winnie was quiet for a moment before the other line quieted. "I may have spent the night at someone's place last night," she said, voice dripping with excitement.

"Win! Who are they?" Whitney squealed, startling Gus as he was about to leave his mark on a neighbor's unsuspecting mailbox.

"Her name is Mari, and we met at a young professional's mixer last month. She's on this retreat with the other firms."

Whitney couldn't resist the sisterly dig. "You're still considered a young professional?"

"Easy there, I'm still young enough to whoop your butt." Whitney didn't doubt it, so she clamped her mouth shut. "Mari is a paralegal, and we bonded over our love of the legal system, pralines, and Netflix documentaries. I'm seeing her again for dinner tonight."

Winnie's dating history varied over the years, depending on her schooling and career. Law school and making partner were Winnie's chief priorities, which meant dating long term wasn't always easy.

"Sounds like Mari's perfect for you," Whitney said, her

grin spreading at her sister's happiness.

Lawyer Winnie came out to play. "Let's not get ahead of ourselves, but yeah. Mari's cool, and I like her." The background noise grew louder and Winnie sighed. "I need to get to this meeting, but you're okay?"

"I really am. I got a job here in Pinegrove, at a boutique downtown. I'm going to rent a room from Daisy and stick around for a little while." She bit her lip, nervously waiting for Winnie's reaction.

"You're thinking of staying there?"

"For a little while. Kim, the shop owner, needs help with the Fourth of July tourist crowd, and I need a little cash to tie me over."

"I can send you money," Winnie offered, as quickly as Whitney anticipated.

"I know you can, but that's not what I want. Let me figure this out."

Winnie sighed into the phone, her big-sister status on full display. "Does this have anything to do with a certain fireman?"

Whitney stopped as Gus did his business, carefully scooping up the mess while holding onto his leash and her phone. Her demonstration of acrobatics was witnessed by a group of elderly walkers, waving from the other side of the street. She waved back and nearly tripped over Gus as she tossed the bag into a nearby trashcan.

"No," Whitney said, the lie bitter on her tongue. Well, maybe it wasn't technically a lie, but it certainly wasn't the truth. She liked Trevor, and while she didn't know where that feeling was going, she was along for the ride while it lasted. Perhaps a change of scenery and a new job could bring her closer to herself?

"I'm choosing not to believe you, but I don't have time to argue. If this makes you happy, and since I know Daisy isn't the next Ted Bundy, I'll allow it."

"Thank you, Counselor."

"You tease me, but it's my job to look out for you."

"I don't know if it's your job, but it's certainly your favorite hobby," Whitney teased, directing Gus back toward Daisy's house. *Back to her temporary home.*

"Be safe and keep me posted on everything, okay? I want to know when you're coming back. Xena and I need you."

"We've established, Xena hates me and you probably miss your own space." Whitney wasn't ready to think about coming back to Savannah. Things were finally starting to turn around; there hardly seemed any rush.

"I really gotta run, but you know Xena loves you. And so do I!"

"Love you, too. Have fun with Mari tonight, you deserve it."

Winnie hung up, leaving Whitney and Gus to walk in silence the last block home. When they reached the porch, he barked and rolled onto his back, legs akimbo ready for his belly rubs.

"Silly doggo." She laughed, rubbing his tummy.

Daisy opened the front door and stepped outside, ready for her day in khakis and a sleeveless blouse. Her hair was tucked up under another straw hat, her smile was infectious. "How do you feel about a trip to Kim's shop and then the Cracked Spine? I want to show you the romance section after you and Kim finalize everything for your job."

Whitney nodded, eager to get her hands on a new book. In her haste to leave Savannah, her romance book collection was the only thing she really missed. *Sorry, Xena!*

"Give me thirty minutes to get ready?"

"You can have forty-five." Daisy held the door for Gus to follow them inside.

Whitney got ready for her day with a sense of hope she hadn't realized she was missing. The people of Pinegrove had opened their arms to her, and she appreciated their kindness more than they knew. Meeting Daisy at her car, Whitney barely contained her enthusiasm as she drove into town with her new friend. Life was good, and she was going to savor the moment.

*

Trevor was disappointed he and Javi didn't have time for breakfast at his mother's house, as he was dying to see Whitney again. Plus, a short stack on the way to a grueling day never hurt. Alas, it wasn't to be, and he and Javi rolled in as the chief and captain strolled out of their offices with matching worried expressions.

"Team!" Chief Warren called out, his voice booming over the busy bullpen. "Gather round, we're having a huddle and getting new assignments." He opened his mouth to continue, but Hastings cut him off.

"Who has the budget reports for the city council meeting?"

Chief cocked an eyebrow. "The budgets were approved last month, Hastings. What are you needing them for?"

Hastings blinked, swallowing hard before he laughed. To the untrained ear it might have been carefree, but Trevor had worked with him enough to spot the tension in his gaze.

"Nothing, Chief. Just wanted to get a jump start on planning next year." He ran a hand over his head, causing his hair to stick up in all directions.

"Maybe you can tweak the budget and get yourself a new haircut, Cap," Javi teased.

Anyone in the huddle could see Hastings was agitated. There were dark smudges under his eyes, and his lips were drawn tight in a frown that would have been comical under other circumstances. His eyes darted over the team as the chief spoke, almost like he was planning a hasty retreat.

"My haircut is fine, Ortiz. Maybe we should look at the budget and hire someone who—"

"Knock it off," Chief barked. "Hastings, don't worry about the budget. I need you on the reports on zoning. Remember?" Hastings nodded, then darted back to his office and slammed the door. Chief had been asking for those zoning reports for months, and it was just one of many little projects Trevor wanted to help with. He had the background knowledge and the desire to learn, whereas Hastings had a short temper and was as dumb as a post.

Pushing Trevor from his spiral, the chief knocked his knuckles on a clipboard. "Here's our next round of assignments. Come on over and see what's planned for this schedule rotation."

Smithy joined Javi and Trevor, handing them each a donut. "I picked these up on my way in and hid them from Hastings. That idiot tried to steal the last two jellies, and I just about lost it."

"Thanks, Smithy," Trevor said, biting into his donut and narrowly avoiding getting jam on his uniform shirt.

"What's on everyone's agenda today?" Javi asked, dusting powdered sugar off his hands.

Maxwell joined them, holding up the clipboard and beaming at Trevor. "We're on inventory duty, dude!"

"Yeah," Trevor agreed, but half-heartedly. "Let's get counting."

Smithy and Javi gave him supportive grins, but Trevor knew they were just as fed up with the current situation as anyone. It was the lamest of grunt work, but at least it kept him away from Hastings. Plus, he liked working with Maxwell. Her positive attitude was a welcome counterbalance to his newfound surliness.

Twenty minutes into color-coding a rather impressive Excel spreadsheet, Chief Warren appeared at his desk. "You got a minute, son?" he asked, hands clasped behind his back.

"Absolutely." Trevor saved his file and stood, biting his tongue so he didn't say what he really wanted to. *All I've got is time …*

Turning to Maxwell, he asked, "You mind merging those two spreadsheets? It'll help us when we count the uniforms in storage."

She shot a thumbs-up and slid into his seat, seemingly enthralled with her assignment.

"Good work, Maxwell," Chief said before turning back

to Trevor. "Let's chat in my office."

The chief's normally confident gait slowed the nearer they got to his office. Trevor swallowed past the lump in his throat, fearing he was about to get another blow to his career.

Chief Warren held the door for Trevor, who immediately sat down. The shaking in his knees gave away his current mental state. He balled his hands into fists and rested them on his lap, praying his pulse slowed.

Taking longer than necessary to close the door and walk around to his own seat, the chief sighed. "Let me start by saying, I'm aware that those zoning reports were due last month."

"Um. Yes, I believe they were." Trevor's ears perked up, but he wanted to hear the chief's perspective.

Resting his elbows on the desk, Chief Warren dipped his head and groaned. "What I'm about to say doesn't leave this office." Trevor bit down on his tongue, nodding until the chief spoke again. "It's a God damn quagmire, if you'll excuse my language. Hastings is an idiot, Trevor. The man can't use Excel, I don't think he knows how to attach files to email, and yesterday he asked me who my boss was."

Chief rarely swore, and he attended church regularly. He'd never seen the other man so flustered. "Sir?"

Flapping his hands again, he leaned back in his chair. "Cut the 'sir' for now. I'm Paul, and you're Trevor."

"Okay?" Trevor tried to stop the bouncing in his legs, but it was no use.

"I know it may not appear like it, but I am trying to figure out your role here, son. City council has their say, but there are ways for you to move up the ranks. I'm also trying to figure out what to do with a captain who isn't qualified."

Trevor squeezed his eyes shut, sensing where this was going. "So city council hires a moron and I get transferred?" He was incredulous. "You're really going through with it— you're going to transfer me to another station, aren't you?"

Chief opened his mouth, closed it, and opened it again.

"I can't give specifics yet, but I'm doing everything I can to make this right. You'd make an excellent captain, Trevor. We both know that. I need you to trust me." His eyes pleaded with him to see sense, but Trevor was still too bitter.

"Is there anything else, sir?" Trevor put his hands on the arms of the chair, leaning forward to get the hell out of this office. His gut churned with frustration but also annoyance. Deep in his bones he understood that Chief Warren didn't get to make the final decision, but it didn't change Trevor's current situation. At the end of the day, Trevor wasn't reaching his professional potential, and he was sick of pretending he was okay with that reality.

"Actually, there is, son, but it's a personal matter."

"Personal?" Trevor asked, just as dispatch announced through the overhead speakers, *"Fire in progress, Station 33 respond with engines and medic."*

Trevor was already to the doorway, when Chief said, "We'll finish this conversation later."

Following some of the other firefighters to the garage, Trevor pulled on his bunker gear in less than a minute and hopped in the truck. Javi was behind the wheel, laser-focused as Trevor navigated to the scene. Fortunately, it was a minor fender bender with a car that was merely smoking, not burning. Smithy assessed the damage while Trevor helped with directing traffic away from the scene.

One of the little old ladies from church, Mrs. Neely, walked by with her poodle and spotted Trevor. "Trevor? What's all this?" she asked as she lumbered over to him, the dog barely keeping pace. If Mrs. Neely was in her eighties, that hound had to be nearly two thousand in dog years.

"Hello, Mrs. Neely. How are you doing today?"

"Oh, you know, dear. Mr. Puddles and I love our walks." She gestured down at the poodle, who looked prepared to meet his maker. Tail barely wagging and tongue lolling out the side, he looked ready for a nap and a guzzle of water.

"I bet you do," he replied, one eye fixed on the flow of traffic. When there was a break in cars, he held up his hand.

"I'll be right back, wait here."

He sprinted to the truck and retrieved a pair of water bottles. Not only did Mr. Puddles need a drink, he wagered the older woman was dehydrated in this heat. "Well, aren't you a sweetheart?" Mrs. Neely cooed as she took the first bottle and whistled for her dog. Pouring water into a gap in the sidewalk, Mr. Puddles lapped up the water, his tail finally shifting back and forth.

"Much better," Trevor said. "Do you need a ride back, Mrs. Neely? You're a ways from home, aren't you?"

She waved away his concern with the empty water bottle. "No, I'm visiting with Douglas over on Maple."

"That's nice," he said, taking a step to go back to work. He'd helped her and her dog, but he didn't have time for neighborhood gossip.

"It is nice, love after loss is always a pleasant surprise."

"Love?" Her admission caught Trevor off guard, and he nearly stumbled into Mr. Puddles.

Her eyes sparkled with mischief. "Yes, young man, I said love. Women after fifty can fall in love, look at your momma."

"Momma?" Trevor was incredulous, thrusting his hands on his hips. "What are you saying, Mrs. Neely?"

The old woman threw her head back and laughed, startling poor Mr. Puddles. "Oh, darlin', that's not my story to tell." She patted his cheek as if he were misbehaving in Sunday School before shuffling off toward Maple Drive."

Love.

Love?

Trevor pushed through the fog of her comment until he reached the truck. He knew his mother and the chief were seeing each other in some capacity, but to smack the L word on it seemed rushed. Taking his momma out for a low country boil is one thing, but love brought a whole new slew of fears Trevor didn't anticipate.

Javi joined him and updated him on the status of the accident, taking Trevor out of his ongoing turmoil. "We're set to go, Lieutenant."

"Why do I have a feeling I'm missing something?" he asked, rubbing the back of his neck.

"With the fender bender?"

"No, with … never mind."

Javi shrugged. "Dunno, man, but let's roll. The cops have traffic moving, and I'm ready for lunch. Smithy said the injuries are minor, no hospitalization needed."

Trevor followed the rest of the team back to the truck and sighed. He loved the job, even the silly parts like hydrating ugly dogs and their quirky owners, but he couldn't shake the fact that something was happening right before his eyes.

Keeping his head down for the rest of his shift, Trevor left right on time and headed for his momma's house. He wanted to have dinner with the two ladies in his life, but he also wanted to know what in the world Mrs. Neely was talking about.

Trevor prayed he'd like the answer. Momma deserved every happiness, but falling in love again? He wasn't a boy, and he knew no one would replace his father or the memories they all shared. Perhaps his hesitation was that he was stuck, barely treading water in his life.

Although, if Daisy Mays could find love again, maybe there was hope for him after all.

CHAPTER NINE

"I can't believe I got so many books," Whitney lamented as they carried two sacks' worth of paperbacks into the house. Her shoulders drooped with effort, but she'd gladly carry twice as many tomes. *It isn't hoarding if it's books, right?*

Daisy followed her, weighed down with her own finds. "I told you, sugar. You can't go wrong with The Cracked Spine. Their romance section can't be beat."

Whitney couldn't remember such a lovely day in recent memory. She'd met with Kim to discuss the job and was set to start the following day. They agreed on a wage that Whitney thought was too generous for being a clerk, but Kim insisted was the least she could do. Then Daisy took her out to lunch at a noodle bar that had the best ramen she'd ever eaten.

Daisy pulled off her hat and fluffed her hair. "Why don't you meet me in my room in a few minutes, and I'll fix us some sweet tea? I'd love to show you my romance book collection." She rubbed her hands together, bracelets clacking.

"Deal." Whitney washed up and let Gus outside for a moment before joining Daisy in her room.

It was the master bedroom, and it looked exactly like

what Daisy's room should look like. A vase of fresh flowers, her namesake, sat on the nightstand. Framed photos of her children and late husband filled the opposite nightstand, along with a small stack of books.

Against the far wall were four lengths of bookshelves, each stacked two-deep with romance books. Their red, pink, and purple spines looked like prized jewels to Whitney, who eagerly started perusing the collection.

Daisy carried in two glasses of tea and placed them on the windowsill. Gus followed her in and jumped onto her bed, his eyes already drooping with fatigue. "You silly hound," Daisy said lovingly, patting his head and kissing his snout before joining Whitney at the bookshelves.

"You have an amazing collection," Whitney said as her finger trailed over the spines, recognizing some of her favorite authors.

The collection spanned both new releases, modern classics, and old standards like Jane Austen and the Bronte sisters. There were at least thirty of Darla Champaign's books, and Whitney couldn't help but smile at the memory of their first meeting at The Pecan Pit. Whitney still marveled at the fact that spotting one of her favorite romance books would lead to everything that had transpired. She had a new, although likely temporary, job, and had found friends that already felt like family.

Returning her attention to the books, she ran her fingers along the edge of the shelf. Every book looked like it had been read and thoroughly enjoyed, their spines cracked and pages worn. Whitney pulled out a historical romance she hadn't read before and studied the cover. It was prime Fabio, with an unbuttoned shirt and heroine splayed across his lap. "That one is hotter than it looks," Daisy said with a wink. "Feel free to borrow it and report back later." Spying another book next to it, Daisy snatched it and handed it to Whitney. "But read this first—it's our book club book for next month."

Whitney raised an eyebrow. "You're inviting me to your

book club?"

Daisy sniffed, covering her nose. "Sugar, we agreed you're living here. You just agreed to work for my friend, and fellow book clubber, and you've proven you know more about romance books than I do. You'd think I'd let you miss out on the joy of book club? Bless your heart."

Taking the proffered book, Whitney held it to her chest as she fought back tears. "I'm sorry, it's …"

It's just that at the beginning of the year she thought she had a good life. She had a boyfriend who loved her, a job placement she didn't hate, and a general rosy view of the world around her. Fast forward to now, and Whitney hadn't known true happiness in far too long.

Yes, her love life was far from perfect, but a seed of hope threatened to bloom if she let it. Trevor was kind, sweet-natured, and treated his family well. These were attributes she'd let slide with Baxter, but those days were done. Whitney wouldn't be blinded by platitudes and flashy gifts; she was ready for more, something *real*.

Whitney rallied. "Thank you. I don't mean to get all weepy, but you've treated me better this week than people I've known for years. It's taking some getting used to is all." She dabbed at her eyes with a tissue that Daisy handed her.

"No worries, sugar. Feel free to tell me to mind my business." She let out a long breath and sat on the edge of the bed, making room for Whitney to join her. "Now, I know you've had your heart run through the meat grinder, and that's nothing you can overcome like that." She snapped her fingers to punctuate her point.

Whitney nodded, but it wasn't merely Baxter's carelessness that wounded her. "I agree, but I'm not even thinking about Baxter anymore. It's more that he made me feel worthless. I'm not pining over him, Daisy, rest assured it's my pride I'm more worried about, not my heart."

Sensing she needed a moment, Daisy whistled for Gus to follow her out the room. "Why don't you take a few minutes, and I'll get the fixings for dinner ready?"

Whitney opened her mouth to offer help, but Daisy was faster. "You've done more than enough today. Now crack open one of those books so we can start discussing your thoughts on pirates vs. Vikings."

"Yes, ma'am." Whitney saluted with her free hand.

She let herself into her room and stacked the books on the small desk in the corner. Selecting a title, she eased onto the bed and read the first two chapters before the day caught up to her and she fell asleep.

An hour later, she woke to the sounds of clattering pans and Gus barking excitedly. She jumped from the bed, pinched some color into her cheeks, and ran her fingers through her dark curls to dissipate the bedhead.

As she reached the doorway to the kitchen, she heard hushed voices. One of them was low, clearly a man's, and Daisy's voice seemed strained. Since the man's voice wasn't Trevor's, she dipped her head over the threshold to investigate. A man in his late fifties stood in the kitchen, clad in a navy-blue fireman's uniform. Unlike Trevor's, his chest was decorated with adornments of a higher rank. Judging from the concerned look on his face, she wagered it was Paul.

"Honey, I tried to tell him today, but we got a call." He reached out, resting his hands on Daisy's shoulders, his brow knit in concern.

Daisy nodded, leaning into his touch with a sigh. "I know, but he's not going to handle this well without knowing the full story. He hates being in the dark, especially with family."

"We'll tell him together. That should have been the plan all along, because it isn't just your or my news to share."

Tipping her head up to meet Paul's gaze, Daisy wilted a little. "I should tell him. He's had a rough summer, and his ego took a hit. Waltzing into family dinner with his boss as my ..."

"Boyfriend," Paul said the word with conviction, melting Whitney's heart with his concern for Daisy. "Although that title doesn't seem right for what we are."

Daisy's head fell forward, her forehead resting over Paul's heart. "I need a little time to tell him everything. Okay? I'm not ashamed of us, but I'm worried for Trevor."

"Okay, that's your call." Paul dropped his arms to his sides and turned around to find Whitney spying in the hallway. She jumped when their eyes locked.

"So sorry, I heard voices, but I'm leaving." She held her hands up like she was being arrested. In her haste to retreat, she tripped over her own feet and fell against the wall with a sad thud. "Oof," she exhaled, steadying herself against the doorjamb.

Daisy sidestepped Paul and reached out for Whitney's arm, pulling her into the kitchen. "Don't be silly, sugar. You need to meet Paul."

Paul stepped up and held out his hand for her to shake. "I've heard a lot of good things about you, Whitney. Welcome to Pinegrove."

"Thank you. It's a pleasure to meet you too, Paul. Daisy and Trevor have had nothing but nice things to say about you." She smiled when he relaxed at her words. He seemed like a nice man trying to do the right thing—in other words, he was perfect for Daisy. "Are you joining us for dinner?" she asked.

Paul winced and faced Daisy. "That's entirely up to our fair hostess."

Daisy hurried to the stove to stir a pot. "There's plenty of food. Please stay, but I'd like it to be as a friend. I will talk to Trevor, but not tonight."

"That's fine. Let me set the table." Paul went to work, pulling out dishes and glasses, proving he was more than comfortable in Daisy's home.

Not for the first time, Whitney feared she'd be cramping the other woman's style. As Paul went into the pantry in search of more napkins, Whitney snagged Daisy's hand and whispered, "Do you need me to make myself scarce?"

Daisy scoffed. "Right now? Sugar, I appreciate the

willingness to play wingman, but Paul and I can wait to have a moment." She waggled her eyebrows.

"What? No, not now. I mean in general. You likely *entertain* here, and I don't want to be in the way of your life. I really can find a hotel or something."

Daisy tapped her wooden spoon on the side of the pot before pointing it at Whitney. In an exacerbated tone, Daisy scolded her. "Listen, young lady, and listen good. Not only are you welcome in this home, but there is still the matter of not having hotels available. I'm a grown-ass woman, and if I want to have a"—she lowered her voice—"booty call, I'm perfectly able to drive to Paul's house."

The color drained from Whitney's face as Paul appeared sans napkins. "Honey, I cannot find the napkins anywhere."

"Honey?" Trevor asked, a look of confusion on his face and two bouquets in his hands.

Daisy whirled around and practically pushed Whitney into her son's path. Catching herself in the nick of time, Whitney clung to the edge of the counter. "Trevor, I wasn't expecting you so soon."

Trevor pursed his lips, his eyes darting back and forth between his boss and mother. Whitney tried to make herself small, hunching her shoulders forward to escape what was surely a family matter.

"I didn't think I needed to schedule my visit," he said, the muscles in his neck tense as he stepped closer to Whitney. "These are for you." He pressed one of the bouquets, a lovely assortment of summery blooms in an array of pinks and purples, into her hands. Turning to his mother, he handed her a gorgeous array of daisies. "I'm sorry, Chief. If I had known you'd be here, I would have picked up some roses."

Paul laughed, but his eyes remained tense. "I'm more of a dahlia man myself," he teased, but Trevor didn't crack.

"Chief Warren was in the neighborhood, and I invited him to supper." Daisy gestured to the table set for four and the oversized pot on the stove. "I'm making gumbo—

everyone, take a seat."

Whitney sniffed her flowers and smiled. Despite the tension in the room, it had been years since a man bought her flowers. Baxter always told her they were a waste of money, so she never bothered asking for any. *They'll be dead in a few days. Why bother?*

Idly, she wondered if his fiancée was the one getting all the flowers. Little trinkets and tokens of affection had never been Baxter's forte, and Whitney had let that be. Now though, she wondered if she had been a placeholder while he wined and dined the real woman in his life.

If she would have been back in Savannah, Whitney would have let that notion ruin her evening. But the air was heavy with the aroma of sausage, peppers, and flowers, and she didn't want to give Baxter freaking Hollingsworth another moment of her time.

Instead, she put Daisy and her flowers in water and took a seat at the table. Paul sat with his hands in his lap, his gaze anywhere but on Daisy and Trevor. Trevor looked as miserable as he toyed with his fork and spoon.

It was going to be a long night, but at least it wasn't her drama. Not yet anyway …

*

"Well, isn't this a lovely surprise?" Daisy said as she ladled heaping servings of gumbo into everyone's bowls.

"This looks delightful, hon …" Chief Warren cleared his throat before chugging half of his sweet tea. "Excuse me, Daisy. I have a frog in my throat." He flashed a smile to Whitney, who looked too uncomfortable for Trevor's taste.

Her beautiful eyes were downcast, and she'd hardly said a word since she thanked him for the flowers. Trevor wished he had a little time with her, because he wanted to see what was troubling her. The last he'd heard, she and his mother planned a full day on the town. He wondered if they'd had another run-in with Virginia, or maybe her job at

Kim's shop fell through?

Trevor reached for his napkin, finding a paper towel instead. "I can run to the market for you tomorrow, Momma. Looks like you're out of a few things?"

"Thanks, sugar, but I'll handle it. I know you're busy."

Trevor swallowed his retort, since the reason he wasn't very busy was currently seated to his left. To his right was the real reason he wanted to be busy, but she wasn't meeting his gaze. Something was up.

"Did something happen today?" he asked, his voice low so only Whitney heard.

Her expression shifted for an instant before she recovered. "No, it was a lovely day. Daisy and I went shopping. You should see my book haul. I would be embarrassed if it didn't make me so happy." She paused her story to take a bite of gumbo, covering her mouth as she chewed. "Oh, and we stopped by Kim's shop."

Chief interrupted. "Daisy said she's worried about Kim's workload. How'd everything look when you stopped by?"

His mother had been saying? Okay, Trevor was officially about to lose his mind. "And when ..."

"Cornbread!" Daisy shouted, springing to her feet so quickly she nearly tripped over Gus on her way to the oven. "I nearly forgot." She made a show of shoving on hot pads and narrating her actions as she pulled out a golden pan of cornbread. Temporarily distracted, she cut everyone a slice before passing the butter.

Whitney heaved a forkful in her mouth and hummed her approval. "Daisy, you need to share your recipe. I haven't had gumbo this good since my nana passed."

"No secret family recipe here, I'm afraid. Just something I picked up from the church ladies. First you need to find a couple sweet onions ..." For nearly ten minutes, his mother painstakingly described the entire gumbo-making process, from the roux to the best types of sausages.

Whitney hung on every word like she was learning state secrets, not a basic recipe. She *ooh*ed and *ahh*ed at all the right moments, as if she was a guest on the Food Network.

For his part, Chief Warren seemed enraptured. Trevor had seen the man eat everything at the station from canned soup and corn flakes to barbecue and frozen pizzas. Yet he'd never shared much in the way of a glimpse into his personal skills in the kitchen. "And you don't blanch the vegetables ahead of time?" he marveled, jaw nearly unhinged.

Trevor snorted into his glass of water. "Momma, as thrilling as the nuances of dicing vegetables are," he said, hiding his smirk behind a forkful of food, "what else happened today?"

Whitney perked up at his question and beamed. "Well, since you asked." She dabbed at the corners of her lush mouth with her paper towel. Trevor would give his next paycheck for the chance to reach out and kiss her lips clean.

Daisy sprung to her feet and went in search of more drinks for the table. As she walked past the chief, her hand rested on his shoulder as she refilled his water glass. Considering she did the same thing with Whitney and himself, Trevor tried not to read too much into it. This evening had crossed into Bizarro World territory already.

"Yes, sugar, tell Trevor all about it."

Trevor helped himself to another spoonful of gumbo as Whitney lit up the room with her smile. "I don't want to brag, y'all, but you're looking at the newest clerk at Kim's Creations." She did jazz hands and giggled.

Paul clapped and Trevor joined in the applause. "Darlin', this is great news. Congratulations." It was great news for a lot of reasons, the most obvious she'd be sticking around Pinegrove. He was far from done spending time with this woman.

"Kim runs a fine store. She's lucky to have you," Paul agreed, shooting Whitney an encouraging thumbs-up.

"That's what I keep telling her, Paul."

Whitney's head dipped low as she absorbed everyone's praise. "It's a retail job, you're the ones saving lives."

Trevor opened his mouth to say he wasn't saving much of anything lately, but instead, he rallied. "I'm pretty sure Kim would say you're saving *her* life, darlin'. Don't sell yourself short." He kept his gaze locked on her profile until she turned and faced him. Her cheeks plumped as she smiled, and his heart squeezed. Those smiles were quickly becoming an addiction.

"I'd say this calls for dessert. Anyone want pie?"

"You had time to bake a pie today?" Whitney was incredulous. "I'm still trying to figure out how you made gumbo since we came back from our day on the town." Rising, Whitney stacked the dirty dishes and started loading the dishwasher.

Chief joined her at the counter and started scrubbing the pots and pans. Daisy poured herself a glass of sweet tea and eased back into her chair, studying the domestic scene. "A girl could get used to this," she teased, elbowing her son in the side.

"Considering we're about to get pie, we're all winners." Whitney put the last dish in the dishwasher as she picked up a towel to dry the pots. When she got to the last one, she held it up and asked where it went.

"On that hook over the island," Chief said, wiping down the stovetop with a sponge.

Trevor slowly turned to his mother, who looked very interested in the pattern on the placemats. The chief seemed awfully familiar with the layout of his mother's kitchen—of his mother's favorite place on this planet. "How does—?"

"I'll start slicing that pie," his mother interrupted, patting his hand as she stood and pulled the pie from the fridge. "Anyone want ice cream?"

Whitney rubbed her stomach and grumbled. "I probably shouldn't have the pie, to be honest. I've fallen off the wagon since I arrived in Pinegrove." Looking down at herself, she frowned. "Actually, I don't think I've been on the wagon since I stopped playing with Barbie dolls."

Daisy swatted Whitney's hip with a tea towel. "Hush up,

sugar. I won't have that talk in my house. You're gorgeous, and that's that."

Trevor swallowed past a lump in his throat. The look of determination on Whitney's face to deject herself put a sour taste in his mouth. Sure, she was curvy, but she was stunning. As soon as Trevor watched Javi walk up to Whitney in The Pecan Pit, he knew he had to meet her. She was effortlessly pretty, with soft curls and even softer curves. Whoever put this poor image in her head needed to pay.

"Why don't you and Chief get the patio table set for dessert? A night this lovely deserves al fresco pie."

Daisy nodded, reaching out and directing Paul by his elbow. "We'll see you kids outside."

Whitney didn't turn around at first, busying herself with folding the damp towels and hanging them from the stove handles. Trevor approached her slowly, afraid he'd spook her right out of this house and all of Pinegrove.

"Whitney, if you think …"

Spinning around to face him, she offered a sad smile. "Trevor, please don't. I've been battling my body issues and weight since I got my first training bra. It's between me and my darned brain." She tapped her temple and sighed.

"Well, if I get a say in the matter," he replied, stepping closer until they were only a foot apart. "I haven't been able to keep my eyes off you since I got here."

She raised an eyebrow. "I'm pretty sure that's because I had sauce on my mouth."

"And you wore it beautifully." He reached out, smoothing his thumb over her cheek. Her skin was smooth and flawless, just like the undriven snow he'd seen on their family vacation to Banff.

She closed her eyes as his thumb smoothed down to her lips, caressing over the tender skin once before he reluctantly pulled back. He wanted more from this woman, but he wasn't about to make a move in his mother's kitchen with his boss out back.

As if sensing the shift in the air, Gus arrived at their feet and barked his discomfort. "Looks like our boy needs a nature break," Whitney said, leaning down to rub behind the hound's ears.

Our boy. Trevor liked the sound of that, a little too much.

He and Virginia rarely shared ownership of anything during their relationship. She was fiercely independent, yet simultaneously dependent on her father's approval—and the CVC code on his major credit cards. Despite putting a ring on her finger, they'd never discussed their future in detail. He assumed they'd have kids and get a Gus of their own, but with just two words from Whitney, he was ready to pick out baby names and find a house with a two-car garage. He wanted a future with this woman, and he didn't know how to get it.

"I'm sorry to interrupt, kids, but I need to go. We had two call-offs from the C shift, and no one is available to come in." Chief sauntered into the kitchen and pulled his uniform jacket from the back of his chair.

"Can I help, sir?" Trevor offered, but the older man shook his head.

Chief rested his hands on his hips. "We've been through this, son. I'm Paul when we're off the clock." He admonished Trevor, but kept going. "I should only need to be there through the first half of the shift." He shrugged. "At least I can finish up some of those reports. Thank you for dinner, Daisy. As always, it was delicious."

Daisy practically bloomed from his praise, and it rankled Trevor. The trouble was, he wasn't sure why.

"Let me get you some pie to go," Daisy insisted, strolling over to the pantry to retrieve a roll of aluminum foil. A minute later, she walked the chief outside, leaving them with a very impatient Gus.

He woofed, head-butting Trevor in the shin. "And it looks like we forgot about our buddy here." He laughed, opening the back door as Gus loped out and relieved himself on Daisy's favorite shrub.

"I'll meet you out there with some pie," Whitney suggested, already turning to slice and serve the rest of dessert.

Trevor headed outside to ensure Gus didn't try to escape through the gap in the fence. He leaned against the railing of the deck and sighed into the cooling night air. He had so many memories in this old house, he'd lost track. Happy times like holidays and birthdays with the four of them laughing, always surrounded by love.

Even after two years, Trevor missed his father with a fierceness that worried him. His therapist loved to remind him how much progress he'd made in that time, but at the end of the day, he still missed his old man. Even as he thought back to tonight's dinner, he couldn't say he didn't enjoy himself. Having Whitney at the table filled him with a sense of hope so tangible, he was surprised he couldn't reach into his own ribcage and hold it.

His mother seemed to enjoy herself, too. He hadn't seen that particular look on her face since losing his father. Kicking at a loose deck board, Trevor sighed. Who was he kidding? All signs pointed to his mother and the chief dating. It seemed like all of Pinegrove knew it, and perhaps deep down he knew it too. Trevor recognized he had to pull his head out of his own ass, needed to have a conversation with his mother.

Before he could chastise himself further, Whitney appeared with his dessert. Their fingers grazed as she handed him a slice of peach pie surrounded by ice cream scoops. "Daisy said you like extra ice cream, but let me know if I went overboard."

Trevor pretended to drop the plate, as if it weighed a metric ton. "I don't know, darlin'. I think you could have fit another scoop on the corner here." He pointed with his fork, earning him a theatrical eye roll that had no right being that cute. *God, this woman* ...

Thoughts of his mother's love life forgotten, Trevor focused on this goddess before him. "You nervous for your first day tomorrow?" he asked, mesmerized by the way she licked the ice cream from her fork.

Whitney lifted a shoulder. "Yes and no. The biggest benefit of being a temp is that I'm used to first-day jitters. I'm more excited than nervous."

"Good, because I know you're going to do great."

A shy smile tugged at her lips. "Thanks, I appreciate that."

Holding up his free hand, Trevor said, "I speak the truth."

For a moment, neither of them spoke. It was the kind of companionable silence Trevor loved. The silence of people who were comfortable enough being quiet with each other. It didn't mean anything, it just meant they didn't have to talk for talking's sake.

Then Whitney broke the silence. "Paul seems like a nice man." She observed, staring out in the lawn as the light dwindled.

Trevor took a bite of pie, buying time. "He is," he agreed through a mouthful of peaches.

"He's been a family friend for a while, Daisy said." Whitney wouldn't face him as she spoke, but she seemed to be holding something back. "It's nice when you have long-term friends like that."

"Yeah, I guess." Trevor swatted at a bug who was far more interested in his skin than the pie in his hand.

"The type of man I'd want my mother to see if something happened to my dad." Whitney announced to Gus as he approached for more belly rubs.

"Huh, I guess so. Never really thought about it." That was technically the truth, but now that Whitney had planted that seed, it's all Trevor thought about.

Momma moving on from his daddy.

Momma moving on *with* his chief.

The revelation should have left a bitter taste in his mouth, but Trevor swallowed past the fear. If things were serious between the chief and his momma, surely his momma would have said something, right?

Trevor pushed aside thoughts of his mother and the chief, focusing instead on the setting sun and the shadows falling around them. Whitney hummed as she chewed her dessert, pausing the tune long enough to coo over Gus. She looked happy, and judging from the swelling in his ribcage, she wasn't the only one. Trevor hoped this was the first of many nights under the stars with Whitney by his side.

CHAPTER TEN

Whitney's heart was a flutter by the time she'd collapsed onto the recliner, the dinner dishes put away and Paul and Trevor back home. "You got a few minutes for some vino and terrible television?" Daisy teased, jostling a wine bottle and wearing her pajamas.

Knowing all that waited for Whitney was more rambling thoughts about Trevor, she eagerly agreed. "Yes, please." The pair settled in for an episode of a true crime show with half glasses of wine.

The wine was on the sweet side, but Whitney wouldn't complain. By the time the suspect was arrested, Daisy was asleep on the couch. Her head rested on a pillow, her mouth already open. Gus was asleep as well, curled up under the coffee table. Whitney quietly gathered their glasses and rinsed them out before heading to the bathroom.

While she brushed her teeth, she realized they were almost out of toothpaste. She also discovered she hadn't packed any tampons for her upcoming period, so a trip to the drugstore was needed.

Whitney checked the time on her phone and Googled the nearest chain drugstore, which was fortunately only a few minutes away. She slid on a pair of sandals and covered

Daisy in a blanket before scrawling a note and leaving it on the coffee table: *Be back soon, running to the drugstore.* She managed to be so quiet, even Gus didn't stir from his dream state.

Less than ten minutes later, Whitney stood in the toothpaste aisle, lost in a sea of red and blue boxes, her attention anywhere but the matter at hand. The longer she stared at the boxes, the more her thoughts roamed. *Had she left enough toothpaste at home for Winnie? Was Xena behaving with Mrs. Rodgers? Most importantly... did she care?*

As she dropped a tube of toothpaste into her basket, she idly wondered what type of toothpaste Trevor liked. It was silly, really, to ponder something as trivial as the brands he used, but she was curious.

Baxter had always made a deal about what she bought, mostly because it was never what he used. She gravitated toward the generic over brand names, while Baxter would gladly spend double digits on something that worked half as well as the cheap stuff. He was all about labels, regardless of what the product was for.

She had just picked up a package of dental floss, lost in thoughts of her past and present, when the sound of footfalls echoed behind her. She scooted closer to the display; it was getting late, and she assumed most shoppers were like her—desperate to get in and out with what they needed.

Yet her attempts at hiding were fruitless as Trevor stepped up to her side, startling her right out of her wits.

"Whitney? Fancy seeing you here," he mused, joining her at the display case.

The dental floss tumbled to the floor, along with Whitney's tongue. Trevor was always attractive, but since changing out of his uniform after dinner, he was a dish best served hot. His shorts hung low at his waist, and he wore a Pinegrove FD T-shirt that did very little to hide his assets. His biceps bunched and flexed as he retrieved the fallen floss, but dental hygiene was the furthest thing from

Whitney's mind.

Well, that wasn't true. Right now she desperately wanted to test the staying power of her toothpaste, but she shook herself back to the moment. Ogling him in public like this didn't feel right, yet it took Herculean strength to wrench her gaze from his arms to his face. Although it was hardly a bad view.

His dark red hair was damp, and judging from the smell of soap, he'd come from the shower. Whitney allowed herself a moment to picture Trevor all lathered up, until she became too lathered up. Cheeks burning with embarrassment, she coughed and fumbled with her basket.

Whitney pushed through her lustful thoughts and attempted an intelligent conversation ... or at least a *hello*. Fate had thrown them together in the toothpaste aisle, and she wanted to enjoy the moment, no matter how long it lasted.

"Trevor! You scared the living daylights out of me. I wasn't expecting to see anyone."

His hand reached out, gently grazing her shoulder. The quick pass of his touch sent a bolt of awareness from her neck to her belly. "Sorry, I didn't mean to frighten you."

"No harm done." Her voice cracked on the last word. Any attempts at keeping her cool in front of Trevor officially up in smoke. "Goodness, I'm a mess. Your momma and I were enjoying a glass of wine with *Dateline* when I noticed I'm out of a few things." She held up her handbasket, shaking the contents.

Trevor raised his hand. "Same. After all that pie and ice cream"—he chuckled, winking at her—"I went out for a run and, well ..." His words faltered, but his smile stayed fixed in place. "You look great," he blurted. "I mean, don't say you're a mess."

They both chuckled nervously, although she wasn't sure why. This was hardly their first time alone together, but she craved more. An idea sparked, but she hesitated. It was already late, and she knew he had to work early in the morning. More importantly, *she* had to work in the morning.

Whitney adjusted her shopping basket, deciding to go for broke. "Fancy a drink?" she asked just as Trevor said, "You wouldn't be up for a drink at The Pecan Pit?"

They both burst out laughing, the sound reverberating around them. Trevor's answering smile caused the dimple in his chin to pop, and Whitney damn near swooned. She'd give anything for one of Scarlett O'Hara's fans and a fainting couch.

"Give me a second, and I'll meet you at the register?" He was already sidestepping to grab a bottle of Scope.

"Sure," she chirped. On her way to the checkout lane, she hastily grabbed a tube of lipstick. It was the least she could do to gussy herself up, especially since she was in leggings and her old *NYSNC T-shirt. But Trevor told her she looked great, and she was going to believe him.

Once they paid for their items, the pair walked out into the summer night. A block up, she saw the flickering lights of The Pecan Pit's parking lot. And to think, only last week, she'd stopped and started this fateful journey.

Trevor held her hand as she stepped onto the gravel lot. It could be his Southern manners, but Whitney relished these brief interactions. A man hadn't held her hand like this since before Baxter, and that was a sad fact. Whitney understood she deserved affection, and she was tired of pretending she didn't.

They left their purchases in their cars and walked toward the hubbub of The Pecan Pit. Dipping low so he could whisper in her ear, Trevor said, "It's wing night, so it might be rowdy."

"Wing night?" Whitney raised an eyebrow.

Trevor snickered. "Here's the thing. Buster hates wings. He claims they're more mess than they're worth. So he took them off the menu last year out of protest, until half of Pinegrove rallied to get them back on the menu. His concession was they were only available one night a week." He kicked the door open with his foot, reaching out to keep it open for Whitney to pass.

"Geez Louise!" She exclaimed as they entered the packed bar. Nearly every table was full, the music from the jukebox rattling through the hot sauce-scented air.

Trevor drew her closer, maneuvering them toward the bar. "Let's snag those two seats on the corner." It wasn't lost on Whitney that was where she'd sat during her first visit. They settled onto their stools, Trevor's arm protectively draped over the back of her seat. He waved down Buster on his way to the kitchen, holding up three fingers. "One order of wings and two sweet teas."

Buster leaned on the bar, his eyes tired but his smile genuine. "I curse the day I created wing day." He stuck his hands in the air, waggling the chubby digits. "These bad boys are going to smell like hot sauce for the rest of my natural-born life."

"You know," Trevor started, "there is this wild invention out there called … gloves!"

The other man barked out a laugh. "I see how it's going to be."

Trevor fist-bumped Buster, chuckling under his breath. "Calm down, man. You still managed to outlaw karaoke."

"Shhh!!!" Buster waved his arms in the air to stop Trevor. "Are you insane, Trev? Don't even mention the 'K' word in this bar." Turning his attention to Whitney, he said, "It's a pleasure to see you back here. I've heard nothing but great things from my auntie."

Whitney flushed. "Oh, um. Thanks?" She nervously toyed with her curls, fluffing them and adding more volume. It was a nervous habit she'd picked up over the years, and some days Whitney feared her hair would consume the entire eastern seaboard.

"Kim is Buster's aunt. Word traveled fast that you're going to be helping her at the shop." Trevor's breath tickled her ear lobe, and Whitney shivered. She made a mental note to have him do that again when they were in private. *Lordy, look at her making plans!*

"Wow! News really does travel fast in Pinegrove." She rested her hand over her heart, which pounded louder than a timpani.

Buster winked and disappeared a moment before returning with two large mugs of sweet tea and a stack of napkins. "Julia will be right back with those damned wings." He muttered something under his breath and disappeared into the kitchen.

This was new. Working the life of a temporary worker meant she rarely made attachments, let alone announcements about where she'd be working. In the blink of an eye, Whitney had managed to reinvent herself as someone with a job, with connections. Neither of those things waited for her back in Savannah, but she shoved that thought down.

Sipping from her sweet tea, she peered at Trevor from underneath her lashes. He rested his forearms on the bar, peeling the paper off his straw. When he caught her staring, he flashed her a smile that made her knees weak. Thankfully, she was rooted to her stool.

Whitney gave herself the time to really absorb the moment, to sit there and picture a future in Pinegrove. Granted, she had no idea where this chemistry with Trevor would lead, but she was eager to find out. She was also excited about work for the first time, ever!

By the time a basket of wings arrived, Whitney made herself a promise. She was going to keep seeing Trevor; she was going to keep stepping out of her comfort zone. She was done being afraid. It was time to live.

*

Julia sashayed out of the back with a tray full of wings and a seductive look in her eye. Trevor liked her fine, as a neighbor, but he grew tired of her flirtatious banter, especially when a lady was present.

Instinctively, he scooted his seat closer to Whitney. He

adjusted his position so he was in profile, all his attention focused on the beauty beside him. Unable to stop himself, he reached out and gently tugged on a curl at Whitney's neck. "I'm really glad we both needed toothpaste," he whispered.

Whitney smirked, moving their drinks out of the way as Julia slid their wings over. "Here y'all go," she said, jutting her hip out and leaning a little too close to Trevor. "Haven't seen you here in a minute, Trev."

Whitney tensed beside him, and he couldn't stand her discomfort. "Julia, good evening. I've been busy, but I thought I'd take my girl out tonight."

"Oh," was all Julia could muster before she shrugged and trudged off to the other side of the bar.

Whitney grabbed some napkins, pressing a few into Trevor's hand before snaking a wing for herself. "Friend of yours?" she asked, dunking a wing in a cup of blue cheese before delicately taking a bite.

He sat there like a damn slack-jawed fool watching her expertly eat the wing without smearing her lipstick. It was simultaneously seductive and impressive. He couldn't decide if he should kiss her or take notes.

Trevor cleared his throat, took a slug of his tea, and confessed, "Julia's good people, but she's always sniffing around for dates." He held up a hand to stop Whitney's protests. "Which I'm not in the market for, but she never seems to mind trying."

That answer seemed to please Whitney, who smirked and selected her second wing. "I see. And if you don't mind me asking, how many *girls* do you bring to the Pecan Pit?"

Trevor took a wing and held it aloft, wanting to put Whitney at ease before delving unceremoniously into his own snack. "I hope that comment didn't bother you. I didn't mean to go all caveman and stake my claim."

Whitney raised an eyebrow. "Did you hear me complaining? I'm merely asking for clarification."

"I like you," he said, shocking himself with his bluntness.

His time with Virginia had been all about games, toying with emotions when it was best just to be honest. He didn't want that with Whitney, so he repeated, "I like you, Whitney."

Whitney recovered. "I like you, too."

"Good, I'm glad that's settled." Trevor chuckled, snagging the cup of ranch and making a royal mess.

Whitney handed him another napkin as a blob of sauce slid down his chin, getting stuck in his dimple. "Let me," she offered, swiping her thumb over the spot and then licking it clean. Trevor needed to adjust himself before he could catch her eye again. *Was it getting hot in here?*

While Trevor spiraled into a lust-induced haze, Whitney rocked on her stool to the sounds of the jukebox. Somewhere over the course of their hot sauce-induced flirting, someone had swapped from country music to boy band pop.

"Oh my Lord!" Whitney gasped when a familiar song came on.

"I take it this is a favorite?" he teased, loving how animated Whitney grew the longer the song played.

She dabbed at her fingers with the last clean napkin before balling it up and tossing it at his forehead. It bounced off and landed at his feet. "Excuse me, Trevor Mays. I will not have you mocking *NSYNC or 'Bye, Bye, Bye'. This is arguably the best pop song of all time."

"I'll take your word on that, darlin'." He nudged her with his elbow, and she leaned into him.

"Stick with me. I'll bore you to tears with my useless music knowledge."

"So you're more than a country girl?" he asked, offering her the last wing, which she politely declined with a shake of her head.

Whitney drained the last of her tea, sliding the glass forward for a refill. Buster came over with a pitcher and topped both their glasses. "I hope everything's good, even those damn wings."

Trevor chuckled. "Buster, I don't know if anyone told

you, but this is *your* bar. If you hate these things, get rid of them."

Buster gestured around the crowded space. "And miss my biggest day of the week? Are you crazy?" He rolled his neck and stomped back behind the swinging doors.

"Now that we've harassed poor Buster, let's get back to music." He pointed to Whitney's T-shirt, which fit her curves like a second skin. He was well aware of *NSYNC and their songs, Jessie had gone through a belated boy band phase, but he wanted to hear every detail from Whitney's perspective.

"Well …" Whitney let out an exhale. "I became obsessed with these guys"—she gestured at her shirt—"when Winnie was in third grade, and I was barely in kindergarten. Our daddy got her concert tickets with her friends and Mom, but I was too young to go. While they were at the concert, he took me out for ice cream and played his old CDs in the car. We listened to everyone from Johnny Cash and Hank Williams to Bonnie Raitt and Reba."

Trevor watched Whitney's face as she described the memory in detail, her cheeks plumping as she smiled, her dark hair framing her lovely face. A few freckles on her nose bunched as she spoke, and Trevor committed every constellation to memory.

"That day sort of started our tradition of listening to music together. When Mom and Winnie were busy, Daddy and I listened to music and picked our favorite songs. Last year for Christmas, we made each other playlists." She sighed contentedly. "I miss my parents, and I don't get down to Florida enough. Yet when I listen to those songs, it feels like home."

She turned to face him, and everything around them went silent. Trevor had countless memories with his daddy that still brought a lump to his throat, but sitting with Whitney and simply talking made those memories seem less painful—made them feel like the treasures they were.

"You ever share music with your daddy? What are your

favorite memories?" She reached out and covered his hand with hers. "What keeps him alive in your heart?"

Her question nearly knocked Trevor off his stool, but he rallied quickly. "Good gracious, darlin'. You're coming in hot with the questions."

"I didn't mean to ..." She started to pull back, but he placed his other hand on top.

"You're perfect. In fact, it's nice to talk about parents and childhood without feeling so dang melancholy." He huffed and straightened his shoulders. "Daddy and I were obviously obsessed with anything related to the firehouse. From drills and best practices to frivolous stuff like the charity fundraisers, we were always talking shop since I was old enough to ride the Ferris wheel at the fireworks extravaganza. But we also loved to go hunting and craw dadding, anything that got us in nature." Whitney nodded along, not interrupting as he fell down memory lane. "Momma and Jessie aren't very outdoorsy, so that was our time. We'd get outside and be, you know?" That was only one of the things he missed the most, having someone in his life who he could just be Trevor with.

That loneliness melted away the longer he spent time with Whitney. He wasn't worried about his career, the loss of his father, or even his broken engagement. He was a man, out with a woman, having a perfectly lovely evening.

Behind them, a pair of women stood on their chairs and started singing a Beyoncé song. The other diners began to clap and cheer, which brought Buster out of the back with a murderous expression.

"That's a wrap, folks! Pay your server and get the hell home." Before anyone could argue, he marched over to the jukebox and yanked the cord from the wall. The music died and the bar quieted where only the sound of popping bubbles in beer glasses could be heard.

Their trance broken, Whitney glanced at her watch and gulped. "Good Lord! It's after ten."

Trevor helped Whitney to her feet and tossed a handful

of bills on the bar top. "Let's get you home," he said over his shoulder.

They followed the masses outside and strode down the street to the drug store parking lot.

"Thanks for tonight. It was really nice." Whitney opened her arms awkwardly, as if going in for a hug. She stumbled back on a cluster of gravel.

"It was," he agreed, taking the opportunity to steady her on her feet. Just as he was about to second-guess himself, he looped his arms around her waist.

She immediately melted into his embrace, and he could have floated away on a cloud of bliss. Trevor's grip was firm, yet gentle enough she could pull away. Fortunately, she didn't, not for a long while. He savored the dips and swells of her curves, resting his chin on top of her head. She smelled like lilacs, and he wanted to stay in this floral-scented haze forever.

"You're gonna do great tomorrow," Trevor promised, spooling a curl through his fingers. He had no idea how he'd gotten so bold. Bumping into her had been the highlight of his day, the perfect distraction from everything happening in his life. She brought out happy memories that had felt painful for too long, and there was no way to thank her.

Whitney let out a shuddering breath before pulling back, her face tipped up to meet his gaze. "Thank you," she said on a sigh. "This definitely helped my jitters. Sleep tight, Trevor." With a final nod, she walked away.

He watched the sway of her hips as she strode to her car.

Their impromptu meeting had done more for his spirits than any run, beer, or night out with the guys. Whitney put him at ease like no one before, and he craved more.

Trevor needed to see Whitney again, for a proper date. No more chance meetings at the drug store, no more stealing glances over slices of pie at his momma's house, no more rushed drinks in a noisy bar.

No, sir, Whitney Kerr deserved a real date. Now Trevor needed to man up and ask.

CHAPTER ELEVEN

"Are you sure I don't need to do some HR paperwork or something?" Whitney asked, tucking her purse under the counter. She'd worn the only other dress she'd packed, a blue shift that flattered her pale skin tone and ample hips. She wasn't sure how she'd managed, but she wanted to find a few more pieces to wear through the Fourth of July celebrations. Shopping outside her new employer's store seemed wrong, but Whitney didn't see anything that would fit her—physically or age wise.

Kim snorted, adjusting her glasses. "Honey, we'll handle all that later. I'm more worried about keeping people moving through the store."

Whitney nodded, checking the time on her watch. "What time do you open?"

"*We*," Kim corrected, "open at ten. I thought I'd walk you through the opening procedures so you're all set for tomorrow. I have a key for you and everything."

Used to having probationary periods at her other jobs, Whitney was incredulous. "You're giving me a key to your shop after day one? Don't you want to vet me or something?"

"Enough with the concerns, honey. Daisy has vetted you

from here to Atlanta and back. Plus, as you're about to discover, there isn't much to steal around here." She rested her hands on her hips and sighed. "Business isn't bad, but sure as shoot ain't good. I need a fresh eye to help me shift things around, you know?"

Whitney saluted, feeling her pulse slow. Kim and Daisy trusted her to do a good job, and that's exactly what she planned to do. "You got it. I'm ready to learn."

An hour later, the store was open, Whitney had notes on how to use the register, and a few women browsed through a display of blouses. The women were closer in age to Whitney than Kim, and they ended up leaving the store empty-handed.

Kim emerged from the back with a fresh pitcher of lemonade. "See, that right there is what I'm talking about. Neither of those ladies bought a thing, and they clearly had the money." She set up the lemonade station by the door and huffed. "I don't get it."

Whitney took the proffered glass and sipped, thinking to herself for a moment. "Can you show me your ordering site? Where you get your inventory?"

Kim didn't hesitate. "Sure, follow me." The pair walked back to the counter, their footfalls echoing in the empty store. Kim clicked away on the ancient laptop, pulling up a site Whitney had used before at other jobs in Savannah.

"May I?" Whitney asked, gesturing to the mouse.

"Honey, as long as you don't look up naked people on that thing, you can do whatever you'd like." Lowering her voice, she suggested, "But if you find any naked pictures of Daniel Craig, I wouldn't mind a look." She giggled and went to work tidying up the fitting rooms.

Whitney leaned against the counter and scrolled through countless pages of dresses and accessories. The vendor promised overnight delivery on rush orders, and the return policy seemed standard. In between customers, she made a cart of merchandise for both younger clients and those with a little more meat on their bones.

"Lunchtime," Kim announced. "I usually shut the shop down for thirty minutes at noon. Care to pop across the street for some barbecue? I'm as hungry as sin."

Whitney covered her stomach, which rumbled to life at the mention of barbecue. "Yes, please."

Kim flipped the *Closed* sign and held the door for Whitney. "C'mon, honey, no time like the present."

The older woman ushered Whitney across the street to a food truck that was double parked in front of the library. The heavenly smells of molasses, pork, and mustard tickled her nose as she joined the growing line. A few locals she recognized from her day on the town with Daisy waved, and she beamed at their friendliness.

"I'm a fan of the pork platter, because I don't have to pick a side." Kim chuckled, gesturing to the menu.

"You don't get a side?" Whitney frowned, eager to eat whatever smelled so dang good.

"Honey, no. You get all the sides with the platter. Cornbread, greens, and baked beans."

Whitney pretended to wipe drool from her chin, although it wasn't far from the truth. "Um, that sounds delightful. I'll join you."

Kim marched up to the front of the line and ordered their lunches, shaking off Whitney's insistence on paying. "You're my guest today, honey."

"I'm your employee," Whitney countered. "You should let me pay."

"You can pay tomorrow," Kim insisted, but Whitney wasn't sure she trusted her.

After their meals were ready, they found a picnic table in the shade beside the library. A few other diners had perched nearby, and the general atmosphere was jovial, if not pork-scented.

"This is delicious," Whitney moaned as she took a bite of the pork. The tender meat was smoky and savory with a sweet kick from the BBQ sauce.

"You can't go wrong with Jefferson's. They know

barbecue in Pinegrove."

Whitney wiped her hands with a wad of napkins and nodded. "No argument here."

Lost in the sounds of chatter and her own chewing, Whitney didn't notice a familiar face milling through the maze of picnic tables. "I thought I'd find you ladies out here." Daisy leaned down to squeeze both women on the shoulder before sliding her own tray onto the table.

"Have to show the new girl the culinary ropes of Pinegrove," Kim said, draining the last of her Coke.

"Consider me schooled," Whitney replied, trailing her cornbread through a puddle of sauce.

"How's the first day going?" Daisy asked, stabbing a slab of brisket with a plastic fork.

"Good," Kim and Whitney said in unison.

Kim hitched a thumb at her employee. "She's a quick learner."

Whitney shrugged. "You're a good trainer."

Daisy swiped a splotch of sauce from her cheek and beamed. "I knew you coming to town was the answer to a lot of prayers, Whitney."

Whitney was flustered, nearly dropping her fork. "Oh, I don't know about that."

Kim nodded. "I do. I was telling my nephew the other day, Buster, how stuck I was feeling at Kim's Creations." She took a bite of her lunch and spoke with her mouthful. "Then Daisy brings you into my life, and poof." Her hands flexed like fireworks. "I saw you looking at the vendor site. You have an idea or two, don't you?"

Daisy leaned closer, as if Whitney was about to share state secrets. "Oh, I don't know." Whitney cleared her throat, afraid she'd overstep and ruin the harmony of the moment. It was Kim's shop, and she had no right to come in and make sweeping suggestions—especially on day one. Although Kim's enthusiasm was infectious.

"Spill it, honey. I'm not paying you to waste time," Kim said, her mouth tipped up in a smirk, BBQ sauce covering her lipstick.

Daisy chuckled. "Kim's a real hard ass. She'll fire you if you don't start talking."

"Well"—Whitney exhaled, hoping she wasn't about to offend these sweet women—"I was looking at the inventory."

"And you realized it's clothes for old bitties?" Kim asked while Daisy choked on her greens.

"Excuse me, ma'am. I happen to frequent your shop weekly, and I'm not an old bitty."

Whitney relaxed at the ease between these two friends. They reminded her of Winnie and her, and she missed her sister a little more in that moment. Although their reaction bolstered her to soldier on with her plan.

"Well, sort of? I think you want to keep the key items your regulars like, such as jewelry and some of the summer outfits. But what about bringing in some new things for a slightly younger crowd? You don't want to spread yourself too thin and try to please teenagers, but what about something for young professionals who are visiting during the festival?"

Daisy leaned back and grinned; Kim leaned forward and blinked. "Keep going," she urged.

"Bring in some sun dresses and sandals, something a woman could wear to the fireworks or out to dance at the barn. Offer something special they won't find in the city, but keep the price right that they don't feel guilty splurging. Lastly, I would expand your size offerings beyond a 12. Shoppers come in all shapes these days, and you don't want anyone feeling left out."

"Genius," Daisy said, slowly clapping like she was at a golf tournament.

"You have some options pulled up?" Kim's eyebrow was raised, her interest piqued.

Whitney's cheeks flushed. "I, um, started a cart. With priority shipping, we can have new inventory here in less than forty-eight hours."

Kim tossed her napkin onto her tray and stood. "Let's roll, honey. It's time to get back to work."

The three of them collected their trash and crossed the street to the boutique.

Daisy hovered at the doorway. "I think I'll leave you two to it. Whitney, enjoy the rest of your first day."

"Thanks, Daisy. Will I see you for dinner?" Whitney liked the notion of coming home to someone, especially Daisy. Yes, she wanted to see Trevor again, but she didn't want to get too far ahead of herself. Every interaction they shared was like eating a potato chip; it was getting harder to stop with just one.

Daisy winked. "Don't you worry about dinner, sugar. Bye!"

And with that, Daisy was gone, and Kim and Whitney ordered thousands of dollars of merchandise. Lost in the task at hand, Whitney didn't have time to ponder Daisy's parting words.

*

"Wanna grab some beers and nachos? It's trivia night at The Pecan Pit, and that always brings out the smart girls," Javi suggested, waggling his eyebrows.

Trevor rolled his eyes and tossed a balled-up paper at his head. "If they're smart girls, they'll stay the hell away from you, Javi."

Javi splayed a hand over his chest and threw his head back in horror. "Ouch, man. You wound me."

Trevor logged out of his computer, pushed in his chair, and was careful to use the other exit to avoid Hastings. "Have fun hitting on the brainiacs of Pinegrove, but I'm heading out."

Javi jogged to catch up to Trevor in the parking lot. "Do your plans this evening have anything to do with a certain brunette whose name rhymes with Britney?"

Unlocking his car, Trevor threw his messenger bag on

the back seat and sighed. "I cannot confirm nor deny."

"You gotta give me something, man. She's been staying with Daisy for a week now. I'm not the sharpest crayon in the box, but I know you two are into each other." Spreading his arms wide, he added, "Half of Pinegrove knows it."

Trevor's neck heated with embarrassment, but not for himself. He didn't want Whitney to feel like a spectacle. He wanted her to belong here, feel like she could put down roots ... feel like she could put down roots with *him*. Last night at The Pecan Pit felt like the start of something.

"I'm going to drive the long way home past Kim's shop, and if she's free for dinner, I thought I'd take her out."

Javi whooped and clapped like he'd bought a winning lotto ticket. "Hell yes! It's about damn time."

Trevor scrunched up his nose. "I think a week is really fast for me. It took me nearly a year to make a move on Virginia."

"And we both know how well that turned out," Javi said with a sigh. "Have fun tonight. Don't overthink this."

"Sure, easy," Trevor deadpanned, earning a playful gut punch from Javi.

"You two obviously get along, so go with the flow and remember to take her back to your place for funny business. Ms. Daisy seems cool, but bringing a girl back to Mom's place really kills the mood."

Now it was Trevor's turn to not-so-playfully punch Javi in the ribs. "I'm sorry." He huffed. "I don't think we've been introduced. I'm Trevor and *you're* Javier. I haven't slept with a girl on the first date since that one time at the academy."

Javi rubbed his side and groaned. "Okay, that was a little much, man. Have fun." He shuffled back to his car, opened the door, and promptly flipped off Trevor.

Trevor laughed the whole way to Main Street, despite his sweaty palms and racing heart. He was going to do this, properly ask out Whitney. After everything that happened with Virginia, he was tired of playing games with women.

And judging from what Whitney told him on their walk with Gus, she was as well. So, he'd be a grown-ass man and march up and ask her to dinner.

Luckily, he arrived right as the shops on Main Street were closing. He snagged a parking spot as he saw Kim approach the front door to flip the *Closed* sign. He waved and pointed to the door, mouthing *Can I?* She nodded and held it open for him.

"Good evening, Mr. Mays. How's the station treating you?" She rested a hand on his arm as he strode inside.

"Cannot complain, Miss Kim. How are you doing?"

Kim patted his arm and lowered her voice. "A whole lick better since Whitney joined me. I didn't comprehend how much I wasn't getting done until today. Are you taking our girl out for supper tonight?"

Trevor held up his hand, where all his fingers were crossed. "That's the plan, ma'am."

Kim laughed, the sound alerting Whitney they were not alone.

"Oh, hi." Whitney emerged from one of the fitting rooms with an armful of clothes. Her hair was different today, spun up into some type of knotted braid, allowing her rosy cheeks to pop more than usual. She was in a blue floral dress that hugged her delicious curves and hung to her knees. Despite it being June, her porcelain skin was barely touched by the sun.

Trevor's heart lurched up his throat. Suddenly he wasn't feeling very brave about asking her out properly. "Erm, hello." He uncrossed his fingers and waved gracelessly as she joined them at the counter.

Kim scurried over and took the bundle and shooed Whitney away. "You've done more than enough today. Why don't you kids go out and have fun?"

Whitney looked to Trevor. "Are we going out?" Her tone was playful, and his shoulders drooped a little.

"Yes, darlin'. That is, if you're free."

Whitney opened her mouth to reply, but Kim was too

fast. "She's free."

Turning to face the older woman, Whitney laughed. "I am? Weren't you going to show me how to lock up and get the money ready for tomorrow?"

Kim tapped her chin a moment, as if in deep concentration. "I don't recall saying that, but then again, I'm nearly a hundred years old." She stuck out her tongue and ushered the pair out onto the sidewalk. "See you tomorrow for opening at ten. Good night, kids." And with that, she pulled the door shut, flipped the deadbolt, and turned off the lights.

Trevor took Whitney's hand, slowly rubbing his thumb over her knuckles. The motion made her shiver, and he understood the feeling. "Have dinner with me? We can celebrate your first day, and I can enjoy a meal in town without Javi trying to pick someone up or Buster lamenting his own menu."

"You mean, Javi's done flirting with me?" she teased, turning her palm so she held his hand.

"Ha! A man can only hope. Have I mentioned recently how much I appreciate you turning him down?"

"No, but we have all night." She flashed him a grin, and Trevor stumbled on weak knees to his car. He liked the notion of having all night with Whitney, regardless of where they were going or what they'd do. Just being with her lightened him, made him feel like he was more than a failed fireman still grieving his father.

Holding the door open, Whitney slid into the passenger's seat. Her skirt rode up slightly, showing a splattering of freckles on her knees. Trevor caught himself staring when she looked up with confusion. "Is everything okay?"

"Huh?" Trevor ripped his gaze back up to her lovely face and shook his head. "Oh, yeah." He laughed at himself and closed the door. Jogging around the front, he was pleased she was still smiling when he got behind the wheel.

"Where are we headed?" Whitney asked, tucking a loose

lock of hair behind her ear. She'd shifted in her seat so she faced him, and Trevor wanted to pull her over the console and kiss her senseless.

Instead, he cleared his throat, and asked, "You like low country boils?"

Whitney snorted, a very unladylike sound that endeared her to him even more. "I'm sorry, but I'm from Georgia. I'm offended you had to ask." She pivoted and buckled her seatbelt. "Let's role, Lieutenant."

Trevor had a goofy, wistful expression on his face for the entire drive to Cajun Carl's. The place opened nearly fifty years ago by Carl's father after moving from Louisiana. The food was delicious, the price was right, and the ambiance was perfect for this evening.

Pulling his car into the lot, he parked under a cluster of trees with fairy lights in the branches. That would look even better on their way out, and Trevor was thinking ahead. "Let me get your door," he said before getting out of the car and nearly hurdling over the hood ala *The Dukes of Hazzard*.

Whitney held out her hand as he helped her to her feet. She didn't let go when they started walking, and Trevor could not have been more relieved. After months of wondering if he'd even date again, he was out with the woman of his dreams. Now he needed not to muck it up.

CHAPTER TWELVE

As soon as Whitney stepped out into the warm June air, her nose was greeted to the smells of garlic, creole seasoning, and seafood. Her mouth watered as Trevor led the way to a hole-in-the-wall restaurant guaranteed to be heavenly. Fishing nets and twinkle lights hung over the entrance to Cajun Carl's.

"You all right getting a small boil to share?" Trevor asked when they reached the counter. An old sandwich board menu swung overhead, but there were only a few things listed ...

Low Country Boil, small or embarrassingly large

Coke or Sweet Tea

"Yes, with a Coke, please." She pulled her wallet out. This may be a date, but she wasn't a charity case.

Trevor rested his hand over her wallet. "I asked you out, darlin'. It's on me." She opened her mouth to protest, but he shook his head. "Whitney, you're killing my manhood in front of Cajun Carl himself." He teased as a man who was nearly as wide as he was tall, clad in denim overalls closed the distance.

"Trevor, it's good to see you, son." The older man shuffled to the register and slid two glass bottles of Coke across the counter. "And who do we have here?" He held out a meaty hand for Whitney to shake.

Trevor rested his hand on the small of Whitney's back, damn near singeing the fabric with his touch. "This, here, is Whitney Kerr from Savannah. She's staying with Momma for a little while and helping out Miss Kim at the shop."

Carl's grin grew exponentially. "Well, any friend of Daisy and Trevor's is a friend of mine." He pumped her hand twice before letting go. "Y'all have a seat on the patio, and we'll bring this right out."

"Thank you. It's nice meeting you." Whitney continued to be charmed by Pinegrove and its quirky cast of characters. Trevor led the way to a corner table on the patio with a view of a small creek. The sun wasn't quite done with the day, and she needed her sunglasses.

"I hope this is okay. Carl is a family friend, and the food is amazing. Truthfully, I haven't been out here as much as I'd like these last few years."

Whitney took a handful of napkins from the dispenser and handed a stack to Trevor. "How come? If you don't mind me asking."

Trevor tucked a few napkins into his collar and shrugged. "Honestly? Virginia hates food you have to work for." He waggled his fingers in demonstration. "We came once—she complained there weren't any salads. She whined that her manicure was ruined and she smelled like Old Bay. Then I lost patience and stopped coming."

Striving to hide her dislike for Virginia, Whitney plastered on a smile. "Well, you're in luck. Not only do I detest salads, unless they're made with pasta or potatoes, but I love a good boil, and I plan on eating my share." She shook her hands in front of her and giggled. "And I haven't had a professional manicure since high school prom."

"Good, I like a woman with an appetite." Trevor's statement was banal enough, but Whitney bristled. Her weight had always been a sore spot, and she didn't want Trevor to think the way to her heart was food. Technically, it was, but she didn't want him to see her as another chubby girl.

Her answering tightlipped smile knocked Trevor back in his seat. "Whitney, please don't misunderstand what I mean. You're gorgeous, and I'm simply happy to share a moment with you. I don't care if you eat one potato or the whole damned boil, just be you."

"Just be me?" She was incredulous. No man was this nice, not even those raised by her new favorite person, Daisy Mays. "If only it were that simple," she mused, staring off into the setting sun. Sunglasses no longer needed, she shoved them up her head and sighed. "I'm sorry, I don't mean to project my body issues onto you."

Trevor rubbed the back of his neck. "Look, I won't pretend to understand what it's like being a woman in today's society." Clearing his throat, he pressed, "And I sure as shoot will not mansplain body image to you, rest assured. But I have a mom and sister, and I've seen my share of magazines and influencers spouting nonsense. I want you to have fun with me, whether you eat a lot or a little. I'm not judging, okay?"

Whitney didn't want to bring up the past today, on their first official date, but it seemed unavoidable now that she opened Pandora's Box. Taking a deep breath, she said, "Here's the thing. We're both coming into whatever this is with baggage, right?" Trevor nodded, but didn't interrupt. "Baxter wasn't always kind about my weight, to put it mildly. He'd take me to new fitness centers in town, hired a chef to make only these teeny tiny meals, and even bought me clothes two sizes too small for 'something to work for,'" she said the last line with air quotes.

The vein in Trevor's temple popped the more she described her ex. "I don't mean to stop your story, but if I ever meet Baxter, I will beat him to a pulp for making you feel that way. What a complete asshole."

Whitney flushed at his words and offered a sad smile. "Hopefully neither one of us will have to see him again, but thank you for the offer."

Trevor sipped from his Coke. "I'm sensing there's something else bothering you, but I don't want to pry."

Toying with the hem of her dress, Whitney's eyes stayed locked on the fabric while she shared her final insecurity. "I've met Virginia."

Trevor swallowed. "Did she say something unkind?" He leaned forward, fists flexing on the tabletop, ready for a fight.

"No, nothing like that. But I've *seen* her, Trevor. She's lovely, a size 2, with glossy hair and perky breasts. If you loved her, then I wonder why you like me. I'm an hourglass shape with an extra forty-five minutes of sand."

Trevor stood, walking around the table until he was at her side. Lowering to his knees, he pinched her chin until they were finally locking eyes. "I'm only going to say this once, and then we're going to forget about Virginia and Baxter for this evening." Whitney's eyes shone, sensing this was going to be a moment. "Virginia might look fit for the cover of a magazine, but she's not a lovely person. She cares about money more than people, and she treated me poorly and broke my trust. I know we're only on our first official date, but, Whitney, trust me when I say you're special. You've shown more kindness and compassion in the last week with the people I care about than Virginia did for nearly two years of dating. And in case you couldn't tell from my ogling your chest, but your breasts are amazing, and that needs to be on public record. I happen to like your extra forty-five minutes."

Whitney coughed and covered her face from embarrassment. "Trevor," she admonished.

"Now, I know that's a lot. I can sit here and flatter you all evening, but if you want to head out and try this again another time, that's fine. I didn't want to upset you."

"You didn't upset me," Whitney said, her voice barely a whisper.

Trevor's lips quirked up. He pulled a napkin from his

collar and dabbed at her cheeks. "I'm sorry people can be cruel, especially the ones that should love us the most, but I promise I will never do anything to make you uncomfortable." Shaking his head, he amended, "Well knowing me, I'll muck up that promise. Tell you what, when I inevitably say something stupid, tell me. Breaking your heart will not sit right with me, darlin'."

Taking the damp napkins from Trevor's hand, she placed them on the table before cupping his handsome face in her hands. She didn't know how he did it, but he'd managed to put her at ease and make her feel seen in a matter of days. No man before Trevor Mays made her feel this worthy of love, worthy of attention.

"I'm about to break one of my rules," she said.

Trevor raised an eyebrow. "Oh yeah?"

"I'm going to kiss you before the end of the night."

Trevor met her in the middle, lips warm and inviting. She kept hold of his face as she melted into the kiss. He steadied her with his hands on her hips, fingers softly digging into her skin. Normally, the feel of someone touching her abundant hips brought her discomfort, but she trusted this man. She trusted her body with Trevor, and that thought pushed her forward into the unknown.

Their kiss was sweet, two souls testing the waters with someone new, but Whitney needed more. She angled her head so he deepened the kiss, and she moaned as his tongue slipped between her lips. He tasted like cinnamon gum and sin.

The sounds of a young family entering the patio jolted them back to the moment. "Mommy, can I sit on the blue chair?" A young boy asked, unknowingly popping their lust balloon.

Trevor pulled himself back to standing, running a hand down his face. "To be continued," he warned as he leaned down and pecked her cheek. "As soon as we're remotely alone." His promise made her shiver, and Whitney thought she could die in this moment without regrets.

Carl approached with a bucket that smelled like Southern summers. "Here we are, folks," he announced as he tipped the bucket onto the tabletop. "Eat hearty." He nodded and left to take more orders.

Trevor picked up a plump shrimp, and Whitney picked up a chunk of andouille sausage. They smooshed them together and laughed. "Cheers," Trevor said before ripping the shell off and eating the shrimp whole. Whitney plopped the sausage in her mouth and hummed in delight, ignoring the trail of juice that dribbled down her chin.

"I can see why you like to take dates here," she mused, wiping her fingers after a particularly unruly piece of corn. "It's very glamorous." She framed her face to highlight her smeared makeup and buttery lip gloss. Unlike with the wings, she wore her dinner with pride.

Trevor's smile fell as he swallowed. "I've never seen anything lovelier." He reached out, swiping a spot of seasoning from the corner of her lips. Without breaking eye contact, he brought his thumb to his mouth and sucked it clean.

And it was officially a million degrees outside. Whitney's cheeks flamed as a bead of sweat rolled down her neck. That was the single most erotic thing a man had done, and Trevor made it seem like no big deal. *Yeah, she needed to kiss him again.*

"Oh," was all she mustered as he peeled another shrimp and popped it in his mouth.

"Oh indeed." He smirked, taking a sip from his Coke. She watched his throat in fascination while he drank, her own mouth suddenly parched. Despite the mess of food they were eating, the cleft in his chin remained free of debris. She wanted to dive in head first and live there for a year or two.

They ate in companionable silence, occasionally commenting on the food and the weather. As far as dates went, it was already the best she'd ever experienced. Even if Trevor wasn't a complete sweetheart, the food was tremendous and the mood was light. She trusted him, and she knew that was scary, but she didn't care right now.

When the table was littered with shrimp shells and corn husks, Trevor leaned back in his seat and rubbed his belly. "That was amazing. I hope you enjoyed it." The smile he gave her suggested he was talking about more than shrimp and potatoes.

"I did, Mr. Mays. Best date ever."

Trevor pulled back his chair and rose, holding out a hand for Whitney. "Care for a quick little walk before I take you home? The paths around this place are gorgeous this time of year."

Carl chose that moment to arrive with a sheet of paper. "I forgot to ask you, folks—did you want to hear our desserts of the day?"

Whitney shook her head, eager for something sweeter than banana pudding.

Trevor snatched her hand and pulled her to his side before draping his arm over her shoulder. "No, thanks, Carl."

The older man winked and headed to another table. As they strolled through the patio and the parking lot, Trevor rested his head against hers. "I meant to ask, how was your first day on the job? Was Kim good to you?"

Whitney watched the sky overhead turn from deep blue to purple, listened as the insects came alive and sang their evening songs. "It was a great first day. Kim has things covered, but she needs more hands, you know? I'm lucky she's giving me a chance, especially since I'm really liking my time in Pinegrove."

"I hope that means you're planning on sticking around," he asked, nuzzling her neck as he peppered her with Cajun-scented kisses.

"You're certainly presenting a good case for staying." She hummed as her head fell back, exposing more of her neck for him to devour.

After the day she'd had, the thought of returning to Savannah was ridiculous, but there was still a part of

Whitney that wondered if Pinegrove was too good to be true. A fun job with a nice boss who gave her permission to try new things felt like a pipe dream. Throw in this sexy fireman currently feasting on her, and Whitney didn't know if she ever wanted to return to reality.

Unaware of her inner turmoil, Trevor nibbled a path from her neck to her ear lobe. Suddenly her previous life was the last thing on her mind.

"Whitney," Trevor gasped her name. "You're going to need to set the pace, darlin'. Otherwise, my brothers in blue will arrest me for public indecency."

Despite the warm air, goosebumps erupted all over her body the more Trevor touched her. Her skin tingled with want, and her belly coiled with desire. She had never felt this way with a man before, and it emboldened her.

"I don't know what I'm doing," Whitney gasped in between kisses. She pulled Trevor closer by his collar, savoring the feel of the starched fabric of his uniform in her grasp. Apparently, she was really into firefighter getups.

Trevor cupped the back of her neck to deepen the kiss. "I think you're doing fine." He sighed as he pulled back for air. "Lordy, Whitney. I've never behaved this way in public." Resting his head on her forehead, his shoulders heaved as he struggled to catch his breath. "I'm manhandling you like a horny frat boy."

The air between them was thick with expectation, but also the humidity of summer in Georgia. Whitney's dress clung to her skin, but she wasn't concerned with appearances at this moment. Under the twinkling lights and wrapped in Trevor's arms, she felt simultaneously protected and on display.

"Does that mean we're done kissing?" she teased, trailing a finger along his jaw and down his neck. Her finger paused, dipping into the cleft before disappearing beneath his collar. He shuddered and slammed their lips together, tasting her like she was his last meal. *Guess not.*

The same young family that shared the patio headed to

their SUV across the lot, and the pair finally came up for air. "I won't scar those children for life tonight," Trevor wheezed. "Plus, I know their daddy, and he'd happily clean my clock if we carried on again in front of his kiddos."

Whitney straightened her dress and nodded, even though she wanted more of her fireman. "That's a situation I'm keen to avoid."

"Then let's take a little stroll to the creek." He hitched his thumb over his shoulder.

Whitney wiggled a foot in the air. "As long as we're not craw dadding." She raised an eyebrow and Trevor laughed.

"No, darlin'. It's just over there, and it's so peaceful this time of day." He gently pinched her elbow and steered Whitney a few hundred paces under a grove of trees. In the distance, she heard the din of the restaurant, but they were alone. "Here," Trevor said, gesturing to a bench under a cluster of pine trees.

She gasped, covering her mouth as she eased down on the wooden seat. The creek bubbled and flowed in front of them, fireflies flickering around them. "This is like a scene from a Hallmark movie," she mused, loving the feel of Trevor's closeness as he settled in beside her.

"I like coming here sometimes. It's a good place to think."

"I bet it's also a good place for dates." She winked to soften the dig. "Not that I'm judging, because clearly we both have pasts."

Trevor tapped his chin, his finger landing right on the divot. "I won't lie, darlin', I did take a girl or two here in high school, but I swear it was to enjoy nature."

"Is that what the kids call it?" She turned to meet his gaze, the color of his eyes muted in the night sky.

"I can promise you, you're the only woman I've brought here since then." He held up a hand and made the Boy Scout salute.

Another piece of Whitney's armor chipped away at his admission, because she believed him. She sensed Trevor was very intentional about what he did and didn't do with people. It made her like him more. *He kept giving her reasons to stay, to let him in.*

"Thank you for bringing me here. It's very special." She closed the distance, pecking his cheek before resting her head on his shoulder.

They sat like that, listening to the bugs and the water until her eyes grew heavy. A tiny yawn escaped, a sign of her long—yet delightful—day.

Trevor smoothed back her hair, letting his fingers trail back down her neck. "You must be exhausted. I'll take you home."

Home. It had only been a matter of days, but Pinegrove felt like home to Whitney. Thinking back to Savannah, she couldn't reflect on anything she missed—beyond her romance book collection. There were no close friends, no job that fulfilled her, not even untainted memories from before Baxter. The only thing waiting for her was Winnie, but that wasn't entirely true. Winnie was traveling. Winnie had a career. Winnie had a life. Maybe it was time for Whitney to follow her lead?

Reaching out, she held Trevor's hand, including on their whole drive back to Daisy's house. He pulled into the driveway and cut the engine. The lights were off inside and the house was quiet, save for Gus's barking. He knew they were outside and apparently natured called.

"I guess we should let Gus out," Trevor said, unbuckling his seatbelt.

Whitney pulled out her phone and chuckled. "Your momma texted. Apparently, she heard we were out on a date and thought she'd give us some space."

"Real subtle, Momma. Like I'm going to have my way with you in my childhood home." His eyes darkened as he pinned her against the front door. "Unless you want me to." He winked and pulled back before they started something.

Gus pushed through the gap in the door and promptly relieved himself on the lawn. Done with his business, he flopped onto his back and presented his belly for rubs. "Oh, poor Gussy, have I been ignoring you?" Whitney cooed as she tickled the hound dog.

"I'm getting a little jealous here," Trevor teased, holding the door open for the three of them to escape the humidity.

Whitney walked into the living room, but Trevor didn't follow. "You're not coming inside?"

He rubbed his eyes and muttered something to himself before striding over and pulling her into an embrace. He kissed her temple before stepping back. "Not tonight. You had a big day and deserve a moment's peace before Momma's back and peppering you with questions." He exhaled. "But please don't think it means I don't want to stay. You're like one of the prized caramel apples at the fireworks festival, Whitney."

She wrinkled her nose in confusion. "I am?"

"Yes, darlin'. You're best savored and appreciated in time." He kissed her chastely before rubbing Gus's head and stepping out into the night. "I'll swing by for breakfast on my way to work."

Whitney nodded. "I'd like that. Thanks for tonight, Trevor. It was really nice."

"It was amazing," he agreed, walking backward to his car. "Sleep tight."

She watched him pull away and disappear down the street. Closing the door, she plopped onto the couch and draped her arm over her eyes. Gus sauntered over and climbed up into her lap, barking once until she gave him her attention. "It's bad, Gussy boy," she mused, rubbing the soft spot behind his ears. "That Trevor might steal my heart if I let him."

She knew that wasn't true though, because he already had.

CHAPTER THIRTEEN

Trevor didn't even bother with the radio for the brief drive back to his place. His mind raced with thoughts of Whitney; his lips still burned from her kiss. She was unlike any woman he'd ever met, and he was falling into the clichés of new love. The color of one of the cars zipping past him reminded him of the color of her dress. A couple walking their dog reminded him of their walk with Gus. Hell, even stopping at a red light and seeing an empty park bench reminded him of their moment by the creek.

Nothing brought him down, or so he thought ...

As he crested the hill for the turnoff to his neighborhood, he spied a familiar car across the intersection. In the newly installed streetlights, he clearly saw the two people in the front seat. One was his boss, Chief Warren, and the other was his momma.

The chief was behind the wheel, but his mother's head rested on the man's shoulder. This was more than offering the woman a moment of comfort, this was the body language of two people who were very comfortable with each other—two people with a familiarity that went beyond friendship.

Trevor's brain raced until he pulled into his driveway and

cut the engine. He'd thought he'd come to terms with Momma dating, but actually seeing them being affectionate with each other unsettled him. Unable to move, he rested his head on the steering wheel and tried to steady his breathing. Back after his father passed, he met with a therapist who offered helpful techniques for when he started to spiral. The only trouble was, he couldn't remember a damned one of them in the moment.

Why did his mother keep this secret from him? They seemed so close, yet why wouldn't she share her happiness with him?

Lost in his own musings, Trevor didn't hear footsteps approach until there was a tap on his window. He jumped so quickly, he honked his own horn. "Jesus." He sighed as he turned and faced one of his teammates, Malcolm Smith.

Smithy was a nice guy, a year younger than Trevor, but a hard worker. There was also the delicate fact that he'd dated Jessie on and off again since high school, but Trevor tried to forget that little tidbit.

"Smithy, what's up?" Trevor asked as he stepped out into the night air. He cracked his neck and struggled to get in the moment.

Smithy rubbed his jaw and sighed. "You okay, man? I didn't mean to camp out at your place, but ..." His words faltered and his shoulders slumped. "You got a minute?"

Trevor pulled his keys from his pocket and jangled them in the air like he was taunting a toddler. "C'mon in. I can't guarantee I have much to drink, but you're welcome to what I have."

"Thanks." Smithy followed him into his apartment and collapsed on the couch. This wasn't the first time he'd been over to Trevor's, as he and Javi come over to watch college football or blow off steam after double shifts.

Today was different though. Smithy seemed to have the whole world resting on his broad shoulders. Trevor rummaged in his fridge for a pair of beers and joined Smithy on the couch, flopping down at the opposite end. They clinked bottles before he relaxed a tad.

Smithy took a slug from his beer and sighed. "Look, this is about work, and if you want me to shut up at any point, I can."

"Okay," Trevor said, slowly placing his bottle on the coffee table to give Smithy his full attention. "What's going on?"

"It's, um, about Hastings." He gave Trevor another glance before asking a question that had no right being that funny. "You, uh, ever notice how he's kind of ... dumb?"

Trevor spluttered, his beer going down the wrong pipe. "Are you serious?" Smithy winced but nodded. "Dude, he's a moron. The only reason he passed the academy was because he cheated on his written exam. Javi and I couldn't prove it, but I'd bet my life he couldn't tell the difference between SCBA and SCUBA. I wouldn't be surprised if he brought the wrong tank to a fire with flippers on his feet."

Smithy snorted at that image. "Sadly, I don't doubt it."

The skin on the back of Trevor's neck tingled. "So, what's up? Not that I don't like shit talking Hastings, but you seem concerned."

Smithy was a damn good EMT and firefighter; Trevor trusted his instincts.

Smithy picked at the label on the beer bottle, peeling off strips of paper and letting them flutter to the floor. "Well," he said on a sigh. "Hastings doesn't seem to know what he's doing, with anything. He asked me to help with the zoning reports today, after overspending in the first aid budget."

"Are you kidding me?" Trevor saw red.

"I wish I was. I was out back with Javi and Maxwell, and he came out all excited that there was a project for me. Next thing I know, he's tossing binders at me and heading out to golf with half of the city council."

Trevor frowned. "Golfing isn't technically a crime, man."

Smithy scoffed. "We need a real captain. Someone who knows the job, the equipment, how to manage people. He's too busy ruffling feathers and making enemies with his own team." Smithy's chocolate gaze bore through Trevor, his concern burning through his stare.

Trevor's voice was low. "I really can't do anything about this, man. You need to talk to the chief."

Chugging the last of his beer, Smithy set the bottle down and groaned. "I know, Trev, but I wanted you to know. We all know it should have been you, and I guess I'm just looking for your input. Is going to Chief the right thing to do?"

"I mean, if the shoe was on the other foot, and you had evidence he can't fulfill his duties, it's worth a shot." He exhaled, feeling tired. "Just don't mention you spoke to me. It would probably look like sour grapes."

Smithy pushed himself up and strode toward the door. His steps seemed lighter since he arrived, and Trevor was grateful he was any help.

They stood in the doorway a moment, and Malcolm's gaze strayed to a family photo on the wall taken a few Christmases ago. Jessie had made it home for a whole week to celebrate before hopping on a plane to her next assignment. Trevor remembered Smithy made more than one appearance at the house that week.

"If you don't mind me asking, how is JJ doing in the Peace Corps?"

JJ, the nickname alone brought out the older brother in Trevor. To his knowledge, Smithy was the only person to use that moniker with his sister. The question was innocent enough, but Trevor tensed. "Well enough, still has no desire to put down roots."

Smithy's trademark grin made its first appearance of the evening. "That sounds like our girl." He cleared his throat and jutted his chin toward the exit. "Do you know if she's planning on coming home anytime soon?" His voice squeaked, and he amended, "You know, just to visit?"

Trevor lifted a shoulder. "Don't know, man. I hope so, but ..."

Smithy nodded. "But with JJ you never know." Glancing one more time at the photo, he took another step toward the door. "I should probably head home and crash."

After a quick nod, Trevor opened the door for him. "I appreciate you coming over. I hope I helped." *And I appreciate you not asking more about Jessie, because I don't think I can handle that drama now.*

"You're a damn good fireman, Trev. Someday you'll get that promotion."

Trevor raised a hand in farewell before walking inside and collapsing back onto the couch. What. A. Day.

His date with Whitney might as well have been a lifetime ago after Smithy's visit. He'd known for years that Hastings wasn't worthy of the uniform, let alone a rank of captain. Trevor's mind whirled with questions and thoughts for the chief, but they all went nowhere. Honestly, the only question he had for the chief was what was happening with his momma.

As he got ready for bed and slipped beneath the covers, Trevor thought about the last week of his life, specifically how Whitney had made everything better. He wanted to talk about his conversation with Smithy, but he wouldn't yet.

He wished Whitney were here now, because he'd love to pick her brain on the Hastings issue. Plus, he wouldn't mind another kiss, or five.

Unable to stop himself, and despite the late hour, he snatched his phone from the nightstand.

You up? he texted, immediately feeling like an absolute idiot. Realizing how that text could have been interpreted, he frantically added, *To talk! Geez, this isn't going well.*

Fortunately he was only in misery for a moment before the three dancing dots appeared. Whitney would either call him a pervert or a moron, and he was okay with either so long as she was talking with him.

LOL! Yeah, can't sleep.

Me too, what's your excuse?

The dots appeared immediately, and Trevor couldn't

stop the grin from crossing his face.

Some really hot fireman took me out to dinner, and I guess I'm too giddy to sleep.

You don't say? I went out with this stunning brunette tonight, and she's all I can think about. Weird.

Trevor imagined Whitney giggling at their exchange. Squeezing his eyes shut, he pressed his phone to his chest. His brain tried to remember the exact way her face looked when she laughed, how the skin around her eyes crinkled and her freckles popped. He wasn't bold enough to ask to FaceTime, but he wanted to hear that melodic voice, be the last person he heard before he fell asleep.

Without overthinking it, he picked his phone back up and was about to dial when an incoming call from Whitney rang. The ringtone blared around him as he shot upright and answered on a breathy exhale, "Hey."

"Hey." Whitney's voice sounded small, quiet. "Is it okay that I …?"

"Yes!" He practically shouted into the phone. "I mean, of course."

Finally, he heard a small chuckle that covered his soul like a balm. "I'm going to sound ancient," she started, voice dripping with fatigue, "but sometimes I prefer real phone calls over texting."

Reaching out, Trevor turned off his bedside lamp and nestled back into the bed. He tucked his phone between his ear and the pillow and didn't bother fighting his giddy grin. "I like phone calls too, especially with the right people."

"Well, you answered. I guess that means I'm right people," she teased.

Trevor had to bite his tongue to stop himself from blurting out *You're THE right person.* Instead, he played it as cool as he could, given his rapidly beating heart. "You certainly are."

"I'm glad," she said, voice barely a whisper. "I'm glad you answered," she repeated.

The sound of rustling fabric came through the line, and

Trevor pictured Whitney curled up in the guestroom. Idly, he wondered what she slept in, and if she let her curls loose while she slept. His fingers itched with the desire to run his hands through that sea of corkscrews, to smell the lilac of her shampoo.

Realizing he was getting a little too excited from this phone call, he cleared his throat. "Me too."

"Tonight was," they said in unison, causing both to burst into fits of laughter.

Always the Southern gentleman, Trevor offered, "You go first."

Whitney sighed, a contented sound that raised the hairs on the back of his neck. "I was going to say that tonight was lovely, Trevor. I haven't had that much fun in longer than I care to remember."

"Me either!" he nearly shouted in his haste to reassure her. This was far from a one-sided attraction for him.

"When I left Savannah, I wasn't sure what I was looking for." She chuckled softly, then said, "Guess I still don't know. But today was ..." She took a moment to collect her thoughts, and Trevor patiently listened to her breathing. If this was all this call turned out to be, he'd gladly take whatever Whitney would give him. "Today was amazing. It started with a great day at the shop, and I feel like I'm making real friends here. I know Daisy's your momma, but she's wonderful and warm. I don't get to see my own mom very often, and I didn't realize how much I missed having someone to talk to without having to filter myself, you know?"

"I do know," Trevor quickly agreed, understanding his momma was one in a million.

"But that's not the only reason today was great," she breathed, her voice tinged with fatigue. "Tonight was perfect, Trevor. I truly had a lovely time, and I hope we can do that again."

Pulse racing, Trevor thought his heart would explode from excitement. "You free right now?" he asked, only half joking.

"Give a girl a chance for her beauty sleep, mister."

"You don't need it, darlin'."

Whitney hummed. "You better not break my heart, Mr. Mays, because I think you're dangerously close to taking it."

The admission shocked Trevor, but only because it was so close to how he was feeling. Even with Virginia, he'd never felt this relaxed and *seen*. Whitney let him be Trevor... flaws and all.

"I won't break it. I promise." Even though she couldn't see him, he crossed his index finger across his chest.

Whitney yawned, and Trevor pulled back the phone to check the time. It was after midnight, and she had to work in a few hours. "I'll let you get your sleep, Whitney. I'll see you at breakfast."

"Hmm, I'm glad. Good night, Trevor."

"Good night, darlin'."

Trevor hung up first, fearful he'd do something stupid like kiss the phone.

The call with Whitney had worked wonders, erasing the tension after Smithy's visit. The more Trevor thought about Smithy and his sister, the more he wanted to spend time with Whitney. Life wasn't always fair, and it didn't always bring people together. He wanted to enjoy his time with Whitney, no matter how long it lasted.

CHAPTER FOURTEEN

Whitney slept like the dead. With a full belly and a giddy heart, she expected to spend the night tossing and turning, but that was until Trevor texted. Chatting with him had been the cherry on the fabulous sundae that was the day, and her cheeks hurt from how much that man made her smile.

Yet as soon as her head hit the pillow, she was out like a light and counting sheep. Well, they weren't sheep so much as dalmatians jumping over a fire truck. She was no dream expert, but she knew Trevor was to blame.

After waking up, she took a little extra time in the bathroom, fluffing her curls and putting on a full face of makeup. She had work in two hours, but, more importantly, she had breakfast with Trevor and Daisy. Their little morning routine was quickly becoming her favorite part of the day. *Except for hungry kisses after dinner and sweet text messages* ...

Inspecting herself in the mirror, she was pleasantly surprised at her reflection. The dark circles around her eyes were gone, replaced with a glint that made her look youthful and happy ... a far cry from the puffy face of earlier that month.

Whitney smeared on some foundation and blended it while she planned for her day. Work was exciting, as today she and Kim were shifting around the racks to make room for their new inventory. Kim had given her carte blanche on setting up the store, so long as the favorites of her regulars weren't buried in the back of the shop.

Adding a swipe of blush, Whitney's cheeks flushed even deeper as her thoughts strayed back to Trevor. He was the polar opposite of Baxter in every way, and she couldn't keep him from her thoughts for long. Yes, he was attractive. It was hard not to be intrigued by his biceps and the little cleft in his chin. And don't get her started on his mouth ... Lordy.

"Whitney?" Daisy called from outside the bathroom door. "You ready for coffee? I was going to start a pot."

"Yes, ma'am. I'll be out in two shakes."

"Make it three," Daisy said with a chuckle. "I haven't found the coffee filters yet."

The other thing that Trevor had that Baxter and her previous exes didn't was a welcoming inner circle. Daisy had quite literally opened her home to Whitney, but also was becoming a friend she couldn't live without. Whitney had a good enough relationship with her own mother, but Daisy was different. Of course she gave motherly advice, but she was also welcoming beyond what was expected. And it was clear Trevor was devoted to Daisy, so much so she worried how he'd handle the Paul news.

Deciding it was better to caffeinate than ruminate, she pushed open the door and strode into the kitchen.

"Morning, sugar. I finally found the filters, coffee's brewing, and I've got biscuits and gravy going."

"So early?" Whitney marveled, helping herself to a mug and pouring two cups. She added the spoonful of sugar that Daisy liked before sliding her mug over to the stove. "What can I help with?"

Daisy shook her head, her hair already pinned back for the day. "Nothing at all. I pulled some biscuits from the freezer, and this gravy isn't that complicated." She sprinkled some flour into the frying pan, whisking until it melted into the waiting puddle of butter.

The smell brought Whitney right back to her childhood and making breakfast with Winnie and their Nana. The girls got more flour on the floor than into the pan, but the memories were cherished. Sitting here now, with a comforting cup of coffee and the company of a sweet-hearted woman, Whitney settled into that same feeling of contentment ... of being where she belonged.

"So, how was your night last night?" Daisy asked over her shoulder, pouring milk into the pan.

"You stole my question. When Trevor dropped me off, the house was quiet. I hadn't realized you and Paul had a date."

"I didn't realize you had a date with Paul either, Momma," Trevor said from the doorway, his jaw slack and eyes pinched. He wasn't dressed for work, instead clad in shorts and a T-shirt featuring the logo of Pinegrove's Fourth of July festivities.

"Trevor, I ..." Whitney said, covering her mouth as her cheeks flamed with embarrassment. "Daisy and I were ..." She stammered, her tongue as heavy and dry as a cinder block.

Daisy slowly dusted her hands off on a towel before hanging it on a drawer handle. Her hands shook slightly, her lips pursed together. "Have a seat, son," she said, her tone leaving no room for argument.

Whitney took a step back, eager to leave the fray. "I can ..." she started as Trevor said, "I'll stand, Momma. I have a feeling this won't take long."

Daisy sighed, striding to the table where she plopped down and sipped her coffee. "Y'all better sit, because I'm only doing this once."

Whitney covered her heart with her hand. "I really don't need to intrude on a family discussion."

Trevor stood ramrod straight, his shoulders bunched up

at his ears. "I don't know, darlin'. Looks like you're already in the know. Might as well join the fun." He kicked a chair out with his foot before sitting across from his mother.

Whitney gasped, unsure she even wanted to stay in this house another moment, let alone this room. This wasn't the Trevor from last night. Gone were the easy grins and dimple popping in his chin. In its place was a sour expression and a glare that sliced through her faster than a warm knife through butter.

"Trevor Nicholas Mays," Daisy spat, slapping her hand on the tabletop. "You use your manners, or you don't get an explanation."

"Sorry, Whitney," he said, finally meeting her gaze. "I guess I expected biscuits and was served a dose of bull—"

"And minding your manners means watching your mouth," Daisy added for good measure, raising an eyebrow at her son. "Whitney, will you join us, please?"

Whitney pulled out the furthest chair and lowered herself down, knees shaking at the effort of keeping her cool. This should be a private conversation between Daisy and Trevor, but she wasn't about to cause more of a stir by leaving.

"So, you *are* dating Chief Warren," Trevor stated, hands curled into fists on the table.

Daisy tucked a lock of hair into place before answering. "Yes. I've been seeing Paul for several weeks." Trevor opened his mouth, but she held up a hand. "To be fair, Paul wanted to tell you right away, but I wasn't ready. I felt like I needed to figure a few things out for myself before I spoke with you and Jessie."

Trevor gestured to Whitney, who was slumped in her seat like she awaited execution. "But Whitney got the full story before I did. A stranger knew before your own son." It was a statement, not a question. His choice of words hit their target, causing Whitney to flinch as Daisy rolled her eyes.

"Now, what did I just say about manners? Whitney is

hardly a stranger, and she only knows because she was here when Paul arrived for dinner the other night. There was no use lying to her when I knew I would tell you." She reached out for Trevor's hands, but he pulled them back and rested his clenched fists on his lap.

Ignoring his mother's explanation, Trevor went for blood. "And you thought dating Daddy's best friend and my boss was a good idea?" The vein in his temple pulsed with the ticking clock on the wall, worrying Whitney as his complexion turned beet red.

"Young man, who I see socially is none of your concern." Daisy was defiant, sipping from her coffee without shaking. "And I remind you, please show respect in my house."

Trevor shoved a hand through his hair, pulling on the roots before exhaling. "I'm trying to understand how you could keep this secret from me. Why did you keep me in the dark? And how could you do this to Daddy's memory?"

Daisy's cool exterior melted as fast as an ice cream cone on an August afternoon. "Trevor, this is ridiculous. I loved your father more than anyone else God saw fit to give life, and I'll be damned if my only son acts a fool in my kitchen." She pushed back her chair and reached out for Whitney's hand, pulling her to her feet as well. "I suggest you take your day off to cool down, and we can discuss this like adults when you're ready." Turning to Whitney, she ordered, "C'mon sugar. I'll take you to Kim's myself today."

"You're making a huge mistake, Momma. What do you even know about Chief Warren anymore? This isn't high school."

Daisy cocked her head. "Are you sure? Because I feel like I'm in the middle of a teenage meltdown."

And with that, Daisy marched right outside with Whitney's hand in her grasp. "I'm sorry to barge out, but I'm mad as a hatter," she spat as she unlocked the passenger's seat for Whitney.

Whitney, having left her purse inside, wasn't sure if

Daisy driving was a good idea or not. "Daisy, maybe I should drive?"

"Sugar, I'm not about to drive into traffic. Now, let's roll."

Whitney slid into the passenger's seat and stared out the window at the house. Trevor stood in the doorway, hands shoved in his pockets. He looked simultaneously defeated and blameless. He didn't look like *her* Trevor at all. Suddenly, Whitney feared she'd put more of her heart on the line than she realized. What was she thinking falling for a man she'd known less than the lifespan of a gallon of milk?

Ten minutes later, Daisy pulled up in front of Kim's shop and killed the engine. "How about we walk up to the corner for some donuts and coffee? I cut our breakfast short."

Whitney wasn't really hungry anymore, so she shook her head. "Thanks for the offer, but I might as well get inside and use the time to move some displays," Whitney said, leaving out all the questions swirling around her brain.

Is this my fault?

What does this mean for Trevor and me?

Do I want this to mean anything?

Why don't I just go back to Savannah?"

"It's the least I can do," Daisy replied on a sigh. "My son was a first-class moron this morning, and I didn't mean to drag you away."

"Trevor will come around," Whitney urged, hoping her words rang true. She didn't know enough about Trevor to know if that was accurate or not, but she saw the bond he shared with his mother, and it took more than one episode of immaturity to ruin that.

Daisy opened her door and reached out, taking hold of Whitney's left hand. "He will. I want to apologize for dragging you into the middle of Mays family drama. I guess I should be lucky Jessie isn't here now, as she'd likely team up with her brother on me."

"You really don't think she'd be happy for you?"

Whitney asked, incredulous.

"What in the world are you two doing out here?" Kim interrupted the moment, sticking her head through the opening in Daisy's door. Her glasses were blue today, making her eyes pop like a pair of sapphires.

Whitney got out of the car and walked around the hood. By the time she'd joined the other women, Daisy was hugging Kim. "Trevor found out about Paul, and he didn't take it well."

"It's my fault!" Whitney blurted. "I should have kept my fat mouth shut."

Kim raised her hand to interject. "First of all, you're not fat. How many times do I need to repeat myself, young lady?"

"And second," Daisy said, narrowing her eyes, "this is my fault for not being honest with my son. You have done nothing wrong, and I hope Trevor gets his fool head out of his ass and apologizes to you."

"Me? Daisy, he should apologize to you," Whitney insisted, shoulders slumped in defeat.

Kim craned her neck around them, taking in the growing crowd of Pinegrove's lookie-loos. "Why don't we continue our gripe session inside? The store is closed, and unless you want the whole free world hearing your issues, we better skedaddle."

"Good Lord, that's all I need." Daisy huffed and led the way inside the shop.

A few folks looked familiar to Whitney, but she didn't have the brain power to put faces with names.

Once they crossed the threshold, Kim flipped the lock and strode toward the office in the back. "Coffee's on, and I need the full story."

Daisy and Whitney took seats by the fitting rooms, flanked by a pair of naked mannequins. "Start at the beginning, and don't leave anything out. My life is about as exciting as a box of hair these days." Kim blew on her coffee mug, easing down onto a bench that split the fitting area into two halves.

Daisy nodded, taking her drink. "I'll give you the abridged version, since you're about to open and I need to pee." Kim snorted at that, but didn't interrupt.

After ten minutes of talking, Kim more or less had the full story. Whitney slurped from her mug, trying to keep her own warring emotions at bay.

"When did you know men to make any wise decisions?" Kim chastised, draining the last of her coffee before dropping her mug onto the floor with a thud.

"Never?" Whitney supplied, gathering the empty mugs and taking them to the kitchenette to rinse out.

Kim punched the air and sighed. "Exactly. I say you give that meathead son of yours a day to cool off, but then he needs to come correct." Pointing to Whitney, she added, "To both of you. I heard about your low country boil date, and it sounds like our boy is smitten with you."

Whitney's cheeks flamed as she stumbled over her reply. "No, what? We're … we're friends."

Kim laughed. "Friends who suck face at restaurants."

Daisy's head whipped to Whitney, her jaw on the floor.

"I can explain," Whitney spluttered.

"You don't need to explain anything, sugar." Daisy stood, closing the distance between them before wrapping her in a warm hug. "I knew you'd be special," she whispered into Whitney's ear. "Give him time. I won't let Trevor muck this up because of my love life."

But Daisy's promise was a cold comfort. A tiny seed of doubt was planted in Whitney's gut that morning, and she feared it would take more than platitudes to squash her fears. She knew Trevor wasn't Baxter, but that didn't mean she hadn't been hurt by his words, by his willingness to push her aside like a stranger.

There was also the sad reality that there really wasn't anything permanent here for Whitney. Trevor could just be a summer fling, and would she really move away from her sister for a retail job? She could practically hear Winnie in her head screaming *Your life is in Savannah.*

"I better get ready to open," she said, her eyes downcast. What she needed now was a distraction, any distraction.

The rest of her shift flew by in a blur of clearance tags and customer interactions. Whitney tried not to let it bother her that Trevor kept his distance all day. When Daisy's truck pulled up to take her home after work, she hid her disappointment behind a smile. As she got ready for bed, with Daisy sitting beside her in the living room reading a romance book, she tried not to compare the fictional man in the story to the real flesh-and-blood man across town who was ghosting her.

Whitney had been ghosted already this summer, and she decided that it had been enough for her. If she didn't see Trevor again, maybe it wasn't meant to be.

After all, looking for love so soon after Baxter was a fool's errand. Whitney needed to stick to what she knew was important, like her sister and her new friendships. Men were a dime a dozen, but women like Daisy and Kim were priceless. And no one could put a price on her sister.

Now, if only her heart could get the memo…

*

This was not how his day was supposed to go. Trevor muttered a slew of obscenities as his car crested over the hill leaving Pinegrove. He'd planned to take Whitney out for lunch and help his mother with the loose floorboards on the deck, but instead he'd yelled at both women like a first-class tool.

The only problem? He was still mad as a hornet.

His boss and his mother. His mother was dating someone new … and Whitney had known before him.

Had she known when they had their date at Carl's?

Was she keeping secrets this whole time?

Was he destined to be with women who kept him in the dark?

Countless images of Virginia's secrets flashed through his mind the longer he fumed in his car. Driving around the backroads usually lowered his blood pressure and put him at ease. Yet today, every mile he drove taunted him.

You chose the wrong girl, again.

Your momma has more of a love life than you do.

Chief Warren is dating Momma, and he wants you out of the station ...

Finally realizing he was emptying his gas tank for no good reason, he turned and went back home, eager to drown his sorrows in beer and whatever game was on TV. Yet as soon as he parked in the driveway, he saw two familiar faces that promised anything but a relaxing evening.

"Who pissed in your corn flakes?" Javi asked, pushing himself off the hood of his car. He was dressed in civilian clothes, his black hair swept back with too much hair product.

Smithy shrugged apologetically, but followed Javi and Trevor to the door. "Sorry to show up, but we wanted to check on you."

Javi held up a hand. "Which is a good thing, since you look like shit. Spill it, man, what's going on?" He gave Trevor a long scan, furrowing his brow.

Trevor debated how much honesty he wanted in this current situation. On one hand, it was no one's business what was going on with his family. Yet the chief was involved, and that only muddied the emotional waters.

"Nothing I want to discuss with you two goobers," Trevor spat, pushing past to get to his front door. When it was clear the two men weren't going away, he sighed and held the door open.

"Such manners and class, man." Javi scoffed as he strode to the couch and fell onto the cushions.

Trevor went to the fridge in search of liquid courage. He handed Javi a beer, even though that only encouraged them to stay. Javi cracked it open and downed half its contents in one pull. He let out a belch that peeled the paint off the walls, and asked, "So did Whitney dump you?"

"What?" Trevor asked, jaw on the floor. "What are you talking about?"

"This." Javi swirled his finger around his own face and frowned. "You look terrible, and that usually only happens when you get dumped."

"Or lose a promotion," Smithy helpfully supplied from across the room. He was lucky Trevor was too wrung out to fight, because suddenly the lieutenant had a very punchable face.

Javi barked out a laugh. "Considering there aren't any promotions to lose right now, I'm sticking with my Whitney theory." He cocked his head and tapped his chin. "I also heard from a little birdie," he said, raising an eyebrow. "That Ms. Daisy and Whitney looked upset this morning."

Trevor was incredulous. "A little birdie?"

Smithy covered his smirk with his hand. "It's Julia. They're seeing each other, again." Under his breath, he muttered, "Since you keep turning her down."

Javi shoved Smithy playfully on the shoulder. "Fine, okay. I'm seeing Julia, kind of. But the point is, she was out getting donuts and walked past Kim's Creations. She saw the ladies gabbing, and everyone looked upset." He took another swig of his beer and pointed at Trevor. "My money is on you, since you're pissed off and alone."

Trevor ran a hand down his face. "Thanks for the reminder." Right now he actually wanted to be alone, but judging from Smithy and Javi's current state of comfort in his home, he was out of luck. Tossing his head back, he stared at the ceiling for inspiration. Finding nothing but cobwebs, he sighed. "I had a fight with Whitney and Momma, but I'm not going to talk about it with you."

Smithy opened his mouth to respond, but Javi flapped a hand to stop him. "Is this about Chief and your mother dating?"

Trevor was incredulous. "No shit, man. I didn't realize how serious it was until this morning." He shot a look to

Smithy, who looked like he wanted to crawl under the coffee table. "Did you know about it?"

Rubbing the back of his neck, he grimaced. "Kind of? I mean, Chief talks about Ms. Daisy all the time, and I saw them at the ice cream shop last month. I kind of assumed you knew it was serious."

"Yeah, and we all know what they say about assuming."

"Why does it bother you so much anyway?" Javi asked, and the question knocked the wind from Trevor's lungs.

"Um, it's …" but the words wouldn't come. The yawning pit in his stomach proved Trevor had issues with this, but he'd also tried so hard to be on board with the changes. If his mother was happy, he needed to be as well.

Smithy cleared his throat, earning both men's attention. "I know I don't understand what it's like to lose a parent yet, but you know Chief isn't going to replace Nick. Your dad was amazing, and if your mom can find happiness again, what's so bad about that?"

Trevor reached up and cupped his face, tugging on his ears to center himself. He had been a complete idiot, and his mother deserved better from her only son. "What do I do?" Always a man of action, Trevor struggled not to have a plan.

Javi drained his beer and went in search of another. Being a smart man, he returned with the rest of the six-pack. "You gotta fix it, Trev. Not just for your momma, but because girls like Whitney don't come around often."

Smithy looked down at his empty bottle and sighed. The somber expression was new for his buddy, who usually laughed at all of Javi's jokes and took pride in his positive attitude. "You have to be careful, man. She could leave Pinegrove. Then you're the loser waiting around with a broken heart."

Javi nudged Smithy. "We'll figure out your broken heart later, man. One crisis at a time."

Smithy dipped his head, and mumbled, "Fine."

Trevor knew he was in a state, because Smithy's mention

of Jessie breaking his heart barely registered. He was too focused on losing *his* girl. "Leave Pinegrove? Whitney isn't leaving. She just got a job."

Javi waffled his hand back and forth. "I mean, yeah. But, c'mon, she's been here like a minute, and homegirl isn't going to stay in your momma's house if you burned your bridges."

Trevor swallowed down the bile rising up his throat. Whitney couldn't leave, she just couldn't. He knew he'd mucked things up with his mother, but that could be fixed. He hadn't known Whitney long enough to judge her reaction to his horrid behavior. After everything Baxter had done, would she be quick to forgive?

"I kind of feel bad coming over here and drinking your beer and making you sad," Smithy lamented, opening the last beer and sliding it across the coffee table to Trevor. "Can we at least order a pizza?"

"And some chips or something." Javi snapped his fingers and cheered. "Julia said that The Pecan Pit does DoorDash now." He pulled his phone out and had greasy takeout delivered within the hour.

Even after watching the Braves game and eating their weight in pizza and French fries, Trevor didn't feel better. His whole world had collapsed since Virginia left and the promotion fell through. The first time he'd felt like himself, like a *better* version of himself, was with Whitney. And what did he do? Treated her horribly and acted like a baby to his mother.

Javi popped the last fry in his mouth and crumpled up the bag, tossing it in the general direction of the trashcan. It landed three feet short, and Trevor had to stop himself from bolting up and putting it away. If there was ever a reboot of *The Odd Couple*, he and Javi would star in it.

"Yeah, I think I'm ready for our male bonding to end for the day." Trevor stumbled to his feet.

Smithy, bless him, gathered the rest of their empty to-go boxes and tossed them on his way to the door. "C'mon, Javi.

I'll drive." He clapped Trevor on the back, and said, "I hope this helped, but I'm sorry if all we did was give you indigestion."

"It helped," Trevor reluctantly agreed. It was nice of his buddies to check on him, even if it resulted in higher cholesterol and more concerns than solutions.

"Cheer up, Trev. If you botched it with Whitney, maybe I'll finally get a chance."

Trevor put Javi in a headlock until Smithy pulled the two men apart. "Javi, man. You just told us you're seeing Julia."

Javi smoothed his shirt and ran his fingers through his hair. "Pfft, casually. You know I don't get serious." Trevor shot him a murderous glare, which Javi took as his cue to exit. "We'll, uh, see you tomorrow."

And just like that, Trevor was alone with all his warring thoughts.

He debated calling Whitney right now, but he didn't know the right thing to say. Scrubbing a hand over his face, he pulled out his cell phone and discovered that no one had bothered reaching out to him. He'd truly have to make the first move, with both of the women in his life. And for someone like Trevor, who used to be the king of confidence, he felt as inspired as a used tissue.

Sighing, he turned up the volume on the game and settled in for a night of baseball and self-loathing. Trevor needed to figure out his life, and fast.

CHAPTER FIFTEEN

"You haven't heard anything either?" Daisy asked Whitney as she padded into the kitchen still in her pajamas. Her dark curls were piled on top of her head. Between the heat and heartbreak, her hair could stay in that position all morning with how little she cared.

"No, ma'am," Whitney said on a sigh, pouring herself a cup of coffee and joining Daisy at the table.

Her friend was dressed for the day in a matching ensemble Whitney knew came from Kim's Creations. The gingham shorts and tank were a lovely green that made her eyes pop. Her graying hair was loose, hanging to her shoulders. The stove was off and the kitchen was cool, no sign of breakfast or the warmth that came from a shared meal.

Daisy's finger trailed along the rim of her mug as she mumbled something under her breath. Despite being dressed, it was clear the older woman hadn't slept well. Her makeup was slightly off, as if she couldn't keep her hands from trembling. Whitney glanced down at the floor and saw Daisy wore mismatched socks.

"I reckon he's cooking up a grand gesture for both of us, seeing as how my son acted like a first-class jackass."

Daisy nodded at her own assumption before standing and striding to the stove. "You okay with oatmeal? I'm not feeling very inspired."

Whitney joined her, resting a hand on her shoulder. "Have you spoken to Paul about all this?"

Daisy placed her hand on Whitney's and patted it. "Yes, yesterday after Trevor stormed out like a bat outta Hell. He agreed it's best to wait for Trevor to come to me, but you best believe I expect an A-plus apology. That boy better grovel and beg until he's hoarse and we're both satisfied."

Whitney pulled back. "Daisy, that man doesn't owe me anything."

"Hogwash," Daisy spat, her cheeks flushing. "My son said some pretty nasty things yesterday, and he *will* make amends." She turned toward Whitney, locking their gazes. "Now it's pretty obvious I'm team Tretney, but ..."

Whitney scrunched up her nose. "You came up with a name for us?"

Daisy rolled her eyes. "Focus, please. You know I clearly want you two to ..." She waggled her eyebrows and flapped a hand in the air. Whitney had no idea what the gesture was supposed to mean, but she didn't interrupt. "But you're a good woman, Whitney. You deserve a man who treats you as good as gold. If my fool son can't come correct, then you find someone who can."

Whitney rubbed over her heart, the organ squeezing in frustration. *Don't get too wound up*, she told herself. *We don't know if Trevor is worth the hassle.*

Yet as she chopped and toasted pecans for oatmeal, Whitney knew that wasn't true. Trevor had already made his mark, and she needed to figure out what that meant. She refused to follow the path she took with Baxter. Being a passive participant in their relationship wasn't for her. She wanted passion, she wanted trust. Right now, Trevor didn't trust her, and the only passion he showed was anger.

After five minutes of silently snacking on her oatmeal, Whitney had had enough of the sullen atmosphere. She was done wallowing for the morning. "I better get ready for work. Kim has more, new inventory arriving this morning," Whitney said, wiping her mouth and stacking the dirty dishes.

"Sugar, I'll handle this. Thanks for your help with breakfast."

"Anytime," Whitney replied and got ready for another day on the job.

As she pulled up to the shop and walked inside, she relaxed at the now familiar sights and smells. The air was cool, thanks to the industrial AC unit churning, and it smelled of fabric and vanilla. Kim had a habit of lighting candles throughout the store, adding to the cozy atmosphere. The woman herself was perched on a stool at the counter, typing away on the computer.

"Good morning, Kim. Has the new inventory arrived?" Whitney smoothed down her skirt and joined the older woman.

"Sure did, and I'm logging in so we can start the fun. There's still a batch of boxes coming later today. I believe this is the plus-sized collection."

Whitney nodded, nibbling her lip. "I hope you don't mind me adding a few things."

Kim pushed her reading glasses up on her head, her lips pursed. "Honey, if it weren't for you, this place would be a ghost town. I hadn't thought about expanding anything in ages, so please do not apologize. You're doing a good job, and I appreciate you."

"Oh," Whitney said, her cheeks heating from the praise. "Then in that case, I'll start tagging."

Kim handed her an old-fashioned price tag gun and laughed. "Locked, loaded, and ready to go."

It took less than an hour for Whitney to tag and hang the new arrivals. She'd selected a variety of tops, tunics, and dresses in sizes from 14 to 3X. As a curvy woman herself, she understood firsthand the frustration that came from going to a cute boutique and not finding anything remotely close to her size. Her closets were always full of purses, shoes, and jewelry—accessories she used to supplement to her tired wardrobe when she couldn't find something in her size.

She was hanging up the last of the tunics when the door opened and a pair of women stepped in. Coincidentally, they were both sturdy women like herself, and they immediately headed in her direction.

"Hiya," Whitney greeted with a wave. "Welcome to Kim's Creations. Can I help you find something special today?" She made a point of stepping back from the rack of dresses.

The younger woman gasped and strode over, snatching a pink and purple dress and holding it out in front of her. "This would be perfect for that party, don't you think, Mom?"

The mother reached out and pinched the fabric between her fingers, covertly checking the label for the size and price. "I think it would, sweetheart. Why don't you try it on?"

"I've got an open fitting room right here—let me get you set up." Whitney went to work pulling a few other options in the same size and hung them outside the door. She poured two glasses of lemonade before rejoining the customers.

"Isn't that nice?" the older woman exclaimed, sipping from her lemonade. "Thank you. We've been shopping all morning and haven't taken a break." Lowering her voice, she added, "Sometimes it's so hard to find clothes that fit us, you know?" Her eyes quickly flicked over Whitney, her smile genuine.

"I certainly do, ma'am." Extending her hand, she said, "I'm Whitney by the way, and you two let me know what you need."

"I'm Marge, and that's my daughter Megan."

Just then, the fitting room door opened and Megan stepped out. The smile on her face lit up the shop as she twirled in front of the three-way mirror. "Oh, Mom, isn't this so cute?"

Whitney handed her the lemonade and beamed. "It flatters your figure, and the pink works well with your skin tone."

"Right?" She took the lemonade with a *thank you* and downed it in one go. "Do you have this in other colors? I might want two."

"Megan, I'm way ahead of you." Whitney pulled the dresses from the fitting room door and fluffed out the skirts. "I've got this dress in two other colors, but there's also another silhouette you might want to try."

Twenty minutes later, Marge and Megan were at the counter buying nearly five hundred dollars' worth of clothes. Marge handed Kim her credit card, and said, "Your shop is so charming. We're visiting from Auburn, but we're going to tell our friends about this place."

"Thank you, Whitney." Megan held up her bags in victory, her excitement warming Whitney from the inside out.

"You're welcome. Now go off and enjoy the festival. We'll see you next time."

As soon as they were gone, Kim pulled Whitney into a bone-crushing embrace. "You're a miracle worker, and I already need to give you a raise."

"Oof." Whitney extricated herself from the bear hug. "Doing my job."

"You're doing more than that, honey. Did you see how happy they were? Here I've been ignoring so much about what people want and need." She tapped her chin, staring outside for a moment. "Do you know anything about social media?"

Whitney shrugged. "Yes?" Truthfully, she had a few pages she'd let collect virtual dust. When it became clear she didn't have a career, home, or love life to brag about, she rarely went online. Her book collection was a testament to her preference of reading to doom scrolling.

Kim applauded, as if Whitney proved herself to be the

next Mark Zuckerberg. "Excellent. I think it's time we got on ClockTock or Instantgrandma."

Whitney covered her smirk with a cough. "I'll, uh, see what I can do."

Before she fell down the rabbit hole of social media planning, she went to work unpacking a new box. Whitney folded a stack of capri pants, her workload growing with every UPS delivery. Lost in her task, she missed the chime of the bell over the door.

"Oh, goodie!" Kim exclaimed, clapping her hands as if another customer was worthy of a standing ovation. "I love me a good old-fashioned grovel."

A star-spangled crop top slipped from Whitney's grasp, her attention on the man in the doorway with his heart— and a lovely arrangement of flowers—in his hands.

"Good morning, Trevor," Kim said from her perch behind the register. She paused entering their new merchandise to gawk. Leaning over so only Whitney heard, she asked, "If I offer you another raise, can I stay and watch?"

Whitney dipped her head to hide her smile. "No, ma'am. It's your shop, and I have a feeling it'll be Pinegrove gossip lickity split anyway." Already outside, a few women stopped and peered through the window. Whitney hoped it was for her styling skills, but she knew it was for the fireman before her.

"Good morning, Miss Kim," Trevor greeted, his voice tinged with sadness. He turned to face Whitney and offered an approximation of a grin. But it wasn't his normal crooked grin, as his eyes remained tense, his shoulders up to his ears. "Good morning, Whitney. Do you have a minute?"

Did she have a minute?

Yes, she did—yesterday when he made a fool of himself. Today, however, she wasn't sure she wanted to hear what he had to say. He'd accused her of lying, which, technically, she may have done, but he'd also ghosted her for an entire day. She hadn't tasted the bitterness of betrayal since Baxter, and two men dropping her in one summer felt like too damn many, in her humble opinion.

Letting out a long exhale, Whitney blinked. Before she said anything, Kim ushered them both to the back of the shop to the office. "You two might as well chat in here. Patsy Williams pulled up out front, and she'll be all over you two like white on rice. Now get," she ordered, practically shoving Trevor.

"Trevor   insert-middle-name-here-because-I-forgot Mays." Whitney pulled the door to the tiny office closed. "You have a lot of nerve acting the way you did and *then* interrupting my work day. Are you crazy?"

"Nicholas," he replied, throwing her off her rant.

"Excuse me?"

"My middle name is Nicholas."

Whitney deflated slightly. "That's nice, being named after your daddy."

"I like to think so." They stood awkwardly in the office, both staring over the other's shoulder. "Were you named after kin, or—?"

Cutting off his line of questioning with a raised hand, Whitney soldiered on. "We are not here to discuss our names, lineage, or anything else family-related."

Trevor's shoulders sagged as Whitney chastised him, but she wasn't finished. After the way he'd carried on at breakfast and then ghosted Daisy and her that night for dinner, she had a good mind to kick his fanny from Pinegrove to Tallahassee.

"Well, that's not true. I do have a few things to say about family. Do you have any idea how crushed your momma is?" She thrust her hands on her hips and scowled at Trevor, whose ears were turning a perilous shade of violet.

"I'm, um, dropping by the house next." He held the bouquet out, shaking it gently so the petals and leaves rustled together. "She's getting the same groveling treatment, although with thirty-one years of guilt piled on top."

Whitney raised an eyebrow. "I'd make it thirty-two years, to be safe."

Trevor was in his fireman's uniform, despite the sweltering weather outside. Sweat pooled at his collar, and Whitney's resolve crumbled ... only a little. "I really am sorry for how I carried on. It's not who I am, and I've been beating myself up about this all day. Please, Whitney, accept my apology, or at least take the flowers."

He jostled the bouquet again, and Whitney huffed, taking the flowers and holding them against her chest. "No use letting gorgeous blooms go to waste, but I'm still not forgiving you completely. I know that must have been a shock, but I wasn't in a great space with the news either. I felt stuck in the middle, and I'd rather like to avoid that in the future."

"I shouldn't have called you a liar." Trevor ran a hand down his face, his eyes dark and sullen. "I've been kicking myself since it happened. It ain't right."

"No, it ain't." Whitney toyed with the ribbon on the stems, eager for something to do with her hands. If they stayed in this cramped space too long, she was likely to close what little distance remained between them and smooth those worry lines from his forehead. She had to admit, he looked terrible.

Trevor perched on the edge of the desk, careful not to disturb the piles of paperwork and receipts. "Look, Whitney. I'm not about to treat you like a free therapist, mostly because I have one that likes to take my money, but I'm clearly working through some stuff." He muttered something under his breath before continuing. "And I'm discovering I'm not as over the death of my father as I thought, in all aspects of my life. I lost my boss and my dad when he passed, and suddenly having my career tank as my boss dates Momma, well ..." he swore and shook his head. Finally, he met her eyes, his own glistening with unshed tears. "What I'm saying is that I'm truly sorry I dropped my baggage at your feet. You are the nicest person I know, and you've been nothing but kind to my mother. My reaction was uncalled for, and I'm sorry."

Whitney put the flowers on the desk, not paying the same attention as Trevor to the stack of invoices teetering on the edge. "Trevor." She said his name with reverence, absorbing his apology. "That was the nicest, most sincere apology I've ever received. Thank you."

Trevor covered his face with his hands. "You don't need to forgive me, because I did a terrible thing." His shoulders shook as he let the tears fall, and Whitney couldn't stand the distance a moment longer. The man was in pain, and she'd give him what she had.

"Shhh," she cooed, wrapping her arms around his shoulders, pulling him to her middle. She held him firm with her left arm, using her right hand to rub circles on his back. "It's going to be okay. You'll see."

Whitney didn't know how long they stayed in the office, but she wasn't in a hurry. She'd done more in half a week on the job at Kim's Creations than she'd managed at her last three temp placements combined. It felt good to have a purpose, but right now it was best to comfort Trevor. Granted, she required a little more groveling to fully forgive him, but she appreciated the time to speak her peace.

That was what Baxter had robbed her of when he left. He hadn't even tried to reach out after she returned his car; a fact she still couldn't believe. That almost upset her more than the breakup—learning that her petty revenge hadn't garnered a reaction.

Now, though, with Trevor, Whitney understood this was different.

"What time is your shift today?" she asked.

"I have to be there in an hour. I'm working second shift to cover for someone on leave." He rested his head on her shoulder and let out a breath. "Thank you for hearing me out. I don't expect you to welcome me back into your life with open arms, but I will continue to make amends."

"I believe you," Whitney said, smoothing back his

cowlick. And she *did* believe him; she hoped it wouldn't cost her her heart again. "Now, go talk to Daisy."

"How is she?" Trevor asked, lips turned down in a grimace.

"She'll be better after you stop by." Whitney's hand dropped as she straightened her skirt and opened the door to the office.

Kim was outside the doorway, very interested in hanging up the new swimsuits. She darted behind a box as if they wouldn't see her hiding. "Oh, leaving so soon?"

For the first time since he arrived, Trevor laughed. "Yes, Miss Kim. I'm off to see Momma."

Kim sniffed. "I hope the bouquet you brought her is twice as big. Mother's hearts need a little more mending."

Trevor saluted. "Don't you worry, I bought out the shop."

"Good," both Whitney and Kim said in unison.

Hesitating, Trevor reached out and took Whitney's hand. Tracing a thumb over her knuckles, he said, "I know I'm working late tonight, but can I see you later?"

Whitney cocked her head to the side, as if deep in thought. "You still owe me an ice cream cone."

"Pick you up at eight for the best banana split of your life?" Trevor offered, his bravado slowly returning.

"I'll be ready, but only if you do a good job with Daisy." She winked, squeezing his hand before letting go. "Get out of here. I've got work to do."

"See you tonight." Trevor grinned, his chin dimple popping. The appearance of that divot had her heart doing somersaults.

She watched Trevor hop in his truck and head toward Daisy's place. Whitney only hoped that Trevor worked some magic and made Daisy feel better, because that woman deserved more than a broken heart.

They both did.

*

Trevor sat in the driveway of the family home for an eternity. After seeing Whitney, after sharing the burden of the truth of his feelings and worries, he simultaneously felt buoyant yet exhausted. He had no idea what to expect from his mother, but he knew he needed to stop being a coward and get out of the car.

Gus announced his arrival as he trudged up the sidewalk to the front door. He let himself in, reaching down to greet the hound. "Hey, boy, is Momma around?"

"I was giving you another five minutes in the driveway before I came out to you," Daisy said from the doorway of the kitchen. She wore an apron, her hair pinned off her face, a dusting of flour on her cheeks. If his daddy was a stress cooker, his Momma was a stress baker. The air was heavy with the scents of cinnamon and vanilla, the smells of his childhood.

"Momma, I'm ..." Remembering the flowers in his hands, Trevor took a step closer and handed them to Daisy.

"I'll put these in water," she said, turning her back as she strode with purpose into the kitchen. Trevor wasn't certain, but Gus glared at him as he followed her inside.

"I hope when you're done with your flower delivery, you're on your way to Whitney." Daisy retrieved a vase and slammed the cabinet door, the glassware clinking. "That girl is sweet as peach pie in July, and you acted like a damn fool. Son, your daddy would be so disappointed."

His mother knew exactly how to deliver a blow, and Trevor fell into a chair, his knees shaking at her words. The trouble of it was, Trevor knew he deserved it. *And worse.*

"I saw her first, over at Kim's shop."

Daisy gestured to the flowers, which she'd arranged in a vase his daddy gave her on an anniversary. "I hope you got her some flowers, too."

Trevor nodded, resting his elbows on the tabletop. "Blooms on Main now has my next paycheck. I spared no expense."

Daisy sniffed, but finally turned toward her son. "Good. You'll need to take her out, that is if she wants to see you again."

"She's working on forgiving me, but I know I'm on thin ice."

"She's a good woman, our Whitney. I'm still thanking the good Lord every day that she stumbled into our lives."

Trevor sighed but didn't disagree. "I'm grateful we found her, too." Snagging his mother's gaze, Trevor laid it all out on the line. "I'm sorry, Momma. I know talk is cheap, although those flowers aren't," he said with a smirk, "but I know I was in the wrong. It's just that ..." His explanation faltered.

Daisy sat down beside him, resting her hand on his. "Trevor, you're human. I know you like to think you're not, but you are. Being human means we muck up situations, and I'm no different."

Trevor turned his hand over to squeeze his mother's. "You didn't muck up anything, Momma. If you and Chief want to date, it's none of my business."

"That's true, but I should have told you the truth before. At first, I didn't think much of it, since I know you love and respect him as I do, but now I'm seeing it through your eyes. It wasn't right to go behind your back like that, son. I apologize."

"Apology accepted, but I need to say something else." He released his mother's hand and covered his face. "I'm a mess, Momma."

"I'll put the kettle on," she said, rising and retrieving a set of tea cups before fumbling for her favorite mix of herbal teas. "Cookies are almost done, then we can have a proper chat."

Trevor squeezed his eyes shut, focusing on the sounds of his mother pottering around the kitchen. If he fixated on her footfalls and clattering utensils, he'd swear he heard Jessie down the hall playing the piano or Daddy out back with the lawn mower. For all the time he came to the family home, he tried to keep these memories at bay, because as much comfort as they brought, there was still someone missing.

"I know you're going to think this is crazy," he started once Daisy was seated again. She poured two cups of tea and slid a plate of snickerdoodles over to him. He picked up one of the cookies and ate it whole, savoring the warm, spicy dough.

"Try me," Daisy retorted, breaking a cookie in half and tossing a piece to Gus.

Gus snarfed the cookie down nearly as quickly as Trevor had before sauntering off to the spot by the door and dozing in the sunlight. *Ah, the life of a dog.*

"I know you loved Daddy," he said, dusting crumbs from his fingers.

"Love," she corrected. "It never feels past tense to me. My relationship changing with Paul isn't going to change that."

For some reason, that made Trevor feel a little better. Deep in his soul he knew his mother would not, and could not, replace his father, but hearing the truth from her directly put him at ease. "I need to talk with Chief about this," he groaned.

Daisy laughed. "Maybe you could start calling him Paul when you're off the clock? I'm not saying he's moving in or anything, but your paths are going to cross. It would be nice if he didn't feel like your boss when we all spend time together."

Trevor raised an eyebrow. "You want to spend time with me and Paul?"

"No, Trevor. I'm going to cut you completely out of my life now that I have a ..."—she hesitated—"boyfriend?"

Wrinkling his nose, Trevor barely contained his laughter. "Gentleman friend?"

She swatted his arm. "Son, that makes me sound ancient. I'm still in my fifties, thank you very much."

"I know, Momma."

Daisy reached out and gently tugged on Trevor's earlobe. It was a nervous habit from his youth. Whenever he got overwhelmed, young Trevor pulled on his earlobes. Once they were out at an amusement park and he'd gotten lost. By the time Jessie and his dad found him, he'd practically yanked his ears clean off his head.

"I love you very much, son. I know this is a lot to take on, especially with losing the promotion, but please trust Paul and I only want the best for you."

"I know, and I love you, too." The silence stretched around them, and the tension in Trevor's shoulders slowly eased.

Daisy stretched, the pressure of their spat melting away. "I think we should get everyone over to the house for a picnic after the festival is done. I haven't seen Smithy in ages, and he keeps dodging my invites for breakfast with you boys."

This was news to Trevor. "He does?" He racked his brain, trying to remember when Smithy started pulling back. It usually coincided with Jessie's visits home, or in some cases *the lack* of visits home.

Daisy nodded sagely. "I haven't seen him since Jessie's surprise visit a couple months ago."

Trevor had been out of town for a training session, expecting to be promoted, and missed his sister's brief stay. "I didn't know he'd come over while she was in town." His mother's expression was coy, but Trevor's gut tightened. "You know something, don't you?"

"I'm not saying I know anything, but those two are still…" She flapped her hands in the air, head tilted up in thought. "They're like a match and a stick of dynamite. On their own they are fairly harmless, but put them together and KABOOM!" She held her hands out and wiggled her fingers.

Trevor scratched his chin. "You know, Smithy asked about Jessie again."

"Poor boy is still smitten. If I ever get my way, she'll

move home and appreciate there's good stuff in Pinegrove."

"Good stuff meaning her high school sweetheart?"

Daisy was exacerbated. "Good stuff like her mother, brother, and a man who always treats her right."

"But she likes helping people," Trevor said, jumping to his sister's defense.

"Pfft, like she can't help her own neighbors? For heaven's sake, sugar, if I want to hear that load of nonsense I'll call Jessie herself." She patted his hand and stood, gathering their tea cups and putting them in the sink to wash later. "You're about to be late for work, not that I'm not enjoying our time together."

Trevor kissed her cheek before leaning down to rub Gus's belly. "Thanks for talking, Momma."

"Anytime, sugar. Now you go talk to Paul and come by and see Whitney."

"You're as bad as Gus with a bone," Trevor teased. "We're taking our time here. In case you didn't notice, I dug myself into a hole."

"And you'll find a way out. I've been praying for Whitney for years, you know."

Trevor wrinkled his nose. "You've only just met her?"

Daisy rested a hand on Trevor's shoulder. "Son, a mother wants the best for her children. At night, when I'm talking to the Good Lord"—she paused and pointed up at the ceiling—"I ask him to bring Jessie home safe and sound. If I'm feeling particularly frisky, I ask that Smithy and she reconcile."

Trevor winced. "Please tell me you're not wishing for me and Virginia to get back together."

"For the love of ..." She scoffed and whacked the back of his head. "No, you dope. I prayed that a sweet woman who will love and respect you would come into your life. Little did I realize she'd fall right into our laps at The Pecan Pit."

Ever since he'd met Whitney, Trevor thought back on that night with fondness. He would never have forgiven

199

himself if Javi had made a move, or worse, if she'd gotten back on the road. Whitney was everything Virginia wasn't, and it was high time he showed her that. "I'm going to swing by after my shift tonight. I'm taking Whitney out for ice cream."

Daisy beamed. "Perfect. I'll make sure she doesn't fill up on cookies. Now, get to work, sugar."

Trevor slid behind the wheel of his truck and pulled out onto the road. As the familiar sights of Pinegrove zipped past his windshield, he pulse slowed. He felt better now than he had in months. His momma seemed truly happy, and he couldn't deny having Whitney around was the brightest spot of every day.

When he pulled into his parking spot at the station, Chief Warren was already there, standing in the parking lot talking to one of the guys from the B shift. Trevor raised his hand in greeting as he strode to the front door.

"Wait a minute, son," Paul called out.

When he and Trevor were alone, he rested his hands on his hips, and said, "Do you have a couple minutes? I'd like to talk to you about something."

Trevor squared his shoulders, ready for whatever the chief had to say. "Yes, sir, let me drop my gear at my desk and I'll …"

But Chief Warren shook his head. "Why don't we take this conversation on the road? I haven't had lunch yet."

"I'm covering for Waller today, so I'm …"

Chief reached out and clapped Trevor's shoulder. "It's handled, son. Let's go get some lunch."

And with that, Trevor got into the chief's car. They drove past the café, Carl's, and the barbecue place, right through Main Street.

"Where are we going?" Trevor asked, his pulse kicking up as they passed the *Thanks for visiting Pinegrove* sign at the edge of town.

"I've got an issue at the station, son," Paul said, his hands squeezing the steering wheel, knuckles turning white as the rare Georgia snow. "And I need your help to figure it out."

CHAPTER SIXTEEN

Chief Warren drove out of town to a small diner on the side of a country road. It was the type of establishment you'd expect to find in a country western song, or in this case, middle of nowhere Georgia. It looked like an Advil capsule if it was covered in tin and rested on the side of a winding road. The sign boasted the *best pie in Georgia,* which was all Trevor needed to see. Their drive lasted less than twenty minutes, most of it filled with crippling silence.

Trevor pulled on a loose thread of his uniform shirt, eager for a distraction from the moment. In all his time working with Chief, he'd never seen him this on edge. They pulled into the diner's parking lot and Chief cut the engine.

Swiveling in his seat, Paul reached behind him for a pair of T-shirts, tossing one at Trevor. "Put this on over your shirt. I know I sound paranoid, but I don't want people seeing a bunch of Pinegrove's finest."

Trevor raised an eyebrow but did as he was told. Placing his hand on the door latch, Trevor was ready to get out of the stifling car, but Chief stopped his progress with a hand on the arm. "Wait a second. The rest of our party isn't here."

"Okay, now you're sounding like a conspiracy theorist in a John Grisham novel." Trevor fought an eye roll as he shut the door and sat back in his seat.

"Before we get to all that, I need to say my peace on another matter." Paul cleared his throat, seemingly as anxious as Trevor.

"I've spoken to Momma and apologized this morning. You can spare me the fatherly routine, Chief." Trevor crossed his arms over his chest, keeping his eyes focused outside at the diner.

Paul scratched his neck and muttered something about the road to hell being paved with good intentions. "I need you to understand something, son," he started, licking his lips and slowing his breath.

It wasn't that Trevor hadn't seen the chief upset before. Heck, he was nearly as broken up as Jessie, Daisy, and Trevor were at the funeral. Yet there was something about how Chief was in this moment, frown lines etched into his skin, eyes so tired it was amazing he was awake enough to drive. Whatever he was about to say was going to be heavy, and Trevor wasn't sure he was ready for that type of revelation.

Trevor held up a hand and sighed. "Please, Chief. If you're about to say anything about my mother, I beg you to stop."

"Call me Paul, damn it. Right now, we're two men having a conversation." He ran a hand through his hair and muttered, "Or we would be if I found my words."

"We really don't need to do this whole routine, Paul. I trust you'll treat my mother right."

"I love your mother," Paul blurted out, eyes wide. He seemed as shocked by his admission as Trevor.

"You what?" Trevor had not expected this. He wasn't sure what he thought Paul would say, but confessing *love* for his mother was not one of them.

"I am in love with Daisy, have been for quite some time." He shook his head when Trevor's face fell. "I'm not saying I ever did or said anything while Nick was with us, because that's not the man I am. But I need you to know that I've cared for Daisy since we were in high school, and those feelings shifted the more time we've spent together recently."

Trevor waited for a feeling of revulsion to wash over him, but instead, he was relieved. Paul wasn't looking for something casual with his momma. Deflating in his seat, Trevor sighed. "I'm actually relieved to hear you say that."

"You think I'd try to play fast and loose with your Momma?"

Trevor barked out a laugh. "Yeah, actually. I kind of did. It was like you were trying to push me out of the station, and then when you and Momma kept the secret of your relationship, it all felt so sordid."

"First of all, son, I've never wanted to transfer you to another station. I only wanted to show you there were other options for promotion while I figured out what to do with Hastings. He was never the captain I wanted on my force, but I've been trying to keep the peace." Rubbing at the back of his neck, he groaned. "Which, clearly, I was doing a terrible job."

"So, you weren't trying to get rid of me?"

"Not at all. You're a damn good fireman, Trevor. Your instincts and teamwork cannot be beat, and I only want you to shine."

The news washed over Trevor, taking the wind from his sails as he caught his breath. His boss was not trying to oust him, but rather help him. "I feel like a damn fool." Trevor huffed. "I thought after Hastings was promoted, that was it for me. It was hose duty for the rest of my career."

"Your career is far from over, and after this little lunch meeting, I'm hoping to make some changes."

Out the rear window, Javi's car approached and parked beside them. Smithy stepped out first, a ballcap pulled low over his face, hiding his black curls. He wore jeans and a flannel with clunky work boots, despite the sweltering summer heat. Javi emerged dressed for the gym in basketball shorts and a tank top. His hair was hidden under a beany.

"Why are you two dressed like lame versions of yourselves?" Trevor trash-talked, stepping into the parking lot.

"Didn't Chief tell you? We're incognito." Javi smirked.

Chief rolled his eyes and joined them, striding ahead to the diner's entrance. "I meant you didn't need to wear your uniforms, goofballs."

"Oh, well, now I look like a lumberjack in Witness Protection." Smithy tugged on his flannel and groaned.

"Who is also a Braves fan," Javi teased, flicking the hat off his head.

When they stepped inside, a cute hostess with a shock of red hair greeted them. "Hi, y'all. Welcome to Bucky's. Table for four?"

"Yes, please, darlin'." Javi stepped forward, leaning against the hostess podium, his grin on full display. "Maybe after my buddies and I have lunch, you could give me your number for dessert." He winked, and Trevor made a gagging noise.

"Oh, well," the poor girl stammered as Chief shoved Javi back.

"I apologize for him, ma'am. Our boy here is part of a social experiment to see if he's fit to be out among real humans," Smithy said, putting Javi in a headlock.

"Unfortunately, he failed the test and will go back into his cell." Trevor added a head noogie while Javi was trapped in Smithy's hold. Chief fought a smile the whole walk to their table.

Malcolm dropped Javi into a chair and chuckled. "You need to work on your game, man. She was clearly not interested."

"Pfft, come on. I saw how she smiled at me."

Trevor opened his menu, keeping his gaze on the delicious options. "It's called customer service, idiot."

"I think her eyes were offering more than ..."

Chief reached across the table and swatted Javi on the back of the head. "And I think we're done, boys." He looked back at Javi. "I thought you were dating that girl from The Pecan Pit?"

Javi shrugged. "Julia and I broke up."

Smithy was incredulous. "You told us last night you were seeing each other."

"That was true, then. We broke up this morning."

Chief muttered something Trevor couldn't hear but rallied quickly. "As much fun as it is discussing your extracurriculars, Ortiz, let's order and get down to business. We only have an hour, and I'm sure the Forestry Service needs Smithy back on the job."

Trevor and Javi burst out laughing, but poor Smithy only slid further down in his seat. "Thank God I didn't borrow my uncle's construction uniform."

Dabbing away a tear, Javi jibed, "But then you'd be eligible to join the Village People."

Their waitress arrived and took their orders, delivering a round of sweet teas before they could ask.

"I want to start by saying," Paul said, slurping from his glass. "You three are my top guys. I trust y'all won't share what I'm going to say, but I need your advice. Usually I take staffing concerns to the city council, but since Hastings is practically married into Pinegrove politics, I'm coming to you." He turned briefly to Trevor, and added, "Sorry."

Trevor held his hands up in surrender. "I'm over it, Chief. Hastings and Virginia can ride out into the sunset for all I care."

"That's actually my point. I need help documenting Hastings's slips." He focused on Smithy. "Thank you for telling me about the zoning reports." Gesturing to Javi, he said, "And I wouldn't have known about the budget errors if you hadn't caught them. The point I'm getting at is, I want to document everything and start counseling sessions with Hastings. If he isn't cut out to be captain, I need to confirm it sooner rather than later. This station deserves real leadership, not someone who teases and taunts his team. I curse the day the mayor expanded the fireworks festival."

Trevor's ears perked at that. "What do you mean?"

Scrubbing a hand over his mustache, Paul sighed. "When the mayor decided to grow all of Pinegrove's festivals, he put more stress on the council with the 'less exciting,'"—he paused his explanation for air quotes— "tasks like personnel. When Hastings and Virginia started dating and the promotion came up, I think LaPlante saw a way to get his future son-in-law a cushy job. He wasn't thinking about how Hastings would actually have to work harder, would have to help lead a fire station."

This was news to Trevor. While he'd assumed exactly what Paul described, he didn't realize how much he needed confirmation on that until now. The stall in his career still stung, but he could see beyond his own frustrations to the forces weighing Paul down.

Before any of the men could reply, the waitress returned with the perfect distraction—an array of greasy food. "Here y'all go," the waitress said, balancing four plates on her arms. "Who has the patty melt?"

Discussions of Hastings and his lackluster performance ceased as the men focused on their meals. "Guys, this place is amazing. When Chief said we needed to get out of dodge for lunch, I knew we had to come here."

Smithy sipped from his sweet tea. "I didn't know you were such a foodie, Ortiz."

Javi preened, spreading his hand over his chest. "Smithy, I am *the* foodie. When I was dating that chick from Ohio, she took me to this little diner in this random town." Lowering his voice, he mumbled, "The menu was unbelievable. I mean, the shit they did to …"

Chief shook his head. "Keep it PG, Ortiz. I still have half a tuna melt left."

Scoffing, Javi shoved a fistful of fries in his mouth. "Get your mind out of the gutter, Chief. I was talking about the food. It was this diner in Buckeye Falls, Ohio. You're in the middle of nowhere, but that menu felt like something out of Atlanta or New York."

"Wow, Javi. I didn't realize your dating territory stretched up into the Midwest," Trevor teased, balling up a napkin and throwing it at his head. "We'll need to alert the other single men, so they don't encroach on your turf."

Javi muttered something in Spanish, giving a death glare to Smithy. For his part, Smithy covered his smirk with his patty melt. "He said it, man, not me."

Javi batted away the napkin. "Yeah, but you didn't come to my defense."

"Defense? You literally hit on the hostess as soon as we arrived. And you keep calling dibs on Trevor's girl. And do I need to remind you of Julia and …?"

Chief Warren held up his hands and chuckled. "All right, gentlemen. We're not going to slut shame anyone today."

Javi was offended, jaw on the table. "Chief, I never refer to my woman as anything other than goddesses."

"I don't think he was referring to your women, dummy." This time, Trevor threw a sugar packet, hitting Javi square in the forehead. Smithy couldn't contain his laughter.

Trevor's face hurt from smiling by the time their waitress returned with dessert menus. Despite all four men being stuffed to the gills, everyone ordered a slice of pie. The ease in their conversation, the rapport they all shared, was tangible outside the station. In a matter of months, Hastings had cast a shadow over a place these men held dear.

"Thanks for coming out, y'all. I appreciate your honesty, and I'll keep you posted on what I need. You're damn good firemen."

Chief paid their bill and led them outside to the parking lot. The sun hung heavy overhead, casting short shadows as they strode to their cars. Just as Trevor put his hand on the door handle, all four of their cell phones squawked to life.

"Five alarm in progress at the corner of 5th and …" dispatch said through the walkie in Chief's car.

"You heard that, fellas?" he asked, snagging Javi's eye.

"Sure did, sir. We'll meet you at the station, should be able to get to that side of town in less than twenty minutes."

Trevor yanked off the extra T-shirt and buckled up, ready when Chief turned on the lights and sped down the road. Fumbling in his pocket, he yanked out his cell phone to text Whitney. He hated the idea of keeping her waiting tonight, and he really didn't want her to worry. Most of all, he wanted to let her know he was thinking about her; thinking about how lucky he was that she'd given him a second chance.

Pressing his finger to the *Power* button, the screen remained dark. "Damn," he muttered, opening the center console to look for a charger. "You got an Android charger, Paul?" Trevor caught the smile forming on his boss's face at the mention of his name, and warmth bloomed in his chest.

"Sorry, son. I've got an iPhone."

Trevor tucked his phone back, already sliding into work mode. "No worries."

When Paul pulled up to the station, Trevor jumped into his bunker gear in record time, Javi and Smithy hot on his heels. As they sped toward the scene, Trevor swallowed past the lump in his throat. While he usually was laser focused when they were en route to a fire, something about today felt different. Telling himself if was just indigestion from lunch, he said a prayer that everyone made it out in one piece.

CHAPTER SEVENTEEN

"Sugar, relax. I'm telling you, he's probably wrapped up with reports," Daisy said from her perch on the sofa. Her legs were tucked under her, one hand holding a glass of wine.

One of the many things Whitney loved about staying with Daisy was their new habit of wine nights. They found a Hallmark movie to watch and then cracked open a bottle of wine. Tonight's movie happened to be about firefighters in a small town, causing Whitney to think about Trevor a little more than usual.

"I know, but I thought we were getting ice cream," she said, placing her now empty glass on the end table. She'd taken the armchair, a favorite spot of Gus's. The basset hound sat at her feet, snoring along with the movie. It was more than her sweet tooth preoccupying Whitney, it was her desire to see Trevor, to continue their conversation and get back on track.

Daisy checked her watch and frowned. "Actually, it is pretty late. Wasn't he getting off at eight o'clock?"

"I thought so," Whitney replied, wishing the tension at her neck would stop. She wasn't sure why, but she was on edge. Her earlier texts went unanswered, which felt like more than being bogged down with paperwork.

"It's the life of a fireman's wife," Daisy said, topping off her glass before shaking the bottle in Whitney's direction. Knowing more alcohol was the last thing she needed, Whitney shook away the offer.

This was hardly the first time Daisy mentioned marriage to her son, but Whitney was still embarrassed. "Daisy," she chastised, "your son and I are barely dating. Let's focus those wedding bells where they belong," she said, twirling her hand in the air before pointing at Daisy. "Solely on you, ma'am. Don't think I don't see how you light up when talking about Paul."

Daisy snorted. "I'm not surprised you can see that, considering the same expression is plastered on your lovely face every day since you arrived in Pinegrove."

Whitney was going to come up with a stellar reply when the doorbell rang. Knowing both Trevor and Paul would walk in, Daisy and Whitney sprang to their feet. Whether sensing what was about to happen or just excited over a visitor, Gus ran to the door and woofed like the world was ending.

"Kim?" Whitney asked, stepping back and nearly tripping over Gus while he scampered around them, barking like a lunatic.

"You haven't heard?" Kim asked, her eyes darting between the two women.

Daisy cursed under her breath before covering her mouth. "Is it Trevor? Paul?"

Kim shook her head, then shrugged. "I don't know. I was closing the shop when I saw a group of people on Main Street looking at something online about a warehouse fire. Turns out, it's a five-alarm fire and all hands on deck. I heard they called in medics from Peach Springs. I'm headed that way now and wanted to see if you ladies want a ride."

Daisy was already rushing outside, her purse dangling from her elbow, bare feet slapping on the sidewalk. "I'll grab her shoes," Whitney said, holding up a finger as she darted around the living room. She quickly filled Gus's water bowl, rubbed his head, and dashed out the door. By the time she handed Daisy her shoes, Kim was speeding through the neighborhood.

"They're going to be okay; they're going to be okay ..." Daisy chanted to herself in the passenger's seat.

Whitney's blood pressure skyrocketed as she thought about Trevor in danger. They still had so much to say to each other. Poor Daisy was a mess, having both her son and partner in danger.

How does she do it? Whitney marveled, hanging on for dear life as Kim took a turn too fast.

"Honey, take deep breaths, okay?" Kim ordered her friend. "Not only are Paul and Trevor terrific firefighters, but they're professionals. They know what to do."

"That's right," Whitney added, although her voice lacked the conviction. "They'll be safe." She crossed all her fingers and rested her shaking hands on her lap. Kim blew past three stop signs in as many minutes, but thankfully no one was on the back roads.

"Where are we going?" Daisy asked when she'd collected herself.

Kim clicked her turn signal and turned into a corporate park with dozens of non-descript buildings flanking the street. "Just there," she said, pointing out the windshield. Although her directions weren't needed.

Smoke plumed into the air at the end of the road, a three-story structure burned like there weren't multiple fire trucks trying to put out the blaze. Even in the car, the bitter tang of smoke coated Whitney's mouth. She coughed to clear her throat, but it was no use. The fire was everywhere, and her nerves combusted the closer Kim's car brought them.

Unable to get too close, Kim pulled in behind another group of onlookers. Early night had fallen, but there was still enough light to see the full damage. Nearly a dozen fire trucks were parked, countless firefighters rushing around the scene shouting out orders and running lengths of hose.

"Do you see Engine 33?" Daisy asked, stumbling from the car. Kim rushed to her side and looped an arm around her waist, holding her in place.

"I don't, but let's see if we can get closer."

Whitney took her place on Daisy's other side as the trio marched to the barricade. A police officer Kim recognized waved people back. "Folks, please keep your distance," he ordered, although no one budged.

"Wait here," Kim said, linking Daisy's trembling arm through Whitney's. "That's Greg, Buster's friend. He'll give me answers, or I'll box his ears." She nodded to them and strode off in the direction of information.

"Oh, Whitney." Daisy sighed. "What a nightmare."

"Shhh, this will all be okay. Kim's right, they're all professionals." As she uttered those words, a chunk of the roof collapsed into the blaze, sending a fresh burst of flames from the building. Heat singed Whitney's face, her eyes clouding over with smoke and ash. If the fire had this effect on her from a distance, she shuddered to think of what Trevor was facing.

"Oh, Lord." Daisy gasped, knees giving out. Whitney tugged her up, practically dragging the older woman to the curb for a seat. "This is bad, very bad."

Maybe it was a bad idea for them to be here? What good could it do for a mother and partner to watch the blaze live? Whitney knew what she was feeling, and it paled in comparison to Daisy's experience. As Whitney was about to suggest they head home, Kim jogged over to them.

"Greg said they've called in two other stations to help. As far as he knows, everyone is out of the building, but they haven't had radio contact with all engines. It's possible some folks are still inside."

"Should we stay?" Whitney whispered, motioning to Daisy's catatonic state. Her eyes were unfocused, lips pressed in a firm line.

Kim shrugged. "That's up to you two. I can't see it helping or hurting either way." Crouching down, Kim met

Daisy's eyes. "Honey, do you want to go home and wait for news?"

Daisy didn't respond, simply staring into the scene with unblinking eyes. "Trevor, Paul." Her voice hitched, a single tear sliding down her cheek.

Whitney rummaged in her purse and retrieved a ball of tissues. She wasn't certain they weren't used, but now wasn't the time for concern over germs. "Daisy," she cooed, dabbing at her friend's cheeks. "Do you want to sit in the car at least?"

Daisy's head shook the slightest bit. "Stay here," she whispered, and Whitney wasn't going to argue.

"I have some water bottles in the trunk. I'll go get them," Kim offered, stepping back to give the pair their privacy.

Whitney exhaled, collapsing on the pavement. "Do you know what we used to do as kids when we were worried?" she asked, understanding Daisy wouldn't respond. If Daisy required quiet in times of stress, Whitney needed a distraction.

"My momma asked us to tell her about a book we read that we really loved. If you don't mind, I'm going to tell you all about that book you let me borrow. The one with the sea captain?" She playfully nudged Daisy, but the other woman was catatonic.

Whitney licked her lips, frowning when she tasted soot. "Well, the story starts with a woman on the run from an arranged marriage. Daisy, when I say she was a runaway bride, I mean she was *running*." Whitney regaled with details of the story, glossing over parts that didn't seem entertaining.

The last time she remembered doing this with Winnie after their grandfather had passed away. She'd recently read the *Twilight* series and bored Winnie to death with details of sparkling vampires, long-haired werewolves, and the scenery of the Pacific Northwest. At the time Winnie rolled her eyes and shushed her, but by the time they'd left the hospital, her sister had ordered the entire series from their local library.

"And," Whitney continued, "you should read the sex scenes. I thought I would get motion sickness reading about all these waves and ship voyages, but, oh boy, the author certainly distracted from the open seas."

Daisy's head tipped slightly, her eyes meeting Whitney's. "Is that the one where they make love in the galley kitchen?"

"Yes, ma'am, and practically ruin dinner for the whole crew." Both women chuckled at that, the tension of the moment broken by laughter.

"Well, I don't know what you're laughing about, but it's good to see." Kim handed each woman a water bottle.

Daisy took the proffered bottle and chugged it like she hadn't had water in years. "Thanks, sugar. We were discussing our book club book." She took Whitney's hand and squeezed.

"Oh, did you get to the hot kitchen sex scene?" Kim asked, eyes dancing with mischief.

"Yes, we did, and I was telling Daisy how …" But Whitney's literary recap had to wait. Javi sprinted toward them, helmet in hand and an anxious expression on his handsome face.

"Ms. Daisy, Whitney!"

"Javier!" Daisy yelled, flapping her hands overhead and using his given name.

Javi caught up to them, panting like he'd run a mile … or ran from a burning warehouse. "They're out," he bent over, resting his hands on his knees. "Chief and Trevor are out. They're getting checked out for smoke inhalation."

Daisy's hand flew to her heart, knees buckling, she leaned against Whitney for support. "Thank the Lord," she said, shoulders heaving as she caught her breath.

"Where are they?" Whitney asked, tears prickling her eyes. The reality that they were okay hadn't sunk in, and she wasn't sure when it would. The shock provided a quicksand sensation muffling everything around her. She wanted to run to Trevor, pull him close and tell him it would be all right.

Javi pushed himself to standing, shoulders slumping with fatigue and adrenaline. "They're waiting for the medics to arrive. Smithy was taken first." Javi's voice cracked at the mention of his friend, and Daisy went into action.

Springing free from Whitney's hold, she pulled Javi to her chest, cradling his head. "He'll be okay. Malcolm is a strong man." Although Whitney barely knew the man, it was clear he was a close with the family. Daisy's relief clouded over into worry as she stroked Javi's sweaty hair.

"I should have been there for him," Javi sobbed.

"You were, Javi. You were. He's on his way to get help. Now catch your breath so we can get you checked out." The sole focus of helping someone pulled Daisy from her funk—she was officially a momma bear on a mission. "Do you want some water?"

Javi nodded dumbly, and Kim pressed one of their forgotten bottles into his hand. Whitney stood helplessly watching everyone recover from the lunacy of the moment. While Kim and Daisy knew people, she still felt like an outsider. There was no way for her to understand the years of connection, of love on display in that moment.

Reflecting back to her life in Savannah, she couldn't think of anyone—save her sister—who would comfort and nurture her in a time of need. Hell, she'd had her time of need when Baxter left, and the few friends she had offered nothing more than a handful of awkward platitudes over text. When work took Winnie away, freaking Xena was the only one there to watch her eat peanut cups. *That notion was even more depressing ...*

Just as Whitney spun herself into a tizzy, her cell phone rang in her purse. Dumbly, she wondered if Trevor was trying to call her. With shaking hands, she answered. "Hello?" A sob burst through the line, nearly knocking Whitney to the ground again. "Win?"

"Whit, can you hear me?" Winnie's muffled voice was all wrong. Gone was her sure, confident sister, replaced with a weeping shell of herself. "I…" She hiccupped, and Whitney heard her blow her nose.

Without thinking, she stepped away from the crowd on boneless legs. "What is going on? Start at the beginning."

"It all fell apart," Winnie sobbed, sniffling so loudly Whitney had to pull the phone back.

"Win, you need to take a deep breath, because I can't understand you. What fell apart?" Whitney clutched the phone in her right hand, her left tugging on the end of her ponytail. The world didn't make sense if Winnie was upset, and right now Whitney needed her poised big sister.

"Everything, the merger was a total bust. The managing partners are so angry, and they're blaming me, because I …" She paused her rant to cough and blow her nose, and Whitney's heart broke. Her career, and this merger project in particular, had taken her focus for nearly two years. While Whitney had been falling in love with Baxter, Winnie had been pulling fifteen-hour days at the firm.

"Honey, they aren't blaming you. You've been working yourself stupid. I've seen it first-hand."

Winnie scoffed. "I had been, except for recently." Her tone had gone from distraught to self-loathing, and Whitney wasn't sure which she liked least.

"What happened? You've been on the road, all you've been doing is work."

"No, Whit, I haven't." The other line was silent, and Whitney waited out her sister. "I've been distracted, since meeting Mari."

Whitney stalked to Kim's car, leaning against the trunk. Despite the cooling temperatures, her skin burned with the discomfort of the situation, eyes watering from the smoke. "Okay, that's normal when you meet someone new."

"Not for me!" Winnie shrieked into the phone. "I never put my heart before my career, and look what it got me! The managing partners are talking about making an example out of the team members who didn't follow through. I could lose my chance at being a full partner because I went on a couple dates." She muttered some choice profanities. "I can't believe I did this. It's so unlike me."

Whitney never understood the cut-throat world of the legal professional, but she knew her sister. When their peers were starting families and getting married, Winnie was pulling all-nighters and making deals. "You're entitled to a personal life," she urged, hoping in time her sister could see reason. Her head dipped, Whitney didn't hear Daisy's footsteps approaching until the older woman was at her side. She tentatively reached out and tapped her shoulder, causing Whitney to yelp and nearly drop her phone. "Oh my Lord, you scared me," Whitney gasped, clutching her hand to her chest.

"I'm sorry, sugar," Daisy apologized while Winnie asked, "Who are you talking to?"

Whitney held up a finger to Daisy and mouthed an apology. "I'm out with Daisy and Kim, there was a fire."

Winnie didn't reply with the concern and compassion Whitney expected, and it grated on her.

"Oh, okay."

She waited, hoping her sister would ask about Trevor, ask why she was at the scene of a fire. Instead she got the last response she anticipated.

"Can you please come home?" Winnie's voice was small, as meek as when she was a girl.

Whitney's heart clenched. "What? Now?"

"I mean, I'll be back at the apartment tomorrow. I'm still at the hotel. I need you, Whit. I can't go back home and deal with this alone."

Home. That word used to mean Savannah, but not since she'd arrived in Pinegrove. Home was in Trevor's arms, sharing a meal and laughing while picking out mundane items at the drugstore. Home was in Daisy's warm kitchen, gushing over their latest romance novel. Home was also her job at Kim's Creations, where Whitney felt the first pull to come to work since college. Savannah was no longer home, despite her closest family living there.

"Win, listen. Take the night to have a drink and cry it out in the hotel. I can't get back to Savannah right now. There's too much going on. Give me a couple days, and I'll ..." Explanation dying on her lips, Whitney wasn't ready to commit to anything or anyone.

"What?" Winnie hiccuped, disbelief dripping from her tone. "You're not coming home?"

"I'll call you soon, okay? Love you." And with that, Whitney disconnected, swallowing down the uneasy sensation crawling up her throat.

"Is everything okay?" Daisy asked, patting Whitney's shoulder.

Whitney snuffled. "Shouldn't I be the one asking you that?" She shoved her phone back into her purse with trembling hands, her sister's words ricocheting through her skull. *Come home.*

"I was looking for you. Trevor and Paul are going to be fine, they're over with the EMTs getting looked at. Unfortunately, Malcolm suffered some injuries and he's on his way to the hospital. They think he'll recover, but he's pretty banged up."

"Oh, that's great news. Except for poor Malcolm."

Daisy reached out, latching onto Whitney's hand and pulling her back to the scene. "Trevor's right over here. I'm sure he's dying to see you."

The pair strode through the crowd, stopping briefly to share the news with Kim. "You go find your men. I'll be in the car where the AC is plentiful." She flapped a paper fan in front of her face and sighed. "Menopause is a real bitch."

Whitney bit back a laugh and followed Daisy to a cluster of ambulances. As they approached, she spotted Paul sitting on the tailgate, legs dangling. He had an oxygen mask over his mouth, his eyes dark and exhausted. "Paul, sugar!" Daisy dropped Whitney's hand and sprinted over to him. As soon as she reached him, he pulled her close, knocking his mask to the ground.

The scene made Whitney's heart swell, relaxing her as

she looked for Trevor. A lot had transpired in the last two days, but she knew she wanted to be by his side. She would have time to figure out how to support her sister, but right now she needed to set eyes on a certain fireman.

Footsteps faltering, Whitney headed toward the cluster of ambulances. "Trevor?" she called out over the din. Skin vibrating, she buzzed with nervous energy as she swayed through the crowd. At first she thought she found him, sitting on a gurney and hunched forward. Clad in his gear, his form seemed hulking in the hazy night.

"Trev..." but his name evaporated from her lips when she realized he wasn't alone. Whitney would recognize that lithe blonde anywhere—Virginia.

Virginia leaned over Trevor, eyes darting all around them as if she'd get caught where she wasn't meant to be. Her red lips were moving a mile a minute, but Whitney couldn't hear what she said. Slowly, Trevor's head bobbed and swayed, his arm reaching out to Virginia's arm to steady himself.

Whitney blinked, expecting the scene before her to change, to go back to something that made sense. But the longer she stood there, dumbfounded, the more she understood she'd gotten it all wrong. In his time of need, Trevor chose to lean on his ex. He wasn't looking for her, he was with Virginia.

History was repeating itself; suddenly it all came swooping back ...

Baxter proposing to a faceless blonde, the scratchy fabric of her Savannah Banana hat digging into her skin as she watched him move on—in spectacular fashion.

Weeks alone on Winnie's couch, cookie dough stuck in her hair while Xena whined for scraps.

That feeling that she didn't know the man in her life, wasn't worthy of someone's love.

The sensations threatened to suffocate Whitney, her throat already closing, her heart crumbling to dust.

Suddenly, a strangled sound, much like livestock being

slaughtered on a farm, cut through the din of the scene. It was only when she saw all eyes on her that Whitney realized she'd been the one making the horrid noise. She clamped a hand over her mouth as the tears fell.

Virginia looked over, seemingly disinterested in the audience. Trevor's eyes grew from above his oxygen mask, and he struggled to disentangle himself from Virginia. Whitney stumbled back, bumping into Javi.

"Easy, Whitney, you okay?"

"Excuse me," she muttered, pushing free from his hold as she bolted toward Kim and her car.

Behind her, she heard Javi's confused voice calling out for her and a scratchy grunt that likely belonged to Trevor. It didn't matter who it was or what they had to say, because Whitney needed to get away from here.

And the sooner, the better.

CHAPTER EIGHTEEN

Trevor had been in fires before, this wasn't anything new. He'd had walls and ceilings collapse on him countless times, but he always trusted his training. If he relied on his academy drills and dozens of continuing education sessions, he would be all right.

The last thing Trevor remembered as they sped back to the station from their impromptu lunch was the chief instructing their squads on what parts of the scene to cover. He'd paired up with Javi, and everything had been fine. They followed procedure, communicated with the team, and at first it didn't seem like anything beyond a standard fire. Then a chunk of the roof collapsed and Smithy and Maxwell were trapped. Chief, Javi, and Trevor had gone inside and managed to pull out their teammates before the situation got any worse.

The only problem? He and the chief both suffered helmet malfunctions and took in more smoke than air. Were he more lucid, he'd blame Hastings for ordering the cheaper helmets to cover for his budgeting blunders, but he didn't have the energy for that now. In that moment he needed oxygen, some water, and most importantly Whitney by his side.

As he lay on the gurney, oxygen mask latched in place, he blinked up at the night sky and said a prayer that everything would work out. His throat burned from the smoke, but he knew it would heal with time. He, and the squad, were all lucky to be alive.

Lost in his musings, and the adrenaline crash, he closed his eyes and focused on inhaling and exhaling. His body ached from head to toe, his brain reeling. Trevor had been through this song and dance before, and knew he wouldn't get discharged by the EMTs unless he followed orders. Being a stickler for the rules, he'd play ball.

As he waited for his turn with the medics, the clacking of heels on asphalt alerted him to a visitor. Hoping to see a shock of dark curls, he was crestfallen when he saw Virginia sashay to his side. Despite every cell of his body burning with fatigue, he managed to inch away as far as the gurney allowed.

"Trevor," Virginia said his name in greeting, her hand raising barely above her waist.

Opening his mouth to respond, Trevor succumbed to a coughing fit. Virginia didn't offer assistance. Her blue gaze flitted around them while he caught his breath, finally asking the question that brought her to him.

"Have you seen Scott?" She craned her neck to look beyond the grouping of EMTs and onlookers, not seeming to find answers in the crowd. Trevor shook his head, not giving a fig where his superior was. "It's odd," she continued, oblivious to Trevor's complete disinterest, "no one has seen him tonight."

Trevor gingerly tugged his oxygen mask down, wincing at the blast of warm air on his lips. "Haven't seen him," he croaked out before another coughing fit took hold. He didn't care about any of this, he just wanted to see Whitney.

Virginia nodded, helping him slide the mask back in place. "Thanks, Trevor. I hope you feel better soon."

Just as she turned to leave, Trevor heard a horrid, animalistic sound cut through the ruckus. His head swiveled and he found Whitney, gray eyes brimming with tears, backing away like she was on fire.

Trevor lurched, his body revolting. "Mmoo," he said, struggling to say no through his shredded vocal cords. "Vitmmee," he said, hoping she could figure out he was trying to say Whitney. This was all wrong.

Perhaps he'd died in that fire and he'd woken up in hell?

Trevor shrugged away from Virginia, his eyes locked with Whitney's. Her gray gaze was misty, a hand pressed against her mouth. He yanked the mask from his face, gasping as the cooling air hit his lips. "Wttnee!" he tried to shout, but it came out as a sad whimper.

Turning on her heel, Whitney sprinted away from him, pushing through throngs of people until she was out of sight. Javi joined him, a sour expression on his face that had nothing to do with the fire.

"Sorry, Trev. I tried to stop her."

Trevor banged his hand on the railing of his cot until an EMT strode over. Her eyes were tired yet focused as she got to work. "Mr. Mays, please keep that oxygen mask on until we can get a reading of your saturation levels."

Virginia turned to Javi, and asked, "Have you seen Scott?"

Javi shook his head, his attention on Trevor. "Nah, not all night actually."

Satisfied she wouldn't find answers with Trevor and Javi, Virginia turned to leave, just as a series of flashbulbs popped around them. The EMT shouted over her shoulder for privacy as the press closed in.

"Please, Lieutenant, a comment on the fire!" one of the reporters shouted, earning a middle finger from Javi.

"Give the man some space, you vultures!" Javi's outburst had the desired effect and the reporters took a few paces back. "I'll go see if I can find Whitney," Javi offered, following Virginia to the other side of the scene.

Trevor squeezed his eyes shut, simultaneously exhausted and defeated. This feeling of helplessness was getting old, and he hated the idea that Whitney was suffering because of a misunderstanding. Javi would find her, and then Trevor could explain nothing was going on with Virginia.

An hour later, Trevor and the chief were finally discharged by the EMTs. Both men suffered from smoke inhalation, but neither had serious injuries. Smithy had been taken to the hospital, and Trevor itched to see him.

Javi returned, out of breath from jogging around the area. Reading his mind, Javi shook his head and apologized. "I looked everywhere." Trevor's heart broke, and he knew he needed to find Whitney and make it right. The sooner the better.

"How you doing, sugar?" Daisy asked, cupping his face in her hands. They were soft and warm, and for a moment Trevor allowed himself to be a pampered son.

"I'm fine," he rasped, pulling back to rub his throat. "Exhausted."

Daisy pursed her lips. "I'm sure you are. We'll get you home, and Whitney and I will take good care of you."

Trevor perked right up at that. "Whitney's still at the house?"

Raising an eyebrow, Daisy asked, "I assume. Why wouldn't she be?"

Javi snorted, earning everyone's attention. "Why do I need to be the bearer of bad news?"

Chief shuffled over, putting his weight on the gurney Trevor had vacated. "Because you're the only one of us who can speak without being in agony."

Wincing, Javi rallied. "Sorry, Chief." He faced Daisy and explained. "Well, um. Whitney kind of ran out of here when she saw Trevor with Virginia."

Trevor watched in horror as his mother's sweet, concerned expression melted into a sullen, angry one. "I'm sorry, sugar. Did you just tell me that that she-devil was here, with my son?" Now her ire was focused on Trevor, and he shrunk back. "Someone explain before we need

EMTs for another reason." She thrust her hands on her hips, and Javi gulped.

Rubbing the back of his head, Javi barely met Daisy's eyes. "You see, she couldn't find Hastings and was asking around. Whitney came up when Virginia was with Trevor, and let's just say it didn't look good."

Daisy sucked on her teeth. "We need to find Whitney. Poor girl. I don't know what else is going on with her, but she was on a pretty heated phone call when I found her an hour ago."

Trevor stepped forward, reaching his hand out. "Keys," he ordered to Javi, who hooted in his face.

"Yeah right, I don't think so." Javi patted his pocket, the muffled jangle of his keys sounding like sad windchimes. "EMTs said you can't drive for a few days, and I'm not letting you near my truck. I'll drive y'all back to Ms. Daisy's."

"Now," Trevor barked, coughing as he shuffled to the truck.

Fortunately it only took ten minutes with Javi behind the wheel to get back to the house. Whitney's car was missing from the driveway, and Trevor could hardly swallow down the bile rising up his throat.

As if reading his mind, Daisy sprinted ahead, muttering, "Oh no." She fumbled with her keys before finally pushing through the front door. She turned on a light and called out into the empty house, "Whitney! Sugar, we're back!"

Gus sauntered out from the kitchen, woofing at the invasion. Trevor headed for the kitchen and nearly fell to his knees when he saw the note on the table. "In here," his voice grated, picking up the note with shaking fingers.

Daisy,

I want to thank you for your hospitality. You made me feel welcome in your home, and you have no idea how much that meant to me.

I hope you understand, but I won't be staying here anymore. I think it's best for everyone. Please take care of Paul and Gus.

Love, Whitney

P.S. please don't try to interfere with Trevor. He has every right to follow his heart, and I truly hope he and Virginia will be happy. XO

Trevor let the note flutter to the floor as he dashed to the sink and retched, throwing up the sad remains of his diner lunch.

Daisy gasped behind him, reading the note for herself. She joined him at the sink, rubbing comforting circles on his back. "You'll get her back," she assured him, but Trevor wasn't feeling very hopeful.

Much like his singed vocal cords, his heart was broken, and he didn't know how to piece it back together. Whitney was gone, and he didn't blame her.

CHAPTER NINETEEN

"Kim, this is really too much," Whitney said, clutching a throw pillow to her chest. She was seated on the loveseat in her boss's living room, surrounded by cushions and a surly cat that reminded her too much of Xena.

The cat eyed her warily before dashing under the coffee table with a growl. "Hush up," Kim spat, setting down a plate of cookies and another pot of tea.

Whitney bit her lip. "Sorry," she muttered.

"Not you, honey. I was speaking to Sherlock. Damn cat has been a thorn in my side since the Carter administration."

Whitney couldn't help herself, she burst out laughing. "Kim, there's no way Sherlock is that old."

Kim flapped a hand in the air. "I know that, but he's been a little jackass since Watson passed. I miss that dog too, but that doesn't give Sherlock the right to be rude." Kim plated a few cookies and handed it to Whitney. She dropped a few cubes of sugar into a cup of tea, and slid it closer. "Now, have a snack. It'll help calm your nerves."

Ever the stress eater, Whitney greedily shoved a cookie in her mouth. Through the crumbs, she said, "I don't know if I feel very calm."

Kim tutted and raised her index finger. "But you have

stopped crying, and that's a win."

Whitney slunk back into the loveseat, swallowing her cookie and praying the tears didn't come back. As soon as she'd made it to Kim's car, she'd burst into a fit of tears that could have filled the Mississippi River Delta. Kim hadn't asked questions, simply ushered Whitney into the car and drove her back to Daisy's.

Unable to stay in that house another second, Whitney had hastily packed her suitcase, scrawled a note Daisy, and tried to drive out of town. Kim wasn't having it.

"I hate to state the obvious, honey," Kim had said, blocking Whitney from getting behind the wheel, "but you're in no state to drive anywhere." She hesitated, and added, "Unless you're following me to my place. It's not too far."

Whitney shook her head. "You're right, it's not safe." She squeezed the keys in her hand, unsure what to even do.

"You'll stay at my place tonight. We can figure out the rest later."

Whitney had sniffed, wiping her nose with the hem of her shirt. "Thank you, Kim."

Kim had poked her in the sternum. "It's the least I can do for my favorite employee."

Whitney stated the obvious. "I'm your only employee."

"Semantics. Let's get you to my place. Things will look better in the morning."

And that's how Whitney wound up on another person's couch, with a plateful of cookies resting on her belly and the angriest cat—since Xena—pawing at her feet for scraps. "Sherlock, for the love of all that's holy," Kim chastised the feline, knocking him off Whitney's legs, "leave poor Whitney alone."

Kim brought out a stack of blankets and pillows. She placed the bedding next to Whitney and began collecting their dishes. "Let me help," Whitney offered, standing and knocking more cushions onto the floor.

"No, no, I've got it. You get some rest. Tomorrow is a

big day at the shop, thanks to you." Kim turned off some of the lights, careful to leave the one in the hallway on. "I want to thank you, Whitney."

Whitney blinked. "For what? I should be thanking you."

Kim waved her off and paused her exit. "Listen, honey, I've been running that shop for over ten years, since I lost my husband. I take pride in it, sure, but I know I've let things slip. Having you here, learning about TickyTack and the Book of Faces has brought the store into the twenty-first century."

Whitney schooled her features. "I assure you, Kim, social media isn't the same as web development. Anyone can do it."

With a huff, Kim stamped her foot. "Now there you go doing that again. Don't sell yourself short, Whitney. You're bright, smart, motivated, and just about the nicest person to walk into Pinegrove. You've made so many people happy with your skills. I won't have you sleeping under my roof and treating yourself that way. I won't stand for it."

"Oh," was all Whitney could muster as a reply.

"Oh, indeed. Now get some shut-eye. We open at nine o'clock." With that, she turned on her heel and headed to her bedroom, the door closing behind her with a snick.

Whitney fell back onto the couch, her heart hammering. Kim was right, and she hadn't realized it until the truth was right in front of her. She had been doing good work, and she had been making people happy.

And she couldn't deny that the customers had responded to her changes at the shop. Not only were sales up, but the visitors that left with bags all had a smile on their face. They felt beautiful, they felt cared for. Whitney was proud that she'd made an impact.

Over the years, she'd always tried to make herself smaller. Not merely just with her weight, but in general. Winnie was the star of the family, and Whitney was fine letting her shine. Yet now, the time had come for her luster to show.

There was no use denying how much Trevor had broken her heart, falling back into Virginia's arms, but she couldn't deny it had made her stronger. She was in Pinegrove for more than a man, and that notion made her smile.

Just as she nestled back under the covers and prepared for sleep, her cell phone buzzed. She pawed around and found the infernal device, seeing dozens of messages from Daisy and her sister. Unable to think about the Mays clan, she closed the notifications and dialed Winnie, keeping her voice low.

"Win?"

"There you are! Geez, Whit. I'm in my hour of need and you're MIA." Winnie sounded stronger, more like herself. Although Whitney knew her sister, it could be bluster after a glass of wine, or she was quickly going through the stages of grief.

"Sorry, it's been … a little hectic," Whitney said, pinching the bridge of her nose.

Winnie snorted. "I'd say! I call you to tell you my life is over, and you hang up on me and disappear for hours. Are you on the road?"

Stifling a sigh, Whitney took a second to collect her thoughts. Standing up to her sister was never easy, but especially not when emotions were high. "No, I told you. I'm not leaving tonight."

"That's probably a good idea. You don't want to drive so late, and I won't get back until the morning. What time are you arriving tomorrow?"

"I'm not coming back tomorrow, Win. I'm staying in Pinegrove a little while longer."

The silence through the other line was deafening, and Whitney braced for impact. "You're not coming home so you can have a booty call? This is all for a man?" Winnie was incredulous. "Whit, I need you at home. My life is falling apart, you can have a fling anytime."

Now it was Whitney's turn to be dubious. "I can have a fling anytime? First of all, that's not true. Second, I have a job here."

Winnie sniffed. "At a retail shop. Come. Home." The last two words were a clipped order from her older sister. "I need you."

"What about what I need? Hmm? You haven't asked me how I am, or what happened, or how I'm liking my job. Every time we've talked since I got to Pinegrove, you've been dismissive of my feelings. Winnie, I love working at Kim's Creations. I'm making a difference, I'm making friends."

"Sounds like you're justifying sticking around for another man. Please don't make this fireman the next Baxter. You need to put yourself first, Whit."

Whitney was done being quiet, and she only prayed Kim slept with earplugs. "Winnie, I am putting myself first. I want to help Kim with the festival sales. I want to stay and see the fireworks with my new friends. And not that you care, but I'm not even with my fireman anymore. I'm doing this for me. I'm sorry you're having a tough time, but I know you do excellent work at the firm. Of course this is upsetting, but you'll figure it out." She paused her rant long enough to pull in a lungful of air. "I will come back for you, Win. Just not tomorrow. Instead of running away from my problems, I'd like to stay and make a difference. I will call and check in, but you need to give me space. I love you."

She didn't bother waiting for a response and ended the call. Winnie would be furious with her, she had no doubt, yet for the first time in their adult lives, Whitney didn't care. She was doing what was right for *her* for once, and regardless of where that took her, she was fine with the consequences.

Before she could turn off the phone, she saw a slew of new messages from Trevor.

Please, let me explain.

Whitney, call me?

It's not what you think.

"It never is." She sighed, turning off her phone and dropping it to the coffee table with a sad, lonely thud.

It might not be fair to Trevor, but she wasn't in the mood for excuses and lame explanations. Once again, she'd been passed over for a pretty blonde with high cheekbones and a waist the circumference of a dinner plate. She didn't need a man to prove her worth, and she certainly was finished shedding tears for someone who didn't want her or treat her the way she deserved.

Naturally, as soon as she swore off the entire male population, Sherlock returned. The tabby cat climbed up onto the couch and she froze. She wasn't in the headspace for another moody cat, but the feline surprised her. He pawed at her belly a moment before curling up and purring happily. Whitney tentatively rubbed his head, and he wiggled closer, soaking up her affection.

"You're not so bad, are you?" she cooed, letting her fingers glide through his soft fur.

Letting her eyes fall shut, Whitney listened to the ticking of the clock on the wall and Kim's refrigerator kicking on. These unfamiliar sounds helped lull her to sleep, but they also reminded her that she wanted her own space.

Grown women didn't crash on stranger's couches, or sleep in their sister's living rooms. It was pointless comparing herself to other people, but Whitney knew one thing. Regardless of whether she stayed in Pinegrove or Savannah, she'd find herself a home of her own. She was in charge of her own life. The time for wallowing was over.

Tomorrow she would go to the shop and sell out their new inventory. She would stand tall and not be angry at Trevor for leading her on. They'd had a magical time together, but she wouldn't let him—or any other man— break her. She'd follow the lead of the most iconic Southern Belle. Just like Scarlett O'Hara, she'd take comfort knowing that tomorrow was another day.

CHAPTER TWENTY

Trevor woke after a fitful night of sleep in his childhood bed. Legs hanging off the side, neck at an awkward angle, he struggled to sit up. His head ached and his mouth tasted of soot. Reaching for his water glass, he chugged it so fast it started a coughing fit. He doubled over as he hacked and gagged, throat burning.

Yet for all the physical pain he suffered, nothing compared to losing Whitney. His phone remained free of messages, and the open guestroom door confirmed she hadn't returned. When he'd finally found a phone charger, he was devasted to see nothing from Whitney. Heck, he would have welcomed a *Go to Hell* message over silence.

Trevor went to the bathroom and took a long, hot shower. The steam did little to soothe his throat, but he didn't care. He slid on his gym shorts and a Pinegrove FD T-shirt, then joined his mother in the kitchen.

Well, his mother and Paul.

"Morning, son," Paul said, clad in his pajamas. The sight would usually have shocked Trevor, but instead it relaxed him. At least someone in this family found love.

Despite this, Trevor didn't miss how the chief hurriedly folded and hid the newspaper. He shuddered to think what the other man was hiding. He was too wrung out for more bad news.

Daisy flitted around the kitchen, flipping hotcakes and squeezing oranges for juice. "Good morning, sugar. You're looking better than I expected." She paused her juice making to pour him a cup of coffee. "Slow sips, remember? Sit down."

Paul pulled out a chair and patted the seat. "Best do as she says." He chuckled. "But seriously, how are you feeling?"

Trevor collapsed into his chair and rubbed at his throat. It was as raw as an undercooked hamburger, but it was also the least of his problems. He stared unblinking at the chair that had quickly become Whitney's. He missed seeing her smile over a plate of eggs, missed how she'd tease him over a slice of pie. Lord, he just missed her.

Vocal cords would heal, but he wasn't so sure about his heart.

"Fine," he mumbled, slurping from his coffee and burning his tongue. He truly could not win this morning.

Daisy plated the pancakes and placed the platter between her two firemen. "Eat up while they're hot." She handed a spatula to Paul, who loaded up Trevor's plate before his own.

"Here we go. Eat up, son. You heard the EMTs, we both need our strength." Paul chortled, causing a coughing fit that had Daisy by his side. She patted his back and thrust a glass of ice water into his hand.

The commotion caused the newspaper to fall onto the floor, splaying open to the front page. Trevor would gladly run into ten thousand burning buildings without his bunker gear to avoid seeing the image before him.

Splashed across the paper was a scene from last night. Trevor, half delirious and covered in soot, hunched over on the gurney. Next to him stood Virginia, leaning close to whisper in his ear. It had been when she'd inquired about Scott, but that wasn't what it looked like. The picture looked like a couple, sharing a moment after a horrific event. *Just great …*

Daisy snatched the paper from his hands, balling it up and tossing it into the trashcan. "You weren't supposed to see that," she ground out.

Paul winced as he collected himself. "It's my fault. As soon as I saw that, I should have burned it out back in the leaf pile."

Trevor laughed, but there wasn't an ounce of humor. "Don't worry about it. It's the cherry on this shit sundae." Flinching, he turned and apologized to his momma. "Sorry."

Daisy rolled her eyes. "I'll let the language at the breakfast table slide today."

"Thanks, Momma. Have you heard from Whitney?" he asked, unable to dig into his breakfast. Despite the fact his momma made the best hotcakes east of the Mississippi, he knew they'd taste like cardboard.

Daisy's smile slid away, and Trevor knew that was a bad sign. "Actually, I haven't. I tried calling her again this morning, but her phone went straight to voicemail."

Trevor ran his hands down his face and groaned, then immediately regretted it when it caused a coughing fit. "This is a nightmare. How can I find her? Do you think she's already back in Savannah?"

A rattling at the front door had Trevor's heart soaring, until Javi stuck his head inside. "Good morning!" he cheered, clapping the chief on the shoulder and pecking Daisy on the cheek. "Am I too late for breakfast?"

Daisy tittered. "Never, Javi. Take a seat, we're just digging in."

Javi pulled a napkin and tucked it into his collar, piercing a couple pancakes and dropping them onto his plate. "Mmm, I'm so glad. I could smell that bacon from the street."

The mention of bacon brought Gus shuffling back into the room. He settled at Javi's feet, eagerly awaiting a treat.

As soon as no one was looking, Javi tossed a slice to the hound, who scarfed it down in record time.

"What are we talking about? The crisis in the Middle East? The traffic caused by the fireworks festival?" He raised an eyebrow at Paul, who only shook his head.

"You never cease to amaze me, Ortiz." Paul nudged Javi with his elbow. "We were actually pondering the whereabouts of a certain curly-haired woman."

Through a mouthful of pancakes, Javi said, "She's at Kim's Creations."

Trevor nearly fell out of his chair. "She's still in town? How do you know that?"

Javi raised a shoulder. "Um, I saw her car outside of the shop? Call me Columbo."

"I've got to go talk to her," Trevor said, jumping to his feet and causing another round of coughing.

Daisy tutted and poured another glass of ice water. "Sit down," she ordered.

Trevor was annoyed. "But, Momma! I need to go see Whitney."

Daisy wasn't having it. "Sit. Down. If Whitney's at the shop, she's not leaving anytime soon. Why don't we all take a moment and come up with a plan?"

"I'm with Ms. Daisy," Javi chimed in, already snaking another three pancakes from the platter. "We need to see Smithy, too. I'm sure he's going crazy in the hospital."

A pang of guilt surged through Trevor at the notion his buddy was in need. How easily he forgot everyone else when Whitney was involved.

Unable to let the topic of Whitney go, Javi asked, "Did y'all see the *Pinegrove Herald* this morning?" He shot a look to Trevor. "You need to come ready to grovel, man. Whitney needs more than flowers this time."

Trevor covered his face and groaned, nearly choking on his own discomfort. "Why can't I do anything right with this woman?"

"You want some free advice?" Javi asked, earning him a

swat from Daisy.

"Javi, please don't take this the wrong way, but I think Trevor could use advice from someone with more experience with women."

Now Paul couldn't control himself. "Daisy, I um, don't mean to correct you in your own home," he said, turning to Javi. "And, Ortiz, I don't mean to call your dating history into question, but…"

"What Chief is trying to say is that you have *too much* experience with women," Trevor jibed, unable to hold back his smirk.

Javi was undeterred, happily chomping away on his breakfast. "Fine, fine. Be that way, I'm only trying to help."

"You want to help? Drive me over to the shop."

"All in good time, man. I think we need to see Smithy on the way."

Daisy poured juice for all three men and nodded her approval. "I think that's a good idea. I made the mistake of calling Jessie last night when Malcolm was admitted, and I think she's coming home."

Suddenly his love life was the last thing on his mind. "Jessie's coming home?"

Javi leaned forward. "For Smithy?" Daisy merely lifted a shoulder before topping off everyone's coffee.

Since Trevor had come around to his momma and the chief dating, he decided to spare himself the questions involving his sister's love life. It was painfully clear that Smithy still held a torch for Jessie, and judging from everyone's expressions in this kitchen, it was common knowledge.

"Does Smithy know?" Trevor asked.

Daisy shook her head. "Not that I'm aware of, but maybe the good news will lift his spirits? He's got a long recovery ahead of him, I'm afraid."

The room fell silent as everyone acknowledged Smithy was lucky to have gotten out with relatively minimal injuries.

"Let's eat and go visit Smithy. Then Ortiz can take you

to see Whitney. I'm sure the poor girl needs a grand ..."
Paul trailed off, flapping a hand in the air. He turned to
Daisy, and asked, "What do you call those things in your
romance books, honey?"

Daisy beamed. "Grand gestures. Let me help, sugar."
Sprinting from the kitchen, Daisy returned a moment later
with an armful of books. She dropped the stack in front of
her son, tapping the top book with her finger. "You can
start reading in the car, but these are some of Whitney's
favorites."

Javi reached out and took a book, randomly flipping
through until he found a spicy scene. "Woah! Ms. Daisy,
you've been holding out on us. This is hot!" Javi fanned
himself with the book, earning a shoulder punch from
Trevor.

"Give me five minutes to change, then we can head out."

Shooing away Paul's attempts at tidying up, Daisy
whistled for Gus to go outside. "Wheels up in five, y'all! It's
time for a happily ever after!"

Trevor tried not to get car sick on the drive to the
hospital. He paged through book after book, desperate to
find something he could do to make an impression on
Whitney. He'd already brought her flowers and bared his
soul before, sharing parts of himself that hadn't been seen
outside his therapist's office. Yet, he knew he needed to do
more.

Javi hit a bump in the road, and the stack of books slid
from Trevor's lap. "Geez, man, careful. It's like I'm
cramming for a final exam over here."

Muttering some choice profanities, Javi took the next
turn a little faster than necessary. "You need to make up
your mind, Trev. Am I going fast or slow?" He shot a
warning glance at Trevor, who had the decency to look
embarrassed. His buddy was right. Not two minutes ago he
begged Javi to break the speed limit by double digits.

"Sorry," he muttered, retrieving one of the books by Darla Champaign. Wasn't this one of the ones his mother and Whitney were yapping about? He opened the book and flipped to the back, hoping it would have bold print reading *DO THIS TO FIX YOUR RELATIONSHIP, MEATHEAD.*

Unfortunately for Trevor, all he saw was a sex scene far wilder than anything he'd expected. Snapping the book shut, he tossed it in the backseat like it was on fire. "I did not need to see that." He cringed, earning a raised eyebrow from Javi.

"Do I want to know?"

Trevor pressed the heels of his hands into his eyes. "Let's just say, I was happier before I knew Momma read that smut."

Without taking his eyes off the road, Javi reached back and snagged the book, tossing it into the compartment on the door. "I'll borrow that one." When Trevor scoffed, he lifted an eyebrow. "I can do research, too."

"Brother, given your track record, I have a feeling you could write that stuff." Trevor laughed for the first time all morning. It felt good, until the racking cough returned with a vengeance.

Javi gestured to the glove box. "I've got some lozenges in there. Help yourself."

"Thanks," Trevor said, grabbing a handful and popping two in his mouth. They finally reached the hospital parking lot, and Javi parked near the entrance. For a moment, neither man got out of the car. His plan to woo Whitney back was temporarily forgotten as Trevor prepared to see his friend.

Smithy was a tough guy, but he was also a marshmallow. He was the first one to help those in need, and that extended far beyond his work at the station. Trevor hated knowing someone so nice could be in so much pain. Despite not wanting to get involved in his sister's love life, he was relieved to know Jessie was coming home. Smithy needed something to look forward to.

Javi let out a shuddering breath, his hands still gripping the steering wheel. "He's gonna be okay, right?"

His question wasn't directed at Trevor, and he was glad—he didn't have an answer. All reports from the chief made it sound like he'd make a full recovery, but it still hurt to see a brother in arms laid up from the job.

Trevor ran his hands through his hair, tugging on the roots as he caught his breath. "Smithy's strong. He'll be fine."

"You're right," Javi quickly agreed, unlocking his truck and hopping out before Trevor had a chance to unbuckle. He fished his phone out of his pocket, scrolling through his texts. "Looks like Smithy is in room 212."

Trevor led the way to the nurse's station where they signed in and got visitors badges. He could tell Javi was nervous, because the nurse was a total smoke show and the other man didn't even blink. If this was yesterday, he'd already have her number and their first date on the books.

When they arrived at Smithy's room, Paul and Daisy were already inside with a few of the others from the station. Maxwell sat in a chair with her toddler Juniper in her lap. She had some bandages over the scrapes and minor burns she'd received, but compared to Smithy she was unharmed.

"Hey," Smithy said, voice low and hoarse. "I was wondering when y'all would get here." His raspy tenor broke another part of Trevor's heart. Gone was the jovial marshmallow, in its place was a husk of the man. His smile was forced, partially hidden behind a gauze strip on his cheek.

One of Smithy's legs was in a type of hammock, hanging from an apparatus in the ceiling. His left arm was in an air cast, secured to his side with a scary-looking plastic brace. Javi closed the distance, kneeling down to give his friend an awkward hug, keeping mindful of all the barriers between them. "Of course, Smithy. Nowhere else we'd rather be."

Trevor waved awkwardly before giving Smithy's good

hand a fist bump. "How are you feeling?" He immediately grimaced. "I mean, I'm guessing like shit."

Smithy chuckled, then started coughing. Between the whole crew, none of them currently had a working set of lungs. "Listen to us," Maxwell said with a sigh. She moved her toddler over to her other side and stood, offering her chair to Daisy.

"Sugar, take that seat. You've got this one to carry." Daisy stooped down and tickled Juniper's belly. She giggled and wiggled until Maxwell gave up and put her down.

"No running around, remember what Mommy said?"

Juniper nodded solemnly, wrapping her arms around Maxwell's leg. "Stay with Mommy," she said in a tiny voice.

Clearly he wasn't the only one affected by the toddler's presence, as both Paul and Daisy were on their knees talking to her and offering her money for the vending machine.

Javi nudged Trevor with his elbow, then gestured at the scene. "You better hope you can patch things up with Whitney, because it looks like Ms. Daisy is ready for grandbabies."

Daisy didn't bother looking up from her spot on the floor. "Pfft, please, sugar. I've been ready since Trevor graduated from the academy."

The group fell into discussion of random topics, anything to keep Smithy's spirits up. "When do your folks arrive?" Chief asked, leaning against the wall.

"Tomorrow—they're flying in from Tennessee." Smithy, an only child, wouldn't be able to keep his parents away if he tried. "Guess I'll have to get used to more visitors," he mumbled, resting his head back on his pillows.

Daisy cleared her throat. "Speaking of other visitors. I spoke with Jessie, and she's coming back for a visit by the end of the week."

That news got Smithy's attention, and he nearly catapulted off the bed, beeps and blips erupting from the machines surrounding him. "JJ's coming home?" His eyes shone with excitement, and Trevor could relate to that feeling. When someone had your heart, it was impossible not to want to be near them, not to love them.

Love? Did he love Whitney already? The ache in his ribcage told him he did, but he knew it was too soon to utter those three little words. It'd barely been two weeks since she stumbled into his life, but Trevor had gone full caveman, needing to stake his claim.

They spent an hour with Smithy until his eyes grew heavy and the nurse shooed everyone out so he could rest. On their way out of the hospital, Trevor stopped by the gift shop and bought the last bouquet of roses they had. Snatching a box of chocolates, he tossed a stack of bills on the counter and told the bored clerk to keep the change.

"Geez, man. I thought you weren't doing flowers again," Javi teased.

Trevor scoffed. "It can't possibly hurt."

Javi scanned around the giftshop, hands on his hips. "I'll meet you at the truck in a minute," he said, not giving Trevor his full attention.

Already antsy to see Whitney, Trevor simply shrugged and headed to the parking lot, his grip on the flowers nearly crushing the stems.

Less than five minutes later, Javi arrived with a bundle of balloons and a shit-eating grin. "What the heck is this?"

Javi clapped him on the back, still grinning. "It's call a grand gesture, so I improvised." Opening the back seat, he carefully shoved the balloons inside. "C'mon. Let's go get your girl."

On shaking legs, he slid back into the truck and prayed that he'd come up with the perfect thing to say by the time they arrived. Not only did he need to set the record straight about Virginia, but he needed to convince Whitney to stay.

Pinegrove, and his life, would lose their sparkle if Whitney went back to Savannah. He'd recovered from his broken engagement, but he didn't think he could recover from this.

CHAPTER TWENTY-ONE

As she expected, Whitney had slept fitfully all night. Sherlock had been her shadow, nestling against her while she attempted sleep. Between her sister and Trevor, her heart was in pieces and her mind raced in a million directions. By the time dawn arrived, sunrays cut through the curtains and alerted her to the new day.

The other thing that alerted her to the day was Kim's appearance with a cup of tea and a plate of biscuits and honey. "Here we go," she said, laying her breakfast on the coffee table. "It ain't much, but it'll get you going." Kim was already dressed for work in a pair of peach slacks and a white sleeveless blouse. A pair of orange reading glasses were perched on top of her head, ready for a day at the cash register.

Whitney flung her legs over the side of the couch, knocking poor Sherlock to the floor. He hissed and darted down the hallway. "Thanks so much," she said, covering a yawn. Her hair was stuck to her face, but she wasn't too concerned with her appearance.

"Did you manage to sleep at all, honey?" Kim asked, already frowning at the dark smudges under Whitney's eyes.

"A little," she lied, not seeing the point in wallowing

more than she already was. What was a lack of sleep when her sister was mad at her and the man of her dreams had moved on? "What time did you want to leave? I just want to steal a quick shower."

Kim sat on the recliner and flapped her hand. "Bathroom is all yours. I'm ready whenever you're are, but no rush."

Whitney took her time in the shower, letting the stream of hot water hide her tears. In the light of day, she was still eager to help Kim at the shop. Not only was she not ready to see her sister and fall back into her old life, but she needed closure with Trevor. She had no idea what that would entail, but she needed a proper goodbye. Once she released the ghosts of her dating past, Whitney was convinced she could start over ... wherever that was.

Dressed with her hair up and enough makeup to cover her lack of sleep, Whitney was as ready as she could be for her day. "Ready to go?" she asked Kim as she took her purse from the hook on the wall.

Kim nodded, handing Whitney a to-go mug of tea. "Thought you'd like a little extra caffeine this morning. Hope you don't mind tea. After I turned sixty, I couldn't handle coffee anymore." She opened the door and stepped on the newspaper. "Oof," she exhaled as she stumbled back into Whitney.

In her haste to steady her boss, Whitney dropped her mug of tea. The metal cannister landed with a clang, right in the middle of the front page. Whitney's heart turned to stone when she saw the headline about the fire and the picture of Virginia and Trevor together.

"Geez Louise," she moaned. "It would have been less painful for the paperboy to slap me across the face." She retrieved her mug and the paper, rolling it up and shoving it through the mail slot.

Kim rubbed the back of her neck, grimacing at where the newspaper had been. "You want to talk about it, honey?"

Whitney shook her head so forcefully, a tendril of curls came free from her ponytail. "No, ma'am. What I want is to go to work and sell out the store. I'll drive."

Kim's frown morphed into a grin as she motioned toward the driveway. "Now that's more like it."

In less than ten minutes, they were at the door to Kim's Creations, Main Street already bustling with shoppers and diners.

Whitney turned on the lights and powered on the laptop and iPad for taking payments, while Kim filled up pitchers with lemonade and turned on some country music that included patriotic songs. "I'm building the mood," she said as she shoved a few miniature American flags into the hands of the mannequins.

The fireworks show was two days away, but already the town was full to bursting with visitors for the festival. There was a carnival set up on the outskirts of town for the children, with all the restaurants offering various sales and summer menus. The far end of Main Street was closed down for a craft fair with dozens of crafters and artisans selling their wares.

A chime sounded from the clock on the counter, and Kim fumbled with her keys. "Showtime, honey!" she called over her shoulder as she opened the door. Within a minute, ten shoppers milled around the store, and within the first two hours they'd sold out of their entire swimsuit and sandal inventory.

Whitney relished the hustle, ping-ponging between shoppers to get them exactly what they wanted. "Thanks so much for coming in. Enjoy your new dress!" Whitney bid farewell to a customer and beamed at her reflection in the shop window. There was a rosy hue to her cheeks and a sparkle in her eye that only came with a sense of a job well done.

"That was our last wrap dress in the store," Kim said, jaw unhinged as she scanned through their inventory list. "I'm serious, Whitney. You ordered a dozen two days ago, and they're gone already."

The news made Whitney's heart swell. It was rewarding to see her plans come to fruition and succeed as well as they had. "I'm just glad my hunch was right."

Kim raised her pencil in the air. "Don't you dare sell your instincts short—you're good at this. At this rate, we'll sell out of our full inventory before the fireworks."

Whitney crossed her fingers. "We can only hope." She looked under the counter for the newest shipment of earrings. "Shoot, I never brought out those new hoop earrings. Can you cover the floor for a second?"

Kim shooed her away. "Take a break while you're at it."

"A quick one. It's nearly lunch." She shot a thumbs-up and went into the breakroom to have a glass of water and a few minutes off her feet.

After collecting herself, Whitney went back out with a box of jewelry to tag. Placing the box on the counter, her back was to the door when the chime sounded. Kim greeted the customers and joined her again. "Do you mind giving me a minute? The register is out of receipt paper."

Whitney nodded, distracted by two sets of earrings that got wrapped together during shipment. She was carefully prying two hoops apart when she heard a voice that sent a shiver down her spine.

"Are you going to be a while? I'm starving. I thought the whole point of coming to this stupid festival was the food."

The color drained from Whitney's face and her hands shook so much she fumbled the jewelry. One of the earrings fell to the floor, scurrying under the desk. She used the opportunity to hide and scope out why her freaking ex-boyfriend was in Pinegrove.

A familiar woman with a blonde bob and pursed lips jutted out her hip. "Baxter, I said I wanted to shop before lunch. Our reservation isn't for another half hour. Have a seat and hush up, please." She flipped her hair and walked over to a display of dresses.

Whitney was trapped like a rat, and she didn't know what

to do. She knew if she showed herself, Baxter would make an unholy scene. Of course, she also couldn't stay in this stooped position forever, as her knees already quivered.

Kim made the decision for her as she joined her at the register. "Honey, what on earth are you doing hiding down here?" She stood over Whitney with a puzzled expression.

In a hushed voice, Whitney said, "Dropped an earring. I'm, uh, looking for it."

"Excuse me," the woman said, approaching the desk. "Can I have a fitting room to try these on?"

Kim nodded, rummaging in her pocket for the keys to the fitting rooms. "Of course, honey. Right this way."

Whitney crawled around the far side of the counter, hoping Baxter had his back to her. No such luck. He faced the fitting rooms, although his attention was on his phone. Neither fast nor nimble enough, Whitney knew her best option was continuing to hide for another moment.

Kim came back and chuckled. "If you need a break, you can just tell me. Why are you hiding down there?" Her laughter drew Baxter's attention, and he turned around. Their eyes locked, and there was no use hiding any longer.

Holding her breath, Whitney slowly rose to face her past. Spinning on her heels, she was so glad she did her hair and makeup that morning. The last thing she wanted to do was see Baxter looking anything less than perfect.

"Are you freaking kidding me?" Baxter sneered, mouth hanging open wide enough for a family of birds to nest. "What the hell are you doing here?"

Kim shook her head, confused by his tone. "Is everything okay?"

"It certainly isn't okay," Baxter spat, stomping up to the counter and banging his fist on the display case.

Whitney flinched as his fist pounded the glass, and she hated that he garnered that reaction. She understood he had a right to be angry, but he wasn't blameless in this fight. "Baxter, I think we can discuss this like adults."

"Oh, you want to play the adult card?" He threw his

head back and laughed, the sound echoing between the clothes racks. "The crazy bitch that ruined my car wants to be an adult?"

Kim's eyes grew as she reached for Whitney's arm. "Whitney?"

"Yes, Baxter. I want us to be adults. You know the concept, right? We act like bigger people and take ownership of our choices?"

"Pfft, you have a lot of experience being the bigger person, Whitney."

She saw red. It was one thing to be angry about his car, but it was entirely different to show up at her job and call her fat. "Baxter Hollingsworth, you have a lot of nerve."

At that moment, his fiancée emerged from the dressing room looking radiant in a navy blue and white strapless dress. She found them and frowned, sensing something was going on. "Baxter, what's the matter?"

Kim slowly stepped back as Baxter whirled around to face her. "Take that cheap dress off, we're leaving." Turning back to Whitney, he added, "As soon as I get a check for the damage to my Mustang."

His fiancée raised an eyebrow. "What did I miss?"

Baxter pointed at Whitney, his mouth set in a firm line. "This is the bitch that trashed my car."

Kim's fingers shook as she dialed the police on her cell phone. "Honey, help is on the way." She glared at Baxter as she said, "This is Kim Sullivan. We have a disturbance at Kim's Creations."

Baxter's face turned an alarming shade of red, the muscles in his neck straining. "Sure, call the cops. I'd like to file a report about my baby."

"Oh please," his fiancée groaned, thrusting her hands on her hips. Despite Baxter's objections to the dress, it did give her a lovely hourglass shape. "If I have to hear one more thing about that damn car, I'm going to scream."

"Val, not now." Baxter shoved a hand through his hair, his eyes boring a hole through Whitney. "I cannot believe you had the nerve to mess with my car."

"Your car?" Whitney asked, coming out from behind the desk to face her ex. She'd officially had enough. "You want to talk about your car?"

"Yes, why wouldn't I? To come home to that mess …" he spluttered.

"After nearly three years together, you only want to talk about your car?"

Baxter's eyes flared, but he didn't defend himself. "Whitney, we had some laughs. Granted, with hindsight, I can see that I should have handled our breakup differently."

Whitney and Val snorted in unison. Clearly not expecting his ex and fiancée to be in cahoots, Baxter rocked back on his heels. "Ladies, why do I feel like I'm being ganged up on?" His expression was so incredulous, Whitney wanted to slap the look off his face.

Whitney thought about all the time she'd given this man. The countless hours of love, attention, and care she'd devoted to him. Was she always happy with Baxter? Of course not, but she certainly deserved better than what she got.

"How dare you come into my place of work and cause such a commotion!" Whitney spat, her shoulders heaving as she struggled to catch her breath. "Yes, I admit, I was a little dramatic with your car. When the shop called and begged me to pick it up, I took the opportunity for a little payback. Considering how quickly you moved on, or heaven forbid cheated on me, I'd say it's the least I could do to repay you."

For a moment, it looked like he wasn't going to respond. He stared at her, his eyes assessing yet distant. "You knew we weren't in it for the long haul, " he finally said. "We wanted different things, and besides"—he sighed heavily, body sagging with the effort—"you're not the type of woman a guy like me marries. You knew that."

"Not the type of woman? And what type is that, Baxter? Hmm? What type is that?"

Sweeping his arm in the general direction of his fiancée,

Baxter said, "Clearly Val. We've been in the same circles for years, and when my mother suggested I settle down, the choice seemed clear." He shrugged, unbothered that he bad-mouthed both women to their faces. "I couldn't marry a chubby girl. That doesn't fly in my social circles."

The store fell silent. Kim stood beside Whitney, her phone still clutched in her hand, her jaw on the floor. Val, for her part, looked equally appalled. Whitney took a breath to think through her next move. She could yell, scream, and call him every name in the book. She could turn on her heel and walk out, never to look at this man again. Or, she could do something she never would have dreamed possible. She could make him hurt as much as he'd hurt her. Her fingers balled into a fist, and Whitney fantasized about clocking Baxter right in his smug face, knocking that smirk away with one punch.

But then she thought about all the progress she'd made this summer. She'd gone from wallowing to finding her purpose, to opening herself up to the prospect of loving someone else. For a moment, she pictured Trevor, hand on her back as they strolled by the creek. She thought of Trevor's crooked, hot sauce-stained smile as they shared a basket of wings. She liked the Whitney reflected in his gaze, and suddenly the need for closure with Baxter wasn't important.

"Get out," she ordered, voice calm. "Get out before the cops get here for public disturbance."

Baxter rocked back on his heels. "You're kicking me out? Of your silly store?"

"It's not a silly store, it's a fabulous boutique. Now, please get the hell out."

Val snorted, stepping around Baxter and reaching into her purse. She pulled out a credit card and handed it to Whitney. "I'll take this dress, and that lovely patriotic silk scarf by the window." Her smile was genuine, and Whitney eagerly returned it. "Needless to say, I'm so sorry about all this. I had no idea Baxter was still seeing you when we got together." She huffed, blowing a strand of hair off her face. "It's cold comfort, I know, but I'm really sorry."

Baxter opened his mouth to argue, and Val elbowed him in the ribs. "Be quiet, please, the grown-ups are talking." She arched a manicured eyebrow and sighed. "He really can be a pill. I for one thought your engagement present for the Mustang was brilliant." She winked, and Whitney nearly pulled her in for a hug. The iPad tallied up Val's receipt, and Whitney numbly handed it to the woman who, a mere moment ago, Whitney had sworn she'd push into the Savannah River.

"Val? Are you serious right now?" Baxter wheezed, rubbing his side. He glared at Whitney and Kim before turning a pleading gaze to his fiancée.

"Yes, I am." Val took the receipt and nodded, tucking it into her designer bag before spinning on her heels and addressing her husband. "Now you hush up while I pop next door for some more shopping." She took another step toward Baxter and jabbed him in the chest with her index finger. "And if I hear you're over here pressing charges on poor Whitney, you'll be hearing from *my* lawyer. I'm bored hearing about your damn car. If you keep this up, I might drive it into the Atlantic out of spite." She patted Baxter's head like he was a dog and strode out the door. Before stepping out into the sunshine, she turned to Whitney and waved. "I know it's ridiculous to say, but it's been a pleasure meeting you, Whitney."

"Same," Whitney replied, dumbfounded.

The coward he was, Baxter followed Val out of the shop without an apology or second glance. The door had barely snicked shut when two policemen stepped inside. "Ladies, what's going on?"

Kim flapped a hand in front of her face and sighed theatrically. "Oh, Officers, we're quite all right now. You know how things get when the festival starts—a few out of towners causing trouble."

Both cops looked to Whitney, who could only nod

dumbly in response.

"You're sure everything's okay here?" he asked, dubious of Kim's charade.

"We're good," Whitney said, a smile taking over her face. Because she was good, she was better than good.

By the time the policemen left, the shop was quiet. Kim poured two cups of lemonade and flipped the sign to closed while they both caught their breath.

Pulling out a stool, Kim patted the seat for Whitney to rest. "You okay, honey?"

"Yeah, I really am. Just in a bit of shock, I suppose." Whitney eased down, taking the proffered lemonade but not tasting it. Her brain whirled, her past and present colliding had not been on her BINGO card for the day.

Kim reached out, resting a hand on her shoulder. "I'm damn proud of you, honey. You handled yourself with grace, and I think you're a badass."

Whitney covered her face and groaned. "That interaction just aged me ten years."

"You catch your breath, and I'll see if we have any snacks in the back." Kim excused herself and Whitney welcomed the moment alone.

She exhaled, throwing her head back to stare at the ceiling. Her heartrate was still bonkers from seeing Baxter, but she couldn't deny she'd gotten the closure she craved. Now if she could do that with Trevor, she'd be all set. She knew she needed to reach out, but she was too tired to have that many emotional run-ins in one day. She'd take her break and get back to work.

A few minutes later, Kim came out of the breakroom with a box of Oreos. "This is hardly lunch, but hopefully it'll tide you over. I texted Buster to bring over some pimento cheese sandwiches and coleslaw for us."

"Bless you, Kim." Whitney took the box and helped herself to two cookies before handing it back. "And seriously, thank you for being so nice about all this."

Expression turning serious, Kim rested against the

counter. "I know this is probably the worst time to bring this up, but I have an idea."

Cookie stalling on the way to her mouth, Whitney's heart kicked up. "What's that?"

Kim squared her shoulders. "Would you consider being my general manager?"

The sound of static filled her brain at Kim's offer, and Whitney officially felt like she'd wound up in an episode of *The Twilight Zone.* This week could officially not get any weirder ...

CHAPTER TWENTY-TWO

Whitney spluttered, cookie crumbs puffing out of her mouth. Kim stood there smiling like she hadn't just made an offer that blew Whitney's mind.

"Huh?" Hardly the most articulate answer, but she was gobsmacked.

"I'd like to turn the day-to-day operations over to you, give you a raise, and let you continue to work your magic. This time last year the thought of already selling out of merchandise would have been a fever dream, but you have made it reality."

Whitney gasped, hands flying up to cover her mouth. While she collected herself, she dusted the Oreo crumbs away. She couldn't believe her ears, and she had no idea what to say. Well, that was a lie. She knew exactly what she wanted to say. She wanted to scream *yes* to whoever would listen, but she still hesitated.

"I need to make a few decisions first." She held up her hands. "Please don't think I'm not interested or ungrateful, but with Trevor and my life in Savannah, it's a lot to consider."

Kim wasn't bothered. She rocked back on her heels, and said, "Honey, take your time. You've had a hell of a few

257

days, and I added to the drama."

"But in a very good way," Whitney countered, unable to hold back her grin. "I'm really honored that you would trust me with the store."

"I already do." Kim squeezed her hand, and Whitney nearly fainted with the turn of events.

As soon as she'd heard the offer, she simultaneously wanted to tell her two favorite people, Winnie and Trevor. But that notion was silly, especially since her sister would have a fit and Trevor likely didn't care what she did anymore. She hadn't bothered to check her phone yet today, but she assumed he'd stopped trying to contact her. The newspaper was confirmation enough that they were over with a capital O.

Through her brain fog, Whitney thought she heard Daisy talking outside. Turning to investigate, she saw her friend waving frantically to come inside. Whitney beamed, so happy to see Daisy no matter how much it also hurt.

"I'll get it," Kim announced, striding to the door. "I see Buster's car, so lunch is here too."

The moment Kim opened the door, Daisy pushed inside and dashed to Whitney. "Javi was right, you're still here." She embraced her, rocking her back and forth. "I was so afraid I wouldn't get to say goodbye, and that didn't sit right with me. Not one bit, sugar."

Whitney returned the hug, pleased to have a moment with her. "I wouldn't leave without telling you, but I couldn't stay at the house. I'm sorry."

Daisy pulled back, angrily swiping as a few tears slid down her cheeks. "Don't you dare apologize. In fact, there's someone outside that has a few things to apologize for." She hitched a thumb over her shoulder, and Whitney was shocked to see Trevor standing there.

Much like the last time he was at the shop, he held a bouquet of flowers. Only this time, Javi was behind him, clutching a cluster of balloons that said *Get Well Soon.* Whitney couldn't help herself, she snickered. "What's going on with Javi?"

Daisy rolled her eyes. "Sugar, if I knew I'd tell you."

Time stopped as Trevor crossed the threshold, Javi and Paul on his heels. Daisy blotted her cheeks with her handkerchief and chastised the trio. "I thought I told you goobers to stay outside until I spoke with Whitney."

Trevor took a tentative step toward Whitney, his unblinking gaze locked on her. "Sorry, Momma. I couldn't wait."

Javi stepped around Trevor and thrust the balloons in Whitney's direction. Instinctively, she reached for them. "Thank you?" she asked, wrinkling her nose.

"I'm helping my man with a grand gesture, and I thought balloons couldn't hurt." Javi shrugged, shoving his hands in his pockets.

Whitney's mind whirled like it was in a blender as she tied the balloons to a hook on the counter. "Grand gesture?"

Trevor nudged Javi out of the way, muttering something under his breath. "Could everyone please give us a minute?" Turning to Whitney, he asked, "Can we have a minute? Please?"

Buster chose that moment to arrive with their lunch and joined their motley crew. "What's going on? I heard the cops were here. You all right, Auntie Kim?" He held up paper bags, and Whitney's mouth watered at the smell of cheese and bread. For a split second, she wondered if she really wanted to hear Trevor's explanation.

Paul and Daisy spun to face Whitney. "The police were here?" Daisy gasped, reaching out to Paul to steady her.

Kim shooed him toward the back. "Everyone calm down. Let's give these two a moment, and I'll tell you all about it."

Paul ushered everyone to the breakroom, leaving Whitney alone with Trevor and a million questions. She looked at him, no matter how much it hurt. He was exhausted, eyes drooping and russet hair mussed. Heck, even the cleft in his chin looked weary.

"I'm so sorry," he blurted, placing the flowers on the counter. Gingerly, he took her hands and squeezed. "Why were the cops here?"

"I'll tell you the whole sordid thing later, but Baxter was here." Trevor's nostrils flared, and she quickly promised, "It's fine. Really. I said my piece and met his fiancée, who is actually really lovely."

Swearing under his breath, Trevor shook himself. "I feel like I've missed a lot, and I hate that." Snagging her gaze, he breathed, "You're sure you're okay?"

Whitney smirked, savoring the feel of Trevor's thumb as it glided over her knuckles. "Yes. Let's get back to why *you're* here."

Trevor pulled her hand to his mouth and gently kissed her palms. "I'm here to set the record straight and to beg you to stay in Pinegrove." Looking up to meet her gray gaze, he added, "With me."

"But what about Virginia? I saw you two with my own eyes, and so did the folks at the newspaper, I might add."

Trevor grimaced. "Darlin', as soon as I'm done begging for your forgiveness, I'm driving down to the *Herald*'s office and cracking some skulls. That picture will haunt me for the rest of my days." He shuddered, scrubbing a hand down his face. "None of this is coming out right."

Whitney took a deep breath, relaxing her shoulders and struggling to stay in the moment. She was in the midst of the weirdest sense of deja vu, but she knew she needed— no, deserved—Trevor's A-game.

Crossing her arms over her chest, she demanded, "Listen up, Trevor Mays. I'm going to make this easy for you," she started, watching the light return to Trevor's gaze. She almost felt bad for what she was about to say, almost. "I got a job offer today to be the general manager of this store." Trevor's mouth opened, but she held up a finger. "You're not talking now, I am." His jaw snapped shut so quickly, she was surprised he didn't bite off his tongue. "It's a good offer, an offer I'm strongly considering. But I need you to know something. If I take this job and stay in Pinegrove, it'll be on my terms and on my own. I'm not going to stay with Daisy, I'm not going to stay just for you. If I like what you're about to say, I'll consider taking you back."

From behind a rack of dresses, Javi snorted.

"Javi, I swear to God," Trevor warned, stepping to the side to glare.

Javi ducked behind, and muttered, "Sorry. Pretend I'm not here."

Trevor groaned, which caused a coughing fit.

For a moment, Whitney's heart clenched as he hacked into a tissue. "Are you okay?" she asked, patting his back while he caught his breath.

"I'm fine, darlin'." Once he was upright, he took her elbow and gently steered her to the furthest corner of the store, away from prying eyes. "Please, continue."

Some of the fight had melted out of her, but Whitney stood her ground. "I guess that was the gist of what I had to say, but know this." She poked him in the sternum, her jaw set. "The next time you visit me with flowers, it better be for something sweet and romantic, not to pick up the pieces from a mess." She cast a quick glance at the odd balloon arrangement, and suggested, "You can save the balloons, too." She wasn't certain, but Whitney thought she heard Javi whine.

Trevor exhaled, some of the tension leaving his frame as he nodded his agreement. "That is a stipulation I will gladly follow. Now, can I plead my case?"

Whitney cocked an eyebrow, making him sweat it out a moment. It was rare for her to have the power in a relationship like this, and she took pride in herself for knowing her worth, for demanding the best. She was eager to hear what Trevor had to say, but at the end of the day, she would be okay no matter what. She'd found her home, and she was ready to start life on her terms.

"All right, let's hear it," she ordered.

*

Mouth as dry as the Sahara, Trevor struggled to find his words and not turn into a ball of emotions in the middle of Kim's Creations. Whitney stared at him expectantly, and he prepared to grovel like he'd never groveled before.

From the far side of the shop, he spied Javi shooting him a double thumbs-up before Paul yanked him back into the breakroom. It was simultaneously annoying and comforting knowing his friends and family had his back. *Although he still hated those stupid balloons …*

"Whitney, let me start by saying the most important part," Trevor said, licking his parched lips and hoping his throat didn't spasm. "What you saw after the fire was not real. Virginia was trying to find Scott, and she stopped to ask about him right when you and the reporters showed up. There is nothing going on between us, *not a thing.*" He enunciated the last three words, determined to drive that point home.

Staring into Whitney's gray gaze, he searched for compassion or any sign she wanted him, any sign that she would push past this awkwardness to be together. Yet she was speechless, arms still crossed tightly across her middle, as if setting up barriers to every part of her. He hated this.

Then he thought back to something Whitney said during one of their walks, about how much Baxter had humiliated her publicly. Trevor flinched at the notion he was as bad as her ex, but he soldiered on.

"The very last thing I wanted to do was hurt you, or embarrass you with that freaking *Herald* photo. Darlin', over these last few weeks, you've become the most important person in my life. You need to know that I'm in it for the long haul, as long as you'll have me."

Whitney took a small step toward him, and Trevor felt a jolt of excitement that she wasn't turning tail and running away. "It hurt," she said, her voice painfully small. Suddenly the spitfire of a moment ago morphed into a shaken shell of herself. "I'm tired of being embarrassed by the men in my life," she admitted.

Trevor couldn't take it, he closed the distance in two strides, carefully resting his hands on her shoulders. At first, Whitney didn't drop her arms, her eyes downcast. "Whitney, I am so, so sorry. I can't tell you how much." Trevor wasn't going to pretend he hadn't made mistakes with Whitney, but he also wanted to make things right. "I'm sorry, for so many things, but especially for making you feel less than. You're strong, brave, and gorgeous, and if you'll have me, I'd love for us to try this again."

Whitney let out a long, slow breath. For an eternity, she refused to meet his gaze. Trevor slowly slid his hands up and down her arms, watching her skin erupt with goosebumps. Cold comfort, but at least she was still affected by his presence. Right now, he'd take whatever he could get.

Going for broke, Trevor shared the last part of the truth. "What I'm about to say isn't meant to guilt you into anything, but I need you to know something." Reluctantly dropping his hands, Trevor brought them to his face and scrubbed at his eyes. Not only did he really not want to cry in public, but he didn't think his singed throat could handle it. "I haven't been this lost, this desperate, since Daddy passed. When I thought you'd already ..." His voice caught, and he fought back another coughing fit. Fumbling in his pocket for a lozenge, he prayed he could get through what he had to say—what Whitney deserved to hear.

After a moment, Whitney reached up to cup his cheek. Her thumb dipped briefly into his dimple, her eyes brimming with tears. "Trevor." His name came out in a whisper, but she didn't move her hand.

Their eyes locked, and Trevor felt a bolt of awareness zip down to his toes. He wanted to stare into those gray orbs for the rest of his natural life. "When I was coming out of that fire, you were the only person I wanted to see. I thought about our ice cream date, how much I wanted us to take Gus out for another walk, how I'd love to share wings at The Pecan Pit and laugh at how much Buster hates his own menu." Voice cracking, he chomped down on his lozenge until he could finish. "If you would have left for Savannah, I need you to know I would've been on the road hours ago hunting you down. I just couldn't let you go without telling you that I'm falling for you."

"So you're saying the third time's the charm?" Whitney quipped, pulling his head down until their foreheads rested against each other. Trevor huffed a laugh, but he ran out of words. "We can take it slow?" she asked, her breath tickling his lips.

"Slow as molasses in January, darlin'."

Whitney giggled, angling her head so she could press a soft kiss to his cheek. "Maybe not *that* slow," she teased, peppering a trail of kisses across his face until their lips grazed. "Can I tell you a secret?"

"You can tell me anything," he promised, heart galloping through his chest.

"I'm falling for you, too."

Trevor nearly wept at her admission, wrapping his arms around her so fiercely he feared she'd pop like one of Javi's awful balloons. "Thank the good Lord," he breathed, inhaling her floral scent that smelled like summer memories yet to come.

Unable to wait another moment, he pressed their lips together again, kissing Whitney like his life depended on it, because it kind of did.

"Hooray!" a chorus of cheers erupted from the back of the shop.

Daisy dabbed away tears while Paul hugged her close before she darted toward them. Javi whistled while Kim and Buster hollered and clapped. It was ridiculous, and it was perfect.

Daisy ran up and enveloped them in a hug. "I knew my

books would do the trick," she gasped, kissing them both on the cheek.

Whitney tittered, asking, "Your books?"

Trevor rolled his eyes. "Momma gave me a stack of your romance books to review while we came looking for you. She was convinced they would save the day." Leaning in so only Whitney could hear, he said, "I did learn some things, but I'm saving it for when we're finally alone." He didn't miss the way she inched closer, a tremor coursing down her spine.

Javi joined them, giving Whitney a one-armed hug. "Well, I might borrow a couple of those, because there was some steamy stuff in there." He scratched his chin thoughtfully. "Any chance I can join that book club?"

"No," Trevor spat while Daisy said, "Sure thing, sugar."

Kim joined them, gesturing toward the door where a line was forming. "As much as I enjoy all this love and togetherness, we've got a line forming. My general manager and I have some work to do."

Whitney swiped at her cheeks and nodded. "Kim's right. Today is too busy for more shenanigans."

Trevor knew they were right, but that didn't stop the disappointment from washing over him. "Can I pick you up for dinner after your shift?"

"Yes," Daisy said, ushering Javi and Paul out the door.

Whitney shook her head, clearly amused. "Yes, that would be nice. I get off at six."

Kim pinched Trevor's elbow and led him toward the exit. "All is right with the world, now let our girl get back to work."

Our girl. Trevor hoped that made Whitney as happy as it made him. Despite the cast of characters, he loved Pinegrove with every fiber of his being. Falling for a woman who fit right in with those he held dear was better than any promotion he could hope for. This was more than following his career dreams—Trevor was following his heart.

CHAPTER TWENTY-THREE

The Pinegrove rumor mill kicked into high gear, and within an hour of Trevor and company's visit, Kim's Creations nearly burst at the seams. Kim squeezed between both customers and looky-loos eager for the dirt on why the police were called to the boutique.

Whitney was helping three women at the dressing rooms, each looking for completely different things, when she heard Kim say, "Yes, that's my general manager, Whitney. She can style the perfect outfit and tell off her ex-boyfriend without breaking a sweat."

The rest of the day flew by, despite squeezing through the masses at the shop. An hour before they were due to close up, and more importantly, her date with Trevor, her phone buzzed in her dress pocket. Not needing to look, she tugged her phone free and ducked into an empty fitting room to answer.

"Hey, Win," She exhaled, collapsing onto the bench. She'd been on her feet all day, and she wanted nothing more than a moment's peace. Silence greeted her, but that wasn't the peace she craved.

Finally, Winnie replied. "Hey, Whit. Are you all right? You sound tired."

Whitney exhaled. "I'm fine. It's been a hell of a day. How are you doing?"

"I'd be better if you were here. I just picked up Xena from Mrs. Rodgers, and the apartment feels so lonely."

A pang of guilt surged through Whitney, hating the notion her sister needed her. Yet for all her concern, Whitney still felt the pull to stay right where she was. Pinegrove had quickly become her home, and she needed her sister to know that.

"Win, I gotta tell you something."

Her sister chuckled, the clatter of cat food hitting a bowl echoed through the line. "That you're on the road and will be here in time for a late dinner?"

Deciding to simply tell her, Whitney went with the truth. "No, I'm not on the road. Frankly, I'm not coming back to Savannah."

Suddenly, her sullen sister was gone, replaced with the hard-ass attorney used to getting her way. "You can't be serious. Whit, come *home*." It wasn't a request, it was an order, and Whitney didn't have the energy to fight.

Pinching the bridge of her nose, Whitney swallowed a sigh. "Pinegrove is home. I've met some wonderful people, and I just got a promotion at the shop. I'm—" Before she could continue waxing on about how much she loved her current situation, Winnie cut in.

"But I thought you broke up with that fireman? You can fold sweaters in Savannah. Whit, I need you here, okay? I know sleeping on my couch is no picnic, but I don't want to be alone."

Whitney jumped to her feet, restless energy coursing through her. "What? Because you think I'm single, I can't stick around a new place for other reasons. I love this job, and I've made friends here. I'm in a book club for crying out loud!"

"But ..." Winnie tried to interject, but Whitney wasn't finished.

"And I probably shouldn't even mention this, because

you're going to get all preachy on me, but I am back together with Trevor. We're going to take things slow, and it would be nice if you were happy for me. Because let's face it, Win, I'm always happy for you, but I need to live my own life. I cannot continue to crash on your couch and hang out with Xena while you're working overtime. I deserve more than that, and I'm disappointed you can't see that."

Footsteps approached the dressing room door, and Whitney did not want to continue this conversation another moment. She loved her sister with all her heart, but she was also tired of not standing up for herself, for not getting what she wanted. "I've got customers. We can talk later, and I'll come back soon for a visit. But it won't be today. I love you."

And with that, she disconnected, silenced her phone, and shoved it back into her pocket. With trembling hands, she yanked open the dressing room door and came face-to-face with Kim. "You okay, honey?"

Whitney groaned. "I'm guessing my whole sisterly chat was louder than I expected."

Kim scoffed. "Pfft, who cares."

Glancing around the shop, Whitney saw it was half empty. Shoppers were leaving to prepare for the night's festival activities, and she was eager to join them. Fatigue threatened to weigh her down, but there was too much to be excited over. Trevor was due soon to take her on a date, and she craved the time alone with him. She promised herself they'd take it slow, that she'd set the pace, but that didn't mean she wasn't eager.

"I want you to help me with something," Kim said as she walked toward the rear of the shop. There were a couple stray boxes they hadn't had a chance to unpack with all the chaos of the day. Using a utility knife, Kim carefully opened a box and reached inside, pulling out a handful of lavender fabric.

Whitney retrieved some hangers, ready to help get the dresses on the rack. "That's a lovely color," she observed, helping Kim fluff the dress before hanging it.

"I thought so too, that's why I ordered it. Shame though," she mused, smoothing down the skirt. "It only came in one size." Without saying another word, Kim handed the dress to Whitney.

Curiosity got the better of her, and she checked the tag. It was her size, but that didn't mean she should blow a day's pay on the garment. Although she did like how it was fitted in the bodice with a flared skirt.

"Well, whoever gets it will be one lucky lady." She sighed, spinning around to hang it with the other new arrivals. After such a busy day, it was easy to find open space on the rack.

Kim hummed, seemingly disinterested. She got another stack of clothes from the box and carried them to the counter. "That dress would work perfectly for the barn dance tonight," Kim said, loading the tagging gun with labels.

"It would, huh?" Whitney raised an eyebrow, quickly understanding what her boss was up to. "And I'm guessing you have someone in mind for this?"

Kim cocked the label gun, deftly tagging three shirts in the blink of an eye. "Maybe. You see, when I was looking at the inventory site, I noticed this dress and thought it would look wonderful on someone with dark hair and gray eyes. That lavender really pops, don't you think?"

"I'm flattered you thought of me, but, Kim, I need to start saving money. Leaving half my paychecks at the shop won't help me find a place."

"Honey, it's been a long day, and I'm knackered, so I'll be blunt. Take this dress, it's your bonus for your promotion. Now get ready, because a certain fireman is due any minute to take you out." She pushed Whitney away from the register and toward the rack where the dress hung.

Whitney stumbled, whining over her shoulder, "No, this is too much. I can't take this."

"You're right, you can't take it. You may have it, my gift

to you. Now hush up and get ready. Mr. Mays should be here soon."

Cocking her hip, Whitney couldn't fight back a smile. "Why do I feel like Daisy was involved?"

"Because you're my general manager, which means you're smart. We had this plan cooked up before everything went a little topsy turvy, but it all worked out in the end."

Ten minutes later, Whitney stood in front of the three-way mirror, spinning around in the new dress. The fit was perfect, nearly a second skin from her bust to her hips. The skirt flared out when she twirled, and she couldn't wait to see how it looked while dancing. More importantly, while dancing with Trevor.

Speaking of the devil, the man himself strode into the shop, the bell tinkering overhead. His dark red hair was slicked back, and he'd shaved since they saw each other, the cleft in his chin practically winking at her. He stepped toward her, only to stop when their gazes snagged.

"Darlin'," he said, voice dangerously low, "you're a vision."

Whitney believed him, too. She closed the distance, pulling him in for a hug and a peck on the cheek. "You don't look too bad yourself." Clad in jeans that hung low on his hips, he'd opted for a gingham shirt made for county fairs and warm summer nights.

"I don't know if Kim spilled the beans, but I thought I'd take you to the barn dance tonight." His hands rested on her hips, squeezing gently before pulling her close for one more peck on the cheek. "Is that all right?"

"It's perfect, now get!" Kim ordered, placing a hand on each of their backs and shoving them out the door. "See you at nine tomorrow. If you need your things, Daisy already picked them up from my place and dropped them at Trevor's. Bye!" And with that, Kim slammed the door shut, flipped the deadbolt, and took down the *Open* sign.

Whitney huffed. "Geez, so much for taking it slow."

Trevor pinched her chin between his thumb and index

finger, bringing her attention to him. "You can stay anywhere you'd like. I can sleep at Momma's for all I care. They wanted to give you privacy is all."

Whitney wasn't buying it. "They wanted to set me up for a booty call," she teased. "Your momma has no chill."

Trevor's head fell back as he laughed. "No argument here, but I meant what I said. You set the pace, starting now." He stepped back, holding out his hand. "May I take you dancing tonight?"

As if waking up in the pages of one of her favorite romance novels, Whitney took Trevor's hand and squeezed. "It's a date," she said, nestling against his side for the walk down Main Street. She had no idea what the evening would bring, but she knew it would be magic. Anything with this man by her side felt right, and Whitney was ready to have some fun.

*

Bringing his A-game was Trevor's only option tonight. He knew he was the luckiest man in Pinegrove for Whitney to give him another chance. He wouldn't waste it, and he was grateful—for once—that his momma was a busybody. Within an hour of sharing his plan, Kim and Daisy had jumped into action to make the night as perfect as possible.

Trevor had no intention of forcing Whitney to do anything, but he knew she'd need a place to sleep tonight. Considering the fact that her things were still packed at Kim's, and Kim was a hopeless romantic, she and Daisy teamed up to throw the poor guy a bone. Her bag was packed and ready at his place, but he'd happily take her wherever she wanted to go—as long as she was happy, that's all he wanted.

Those Whitney Kerr smiles had grown rather important to Trevor. It was like when he was a kid and his parents took Jessie and him to the beach. They'd spend hours combing through the sand looking for the perfect seashells, only to inevitably forget the carefully found trinkets on the shore as they hurriedly packed up. Trevor thought the analogy was apt, as he had no intention of hustling away and losing anything Whitney wanted to give him.

Pulling their linked hands up to his mouth, Trevor pressed a kiss to the tender skin of Whitney's wrist. Her pulse bounced against his lips, and he fought a smile. "Want to grab some supper before we head to the barn? I don't know about you, but I plan on dancing up a storm."

Whitney's gray gaze regarded him, her lips quirking. "I could eat."

"Then let's see what the festival has on the menu." After crossing the street, they stopped at a cluster of food trucks. Pointing with his free hand, he gestured to a BBQ truck, a taco truck, and a seafood truck. "What looks good? If you prefer something different, we can be at The Pecan Pit in five minutes."

Whitney tapped her chin, studying their options. Finally, she said, "Tacos?"

Trevor's stomach rumbled to life, and he beamed. "Tacos it is." They got in line, quietly observing everyone around them. "How was the rest of your day?" he asked, dropping her hand in favor of wrapping an arm around her waist. Whitney was a vision in purple, the dress fitting her like a glove. It took every ounce of self-control not to twirl her around and have his way with her right in the food truck stall. Body shaking as she sighed, Trevor noticed how tired her eyes looked. "Are you all right? We can go home if you…"

Whitney shook her head so forcefully her black curls bounced around her face. "No, I mean yes, but no. I'm tired, but I'm fine. I had a stressful call with Winnie right before you arrived. She and I had another fight, and it's the last thing I wanted after Baxter and already busy day."

She nibbled her bottom lip, pretending to study the menu rather than meet his eye. "Sisters are a blessing and a curse," he teased, striving to lighten the mood. "Momma said that Jessie is coming home for a visit."

The topic change did the trick, and Whitney became more animated. "Oh, that's great! You said you haven't seen her in ages. You must miss her terribly."

Trevor agreed, moving them up a few paces in line. "I do, very much. Although she's coming home for Smithy, too."

Whitney raised an eyebrow. "Uh-oh, are you being a protective big brother?"

"Ha! No, I'm actually being a protective friend. Smithy is still in the hospital, and I know he wants to get back with Jessie."

"Malcolm's important to you?" Whitney observed, snatching a paper menu off the side counter at the truck. She trailed a finger down the offerings before nodding and handing it to Trevor.

Trevor took the menu, although he knew he was getting as many shrimp tacos as they'd give him. "Yeah, we've been friends since high school, and then when he joined the academy, I kind of took him under my wing. Plus, he and Javi are tight, so the three of us kind of pal around." He shrugged, but there was nothing casual about Javi and Smithy to Trevor. They were his brothers, and he wanted them to be safe and happy. Unfortunately, while Smithy was likely to make a full recovery, the same could not be said about his heart if Jessie had her way. Their on-again off-again status was exhausting to everyone on the outside, and Trevor had no idea how Smithy could stand it.

Although, that wasn't really true now, because Trevor would gladly suffer for the chance to see Whitney. *God, this love stuff is a real bitch.*

When they reached the front of the line, Whitney ordered two brisket tacos and Trevor ordered three shrimp tacos and a pair of Cokes. She reached into her purse for money, but Trevor shook away her offerings. "I invited you, it's my treat." She pursed her lips together, but she didn't argue.

"Thank you for dinner," she said, walking toward a picnic table another couple had just vacated.

Whitney lifted her skirt to slide onto the bench, and Trevor's pulse hitched at the sight of her creamy thighs. Lordy, he needed to pull it together or he'd faint. Clearing his throat, he eased down next to her, resting his elbows on the tabletop.

He didn't want to upset her with more talk of her sister, but she needed the chance to vent. "I'm sorry you had a rough call with Winnie. I'm sure whatever it is, she'll come around."

Whitney blew out a breath. "Probably, but that doesn't mean I like where we are now. It's kind of precarious, you know? Winnie is very type-A, works hard and barely takes time for herself. If anything goes wrong in her life, she's quick to throw up walls and bury herself in work. I feel guilty that if I'm not there, she'll just become some workaholic hermit or something." She picked at the label on her Coke bottle, the pieces fluttering to the table.

"It's not your responsibility to watch over your sister," Trevor offered, knowing it was easier said than done. "Sometimes we just have to step back and hope our family does what's right for them, but we can't railroad them." He chuckled, thinking of the many of the disagreements between Jessie and him over the years. "Trust me, I speak from experience."

Before they could dive further into family drama, the clerk from the taco truck arrived with two plates of heaven.

"Hello, gorgeous." Whitney gasped as she picked up her first taco and took a bite. "Oh my goodness," she moaned, head thrown back like she was about to recreate a scene from a Meg Ryan movie.

Trevor ate one of his tacos in two bites, eager to avoid getting aroused in public. They inhaled their dinners, both eager to move on with their plans for the night. Just as Trevor collected their trays, Paul and Daisy arrived at their table.

Whitney hopped to her feet before Trevor realized they had company. "Daisy, Paul, hello!"

Daisy kissed Whitney's cheek before sitting on the opposite side of the picnic table. She was focused on Trevor in a way that made his shirt feel too tight. Yanking on his collar, he asked, "What brings you two over here? I thought we'd see you at the dance."

Paul sat next to Daisy, covering her hand with his. "We're on our way, son. First, I need to tell you something."

Trevor swallowed the rest of his taco, hoping he wasn't about to get more bad news. "Is it about Jessie?" He looked to his mother, who merely shook her head.

"Jessie's fine, sugar. She lands tomorrow. No, this is about the station." She nudged Paul in the side until he spoke up.

"I'm just coming out with it, and we'll figure out the logistics later."

Whitney balled up her napkin and tossed it on her empty plate. "Oh dear," she muttered.

"Hastings resigned this afternoon," Paul announced, nearly knocking Trevor from his seat.

"I'm sorry, what?" Trevor was idly aware that Whitney had scooted closer, wrapping her hand around his bicep. "Hastings quit? Just like that?"

"Well, it was a little more nuanced, but yeah. I went in this afternoon to talk with him, to question some of his behavior. On top of everything you, Smithy, Javi, and I discussed this week, he was a no-show at the fire last night. Hence why Virginia was there asking around. Despite it being all hands-on deck, he chose not to assist at a massive fire involving his station. I would have been able to fire him if he didn't beat me to it by quitting."

Beside him, Whitney found her words first, and asked, "What does this mean for Trevor and the captain position?"

For the first time since joining them, Paul beamed. "It means that first thing next week, I'll attend the city council meeting with the *very* short list of recommendations for captain. Not only does Trevor have years of experience, accolades, and references, but he was on the scene first with the team, staying until the end even at the risk of his own safety. That's a leader."

Trevor's eyes welled at Paul's words, his throat burned with the effort. "That's um"—he coughed, dipping his head and wiping his eyes with a rumpled napkin—"that's good news, sir."

Whitney rested a hand on his neck, running her fingers up through his hair. She leaned close, her lips right by his ear as she whispered, "It's more than good news, Captain."

"We'll let y'all enjoy the rest of your evening," Daisy said, pushing to her feet and dragging Paul with her. "Have fun at the dance, and..." She paused, rummaging through her handbag and pulling out the spare key Whitney had returned. "You take this in case you get enough of my fool son." She winked to soften the blow, and Whitney smiled.

"I'm sorry for running away like that."

"Don't apologize," Daisy and Trevor said in unison.

Whitney giggled, tucking the key into her own purse. "Okay, geez. Then I guess we should get dancing."

Trevor hugged both his mother and Paul goodbye, his hands shaking with nerves and excitement. Whitney looped her arm through his as they headed toward the big barn on the outskirts of downtown. Back in the day, it had been a mill, but in the last few years it had been renovated into a community space for the festival and other town events.

When they reached the entrance to the dance, his ears rang from the music and noisy chatter. Trevor pulled Whitney to the side. "Do you mind if we take a minute?" he asked, carefully leading the way around the rear of the barn.

A gravel pathway led toward the creek that meandered through Pinegrove; the same creek they sat by after their date at Cajun Carl's. The water babbled, covered by a canopy of pines and oak trees, the air scented with juniper. These quiet pockets by the creek all looked similar and reminded Trevor of their first official date.

"Where are you taking me, Mr. Mays? I'm still not dressed for craw dadding," she quipped.

"Over by the creek for a minute. At the risk of sounding like a selfish jerk, I'm not ready to share you yet."

When they stepped under the pine trees, the air cooled slightly. Whitney stayed close to his side, her eyes taking in the woods, their footfalls muffled by the din of the dance. "This is lovely; nice and quiet," she mused. "As much as I love dancing, I'm enjoying a little quiet."

Trevor stopped at a rock that was big enough for two to sit, easing himself down before pulling Whitney onto his lap. Their noses touched, breath lingering between them. "Can I tell you something?" he asked, voice strained from fatigue and the emotions surging through him.

"You can tell me anything," she promised, pecking the tip of his nose with a kiss that he craved.

"Despite how this week started, and smoke inhalation and visits from our exes notwithstanding, this has been the best week of my life."

Whitney's smile damn near blinded him. "You earned that promotion, and I know Paul will do his best to—"

Trevor brought his hand up, cupping her cheek and tracing his thumb over her bottom lip. "The job isn't the only reason I'm so happy. I love having you here, and I will make it my life's mission to make you happy and a permanent resident of Pinegrove."

Whitney melted into his hold, and Trevor was grateful they'd skipped the dance. He closed what little distance that remained, lips tangling in a kiss that consumed him. This kiss was more than passion, it was a promise of a future.

Reluctantly coming up for air, Trevor said, "Darlin', as much as I'd love to dance the night away, I'm a little beat."

"Take me back to your place?" Whitney asked, her hands skimming up and down his arms. Even in the July heat, he shivered. Making a face, she warned, "No funny business. This is really about resting. We've both been through it."

"Whitney, you had me at rest." Trevor stood, wrapped

his arm around her shoulders, and led the way back to his pickup.

By the time they made it back to Trevor's, he was surprised they were able to walk under their own power. But it was perfect, having Whitney in his space. He hoped it was only the beginning of more time together.

CHAPTER TWENTY-FOUR

Whitney woke with the sun peeking through the blinds. She wiggled away from the light, only to collide with a hard, warm wall. "Oof," she mumbled into her pillow. The flannel sheets were soft against her skin, but wholly unfamiliar. Pulling herself up a little, the wall at her backside grumbled, tugging her close.

"Not ready to wake up," Trevor protested. "Bed is good." He sighed.

Whitney's eyes shot open as the last evening flew through her mind. She was in Trevor's house, in his bed, and she had no plans on getting up. "Bed is good," she agreed, nestling back into his hold.

They lay there like that, the only sounds the birds outside and their mingled heartbeats. Last night had been a dream of simplicity. While at first she'd loved the idea of dancing, she was exhausted from everything that had transpired. Baxter, Virginia, her—and hopefully Trevor's— promotions, it had all come to a head.

Trevor had taken her back to his place, giving her the tour before they finally collapsed into bed. Despite the pull in her belly urging her to push for more, Whitney was glad they were taking it slow. She was falling for Trevor, and the very last thing she wanted to do was rush things. They would take this new relationship one day at a time, and she was excited to see what that brought.

Unfortunately in that moment, it brought a full bladder. Whitney groaned and wiggled free. "I need to visit the little girl's room." She sighed, tiptoeing into the adjoining bathroom.

Taking a moment to check her reflection, she saw nothing but rosy cheeks, messy curls, and a smile that belonged to a truly happy, carefree person. Yes, she was still upset over everything with Winnie, but they were sisters. They would figure it out. She brushed her teeth and went in search of the coffee maker.

While she measured out the grounds, a pair of arms snaked around her. "Good morning," Trevor nuzzled his nose into her hair. "Darlin', this is the greatest way to wake up. Folgers has nothing on you, let me tell you." He kissed her temple before stepping away to find mugs, sugar, and cream.

"Good morning. How do you feel about breakfast? I can make eggs," Whitney offered, opening the fridge and searching for the fixings.

"Breakfast can wait," Trevor said, resting his hands on her hips and tugging her closer. "You're going to discover this soon enough, but you need to know something about me."

Whitney spun in his arms, the eggs cradled between them. She poked the divot in his chin. "Oh yeah? What's that?"

"I'm a bit of a cuddler," he admitted, taking the eggs and sliding them across the counter.

"You are, hmm?" She looped her arms around his neck, pulling him down for a kiss.

Breakfast, coffee, and the outside world forgotten, they continued their kiss fest from the night before. Whitney was surprised her lips were still functional after all the lip-locking they had done, but she hardly complained.

The coffee maker dinged, alerting them that their caffeine fix was ready. "Coffee," she said in between kisses.

Trevor angled her head and deepened the kiss. "Coffee can wait."

Then the doorbell rang, tearing them away from the moment, causing both to mutter profanities that would make a sailor blush. "Who in blue blazes could that be?" Whitney asked, letting her arms fall to her side.

"Whoever it is has a death wish," Trevor grumbled as he strode to the door.

Assuming Trevor could handle their visitor, Whitney went to work fixing up their coffees. Her ears perked up when she heard a very familiar voice coming from the doorway.

"I'm sorry, you don't know me," Winnie said as Whitney slammed the carton down and sprinted toward the door.

"Win?"

"Whit!" Her sister deflated, dropping her purse to the ground. Trevor stepped back to let Winnie inside.

"How are you here?!" Whitney yelped, squeezing the life out of her sister, mind racing with questions. "How did you find us?"

Winnie hugged Whitney so fiercely, Whitney's ribs nearly cracked in half. "I might have pulled some strings for an address check at the firm. Don't hate me." She sighed into Whitney's neck, her skin damp with tears. "I had to come see you and"—she paused her explanation to sniffle—"apologize and meet your fireman." Whitney's explanation was punctuated by more tears and laughter.

Trevor disappeared into the kitchen, returning with three cups of coffee. "Here we go," he said, handing out mugs.

"Oh, I like him already," Winnie said, wiping her cheeks with the back of her hand before helping herself to a cup. "In case you haven't gathered, I'm the big sister."

Trevor reached out to shake her hand. "Trevor Mays, very nice to meet you, Winnie."

Winnie took his hand, giving it a few pumps before letting go and falling down onto the couch cushions. "It's nice to meet you, too. Hopefully my baby sister hasn't warned you off my company." She waited for Whitney to interrupt, but her sister was stunned into silence.

Trevor shoved his hands in his pockets, taking slow steps back. "I'll let you two catch up. I'm due for a shower anyway." Whitney snaked his hand before he could leave, kissing his cheek and muttering her thanks.

She couldn't believe Winnie was here, with an olive branch no less. Whitney joined her sister, vibrating with excitement over the surprise. Deep down she knew her sister loved her, would do anything for her, but this impromptu visit meant more to Whitney than Winnie could ever know.

"First things first," Winnie said, placing her coffee cup on the table. "You look great, Whit. I mean that in every way." Studying her, Winnie observed, "You're glowing, and I can tell it's more than just good moisturizer."

"Really?" Whitney asked, rubbing a hand over her heart. "I'm just so surprised to see you, and I want you to be happy for me, Win. All I want is for both of us to be happy."

Winnie reached out and took Whitney's hands. "I'll be okay, and, besides, seeing you this happy is going a long way to calm my nerves. I'm so sorry I haven't been a better sister to you." Whitney opened her mouth to argue, but Winnie shook her head. "Let me get this out. I've been practicing in the car all morning." Whitney laughed.

Lordy, it was great having her sister back.

"We've always been different types of people, and sometimes I forget that what makes you happy doesn't make me happy." She chewed the inside of her cheek, finding the words. "I'm sorry I kept pushing you to come back to Savannah. It's clear this is where you're supposed to be, and I won't stand in your way."

Whitney covered her heart with her hand, her bottom lip trembling. "Thank you. I never wanted to disappoint you."

Winnie scoffed. "You never have, and you never will."

The pair caught up on the happenings of the last few days while Trevor kept himself busy making breakfast. By the time he came out with plates of French toast, Whitney could tell Winnie approved.

"Okay, Trevor. I'm starting to see the appeal." She greedily took a bite of her meal before Whitney could thank her boyfriend. "If you feed her this well, I won't worry she's back to eating peanut cups for dinner."

"Hey!" Whitney gasped. "That was only while I was recovering from the breakup. I've been eating like a human being again, mostly."

Trevor crossed his heart, expression serious. "I promise, Winnie. I'll take care of Whitney as long as she'll have me."

Winnie hummed, eyes darting back and forth between them, before nodding. "Fine, I guess I'll let her stay and live her own life." She held up a finger, and added, "But I expect you both to come visit me and Xena soon in Savannah."

Whitney nearly choked on her coffee. "Yeah, I'm in no hurry to see that devil cat again."

"Pfft, she's a sweetheart, and you know it." Winnie stuck her tongue out.

"I think the only reason I'm in a rush to get back is for my collection of romance books and my favorite pajamas."

"You should order some new pajamas for the shop," Trevor suggested, leaning down to collect their dirty dishes. Whispering in Whitney's ear, he added, "Or sleep naked." That suggestion brought a crimson flush to Whitney's cheeks, but she wasn't complaining.

Once Trevor cleaned up breakfast, he continued to impress both Kerr sisters with his next question. "So, Winnie, do you want to stay here with us and go to the fireworks in a couple days? The festival is in full swing, and I'd love to get to know you better."

Winnie swooned nearly as hard as Whitney at the invite. "That's so thoughtful, Trevor. But I'm only here for the day. I wanted to see my sister and confirm she was okay." Letting out a contented sigh, she mused, "Which, clearly, she's more than okay."

"You can't get on the road already," Whitney protested. "Can you at least spend the night?"

Winnie made a show of thinking it over. "Hmm, Mrs. Rodgers has Xena. I guess I can handle one night in the company of you two love birds."

Trevor gestured to the couch. "That pulls out into a surprisingly comfortable bed. You're welcome as long as you'd like."

"Thank you," both women said in unison.

Trevor saluted and checked the time. "Since you two have a lot of catching up to do, I think I'll swing by the hospital and check on Smithy. How about I bring home something from the festival for dinner?"

Winnie cheered. "Oh my gosh, that'd be lovely! Is that food truck with the hush puppies and fish fry still around?"

Trevor retrieved his keys and wallet from the table by the door, nodding as he got ready to leave. "Yes, ma'am. I'll get us a triple order."

Whitney joined him at the doorway, kissing his cheek and tucking rogue hair behind his ear. "You're the best, thank you."

"Happy to be of service," he said, kissing her chastely before he excused himself.

Winnie patted the couch cushion next to her for Whitney to return.

"Uh-oh," Whitney was incredulous. "Why do I think I'm about to get a lecture?"

After swatting her younger sister's arm, Winnie blinked away a fresh round of tears. "I'm not going to lecture, but I will get a little sentimental. I'm really proud of you for doing this, Whit."

Whitney shrugged. "Dating a man who brings us hush puppies?"

"No, you tit mouse," Winnie groaned. "I'm proud of you for following your bliss. You've found a place, a job, and people who make you happy. You're not going to sit on the sidelines and do what makes others happy. You're finally living for yourself."

"Oh," was all Whitney could say. While she understood what her sister was saying, she couldn't deny that it was a shock to hear. Yes, she had made strides to be her own woman, but having her favorite person in the world confirm it felt amazing. "Thank you."

"And as much as I miss you, I am only going to stay the night. You have a life to get to, and I need to head back and fix the mess with the merger."

Whitney nudged Winnie playfully with her elbow. "Can I make a suggestion?"

"Oh boy, now I feel like I'm going to get a lecture." Winnie winked.

"Can you give whatever you have with Mari a chance? Please don't shut yourself off from a love life because of a work issue. We both know that merger had a lot more issues than you going on a few dates."

Huffing out an exhale, Winnie finally nodded. "I thought about that, too. Now that my favorite sister is leaving, it might be nice to have someone else around. Although if Mari and Xena don't hit it off, I'm screwed."

Both sisters burst out laughing, clutching their sides as they caught their breath. "You might want Mrs. Rodgers to keep Xena indefinitely."

"Haha," Winnie teased, pulling Whitney in for another hug. "I love you, Whit."

"Love you more," Whitney replied, resting her hand on her big sister's shoulder, feeling the world around her right itself.

For the first time in a very long time, Whitney was in charge of her own life. And it was a marvelous feeling.

CHAPTER TWENTY-FIVE

Trevor woke with Whitney wrapped around him like a koala bear. Her ponytail had come undone in the middle of the night, her black curls a messy riot against the pillow. Carefully, he sniffed her scalp, relishing her lilac scent.

"Trevor Mays," a groggy voice came from the tangle of sheets. "Are you smelling me?"

Body shaking with laughter, Trevor nestled closer, fingers digging into her soft skin. "Guilty," he admitted. "I just can't get enough of you in my bed."

Spinning around to face him, Whitney tapped his chin divot. "You're only saying that because we're finally alone."

He couldn't argue with his girlfriend. Despite the fact that the visit from Winnie clearly helped Whitney feel more comfortable and less guilty, it was delightful having their own space again. "Your sister is welcome anytime," he promised, earning a peppering of kisses along his jawline.

"Thank you," she whispered.

Pulling Whitney as close as possible, Trevor swallowed down all the words that threatened to erupt from within him. He was completely in love with her, and he planned to tell her today, under the fireworks. *He'd turned into a walking romance book hero cliché, and he loved it!*

In addition to various embarrassing stories of her childhood, Winnie had shared memories of their girlhood visits to Pinegrove for the festival. Trevor marveled at the fact that they had been in the same place for years, their paths never crossing until now. But it was no matter, as he finally had his girl.

"I should probably get ready for work. Kim said that Main Street is already closed off, and I need to find a place to park."

"Pfft, you're with a member of the Pinegrove FD, darlin'. I can get past any barricade."

Whitney giggled. "Is that a euphemism?"

Trevor pinched her bottom, savoring the sensation of her squirming against him. "It can be," he teased. "But, seriously, I can get you to work, and I'll pick you up for the fireworks after."

"That sounds perfect. You heading into the station today?"

"Yep. Paul is going to show me his pitch for the city council meeting. In the meantime, I've been named interim captain."

Whitney's grin expanded, the freckles on her cheeks popping with the movement. She was adorable, and Trevor still couldn't believe his good fortune—in all aspects of his life. He was in love with a beautiful, kind woman, and he was actually excited about the trajectory of his career.

"Let's get ready for the day, Captain," Whitney said, pulling back the sheets. "The sooner we leave, the sooner we can come back here." She waggled her eyebrows, and Trevor enjoyed the view as she tiptoed to the bathroom.

He could certainly get used to this…

Fortunately for both of them, the day flew by in a flurry. Trevor changed at the station into shorts and a polo shirt, and he practically skipped down Main Street to Kim's Creations to get his girl. Whitney was ready for him, wearing a dress he didn't recognize and smile just for him.

"Ready for the fireworks?" she asked, waving goodbye

to Kim as she closed the door.

"I was born ready," he said, taking her hand and strolling through the crowds.

Arriving at the meadow where the fireworks went off, they tiptoed through a sea of picnic baskets and blankets until a familiar voice cut through the din. "Trevor! Whitney, over here!" His momma stood and flapped her arms over her head like she was a windmill in the middle of the Netherlands.

"Apparently everyone is over there." Trevor chuckled, narrowly avoiding a toppled lawn chair.

"Sorry it took us a minute to walk over from the shop. Traffic was terrible. Maybe the fire department should have done crowd control this year?" Trevor quipped as he sat down and helped Whitney ease onto the blanket. Resting his head on her shoulder, he whispered into her ear, "You comfortable?"

"I'm perfect," she said with a happy exhale.

After kissing her temple, he agreed. "No argument here."

They chit chatted with his mother and Paul, greeting neighbors as they found their own spots for the festivities. The longer the evening stretched out, the more nervous he got about confessing his feelings.

He should probably be embarrassed by this fact, but he never really loved Virginia. At the time he thought she was the woman of his dreams, but with hindsight, he saw she was a pretty face who boosted his ego after the loss of his father. With Whitney, everything was authentic. Their laughter, their trust, their time together, it all flowed effortlessly. Every day was better since he'd met Whitney, and she deserved to know the truth. His heart beat for her alone.

"Ladies and gentlemen," the mayor's voice boomed through the loudspeaker. A little feedback hit and the audience flinched. "Sorry about that." He chuckled. "Welcome to the annual Pinegrove Fireworks Spectacular."

The mayor took a moment to thank everyone for attending, spending a little too much time thanking the sponsors.

Paul cleared his throat, and asked, "Is this taking a lot longer than normal? I think the only person who hasn't sponsored tonight is Gus." The four of them laughed, and Trevor marveled at how comfortable he was with the shift in the dynamic with Paul. He was family, and he loved seeing his momma this joyful.

"And without further delay, let's start the show!" The mayor cheered as the audience applauded and the fireworks show began.

Despite being one of the biggest fireworks extravaganzas in the South, the show always started out slowly. Bursts of red, white, and blue fireworks began speckling the sky, their booms ricocheting throughout the fields.

Trevor pulled Whitney closer, his arms wrapped tightly around her middle. She was a vision in this purple dress, and he was tempted to ask her to wear it every day.

She shivered as a golden explosion flickered overhead. "Beautiful," she exhaled.

"No argument here." He kissed her neck, the dark curls of her ponytail tickling his nose.

She admonished. "Are you even watching the show?"

Trevor's body shook with mirth. "I'm paying attention to the only show that matters." He drew one of his hands up to the side of her breast, giving it a playful pinch.

Whitney whispered, "Your momma and Paul are right there."

"Hopefully they're too busy watching the show to be bothered with us." He was only half kidding. Craning his neck, he found his mother and the chief as enamored with each other as he was with Whitney.

A cluster of fireworks popped overhead, building to the show's climax. Whitney jumped in his arms when a silver shimmer ball exploded overhead, sending metallic confetti fluttering to earth. "I've got you," he whispered into her ear, shamelessly sniffing the lilac of her perfume.

"I know you do," she said, wiggling closer still. If she kept this up, he was about to have a very not-PG issue spring up.

"This is my favorite fireworks show of my whole life," he said, drawing her attention from the sky.

"But it's not over?" She raised an eyebrow, her eyes sparkling.

"Tonight is the best because you're here. I was thinking about it, on the walk out. We used to be here at the same time, maybe sitting just feet apart, but we never found each other."

Whitney's face softened, and she slowly spun in his arms so they were facing each other, her legs tucked under herself. "I thought of that, too." She reached out and cupped his cheek, smoothing over his stubble with her thumb, finally poking his chin divot. "It's kind of magic, isn't it? Finding each other after all these years of circling."

"It kind of feels like fate," he agreed.

"Trevor, I …" she said as Trevor said, "Whitney, I …"

They both laughed, not caring who was watching them, too immersed in their own moment. "You got first," she urged, ducking her head to hide her blush.

Trevor pinched her chin between his thumb and index finger, bringing that stunning face back up.

"Never hide that gorgeous blush, Whitney. Do you hear me? I love watching your reactions, it's one of the things that make you, you."

Tears glistened in her eyes, and Trevor hoped he didn't say the wrong thing. *It sure as hell wouldn't be the first time.*

"I don't hide anything from you, Trevor. I never have to, and that's freeing."

For a moment, they simply stared into each other's eyes. Fireworks boomed overhead, people clapped and cheered all around them, but it felt like they were the only two people in the world. Like moths to a flame, they leaned closer, both staring at the other's lips. Just as they were about to kiss, they whispered in unison, "I love you."

Trevor pulled back slightly in delighted surprise. "You love me?"

Whitney pecked his cheek quickly and nodded. "Of course I love you. I've been thinking of the best time to say it. But let's get back to the important stuff, you love *me*?"

Trevor chuckled. "Uh, yeah. Whitney, when you said you were staying in Pinegrove, it was the happiest moment of my life. I was losing sleep over the thought of you going back home to Savannah. I couldn't bear the thought of losing you."

"You're wrong about something," she said, her lips quirking.

"What?"

"Savannah isn't my home anymore. Pinegrove is."

Trevor cupped her face in his hands and pulled her into the best kiss of his life. The finale of the fireworks crackled overhead, but neither of them heard anything beyond their racing heart beats.

Whitney loved him back, and that was all Trevor needed in his life. The future was bright, because he'd found his other half.

EPILOGUE

Five months later

"Would you stop fidgeting, or I won't be able to get your tie straight," Whitney said, reprimanding her boyfriend.

Trevor toyed with the edge of the fabric, unable to stop moving. "Sorry, darlin', but I'm nervous." After tugging once more at the collar of his shirt, he muttered, "Why couldn't we wear our dress uniforms?"

Whitney smiled, smoothing his tie into place and straightening his boutonniere. The sprig of holly matched the green of his eyes, and Whitney fell a little more in love with her favorite fireman. "That isn't what the bride and groom wanted. Now hush up. You look handsome as sin." After carefully tucking his cowlick into submission, her finger trailed down and poked Trevor square in the chin. "Now, go get the bride. We can't keep her waiting."

Gathering the red velvet of her skirt, she stepped back so Trevor could leave the staging area of the church. Outside the door, they heard their friends and neighbors ushering into the chapel.

"I'm doing the right thing, aren't I?" Trevor asked, his frown back in place. "I keep thinking about Daddy, and …"

Whitney gently covered his mouth with her hand and offered her most reassuring smile. "Honey, listen to me." He bobbed his head from behind her hand. "Daisy loves Paul, doesn't she?" Trevor nodded once. "Your daddy loved Daisy, didn't he?" He nodded twice at that. "Paul and your daddy were best friends, weren't they? They loved each other?" Once again, Trevor lifted his head in the affirmative. Letting her hand drop slowly, Whitney blinked away her own tears of joy. "Then I think you have your answer. Life doesn't always go the way we plan, but if we're lucky, we can find love again. Paul and Daisy are head over heels, but I can tell they both still love your daddy. This wedding is a blessing, but I think you already know that."

"How did I get so lucky finding you, Whitney Kerr?"

Whitney shrugged, her black curls bobbing with the motion. "Don't know, Trevor Mays, but I feel the same way. Go out there and give away the bride. Daisy will be mad as a hornet if you're late."

"I love you," Trevor said as he kissed her, careful not to smudge her lipstick.

"Love you, too. Now go be the best, best man Pinegrove has ever seen." She swatted his bottom on the way out and sighed. There was a lot of love floating around today, and she soaked it up with gusto.

Now that the best man was taken care of, Whitney went in search of the bride. She found Daisy in the pastor's office, dabbing at her eyes and chatting with Jessie. Whitney and Jessie had hit it off immediately once Jessie returned home to Pinegrove, becoming another sister to her. Many nights were spent at book club or hanging out at The Pecan Pit. Whitney couldn't imagine her life without this spitfire in it.

"Hello, Mays ladies," she said from the doorway. "Can I join the fun?"

Jessie sprang from her seat and pulled Whitney into her a bearhug. Her reddish hair was pinned back, her freckled cheeks on full display. "Your timing is perfect. Momma's about to spoil her makeup and needs a distraction."

Daisy fluttered a hand in front of her face. "Hush up. I can't help it that I'm crying happy sad tears."

Whitney furrowed her brow. "Happy sad tears?"

Jessie rolled her eyes and flopped back down in her chair, uncaring for the wrinkles in the fabric. "Now you did it." Her mother shot her a look before explaining the situation to Whitney.

"Nick and I got married in this same church over thirty years ago. I guess I have a lot of old memories crashing back as I get ready to marry Paul. It's a lot, sugar."

Whitney closed the distance between them and rested her hands on Daisy's shoulders. The lacy fabric of her ivory gown tickled Whitney's fingers, but she soldiered on. "Daisy, you look beautiful. I'm sure if Nick was here, he'd fall in love all over again. But do you know what's magical?" Daisy sniffed and shook her head. "Paul is outside waiting to marry you, and he's going to faint when he sees his beautiful bride walking down that aisle."

"I know, and I love Paul so much." She swiped at her cheeks as she fought another round of tears. Tapping her sternum with her bouquet she sobbed, "and all these emotions are bubbling up." She hiccupped, blotting at her eyes again.

Jessie sighed from her perch. "I think it's probably gas, and we need to get moving."

Daisy admonished her daughter. "I'm looking for a little more support, Jessica June."

Whitney bit back a smile, loving the dynamic between mother and daughter. What she loved even more was that she was included. Trevor had not only let her into his life, but his family's as well. It was a gift she would never take for granted.

"Erm, heartburn aside"—she shot a look to Jessie—"I do agree we should get moving. It's time to get married and start this next chapter, don't you think?"

From behind them, Jessie snorted. "Damn, Whitney. You're good. Have you thought about a career as a therapist or motivational speaker?"

"I'll stick to retail, thanks." She winked at Jessie and turned back to Daisy. "You ready?"

Daisy straightened her spine and nodded. "Let's go, girls." She picked up her bouquet and waited for Jessie to open the door.

"All right, Shania Twain." Jessie smirked, snaking her mother's hand and squeezing before they headed toward the main event.

When they reached the rear of the chapel, Trevor waited for them. He looked so dapper that Whitney had to dig her heels into the carpeting so she didn't jump him in front of God and their neighbors.

As soon as he saw his mother, his eyes glistened. "Momma, you're beautiful." He carefully hugged her to avoid crumpling her dress.

"You look like your father," Daisy whispered, her voice cracking.

"He would be so happy for you and Paul. I know it." They were the right words to say as Daisy's shoulders shuddered with more waterworks.

"Hush up, now. Whitney just got me to stop crying."

Jessie interjected herself and thwapped her brother on the shoulder. "How do I look, jackass?"

"Language," Daisy scolded, but her voice was light. "We're in God's house."

Jessie shot her brother a look before getting in line behind Whitney. "I still don't know what you see in him."

Their gazes snagged and she mouthed *Love you* to Trevor before it was time to walk down the aisle. Malcolm played the role of usher, and Whitney didn't miss the look that passed between Jessie and him as they got in line. Whitney led the way, with Gus at her side. In lieu of a ring bearer, they'd hooked a little pillow on the basset hound's collar. Whitney held his leash in one hand and her bouquet in the other as she marched toward Daisy and Paul's happily ever after.

The crowd gasped as Daisy and Trevor strode down the aisle, Paul's eyes already misting over. When Trevor gave his mother away, she heard Paul say "Thank you, Captain." Trevor nodded, giving the older man a one-armed hug before standing opposite Whitney and Jessie at that altar.

The ceremony was short but sweet. The church was already decorated for Christmas with poinsettias flanking the aisle, pine branches hung from the altar and the sides of the pews. The air smelled of incense and Christmas trees, and Whitney couldn't think of a better place to get married.

By the time they made it to the firehall for the reception, everyone was rowdy and ready to party. Javi played DJ, a job which he took very seriously. After the couple had their first dance and dinner was served, he started playing pop music to get folks dancing. Malcolm, finally recovered from his injuries, led guests in a questionable rendition of *The Cupid Shuffle*.

"Time to move around, or I'll fall asleep after that meal," Trevor said, reaching out for Whitney's hand. "Care to dance?"

Whitney placed her hand in his and allowed him to drag her out to the dance floor. They shuffled in time with the beat of the song before Javi changed the music to something slow and soulful. Trevor twirled Whitney around, pulling her close to his chest, resting her hand over his heart.

"Are you having a good time?" he asked, his mouth right by her ear. She shivered at the sensation of his breath on her neck, leaning in to absorb his warmth. Since moving to Pinegrove, Trevor had become her own personal charging station—a mere moment in his arms could bring her back to life. Right now, surrounded by her favorite people, she felt at home.

"It was a beautiful service. They look so happy."

"They do, and I'm happy for them, truly."

"I'm glad," Whitney replied on a sigh, as the music shifted to a slow Christmas ballad. This was a magical time of year, but throw in a wedding and Whitney was in heaven.

"I'm proud of you, you know."

Trevor scoffed. "For not ruining my mother's special day?" His body shook with mirth as she giggled.

"Well, that too. But for your promotion, sticking with your job and following your dreams. I realize I sound like a greeting card, but you're a damn good fireman, and I know you'll be a great captain."

Trevor kissed her, chastely given their current location, and smiled. "You've always believed in me, and sometimes I have to pinch myself that you're mine. I love you, Whitney."

"Love you, too. Now let's go get some cake before Jessie eats it all." He chuckled and wrapped his arm around her waist as he led them to sugar town.

*

Trevor was pretty sure he was about to puke all over the dessert buffet. Why he thought this was a good idea was beyond him. A smart man wouldn't plan to propose to the love of his life at his mother's wedding, but he couldn't stop himself. He wanted Whitney as his wife so badly it kept him up at night. He spent so much time fantasizing about their future home and children, Javi threatened to stop talking to him.

Speaking of his buddy, they made eye contact and he shot a thumbs-up. Trevor gulped and nodded, hoping Whitney couldn't sense his sudden discomfort.

"Ladies and gents, it's time for the bouquet toss!" Javi announced to shrieks of delight from the women in attendance.

Smithy barely made it off the dancefloor before a swarm of women rushed the space, hands waving in the air like money was at stake. Kim joined them, elbowing a young woman off the floor with a surprising amount of force.

Whitney stayed put, licking frosting from her thumb with disinterest. "Aren't you going to join them?" Trevor asked, his voice sounding foreign to his own ears.

Shrugging, Whitney reached for another pecan bar. "Let the young ladies have their fun."

"What?" Trevor squeaked as she turned her attention to the chocolate fountain. He was thirty seconds away from flipping the table when his sister joined them.

Jessie being Jessie wasted no time reaching for Whitney's arm and pulled her toward the dance floor. "C'mon, single lady. I'm not doing this solo." She yanked, but Whitney didn't budge.

"You go, Jessie. I'm too busy deciding between another slice of cake or a pecan bar."

"Both will be here after the toss," Jessie urged, digging her heels in.

Whitney turned and stared at the Mays siblings with concern. "Did I miss something?" she asked, eyes darting back and forth.

"No!" they both shouted, a little too obvious.

Smithy saddled up, draping an arm around Jessie's shoulder. "What's taking you girls so long?"

Daisy headed toward them, her flowers hoisted in midair. "Ladies, get your darling fannies out here, please." She made eyes at both men before turning and going back on the floor.

Whitney shrugged, reluctantly leaving the sweets behind and let Jessie drag her out with the crowd. "Geez, Jessie. You're about to pull my arm off."

Jessie muttered something under her breath before they made it to the floor, Trevor discretely following them.

Javi played "Something to Talk About" by Bonnie Raitt until everyone was in place. "Who's ready for that bouquet?" he asked to a resounding cheer from the women.

Whitney gave a half-hearted hoot, earning a nudge from Jessie. "Whit, you're going to need to do better than that."

"What?" Whitney asked, but it was too late for answers.

Daisy strode to the middle, slowly spinning in a circle until her back was to Jessie and Whitney. The music turned down as Daisy theatrically held her bouquet aloft. "Here we go!" she shouted, waggling the blooms in the air.

While Whitney watched Daisy, Trevor crept up beside her, hands shoved in his pockets. He was shocked Whitney didn't hear his arrival from the pounding of his heart in his ribcage. He feared he'd faint before he'd get the ring out of his pocket.

Just as Daisy pretended to throw the bouquet, she spun on her heel and stepped forward to Whitney, placing the flowers in her hand.

"What the?" Whitney asked, before Trevor stepped in front of her and lowered down to one knee.

The room, including Whitney, gasped as he pulled a small velvet box out of his jacket pocket. Jessie was already clapping, even though he hadn't done anything yet, and earned a glare from her brother.

Whitney cupped her face with her hands, mouth agape. "Trevor?" she asked, voice cracking.

"Whitney Kerr, you are by far the most incredible woman I've ever met. You're gorgeous, smart, funny, and you inspire me every day. I didn't realize how much was missing from my life until you stumbled into it. Would you do me the honor of being my wife?"

Whitney was already nodding as she held out a shaking hand. "Yes, Trevor. I'd be honored to be your wife."

Trevor was on his feet and sliding the ring on her finger before anyone could blink. Everyone cheered as he closed the distance and kissed Whitney. To the untrained eye, it looked like any other kiss, but Trevor knew the truth.

This was their first kiss as an engaged couple; the first of many in their new life together. They'd overcome so much, from bad breakups to career missteps and family drama, but they'd found their way to each other. Trevor never planned on letting go.

"I love you," Whitney cried into his neck as he held her. They both shook with happy sobs until breaking apart to accept Daisy and Paul's congratulations.

"You knew all along?" Whitney asked Daisy, incredulous.

"Oh, please, like Trevor planned this on his own." Jessie supplied beside her mother.

Trevor looped his arm around Whitney's waist and held her close for the rest of the night. As Javi announced the last song, couples spilled out onto the dance floor. Jessie grabbed hold of Smithy's hand and they swayed to Sinatra. Paul and Daisy danced in the middle, their love filling the space.

Ushering Whitney off the floor, they reached the buffet as the caterers were clearing it. "Wait," Trevor begged, snagging the last two pecan bars, wrapping them in napkins and tucking them in his pocket.

Whitney giggled. "What are you doing?"

"Taking our dessert on the road. Come on." They went out the back door of the firehall to a small courtyard surrounded by pine trees. Fairy lights weighed down the branches, casting the space in a heavenly glow.

"Oh, it's lovely out here." Whitney stared up at the trees, resting her head on his shoulder.

"I like to come out here on my shifts for a break. It's always peaceful, even now." He steered them to a bench and retrieved the pecan bars. "Here." He placed one of the bars in her hand.

"That's the second nicest thing you've given me today," she teased, taking a greedy bite.

He kissed her cheek as she chewed and rubbed at his chest. His heart nearly exploded from happiness. "Thank you for saying yes," he whispered, kissing her again.

"Thank you for asking," she replied, covering his heart with her hand. The engagement ring sparkled like their own personal fireworks show, and Trevor's world righted itself.

No matter what happened, he knew they would be happy. It was impossible not to be happy with the love of a good woman, the job of his dreams, and his friends and family all in one place.

Trevor Mays was the luckiest man alive.

The End

ACKNOWLEDGEMENTS

Starting a new series is a tall order, and I couldn't have done it without the support and love of the following people:

First, my thanks to the team at Inkspell Publishing, especially Melissa and Yeza. This book would not have the sparkle and swoons without you. Thank you for your patience while I sent back a million and one revisions.

Thank you to Emily at Emily's World of Design for making a stunning cover…and allowing me to request a few dozen changes to make it perfect. You're a rock star.

A huge shout out to my beta readers, Liz Donatelli and Johanna Kraynak. Whitney and Trevor's happily ever after wouldn't have happened without your insight and suggestions. I'm eternally grateful.

I also want to thank Liz for being my fearless cohost for Romance Roundup. You promote my work without hesitation, and I truly thank my lucky stars we both moved to Columbus at the same time. You're the best!

To my friends and family, who listen to me vent and support my insanity during the writing process. Mom, Dad, Kathleen, Thelma, Ernie, and the Jets—you're my heart.

Last, but never least, thank you to my husband for filling my life with so much love and support. It's easy to write romance books with you by my side. Love you to pieces, Curly!

BE SURE TO CHECK OUT ANOTHER GREAT SERIES BY LIBBY KAY

Falling Home

Welcome to Buckeye Falls, Ohio!

'Tis the Season for Second Chances...And this couple is going to need a Christmas Miracle!

When New York transplant Ginny Meyer returns to her small hometown to help her father recover from surgery, she isn't looking for any complications. No Christmas caroling, no cookie decorating, and certainly no time spent with her ex-husband, Max. The trouble is, she's looped into helping with the Christmas Jubilee—and a certain ex is her planning partner. Now all her plans to avoid Max disappear in a puff of tinsel. But she can resist his charms, right?

Max Sanchez has three great loves in his life—his diner, Christmas, and his ex-wife. He's spent two years missing the woman who broke his heart and left town, and he'll use any excuse to spend time with her. Max hopes some holiday cheer, and his famous cheese enchiladas, can help them find their way back together. Buckeye Falls hasn't felt the same since Ginny left, and Max can tell she's warming to the idea of staying in town. Now if only he could get her to stay with him...

With a little help from the residents of Buckeye Falls, this Christmas is bringing more than presents under the tree.

Author Libby Kay's books are perfect for fans of Kristan Higgins' second chance romances or Sharon Sala's smalltown romances. Readers will fall in love with Buckeye Falls, Ohio and the townspeople as they embrace the holiday season. Slip in to this enchanting smalltown and stay awhile! You might just fall in love...

EXCERPT:

Blinking, Ginny begged her eyes to see someone else standing before her. It was as if her memories willed themselves back to life. Beside her, her father perked up and lifted his free hand. "Max, over here." Max turned around, and Ginny felt the air leave her lungs. This was no trick of her mind. It was the real deal. *Well, hell ...*

Time had been good to Max; there was no denying it. His dark hair was longer now, curling at the base of his neck. A few flecks of gray threatened to take over his temples, but he managed to look mature rather than haggard. Instead of the clean-shaven face she remembered, his chiseled jawline was now peppered with a few days of stubble. Suddenly, Ginny understood all the fuss with lumbersexuals.

Max's brown eyes darkened when he saw her, but his steps didn't falter. "Harold, good to see you." He moved one of his shopping bags to his other arm and shook her father's hand. When he turned to her, Ginny felt her breath hitch as he reached out his hand for a shake. *Really? They were in the hand-shaking phase of their relationship?*

Ginny reached out and took his hand, a shot of awareness coursing through her body as his fingers wrapped around hers. "Max," she said his name in greeting, hoping her tone was light, carefree.

"Gin." Max swallowed and squeezed her hand before letting it go. He didn't say anything at first, just studied her. She was glad she had listened to her father about makeup. Bumping into her ex-husband with bedhead and sans mascara would have been mortifying.

Ginny was helpless for a moment, staring at Max like a fool. Perhaps she'd fallen into an alternate universe when she left the turnpike? Maybe her rental car was a time machine where she felt pulled to a man who bruised her heart? A man whose heart was certainly broken by her.

Either oblivious or uncaring of her current slack-jawed state, Max surprised her by stepping closer and giving her a genuine smile. "I'm glad you're back," he said. "It's really good to see you."

In that moment, staring into his warm gaze, Ginny couldn't disagree. Being so close to Max, so close to the worn paths of their past, she felt comfortable. This didn't feel like a foreign place; it felt like home.

Falling For You

Welcome to Buckeye Falls, Ohio!
Sparks fly in this small town as everyone's favorite gruff pastry chef finally gives the sweetest guy in town a chance.

CeCe LaRue knows what she wants in life, and in the kitchen, and that's control. She doesn't have time for distractions—from her past or present. But that doesn't mean a certain bright-eyed coworker hasn't captured her heart.

Evan Lawson is a chronic optimist, and he brings his sunny disposition to everything he does, especially his job at the diner. It's obvious why he loves his job so much, and it has everything to do with CeCe. He's been crushing on her for a while, but he's biding his time. Much like the perfect recipe, love cannot be rushed.

When a major food competition comes to town, Evan is thrilled at the prospect of competing. Despite her stellar culinary skills, CeCe is hesitant to participate. The celebrity chef host is more than a pretty face; he's the painful past she's been outrunning for years.

Can CeCe open herself up to the prospect of love and give Evan a chance? Can Evan's optimism keep them both afloat?

Falling For You is part of the Buckeye Falls series and can be enjoyed as a stand-alone read. Author Libby Kay's books are perfect for fans of Penny Reid and Sharon Sala's smalltown romances. These sweet romances will have readers falling in love with Buckeye Falls, Ohio. Slip in to this enchanting smalltown and stay awhile! You might just fall in love...

EXCERPT:

They were friends, friends with a whole lot of potential. Surely this magnetic pull wasn't one-sided?

"I think I could be serious about you," CeCe finally said, the words shaking Evan back to the moment. "And I don't know what to do about that."

Evan felt his heart explode in his chest. "You do?"

CeCe slowly raised her hand and cupped his cheek, having to stand on tiptoe to make up for their height difference. How easily he forgot her height when they were together. She was such a force, she filled up every space she was in. Her energy, her passion for what she did, radiated around her.

Even now, standing outside with only the din of the pub surrounding them, CeCe was all he could see, feel, and touch. Her thumb swiped around his lips, making him shiver. "I do."

Words escaping him, Evan closed the distance to kiss her. It was slow, tender. They were feeling each other out, finding the angles where they fit best. Cradling her face in his hands, the world around them evaporated. CeCe moaned, and Evan swallowed it, wanting to savor every little thing she gave him. Kissing CeCe felt crucial, like he'd die without her touch, die without having the privilege of her.

Falling Again

Welcome back to Buckeye Falls, Ohio!
Does this small town mayor have the political savvy to negotiate his way back into his wife's heart?

From the outside, Mayor Anthony Snyder and his wife Natalie have it all. Adorable children, a lovely home, and a never-ending supply of free food from the local diner. But behind closed doors, this duo struggles to stay connected. The sparkle they show Buckeye Falls has turned a little dull on the home front.

Over the last decade, things became hectic in the Snyder household. Anthony was elected to office, following in his father's footsteps. Unfortunately, he's reminded regularly that these are big shoes to fill. Being the best mayor takes a lot of time—time he's not spending with his family.

Natalie prides herself on being everything to everyone, but the job of a wife hasn't been smooth sailing. Wrapped up in her own growing business and their kids' activities, her time with Anthony has dwindled faster than her secret stash of Halloween candy. Natalie longs for quality time with the man she loves, but it never seems to be in the cards.

A chance to visit their family lake house promises a week away from it all, but can these two reconnect when there's no distractions? Or is it time for these high achievers to admit that love might be the one thing they can't master?

With a little help from the residents of Buckeye Falls, this power couple will find their way back to happily ever after.

***Falling Again* is the third book in the Buckeye Falls series, but it can be enjoyed as a standalone read. Featuring similar marriage conflicts as in Lyssa Kay Adams' *The Bromance Book Club* and the small-town romance of Susan Mallery's *Fool's Gold* series, fans will love this second chance love story. After all, who doesn't deserve to fall in love again?**

EXCERPT:

"Anthony saw me topless, and vice versa, for the first time in ages yesterday."

Ginny raised an eyebrow. "Isn't that a good thing?"

"It would be if we'd done anything about it. Both times we were cleaning up after the kids and didn't even acknowledge it happened. Or I guess that it didn't happen."

Ginny paused, clearly unsure how to continue. "Has it been a while since you two—" she swirled her mug in the air, gesturing for Natalie to finish the sentence. Apparently, her friend wasn't going easy on her this morning.

"Had sex? Yes. It's been a while. It's been so long that I don't even remember the basic mechanics of the deed. And don't even ask me when it was. Sometime between Otis's conception and last Thursday." Natalie sank back in her chair and groaned. "This is bad."

*

Placing her hand over his mouth to shut him up, Natalie shook her head. "Stop that. You are a wonderful husband and father. Just because we hit a rough patch doesn't mean all the ways you love us don't shine through." Beneath her hand, Anthony sighed. He sounded so defeated; she wanted to wrap him in a blanket and hide him from the world. "I've made some mistakes too. You're not allowed to play the blame game alone. It's a two-player game."

Faking the Fall

***Sparks fly** when a reclusive artist meets his muse in this new installment of the **Buckeye Falls** series.*

Alice Snyder knows her reputation—and if she didn't, Buckeye Falls loves to remind her. She may come from the town's First Family, but that doesn't mean she plays by the rules. After a decade of traveling and going to school, she's back home and ready to settle down, or at least relax for a while. The trouble is, her neighbors are determined to find her a husband. She needs a way to get them off her back...

When James Gibson, a divorced artist, flees New York for the peace of small-town Ohio, he's excited to get painting again. The only trouble is, he's completely blocked. Despite his best efforts, his collection of canvases are blank and he's at a career crossroads. A chance meeting with the mayor's sister throws James's routine off balance, and he's eager to spend more time with this quirky spitfire.

And Alice might have the solution to both their problems...
Fake Date.

She gets the Nosey Nellies off her back, and James gets time with a woman who inspires him both *inside and outside* the studio.

Just a few weeks of pretending, and they'll move on. Simple, right? The trouble is the more time they spend together, the realer their relationship feels. The laughter, the stolen kisses—it all starts to feel like more.

Can these two be honest with each other and find their happily-ever-after, or are they doomed for a *real* breakup?

Libby Kay's FAKING THE FALL redeems Buckeye Falls's spinster troublemaker with a fake relationship romance filled with sweet small town vibes. FAKING THE FALL will bring to mind amazing books like Practice Makes Perfect by Sarah Adams and Fix Her Up by Tessa Bailey. But best of all, it returns readers to the small Ohio town and the familiar characters from the previous Buckeye Falls books. All the zany, overbearing, and well-meaning ones! So sit back and grab FAKING THE FALL for the latest roller-coaster romance by Libby Kay.

EXCERPT:

A lock of chocolatey hair had fallen from her ponytail. James lifted his hand and tucked the silky strands behind her ear. Her skin was as soft as rose petals, and he suddenly forgot this wasn't real. That this sweet woman standing in front of him wasn't his. James dipped his head and saw the moment Alice registered his intent. Her green eyes grew dark and her tongue poked out to moisten her bottom lip. There was no going back now.

"Alice." James croaked her name through the lump in his throat. He had to taste her, just once.

"Kiss me," she whispered.

She tasted like ginger—warm, spicy and inviting. James couldn't believe his luck that he was actually kissing Alice. His hands slid up to cup her cheek, cradling her against him. Their lips nipped at each other, curious yet hungry. He hadn't shared a kiss like that in far too long. The world around him burst into color— bold reds and sharp oranges.

Just when James was ready to deepen the kiss, Alice pulled back. Resting her hands on his chest, she sighed. "I think that worked," she said, her breathing labored.

"What?" James asked, struggling to clear his head.

Alice gestured over his shoulder. "Roxie and Jennie followed us out. I just wanted to make sure they—" But her explanation died on her tongue. James stepped back, his arms falling limp at his sides.

It was all for show. That moment of color and passion meant nothing to Alice. "I'll get you home," he said, keeping his gaze focused anywhere but on her.

Forever to Fall

Welcome to Buckeye Falls, where second chances mend broken hearts for these childhood sweethearts. Wedding bells are ringing, but the sister of the groom is conflicted.

Fifteen years ago, Mallory Lawson "married" her childhood sweetheart, Beckett, in a pretend wedding on his family's apple farm. She treasures not only the memories, but the ring he put on her finger. The trouble now, her brother, Evan, wants to put that family heirloom on his fiancée's finger. Mallory adores CeCe, but she struggles to get past her girlhood fantasies of Beckett swooping back into her life with a certain ruby ring...

Beckett Fox is at a crossroads. After losing his grandfather, he's listless and fearful of coming back to the family farm. There are too many memories, and most of them are tied to the love of his life, Mallory. He doesn't even know if she remembers that fateful day when they were kids, playing make-believe under the apple trees, but he does. Now he's back to help his buddy get married, and he hopes to find peace on the family farm, with Mallory by his side...

When the wedding planning kicks into high gear, Beckett and Mallory are thrust together as maid of honor and best man. The more time they spend together, the harder it is to ignore the sparks between them. Beckett fears Evan won't support him dating Mallory, so the pair date in secret. But true love won't stay hidden forever...

Best-selling author Libby Kay's Buckeye Falls Series reminds readers of small-town life where everyone knows each other. Fans of Sharon Sala's *Blessings, Georgia* series and Susan Mallery's *Fool's Gold* series will fall in love with Buckeye Falls and the childhood sweethearts who are tired of hiding their feelings. Come for the wedding and stay for the whole series.

EXCERPT:

Rubbing the back of his neck, Beckett felt his muscles relax at her presence. Mallory had this amazing ability to calm him down while simultaneously causing him to burn with lust.

For a moment, neither of them spoke. The sound of cicadas in the night air surrounded them, their nightly song echoing through Buckeye Falls. Mallory finally cleared her throat and gestured with the box toward the door. "Can I come in?"

"Erm, yeah." Beckett stepped back and held the door open for her, catching a whiff of her perfume as she slunk inside. Mallory always smelled like summertime: sweet and tangy like a handful of blackberries.

Mallory took a few paces inside and looked around. Beckett said a silent prayer of thanks that he had the forethought to start unpacking. It was a mess, but at least it looked like his mess. "Cute." She said the word with a small smile, plopping the box on top of the coffee table.

She turned like she was going to leave, her presence not required beyond the delivery. Instinctively, Beckett blocked the way, letting the door close behind him on a soft click. "Where are you going?" he asked, his pulse kicking up at the idea that he wouldn't see her for more than another moment.

Shrugging, Mallory pointed to the door. "Home?"

Before he could think better of it, Beckett blurted out the first thing that came to mind. "Stay. Have dinner with me."

Mallory didn't respond at first, but he didn't miss the flush that crept up her neck. "You want to have dinner with me?"

"Yes?" he replied, although it was far from a question. Beckett wanted Mallory to stay as long as she liked—for dinner or the rest of her life. He wasn't picky.

A Buckeye Falls Christmas

On the first day of Christmas, Buckeye Falls gave to me...

A snow storm...

Uninvited dinner guests...

A Christmas pageant...

And a friends' reunion dinner to warm your heart.

It's been ten years since five couples found love in this charming small Ohio town. Families and careers have grown, but the love remains the same.

Max is hosting Christmas at the diner, a final sendoff before the beloved hangout gets a facelift. But the risk of a snow storm and a few uninvited guests threaten everyone's plans. Will it be a Christmas to remember, or will their holiday get plowed away?

Revisit your favorite couples in this holiday novella, which includes favorite recipes from the series. Warning: this story will make you hungry and may cause uncontrollable swoons.

EXCERPT

Ginny kissed Max's cheek, tasting his tears on her lips. "Max, honey. This rarely happens. C'mon, Henry's going to be the lead in the Christmas pageant. He's a tough kid, just like his father." She punctuated her statement with another kiss.

Max coughed and wiped his eyes with the back of his hand. "Oh yeah, I'm a real macho man."

"Yeah, because you know they're my type." Ginny theatrically rolled her eyes.

"I shudder to think of what your type is," Max said, gesturing at his current state. His eyes were red, he was covered in dirt and dog kibble, and he probably could stand another few hours of sleep.

Ginny leaned back, tapping her chin. "Well, let's see. I like a man who can take care of me and my children. Someone who can cook, like really well. And it would be nice if he was a small business owner and took care of my father like his own. Oh, and if he's also best friends with my best friends, that would be perfect." Ginny huffed and pulled herself to her feet. "Looks like that's a pretty tall order."

Max snatched Ginny's hand and pulled her onto his lap. "Okay, Mrs. Sanchez. Point made." He kissed his wife, relishing in the fact they were still together after all these years. Life wasn't always perfect, but it was from where he sat. "I need to get to the diner and start working on the menu for Christmas."

Ginny kissed him one more time before pulling back. "And I'm needed in the office."

"Love you, Gin."

"Love you more."

Now Available In Ebook And Print Where Books Are Sold

ABOUT THE AUTHOR

Libby Kay lives in the city in the heart of the Midwest with her husband. When she's not writing, Libby loves reading romance novels of any kind. Stories of people falling in love nourish her soul. Contemporary or Regency, sweet or hot, as long as there is a happily ever after—she's in love!

When not surrounded by books, Libby can be found baking in her kitchen, binging true crime shows, or on the road with her husband, traveling as far as their bank account will allow.

Libby cohosts the Romance Roundup podcast with Liz Donatelli where they recommend romance books and interview authors, influencers, and publishers. Check it out for your weekly dose of romance!

Website: https://www.libbykayauthor.com/
Instagram and Facebook: @LibbyKayAuthor
Goodreads and Bookbub: @LibbyKayAuthor